THE DEFINITI   *_____*
OR
THE POST-MODERN PROMETHEUS

Khadambi Kinyanjui, a 6-foot-five Kenyan who grew up in London, is from a wealthy family. Joe Smith, quite a bit shorter, is a red-headed orphan who grew up with his Aunt Liz in a hole in the California desert. Both are brilliant scientists. One is a neurobiologist, the other an astronomer, who first meet in 2049 under the Tommy Trojan statue at the University of Southern California. They become the best of friends but a very odd couple. And yet, their brotherhood is more robust than most actual brothers.

Then tragedy strikes the pair. Death is near for one of them. What can fend it off? Can the mind, the *self*, be uploaded to some digital realm? Can one become more than a human and far less than an animal? Or will the fix be something unexpected and mysterious? Can this human survive? Can humanity? Can friendship?

PRAISE FOR SOME OTHER NOVELS BY STEVEN PAUL LEIVA

JOURNEY TO WHERE: A Contemporary Scientific Romance
International Amazon Science Fiction Bestseller

"The author's true strength is in storytelling…Throw this in with a strong cast and a nicely paced plot, and *Journey to Where* is a fun read sure to entertain fans of the classics." — *Amazing Stories Magazine*

"A deftly crafted, inherently interesting, and thoroughly entertaining read … impressively showcases Leiva's genuine flair for originality and a distinctive, reader-engaging narrative storytelling style. Unreservedly recommended." — *Midwest Book Review.*

TRAVELING IN SPACE

"*Traveling in Space*'s humor and refreshing perspective is thoroughly enjoyable." — Diane Ackerman, New York Times Bestselling Author of *The Zookeeper's Wife*

"Many of the aliens' encounters with human beings are downright funny...much to think about, and I'm sure that *Traveling in Space* will play on my mind for some time to come." — Russell Blackford, author of *"Science Fiction and the Moral Imagination*

"A deadpan, laugh-out-loud look at first contact told from the alien POV... Recommended!" — Stephen Webb, Physicist, Author of If the Universe Is Teeming with Aliens ... WHERE IS EVERYBODY?

IMP: A POLITICAL FANTASIA

"Steven Paul Leiva is a master wordsmith able to take on any genre or blend them as in the case of *IMP, A Political Fantasia*. Once started, I couldn't stop reading. I highly recommend this novel." — USA Today Bestselling Author Jean Rabe

"Steven Paul Leiva is a very bad man. His version of US politics 'Trumps' anything the real world has to offer. Hell, you thought the orange one was the only homunculus America had to worry about? You thought wrong. There's always the nuclear option." — Steven Savile, New York Times & USA Today Bestselling Author

CREATURE FEATURE: A HORRID COMEDY
Named a "Top Book of 2020" by the Montreal Times

"*Creature Feature* reads like a comedy, has the weirdness of a *Twilight Zone* episode, and just enough monsters and mayhem to keep the readers on their toes and eager to turn the page....So, curl up on the sofa, and dim the lights and pull the blanket up close because it's going to be a chilling ride. Leiva's fast-paced *Creature Feature: A Horrid Comedy* will take you back to those late-night fright fests with just enough humor to appreciate the writing while remaining loyal to the horrors we grew up with and expect." — Amazing Stories Magazine

"Leiva is witty and engaging, stylistically striking an immediate generational middle ground. At face value, the novel would seem nothing more than a boomer's nostalgic wet dream, but Leiva imbues the novel with an accessible comedic edge... A perfect mix of dynamic action and dry dialogue keep readers turning the pages... *Creature Feature* holds enough rich nostalgia for all of us. It's a tender ode to Cold War-era technological anxiety and is a delightful read for a less than delightful time."— The Daily Californian

"Leiva has such a vivid imagination -- not to mention a vast knowledge of the baby boomer world -- and it shows up on every page of this book. Inspired by all those movies, comic books and late shows, Leiva gives the reader such a rollercoaster ride... And even the scenes with the proliferation of the creatures on the streets of Placidville has a tinge of timeliness to today's headlines that it will have you guessing what the parallels are." — Montreal Times

THE DEFINITION
OF LUCK

OR
THE POST-MODERN PROMETHEUS
A NOVEL OF THE NEAR FUTURE

THE DEFINITION OF LUCK

Or
The Post-Modern Prometheus

A Novel of the Near Future

STEVEN PAUL LEIVA

Magpie

Press

Magpie Press December 2022

ISBN-13: 978-1-7352985-4-2

Library of Congress Control Number: 2022910341

Cover Design by: Juan Padrón https://www.juanjpadron.com/

Edited by Jean Rabe

Author Photo by Miranda Leiva

Printed in the United States of America

For Antonio Damasio
A man who knows his own mind
A man who knows our minds

CONTENTS

"Man is a machine by birth but a self by experience."
— Jacob Bronowski

"You and your body are one—it goes, you follow"
— Philip Roth

"...what the hell, we're all just human, bodies with brains
at one end and the rest just plumbing."
— John Updike

"We humans are born storytellers, and we find it very
satisfying to tell stories about how things began. We have
reasonable success when the thing to be storied
is a device or a relationship, love affairs and friendships
being great themes for stories of origins."
— Antonio Damasio

PART ONE

1
A DRUNKEN NIGHT

"You see, here's my definition of luck," Neuro said to Astro as both sat in a near-empty bar a bit, or maybe a bit more than a bit, drunk.

"You have a definition of luck?"

"Just, just, now—just now occurred to me," Neuro declared.

"You've had a revelation about luck?"

"I have!"

"Have you been searching for one?"

Neuro thought about this for a moment. "No. If I had, then it would be a discovery, not a revelation."

"So this, this—" Astro took another sip of his vodka tonic. "This definition has just burst into your brain like a newly-born star."

"Well, my friend, it could not have been an old-ly-born star."

"That, um, yeah, that's true." Astro had to agree.

"You should have said, I think, *Like a star aborning*."

"Well, sure, if I had wanted to be poetical about it."

"There is no reason why a scientist cannot be poetical."

"Ah, but can a poet ever be scien…scien, you know, scientist-tical?" Astro smiled, proud of his coinage.

More thought, cloudy though it may have been, was given by Neuro. "An intriguing question. I do not have an intriguing answer." Neuro said over his failure, then downed a shot of whiskey followed by a swallow of beer.

"No luck, huh?"

"Luck! I was going to tell you my definition of luck!"

"Okay."

"Here it is. Luck is being born a transexual male—a male who is actually a female inside—and then turning out to be a lesbian!" Neuro laughed one big, wide-open-mouthed, flash of white teeth laugh of delight, which settled down into a broad grin.

"That's your definition of luck?"

"Just think about it! No hormone therapy, no surgery, you can keep your Adam's apple."

"Well—it's a unique definition. Why in the bloody blue blazes has it even occurred to you?"

"Because that, my good friend, is what you are."

"What?"

"A man-lesbian, that is exactly what you are!"

~

Neuro and Astro were not their names but, rather, the nicknames they had given each other the day they had met. They were both twenty-four years old that first day as doctoral candidates on the University of Southern California campus ten years before in 2049. Astro was standing under the bronze statue of Tommy Trojan, the university's mascot. If "mascot" can apply to an image of a physically beautiful ancient warrior brandishing a sword ready to dismember and disembowel. Neuro, who had arrived in Los Angeles only the night before and was still disoriented, felt lost on the campus and wanted to ask someone for directions. Most of the academic humanity he saw in the plaza surrounding Tommy was rushing here and there. He truly hated the idea of stopping anyone in their flow. Then he saw the static Astro standing in the shadow of Tommy Trojan staring up at the statue with curiosity.

"Excuse me. I am sorry to bother you," Neuro said to Astro after coming up on his right side. "But could you tell me where the Dornsife Neuroscience Imaging Center is?"

Astro almost thought that it was Tommy who had spoken, for the voice had come from on high. He turned his head to the right, still looking up, and saw Neuro looming above him.

"Well, *you're* certainly going to stand out in a crowd," Astro exclaimed to Neuro.

"Excuse me?"

"You're very tall, black, and have a British accent."

"Yes, well, I had no choice in these matters."

4

THE DEFINITION OF LUCK

"My Aunt Liz told me that if you are going to go out into the world, try to stand out in a crowd."

"A not unwise piece of advice, I suppose."

"But I said to her that at five-foot-five, it's going to be hard for me to stand out in a crowd."

"Do you think she possibly meant it as a metaphor?"

"Figuratively, you mean? Possibly. But I'm still literally only five-foot-five."

"Well, be that as it may—the Dornsife Neuroscience Imaging Center?"

"Oh, sure, here, I've got a map."

"A map! Brilliant!"

"You can get one at the campus bookstore."

"But how shall I get to the campus bookstore without a map?"

"Here, you can have mine."

"But then you will be without a map."

"Oh, that's okay. I've already memorized it."

"You have memorized it?" Neuro was impressed.

"I've spent my life memorizing the night sky. This map was nothing."

"You're an astronomy student," Neuro stated what had become evident to him.

"Yep. Getting my doctorate in it."

"And since you had a map, you apparently did not do your undergraduate studies here at USC. Where might you have done them?"

"Nowhere. It's all been independent study and online courses."

"Oh."

"And you?"

"University of Oxford," Neuro said with a little too much pride.

"Really? That's impressive. Beautiful buildings there."

"Beautiful, if somewhat in need of repair," Neuro had to admit.

"Is that why you've come here? For *your* doctorate?"

"Yes. In neuroscience. But the conditions of the hallowed halls of Oxford had nothing to do with it. I just needed a change. And USC has a superb program."

"I'm here because my aunt said I had to get the hell out of the desert."

"Well, there must be a story there."

"Oh, nothing interesting, believe me. And you probably need to get to your center."

5

"Yes, I am pushing my time a bit. Well, it has been a pleasure meeting you. My name, by the way, is Khadambi Kinyanjui."

"Oh, no."

"I assure you it is."

"I'll never be able to pronounce that, too many syllables. Since you're studying neuroscience, I'll just call you Neuro."

"If you wish. And might I have your name?"

"Joe Smith."

"Oh, no, I will never be able to pronounce that. Too *few* syllables, you see. However, since you are studying astronomy, I will call you Astro."

Neuro smiled. Astro laughed. They shook hands and parted, both assuming they would never see each other again.

~

"Why would you call me a man-lesbian?" Astro asked Neuro.

"Because of your absolutely uncanny success with women. And gorgeous women, absolutely gorgeous women."

"Not gorgeous, Neuro. Elegant. I prefer elegant women. I am, after all, the 'Leading light of the New Elegance Movement.' Or so *The New York Times* said."

"I fail to see the difference."

"I can elucidate if you wish."

"Please do."

"'Gorgeous' means a certain perfection of classic physical beauty, of which there is, of course, nothing wrong with that. 'Elegance' has to do with a certain perfection of an aesthetic attitude towards dress, presentation, manner. Of course, not all beautiful women—or men, for that matter—are elegant. But all elegant people are beautiful. Do you see?"

"All that means, Astro, is that you overdress in a hot climate. All those layers, vests, and coats and tightly tied ties you wear."

"There is no such thing as overdressing anymore. Not with nanotech air conditioning built into the fabrics."

"Well, there were no nanotech air-conditioned clothes the day we met, and you were wearing a suit on a stunningly hot mid-August day. A rather daft thing to do."

Astro smiled, remembering. "My very first suit, ever. Not much need for suits when you live in a hole in the desert and your only real company is a widowed aunt. But I was coming out into the world. And I wasn't going to come out naked."

"Well, you did when you first came out," Neuro mumbled to no acknowledgement but his own smile.

"It was a beautiful suit. One hundred percent cotton. Skinny lapels. Very 1960s. I loved it"

"It must have been so hot."

"And you were in khaki shorts and a blue tee-shirt that read, um—wait a sec, I'll remember. Um, damn! Wait, no, um, yes—MY BRAIN HAS BEEN DRAINED."

"It was a bespoke tee-shirt made to order. To celebrate my intellectual flight to the U.S."

"And you looked just like everybody else. Except for the fact that you were six-foot-six, black as coal, and talked like King William."

"Standing out above the crowd."

"Yes, well, I couldn't do that. So, I had to stand out within the crowd. Nothing like an elegant suit in the land of tee-shirts and wrinkled pants to do that."

～

They were in a bar in downtown Los Angeles at Figueroa and 7th. Vic's Virtual Sports Bar was popular with the virtual sports crowd, of which Neuro was one, and Astro was not. But Neuro had pestered and pleaded, cajoled, and finally convinced Astro to come with him to see the "Big Game" on the bar's three gigantic 3-D screens. The screens were horseshoed around a pit of wooden tables packed with screaming, yelling, cheering, increasingly more inebriated men and women. And all were engaged in an orgy of vicarious fantasizing of personal athletic glory they would never know in real life.

Not that the games were real life. OUR SPORTS ARE VIRTUAL BUT OUR BOOZE AIN'T was the slogan in plasma light under the large VIC'S VIRTUAL SPORTS BAR sign over the door. But then Vic wasn't even real life as the owner's name was actually Brandon. But Brandon liked the alliteration.

American football was the first sport to go one hundred percent virtual. The sport had become more and more violent to fulfill team owners' fantasies, and there were mounting problems of severe head injuries and chronic traumatic encephalopathy. The Federal government finally had to step in, banning the sport to the dismay of millions. But not before an alternative was waiting in the locker room. A savvy tech investor with a nose for innovative geeks to invest in came to the rescue. She combined fantasy football leagues, virtual reality programs, artificial intelligence, and quantum randomness.

Like manna from heaven, there was suddenly a virtual reality of football players, teams, and leagues. And they played games that could be streamed in natural 3-D to screens big and small. Or be projected as giant holograms into the stadiums that no one wanted to see decay in disuse. The sale of hot dogs, sodas, and beer to cheering crowds did not suffer from progress. The team owners just bought licenses from the clever tech investor and continued on as before. Except now, they did not have to pay multi-million-dollar salaries to star players or worry about liability insurance for sexual or political misconduct. Now they contended with no egos but their own.

And they could make the sport as violent as they pleased to feed the fans' bloodlust.

Except, of course, there was no blood. But that didn't seem to matter. Virtual players were created by work-for-hire digital surrogate designers. They utilized AI, randomness, and a cornucopia of personality quirks established over three hundred thousand years of human evolution. And, of course, the Otsuka-Kinyanjui AI Intuition software was key to the excellence of the game. These virtual players soon became beloved, hated, or dismissed with about the same frequency as the real players had been.

Virtual American Football became so popular that soon most sports transitioned from real to surreal, especially boxing and wrestling (some lovely unrestrained violence here). And the non-helmeted, feet-centric *football* known in the rest of the world. As well as baseball, basketball, tennis, and even—in a cartoonish variation— the more minor, cultish games which dispensed with human or human surrogate players altogether. Kings, bishops, and pawns decided on their own moves. Squidgers tiddlied their winks digitally but without the aid of human digits. And self-motivated marbles sped toward other marbles, momentum-driven to knock them the hell out of the ring.

All profits went to the owners who could license rights. And all concern, genuine or hypocritical, for sportsmanship, could finally be relegated to a storied past.

~

"Bloody hell!" Neuro shouted as others in the packed bar made similar once-obscene exclamations. Vic's three gigantic screens went blank just as the first kickoff sent the oblong digital ball into the digital atmosphere. The sudden death of the streaming sport was disconcerting to the packed-in patrons. Then mystifying. Then it was depressing when Brandon explained to them that something had gone wrong with his computer system. It just quit accepting the streaming service signal, blocking it as if it was something politically incorrect or personally offensive.

"I'm sorry, everybody, but I don't know how to fix it." Brandon made the sad announcement. "But I called over to MaGee's, and they said that their system is working fine. It's standing room only, but at least you can see the game."

The mass of patrons picked themselves up, dusted off their disappointment, and started *en masse* for MaGee's three blocks away.

"Let's go," Neuro said to Astro as he raised his six-foot-six body to a standing position.

Astro remained seated. "Must we?"

"What?"

"Must we follow the crowd like mindless drones? Must we march to the same old drummer—or drum major, as the case may be?"

(Yes, there still were half-time shows, all virtual, of course. Exactly why, no one had figured out. Tradition, most likely.)

"Why don't we just stay here and have a quiet drink, or a few, some finger food, and some sparkling conversation," Astro proposed. "It's been a while since we've gotten together."

Neuro looked down at his elegantly attired friend, who was preemptively putting on the face of pure innocence. Then he got it. He sat down and gave Astro an age-old stare. "You did this."

Astro smiled. "I hacked into their computer. It wasn't hard. And look. We have the place to ourselves."

"And Brandon will lose a small fortune."

"Well, we can do our best to make up for it. And you'll pay the difference, won't you? You being filthy rich and all."

∼

Which is how they found themselves in a near-empty bar a bit, or maybe a bit more than a bit, drunk. A welcomed time after an unusual four months in which they had seen each other only in passing, despite both being professors at USC. But they had been busy. Both had to take several trips for conferences. Neuro almost always worked late in his lab. Astro often had lovely evenings out (and in) with elegant women. When the "Big Game" was coming up, Neuro saw it as an opportunity to get together with Astro to continue his years-long campaign to get Astro "into" sports. He knew Astro thought his attempts were absurd. He knew Astro often found ways to subvert them. And, most pertinently, he knew Astro would see it as a challenge to subvert yet another attempt. Thus, he was assured of getting together with his friend and fully expected to miss the "Big Game." But not, of course, this little game with Astro. Which Neuro conceded with admiration. It was true sportsmanship.

Their conversation had been sparkling. There was much to talk about. Their work, their research, Astro's head in the stars, and Neuro's head in other peoples' heads. Through their conversations over the years, they had given each other a minor education in each other's field. Which broadened both their minds and deepened their thinking about existence. But they also joked around. They shared a love of food from various parts of the world. Both followed politics and had the same concerns. They loved to swim (which Neuro had taught Astro to do), enjoyed museums and the art or science on display in them, and the reading of novels both serious and frivolous. They respected and tried to understand their differences, starting with their heights.

("Or lack thereof," Astro would often say, referring to his own.)

They were well aware of the odd couple image they had on campus when they walked together, usually in the middle of an intense discussion. This near-gigantic, deeply ebony, thin, and lanky Kenyan of English accent. And this near-child-sized, pale, fully red-haired, slightly pudgy, but always elegantly dressed exile from the California desert. They always caught the head-turning eye of anyone new to the campus. Even those who had been around for a while—students, professors, and staff alike, still found them hard to ignore as we all mostly ignore others.

They both stood out in a crowd.

And they, so obviously, were each other's best friend.

~

"But wait a minute," Astro said after Neuro had declared him a man-lesbian. "If the criteria you are using is my success with women, wouldn't that make me a manly man and not a man-lesbian?"

"I think you have misconstrued my point."

"Have I?"

"It is not your success in sexual congress with women that is—

"Wait a minute!"

"I'm trying to explain what—

"I want to run for Sexual Congress! I'm going to need a campaign slogan. Something like, uh, SMITH FOR BLISS! Or VOTE FOR SMITH AND COME TOGETHER!

Neuro was momentarily silent while displaying a passive yet telling face. Then he asked, "May I finish now?"

"Finish what?"

"Finish explaining why you are a man-lesbian."

"Are we still talking about that?"

"I most assuredly am."

"Is this still your definition of luck thing?"

"Correct. You were extremely lucky to be born a man, considering the undeniable fact that you are a lesbian."

"Okay, I'm still not getting this lesbian thing. I told you, I'm a manly man."

"Well, a manly half-man at least."

"Ooo! *A touch, a touch, I do confess't.* Not bad. Not one of your best, though. Perhaps the thin air way up there where your head is at is affecting your wit."

"Perhaps it has more to do with the drink," Neuro said.

"Ah. Could be. We should probably stop."

"After one more, and I explain to you that you are a man-lesbian not because you fornicate with women, but because you seem to understand them so well. You seem to relate to them. They like having you as a friend. A talent I have certainly never had."

"I like women, that's true. As people, I suppose you would say. The sex, besides being *a consummation devoutly to be wished*, is just sort of what you do when conversation lags."

"You confirm my hypothesis. You are my lesbo-bro."

"To lesbo-bros!" Astro offered up a toast.

"To lesbo-bros!" Neuro joined in.

They both downed what was left of their drinks to make way for one more each.

"Oh, guess what?" Neuro said after he had swallowed.

"What?"

"Carmichael reached out to me again."

"Oh, crap." It was an old conversation Astro was not fond of. "What did that antiquated post-humanist want?"

"He still wants me to join his group."

"In the uploading of minds?'

"In the uploading of minds," Neuro confirmed.

"When is he going to give up? Wasn't the *Singularity* supposed to be here already? I don't see it.

11

"He says he's close to cracking it."

"The only thing he's going to crack is himself. If he isn't cracked already. You're not going to do it, are you?"

"Most likely not. But you know why I would if I did."

Astro did. Astro knew the sad story and had felt a full measure of empathy for Neuro's situation. But he just didn't believe it was a path that led anywhere real.

~

After their last drink Neuro settled the bill, adding a tip that could well have covered Brandon's expected receipts for the night. They walked out onto Figueroa and breathed in the cool night air. It was refreshing, but cleared their soggy brains only a little.

"And now for the long walk home," Neuro said.

"Neuro, you live across the street."

In all mock seriousness, Neuro questioned the reality of his residence. "I do?"

He did. Neuro had a penthouse apartment in the Wilshire Grand Center in what had been the tallest building in Los Angeles for more than forty years.

"Well, someone has a long walk home. If it is not me, then I can only assume that it is you because we are the only two here."

"It is me. But it is more of a saunter, two blocks up, two longish blocks to the right, as you well know."

Astro lived in the hundred and twenty-nine-year-old Title Guarantee Building across the street from Pershing Square. It had long ago been converted to lofts.

"Still, you cannot walk it in your condition," Neuro declared. "I will call my car for you."

"No, don't do that. The walk will do me gooo. It will help clear my head."

"Do you *gooo*? Astro, you would have to walk Wilshire Boulevard from here to Santa Monica to clear your head. Besides, why would you want a clear head? No, I will call my car."

"Okay, but not before I walk you across the street."

"You will do no such thing. Am I a little old lady?"

"No. You are a long-legged galoot, as my dear old aunt might have called you. I'm not sure you can make it across the street without tripping on your apparently endless posterior appendages."

"That is absurd, and I take offense to it."

"And I take you across the street."

Astro grabbed one of Neuro's sharp elbows and guided him across the street at the corner to stand on 7th Street by the entrance to the Wilshire Grand Center.

"Thank you," Neuro said in a clipped, formal manner. Then he reached in his pocket to signal for his car with a small black device. "Gathii will be here in just a second."

"Why do you call your car Gathii? I've always wanted to know."

"It is a Swahili name. It means," Neuro thought hard to remember as he slightly swayed in the breeze, "traveler or wanderer."

"Ah. Logical."

"Look at that behemoth!" Neuro commented in a sudden switch of his mind onto a recent massive irritation in his life.

Astro stared up at another skyscraper under construction across 7th, where a shopping complex and a smaller scraper had once stood.

"You're just upset because it's going to be taller than your building."

"Cutting off some of my fine views," Neuro said sadly.

Gathii, Neuro's self-driving car, had come out of the building's garage and pulled up to the curb in front of Neuro and Astro. Its double doors automatically opened like welcoming arms. Neuro escorted Astro to the spacious passenger area with the four plush leather-covered seats, two facing two. He directed Astro in a forward-facing seat because he knew he hated riding backward. Neuro sat his friend down in the seat and strapped him in. "Just give Gathii your address, and he'll take you right there."

"I will if I can remember it," Astor said in the middle of a yawn.

"I am sure you will. Goodnight, you drunken, short-statured, American of dubious lineage, you."

"Goodnight, you drunken Giacometti-statue of an Afro-Anglo commercial prince, you."

The doors closed, and Neuro turned and went to the short run of shallow steps that led up to the entrance of his building. He was on the third step when a sudden high-pitched screech of tortured metal came from above. Neuro swung around and looked up. Twenty stories above on the unfinished building across the street, a massive construction crane bent slowly as if taking a bow, its attached American flag dipping in respect to gravity. Then a frightening explosive-like snap punctured the air, and part of the crane fell. Neuro was fixated. The crane seemed to fall slowly like a feather. Down, down, down it came slamming onto and across 7th Street. In an agonizing crash and crumple and slam, the end of it fell directly onto Gathii, which had just been pulling away.

Neuro screamed. In disbelief, in fear, in horror, Neuro screamed.

2
A RUDE AWAKENING

When Astro awoke in the morning, he was surprised that he did not have a hangover. Never in the past had he not had a hangover after a binge like the one he and Neuro had the night before. He was still young enough to think of hangovers as a badge of honor, although old enough to perceive that they were an absurd badge of honor.

Well, this will make for a pleasant Sunday, was his first thought. It's good to feel good, and he did feel good as he stretched in his bed.

Or rather, strangely, he felt nothing. He was not really stiff—so why did he stretch?—nor felt pain anywhere, not even in his big toes, which often cramped first thing in the morning. Maybe they had medicinal vodka at Vic's? And his sheets. Astro suddenly realized that he couldn't feel his sheets that gently spread under and over his naked body. Yes, granted, they were an expensive set of linen sheets that he had only bought yesterday. But the salesperson had said they would not be as soft at first as they would become over time. But he lay there finding them super soft, extraordinarily soft, so soft they made no impression on his bare skin at all—except for the palms of his hands. He could just barely feel his sheets with the palms of his hands.

Astro removed the top sheet and got out of bed. He stood there, unsteady on his feet, weaving just slightly, feeling weak. He looked around and found he was having trouble focusing on his loft's interior. Everything was just a little fuzzy.

That's it! I don't have a hangover because I'm still drunk!

He didn't have to pee. When had he ever gotten out of bed in the morning and not had to pee? He looked to make sure he still had the exterior apparatus to pee with and, yes, sure enough, there it was, ready and waiting. But where the fuck was his pubic hair? His red, curly pubic hair? And leg hair? And chest hair? Where was the nice manly red chest hair that not one of his sexual partners had not loved running their fingers through?

Astro drew in a quick, fearful breath and shot his right hand up to his head. It was there, his full head of hair. Although it did feel somewhat—what?—wispier. He padded to his bathroom in an enclosed area in the back corner of his open-space loft. He went to the mirror over the sink and was relieved. The hair on his head was as full and thick as always. Or, at least, thick-looking. Who the hell shaved the rest of his body? And his face. For his face was smooth. What man wakes up in the morning with a smooth face?

A splash of cold water on his face was a thought that crept into his mind as a desire that might be at this moment useful. Astro turned the cold water tap on. A clear, gelatinous, yet sparkling substance came out of the faucet and slowly descended into the sink.

That was too dream-like not to think this must be a dream. But Astro had never had a dream like this. Had anybody? His dreams were usually mundane and forgettable, if fluid. More fluid than the water coming out of the tap right now.

He felt—or rather rationally assumed—that he should be in a panic. But he wasn't. He was fretful. And curious. Certainly confused. And naked. Which prompted him to leave the bathroom and cross over to the antique French armoire that stood between two windows in his sleeping area. He opened one of the long side doors, pulled out a pair of briefs from a drawer, and slipped them on.

Wait a minute.

Pink?

He didn't have a pair of pink briefs.

Red, yes, deep red, several of them. But not pink. Did they fade in the wash?

He opened the double center doors of the armoire and looked in. Shirts and slacks hung neatly, as always, shirts to the right, slacks to the left. Except they hung there on no visible hangers. They hung there in mid-armoire-air.

He snatched a shirt, grabbed some pants, and put them on. But he still felt naked.

Astro looked over to his living area. It was neat, clean, and orderly.

16

This is not how he had left it the night before when he had vacated it to walk over to Vic's Virtual Sports Bar to meet Neuro. Where was the pile of books and papers that usually surrounded his computer on his desk? And where were the dirty lunch dishes he had left on his small round dining table by the kitchen? He had meant to clean up before leaving. But he had been too busy at his cluttered desk drafting a paper for *Astronomical Review,* finishing it just before he knew he had to leave. (It was okay, not perfect, but he already had thoughts for the second draft.) He remembered regretting leaving the mess. As no one was going to see it, he thought to himself, it would be okay to just let it slide. But he hadn't listened to his logic. And the regret continued as he put on his coat, checked the straightness of his tie in the bathroom mirror, made sure he had his ID chip activated, told his loft to power down, and left, listening for the assuring click of his door's self-lock as he made his way to the elevator.

He remembered quite clearly emerging from the elevator into the narrow lobby of lavish marble, lovely woodwork, superbly crafted and maintained hand-laid ceiling tiles, and the well-preserved Hugo Ballin murals. It was a century-past elegance he never failed to appreciate no matter how quickly he exited his building. As he did last night. Still wishing he had time to run back up to the loft, clear the dining room table, and wash the afternoon dishes. But Neuro demanded punctuality. And he would never consciously disappoint Neuro.

There was nothing to regret now. The dining table was perfectly clear. And perfectly clean. And perfectly polished. Indeed, it was perfect in every way.

Astro walked into the kitchen. There were no dishes in the sink (he hated the dishwasher and never used it). Everything was spotless.

Surely, he didn't come home and clean up, drunk as he was. If he had, he probably would have dropped something and broken it. He pulled out the kitchen trash drawer to check for anything broken. It was not just empty—it was a space of nothing. Not even, it seemed, space.

Why was he not screaming in existential dread? Why was he feeling nothing but curiosity?

Astro turned to the three just slightly rectangular sash windows that wrapped around the corner of his loft. The blinds were down, as they usually were in the morning. He went over to the windows and rolled up the antique blind of the center window. He hoped to reveal the comfortable view of 5th Street flowing toward Broadway. And the lovely green of the trees and lawns across the street in Pershing Square.

But what he saw was just black, spatter-punctuated with white spots of minutely various sizes. A starfield. He quickly rolled up the blinds on the other two windows. Each showed the same starfield. And all three views were static. There wasn't a twinkle to be seen.

Astro?

The voice came from everywhere. Or maybe it was just in Astro's head. He did not recognize the voice. There was no quality of tone in it. It was not a deep voice nor a high one. It was not a rough voice nor a soft one. It was not threatening, but also not comforting. It was not a shout, nor was it a whisper, if it even had a volume at all. And yet it was there, unmistakably there. *There,* being everywhere.

Astro?

"Uh...who? What?"

Astro, can you hear me?

"Yes," Astro said, feeling apprehensively silly. "I—can—hear—you. Is this God?"

Astro, you don't believe in God.

"Well, I never have in the past, but—

Why would you even ask that?

"Uh—cultural indoctrination? And you are a, um, you know, a disembodied voice."

Who has ever called you Astro but me?

"Neuro?"

Yes.

"But you don't sound like Neuro."

I should not sound like anything. I am communicating directly with your mind. Actually, I am typing my words.

"Why does that make perfect sense to me? Why aren't I panicking? And what the bloody blue blazes is happening?"

Ah, I haven't heard that bloody daft phrase of yours in a long time. It is good to hear it again.

"A long time?"

Well, this is going to be a bit hard to explain.

"Neuro, you're a man of superior intelligence, and so am I. How hard is this going to be?"

There was a moment. A pause in time. Or, possibly, a vacancy of it.

There was an accident.

"An accident?"

Yes.

"What happened?"

To detail that may be too traumatic for you.

"I'm not feeling any trauma. In fact, I'm not feeling much of anything. I'm just...just taking it in."

Suffice it to say, you were hurt quite severely. And that you have been in a coma. A medically induced coma.

"In a coma? For how long?"

These are the first conscious thoughts you have had in seven years.

"What?"

You have been unconscious for seven years, and you weren't supposed to be conscious today.

"Neuro, where am I? Why have I not woken up in a hospital bed? Why is this my loft and yet obviously isn't?"

You are in a place we have created for you. We wanted you to wake up in familiar surroundings.

"Familiar but not real."

Yes, in a manner of speaking.

"Where is this place? Where are you?"

I am in Nairobi. In Kenya.

"Kenya? Okay. And where am I?"

You are here with me, in Nairobi.

"Well—thank goodness I had just renewed my passport."

It is heartening to hear you make a joke.

"Thank you. I just hope the laughs are not on me."

You were not supposed to be conscious yet. We are not finished with creating your world.

"My world?"

Your world and…

The voice in his head stopped. No, not stopped, just existed no more.

"Neuro?" Panic finally hit Astro. At this moment, the absence of Neuro was more profound than a void. "Are you still there?"

Yes. It is too much information to give you right now. I need you to go back to sleep.

"But I just woke up, you said...seven years...I don't want to go back—"

Astro! I am putting you back to sleep.

"But—"

Astro, you are now in your bed.

And he was. Suddenly. Stretched out in his bed, covered by sheets that he couldn't really feel. And fully clothed.

"Hey, I'm—"

One moment.

Then Astro was nude under the sheets.

"No, Neuro, please…"

3
THE LOVE OF HIS LIFE

In the middle of his scream of disbelief, fear, and horror, Neuro leapt off the third step and landed onto the sidewalk sprinting to the crushed Gathii. Parts of the jib and the mast of the construction crane, together with the operator's cab, seemed to still be pushing down and crumpling the vehicle, unwilling to give up its destruction.

Neuro fell to his knees and peered into what little space was left of the door windows, the glass having been pulverized. It was hard to see; it was dark in there, but, yes, he could see Astro, a body folded within the ripples of the roof. His head, his face, where's his head, his face? Neuro could not see them. He got up and ran around to the street side of the car, climbed under the fallen crane, and peered in. Here the street lamps provided some light, although broken up by shadows of the crane. Yes, there! Astro, his head, his face turned toward Neuro, and his eyes open, his lids fluttering...fluttering...fluttering. Fluttering eyelids meant life! LIFE!

The city's emergency AI had become aware of the accident within 1.36 seconds and directed one of the ever-flying self-piloted emergency vehicles to rush to the scene. It arrived within thirty seconds. It hovered over Gathii, beaming down several strong waves of light, both visible and not, to assess the situation.

STEP ASIDE, SIR. GIVE US SOME DISTANCE a booming, amplified voice from above politely asked. Neuro did so, returning to the sidewalk, to the steps of his building.

Then a uniformed emergency medical technician was lowered on a line to the street. He pulled from his backpack a thick metal loop that he attached to a place on the remnant of the crane lying on the car. Then a thick metal cable ending in a hook lowered from the hovering craft. The EMT hooked it onto the loop, the cable stiffened, and the vehicle above rose, slowly pulling the crane off Gathii and setting it down in the street out of the way.

The EMT took another loop out of his pack and attached it to the crumpled roof of the car. He then pulled a device out of his pocket, punched in some numbers, and pushed a button which turned on the electromagnets buried in the asphalt directly under Gathii, securing it to the street. The hovering craft moved over to the car, dangling the cable. The EMT grabbed it and hooked it onto the loop. The hovering craft ascended slowly, pulling on the car's crushed roof as Gathii was held fast to the street by the electromagnets below. This opened up space in the cab, relieving the crush on Astro's broken body.

The emergency vehicle descended and landed next to Gathii. Double doors opened, revealing a large complex of medical equipment arranged around a central space with a gurney on wheels. Three other EMTs emerged, and the four surrounded Gathii to do their job of saving a life.

First, Astro's ID chip was scanned. All of his vital statistics were there, including medical.

"No allergies, no chronic diseases or medical concerns. Prepare the IBN injection."

"What's that?" Neuro, who had come forward, asked.

"Sir, please, you must stand back," one of the EMTs turned to speak with Neuro and walked him back as the others worked.

"Check his ID information. He's my friend. I have a medical power of attorney."

The EMT looked at his scanner. "You are Dr. Khadambi Kinyanjui?" he asked, almost pronouncing it correctly.

"I am."

"May I scan your ID chip?"

"You may." Neuro held up his right hand.

The scan was made, and the EMT was satisfied. "Fine. But right now, your friend's life depends on my team working without

22

interference or questions."

"Of course. You're right. It is just—"

"But to answer your question, IBNs are internal bleeding nanobots. We inject them to check for internal bleeding. If any is found, they cauterize the source."

"No internal bleeding, all organs are intact," one of the ETMs working on Astro announced.

"Multiple fractures in all limbs and extremities, the neck, and the spine," another said.

"Well, this is going to be difficult. What we will have to do is spray a special trauma biofoam on..." The EMT consulted the screen on his scanner. "On Dr. Smith. It will surround him and essentially put his body into a static field and protect it. Think of it as high-tech bubble wrap. Then we will very gently move him into the ambulance and transport him to..." He reviewed his screen again. "To Keck USC. There will be room for you, sir; you may come along."

~

Neuro sat and stared at his friend on the short aerial hop to Keck USC in Glendale. Astro had been given a powerful sedative and was unconscious and rested in an off-white cocoon of semi-solid organic foam, with only his head exposed. It was absurd looking. Almost laughable. His head sticking out like that. Like some kind of cartoon. Astro would have been shocked to see himself. It was not elegant at all.

It was a small head, really. A small head for a small body. But oh so bright inside, beyond the wavy red hair.

"You know who you remind me of, Neuro?"

It was a line of dialogue from the past invading Neuro's anxious present, commenting on his head.

"Who?"

"A young Ornette Coleman."

"And who might this be?"

"He was a jazz musician. A saxophonist. You have the same pursed thick lips, your mustache is pretty close, same nappy hair, of course, and absolutely the same piercing, intelligent eyes."

"Nappy hair?"

"Well, what would you call it?'

"Tightly coiled like the magnificent muscles of a lion."

"Nappy is shorter."

"Was he a good jazz musician, this Ornate Coleman?"

23

"Ornette. *He was considered very* avant-garde.*"*

"Which would pretty much be rear guard today. But then you like all that old music."

"Well, he wasn't my favorite. He played what my Aunt Liz called nervous jazz. I think it was best heard live in a club. Unfortunately, as he died ten years before I was born, I never got the chance. But he had a magnificent head."

Neuro smiled at Astro's distressed-looking, unconscious face, his red hair and his freckles, his head filled with so much data about the sun yet finding the orb's light less than kind, even if necessary for life.

Life. *Remain with life, my friend.*

~

When they arrived at USC Keck, all moved confusingly fast for Neuro. In his biofoam trauma-cocoon, Astro was wheeled in one direction, and Neuro was directed in another to a waiting room. There were others there. Most were quiet and withdrawn into their anxious thoughts. One group of three, two females, one male, one young, the other two not, sat quietly and spoke among themselves of matters possibly mundane. But Neuro assumed otherwise.

Neuro sat. There was nothing to do. There was not even anyone to call. No family, and it was too late—or too damn early—to contact anyone at the university. He did not even have to fill in any paperwork as the ID chips, both Astro's and his, had all the information required by the hospital.

All he could do was feel. He tried to put off feeling by thinking. It was useless. He was fearful, in shock, confused, worried, consumed with dread, dumbfounded with the fragility of existence.

Crushed. Pounded. Gravity can be your enemy. Flesh so fragile. Bones so brittle. Not well tolerant of cold or heat or lack of oxygen or too many rads of radiation that mutates DNA and stops replication. Life ends without replication—from molecules to bouncing babies. That spark, that thing, that ineffable essence, that here now/gone tomorrow, that brief candle, that—

"Dr. Kinyanjui?"

It was a stolid man who stood before him. And a solid one. A man in a white coat, a doctor obviously, middle-aged for he had that bulk of body and squareness of face that comes to a man when youth has passed. Was there authentic experience there, marked by the gray at his temples? Or just melanin hitching a ride with his passing youth?

"Yes," Neuro answered as he stood.

"I'm Doctor Chivers."

He was tall, although not as tall as Neuro. But he seemed to take up more space. Was it the bulk? Or his confidence in his role?

"If you follow me, I will take you to Dr. Smith, and I'll go over the options."

He was certainly no-nonsense.

Dr. Chivers walked Neuro down several of the corridors. Hospital corridors have a reality divorced from the daily one most people are used to. They aren't just passageways, but fields of endeavors with stations for nurses, equipment at the ready, rolling carts with medicines, or nutritious food. Sounds here are unlike those on the outside. Many of them muted except for the occasional burst from a nurse or other medical professional addressing the elderly hard of hearing or the groggy coming back into consciousness. Sometimes there is a moan from this room, sometimes a groan from that one. On occasion, the sound of televised drama, game playing, or news escapes from sick rooms.

Neuro had always hated hospital corridors. Not just because of sad, surreal, youthful times traveling such passageways, but for the essence of the space itself. A space fraught with the crapshoot of life, the *there but for the grace of something or other* of life, the diminishment of past abilities of mind and body of life. Yes, maybe there were sometimes, maybe most times, recovery, healing, health restored. But why was that not reflected in these corridors? Why? Neuro had never known why.

Using his ID chip, Dr. Chivers opened the wide double doors to the Trauma Center and led Neuro to Trauma Room B. Astro lay in a new trauma biofoam cocoon, a more elaborate one with several bio-mechanical connections to monitoring and drug administrating devices under the control of a MED-AI. Astros' head was supported by a large pillow made of the same semi-solid organic foam as the cocoon. This pillow also monitored and administered.

"We have put Dr. Smith into a coma," Dr. Chivers informed with no preamble. "There was no injury to his head, and his brain is functioning normally. It's the same situation with his organs, including the heart. Which is all pretty amazing given the type of accident. That's the good news. Unfortunately, there is much bad to counter it. All four limbs have multiple fractures. And not only fractures. Certain segments of bone are not broken but pulverized.

25

Indeed, his right hand is nothing but, essentially, a glove of flesh filled with powdered bone. He has several spine fractures, but somehow the cord itself escaped injury. He has fractures in the neck also. If it was not for the cocoon, he would be dead from the trauma."

The pain. Neuro knew that Astro, or his brain assuming they were separate entities, could not have taken the pain. Nor could he take the number of drugs that might have killed the pain (a weird way to express it) in the past. But the recent nanobot-tech that could get to and influence key areas of the brain could induce a coma for as long as required with no deleterious effect. At least, none had been recorded so far.

"Right. I understand," Neuro said. "Astro—that is, Dr. Smith—is in a bad way. So what do we do now?"

"Well, if it was just one or even two of the limbs, we could explore cyber prosthetics. But with all the extreme damage Dr. Smith experienced… To replace all four limbs, heal the spine and neck, maybe replace some vertebrae with artificial ones… I don't think he would survive all that surgery. I can't give him more than a fifteen to twenty percent chance."

"So you are saying—" Neuro did not want to finish the question. Nor have it answered.

"I don't believe we should sustain him." Dr. Chivers' statement was blunt. It was not unfeeling, but it was unequivocal.

Neuro was prepared to be unequivocal as well. "No. No, we will not be going down that path."

"But Dr. Kinyanjui—"

"I will not authorize it."

"Against my advice?"

"Understand, Dr. Chivers, that man in that cocoon is my friend, my only friend, and thus my best friend. All my family is far away. I have no wife or children. I have a plethora of acquaintances, colleagues, service people I enjoy short chats with, and the occasional sexual liaison. But being, as Dr. Smith likes to point out, filthy rich, I trust none of them to ever have an honest relationship with me. But Astro—that is my name for him, Dr. Chivers—Astro has been honest with me from the first words he ever uttered to me. He is the love of my life. I mean that as a friend. Do you understand?"

"Yes, I think I do."

"I cannot lose my friend. I refuse to lose him, doctor. I absolve you of all responsibility in this. I will make all the decisions. I am in charge. You have done your utmost, and I do not mean to ever say your advice is wrong. It is just wrong for me."

"But what about Dr. Smith? Is it wrong for Astro?"

It was a question Neuro had to consider. "You bring up the morality of my actions. I suppose you must. I am no less selfish than any other person, Dr. Chivers. That, for the moment, is the only answer I can give."

"Well, as you said, you're in charge. But you will have to come up with a plan of care. I'm not sure you will ever find a recovery plan. All I can do is wish you the best of luck."

"Thank you, Doctor. I appreciate that and do not take it lightly."

~

Neuro found a transport home. Fretfully slept for a few hours. Then, in the morning, he put in a call. When it connected, he said to the AI on the other end, "This is Dr. Khadambi Kinyanjui. Let me speak to Dr. Carmichael."

4
LITTLE JOE FROM CONNECTICUT

Astro should have died at least twice before his traumatic accident in 2059.

The first time was on the day he was born in 2025, five and a half weeks premature. Joseph Charles Smith would have most likely died quickly if he had been born in 1925, or most certainly if he had been born in 1825. He was a tiny bit of pink, wrinkled flesh, suffering not only from premature birth but fetal growth restriction. All because his unwed mother, while pregnant, had been a gleeful and consistent consumer of marijuana. Which had recently been liberated from institutional sanctions. Of course, since marijuana use was not that prevalent on the East Coast of the United States in 1825 or even in The Jazz Age of 1925, he might not have been born premature and ridiculously small at all in those years. But then, there was the liberal use of alcohol in those years, so…

Then Hurricane Aloysius slammed into New York and Connecticut in 2031. Which forced the still rising sea level to pour into Long Island Sound and level much of the coastal communities surrounding. One of which little Joe and his mother resided in. His mother died. And if Joe had been home, he most likely would have died as well. But he wasn't because he was in a hospital a hundred miles away, well on the mend from recent surgery correcting some of the problems of his premature birth.

And if he had died then, he would not have been sent from a devastated Connecticut coastal community to a blistering hot California desert. And he would not have grown up under the care of his Aunt Liz, his mother's half-sister, twenty years her senior.

It was Astro's first plane trip. He took it accompanied by a Connecticut Child Services worker. Who, in Los Angeles, turned him over to a California Child Services worker. Who drove him by car to a remote spot in the blistering hot California desert that her GPS swore up and down was her destination. They parked in front of a strange wedge-shaped structure surrounded by many solar panels on the ground and a bunch of the latest micro windmills sticking up like colorless pinwheels.

The California social worker—whose name is lost to this history—got out of the car, leaving the engine running to keep the air conditioning on for little Joe. Instantly she gasped in stunned disbelief when the midday heat hit her as if it had malicious intent. Fortunately, the worker had a broad-brimmed hat and intensely dark sunglasses. She took a look at the wedge-shaped structure. Its blunt rectangular end was only one story high. It featured a simple door beside a simple intercom featuring a simple call button. She poked it. When no response was immediately forthcoming, she walked to one of the long triangular sides. She could see that the structure was covered on top by dirty brown desert ground giving the illusion that it had been raised up on one end from the desert floor itself.

Hello?

The amplified voice came from around the corner, and the worker rushed back to the front. "Hello. I'm from California Child Services. I have your nephew Joe here."

Oh, yes? I guess that means this is Tuesday the fifth.

"Yes, it is."

I'll be up in a minute.

"Up?" the worker questioned as she heard a click coming from the door.

I've unlocked the door. Come into the reception area and get out of the sun.

The worker went to the car's trunk, opened it, and pulled out her briefcase and a small bag that contained what few possessions Joe had. Then she opened the front passenger door and helped the young, fragile-looking child out of the car. She made sure his I LOVE CALIFORNIA baseball cap, and the small sunglasses she had bought for him in Los Angeles were securely on his head.

Little Joseph Charles Smith hated everything he saw and felt. The extreme heat sucked at him, taking his breath, and needled him, stinging his skin. The surroundings, which he shyly surveyed, were all brown, very brown, dull, dumb, desiccated brown. He hated brown. His favorite colors were blue and green. And although he did see some faded green in some sparse vegetation dotted about the landscape, all of it seemed to be in the process of turning brown. His pink brown-freckled skin protested aggressively, sending signals to his brain that would have been profanity-laced had it been possible.

The social worker quickly walked Joe to the door that opened upon their arrival. Aunt Liz, a late-middle-aged woman of short, graying hair, impassive face, and a comfortable bulk to her body, ushered them into a narrow, rectangular room with no furniture. There were hooks on the wall for coats and hats. A large, dusty mat rested on the floor with some boots. Against one wall was a sink streaked with thin mud, built into a cabinet where bottles of soaps, skin lotions, and sunblocks rested on its countertop. In the back wall, directly opposite the front door, was a large, almost gate-like door.

"My goodness, you are a little one," said Aunt Liz, who wore baggy green pants and a buttoned long-sleeved, oversized men's shirt with pockets over her not insubstantial breasts. "How old are you again?"

"Six," the shy boy replied.

"You look about four. You can thank your mother for that."

The worker opened her briefcase. "I have some paperwork for you to sign, Mrs. Fleming. But first, I'm assuming this isn't your complete, um, home?"

"They didn't inform you?" Aunt Liz asked.

"Who?"

"All the myriad, officious bureaucrats I've had to deal with to secure custody of my nephew."

"No, I'm afraid not, I'm really just a—"

"Courier of living flesh."

"Well… I just started. This is my first assignment."

"And do you trust your new state employer?"

"Yes, of course."

"Then trust that beyond that big door there, I have a perfectly suitable abode for my nephew and me. Now give me the papers to sign."

～

Beyond that big door there... was not an abode but an elevator. A large, hefty, industrial-looking elevator unlike any vertical conveyance Joe had ever been in. His mouth dropped, and his eyes widened as he looked up at the high ceiling of the elevator. Aunt Liz looked down at him and smiled. "Do you want to push the button?"

Joe nodded yes, and Aunt Liz moved him to the control panel. There were only two buttons. UP and DOWN. Joe stared at them with some hesitancy.

"What are you waiting for? You don't really think we can go any more up than we already are, do you?"

Joe looked up at his aunt. She was a tower of a woman, and if she had not been smiling, she would have been as frightening as hell. He looked back to the panel and pushed the DOWN button with a six-year-old resolve.

The giant elevator jerked into motion, descended with a hum, and then jerked just slightly as it stopped. There was a big door opposite the one they had entered by, and it opened slowly. Aunt Liz picked up Joe's bag with one hand and took Joe's right hand with the other, and walked him out of the elevator and into a spacious storeroom.

"Not so impressive, I admit," Aunt Liz said. "But it's damn convenient to warehouse your stores right where the elevator ends. But you just wait."

She walked him to another fair-sized door that slid open upon the push of another button.

Aunt Liz stepped Joe into a large, circular space. "This will be your new home, Joey."

The circular space was, especially to a child of Joe's size, vast, intimidating, confusing, and unlike any place Joe, in his few years, had seen. Yet it was filled with the familiar. There was an area with a couch, several tables, and a few worn, comfy-looking chairs, all facing a big curved digital screen on the curved wall. There was a kitchen with all the cabinets, counters, appliances, and hanging dish towels one would expect. The big appliances did not match in color, although the cabinets did. The counter could have stood a wiping down, and the dish towels were a bit ragged. There were pots and pans on top of the stove. And a row of new magnets on the refrigerator door, although none of them held anything up. Just off to the side of the kitchen was a dining table with chairs. There was a large desk with a computer and a monitor in another area. And papers haphazardly placed on either side of the computer. There was a desk chair. And a standing lamp next to it illuminated this part of the large room. A little way to the side of the desk was a recliner chair with a table by it. On the table was a stack of books, a reading lamp, and a half-filled glass of dark liquid with ice cubes, beads of condensation clinging to the bottom half of the glass. Along the curved wall opposite the digital screen, spaced evenly, were three open entryways to what looked to be corridors.

"Well, let's get you settled in your bedroom first," Aunt Liz said as she directed Joe to the corridor on their right.

~

The bedroom was sparse. Just a single bed with a nondescript bedspread and a white pillow; an unpainted wooden dresser with four drawers; a small desk with a small desk chair. There was an empty closet with no door. The walls were white and bare.

"I know it doesn't look like much, Joey, but I had no idea what a six-year-old kid would like. Or even if all six-year-olds like all the same stuff. I know your stuff was lost in the hurricane so think of this room as an empty canvas for you to fill with what you like."

Joe said nothing. He had nothing to say. It just was what it was, and it was all overwhelming. He didn't want to, but he started to cry.

"Oh, shit, Joey, don't cry."

(Has there ever been a more useless admonition?)

"Maybe you better sit down on the bed."

Joe walked over to the bed and sat, slumping into his sadness

Aunt Liz did not know what to do. She had never had children. She had not liked children much, even when she was a child. And she had spent years teaching in a university dismayed by how many of her students were still children. But by reflex, she gave him a clean tissue she had in one of her breast pockets. Then she quickly cataloged in her mind what more she could possibly do. Get him a glass of water? Or milk? Tell him to buck up? Comfort him? A memory from her own childhood centered her thoughts. A dead pet. The end of life. It had been furry and fun and was now cold and still. Tears welled then fountained and would not stop. Her father, a gentle, joyful man, sat down next to her, wrapped an arm around her, and held her. He agreed that it was awful and undoubtedly worthy of as many tears as she had. She remembered burying her face into his body. Did she want that? To be on the receiving end of that? Joey's crying was beginning to labor his breathing. What choice did she have?

Aunt Liz sat down next to Joe and put her arms around him. He buried his face in her side, and the perception of wetness was immediate.

"My mommy has passed away!" Joe said between sobs.

It was the weirdest thing Aunt Liz had ever heard coming from the mouth of one so young. Passed away? An existential equivocation? And yet it seemed to offer no more comfort than the truth.

"Joey, your mommy died. She is dead. Happens to people every day. She didn't just pass away or fade from the scene. She died. You will miss her, I'm sure. And you should, you should miss her every day. Because that way you'll never forget her. And it will hurt, it will hurt badly. And then it will hurt less bad. And then, eventually, it will no longer hurt. But the memory will remain—*it* will not pass away. That's the only thing you can do about this crappy situation."

Joe pulled his face away from his Aunt Liz's side and looked up at her. The tears stopped, and he became thoughtful. It made sense. Other thoughts arose. He sniffed a big sniff, and Aunt Liz pulled out another tissue and wrapped it around Joey's nose, and commanded him to blow. He did. It was a generous release. Then, she wiped his nose and cleaned up his whole face with another clean tissue. After which, Joe asked, "Why do you live in a hole?"

~

Aunt Liz did not answer the question immediately. Instead, she asked, "Are you hungry?"

Little Joe nodded.

"Would you like some mac and cheese?"

"What's that?"

"You've never had mac and cheese?"

Aunt Liz's incredulity was scary as if it was a reprimand. Joey didn't quite know what to say. But then Aunt Liz laughed a short, joyful laugh and said, "Boy have you got a treat coming. Come on!"

She took him to the circular space and sat him down at the dining table. "Sit here for a second. I'll be right back," she said, then left and exited by another corridor than the one Joey had already been down. Joey sat there, alone and quiet, not daring to move to any other part of the space except with his eyes, which roamed, giving his mind things to note. Soon Aunt Liz returned with a green-covered hardback book in her hand. She placed it down in front of Joe.

"Here. You'll enjoy this. You do know how to read, don't you?"

"Yes. Mommy taught me."

"She did?" Aunt Liz expressed some surprise. "Good for her. Well, that's a book about some animals in England, one of whom lives in a hole. I think you'll find that it's a perfectly natural thing to do for certain creatures. Now, mac and cheese! And tuna! Yes, I'll add a can of tuna."

Aunt Liz went to the kitchen, grabbed a pan, filled it with water, placed it on a burner on the stove, and turned the burner on. She then opened a cabinet door and drew from it a box of Kraft Macaroni and Cheese—still considered by aficionados as the *cheesiest* —and a can of tuna. Then, out of the refrigerator, she took some butter. "I only make it with butter; I never add milk. That's my secret." She then went about the task—or rather the joy—of preparing their lunch.

Joey opened the book before him and thumbed through the pages to see if there were any illustrations. There were, and that comforted him. Then he made his way to the first page of the first chapter and read, *The mole had been working very hard all morning, spring-cleaning his little home….*

By the time Aunt Liz returned with two bowls of hot, steaming, orange mac & cheese infused with the shredded flesh of tuna, he had read three pages of the book. He understood some of it but did not understand a lot of the words. He already liked Mole, though, and did not want to stop.

"Go ahead, take a bite," Aunt Liz said to Joey as she placed a bowl before him on the table.

She had stuck a fork in the middle of the dish, and Joey took it, forked up some of the little cheese-smeared noodles and tuna flesh, and smelled it. Then tongue-tipped it. As his mind and body did not send out any warnings, he placed the forkful in his mouth and began to chew.

It was warm, flavorful, and felt fun in his mouth. That was the only way he could think of it as—fun in his mouth.

"Good?" Aunt Liz asked.

Joey nodded.

"Good," Aunt Liz declared.

Aunt Liz sat down to her bowl and took a few bites and the time to chew, appreciate, and swallow before she spoke again. "Joey, do you know who I am?"

"The people said you were my Aunt Elizabeth."

"That's right. But you can call me Liz. Do you know what an aunt is?"

Joey shook his head.

"An aunt is the sister of one of your parents. In our case, I am your mother's sister."

"But you are old!"

Aunt Liz snorted at this reality. "Well, yes, twenty years older than your mother. That's because I'm actually your mother's half-sister?"

"Which half?"

It was a more intelligent question than Joey knew, and Aunt Liz laughed. "Well, the best half, of course, Joey. But, no, look, what it means is that we had the same father, but different mothers."

Joey's little freckled face fell into confusion and a struggle to understand.

"It's something I can explain when you're a little older. But what it means is, since no one knows who your father was—although he was obviously a redheaded guy—I am your closest relative, uh, you know, family. So they contacted me to see If I could take care of you. And after some reflection—and I've got to tell you, it was much deep reflection—I said okay. I don't really know why. Your mother and I were not close. But then I thought of my father, your grandfather. He's also dead. A couple of years ago. He regretted not getting to see his one and only grandchild. I thought that he would have wanted me to take you on. Not a very logical reason to do it, of course, but, well —here we are. You're going to live with me now, and I'm going to do my best to raise you, you poor little bastard, you."

Joe had finished his macaroni and cheese. The whole time Aunt Liz had been talking, it was his main occupation and concentration, his face bent down close to the bowl so the fork would have but a small distance to travel. But now, he raised his face and looked at this woman across the table from him who had just announced that she was his only family. And that he would now be living with her instead of his mother, who was dead, gone, and buried.

"But why do you live in a hole?" Little Joey asked again.

∼

It was a fair question. But how to answer it was a perplexing one. "Well, Joey, I'll tell you why but, first, let me show you more of this —hole."

Aunt Liz took him down each corridor and into every room (there were four along each corridor with one large bathroom at the ends), some of which were empty, but the ones that weren't were...

"This is my library," Aunt Liz said when she stopped in the middle

35

of a room with floor-to-ceiling bookshelves filled with books of various sizes. And of several kinds: non-fiction and fiction, serious reads and frivolous fun. "I have here books I've collected for years, including all the textbooks I used to assign my students. Also, books from my childhood. This is where I pulled out *The Wind in the Willows* for you," she said, pointing to the green book Joe was clutching…

"This was my father's—your grandfather's room. He lived with me in the last years of his life. See that funny bed, that's a hospital bed. I had a hospice nurse here for the last six months. Just haven't bothered to get rid of it. Who knows, maybe *I'll* need it someday," Aunt Liz said with a bit of a laugh. "On the other side of the room is his music collection. None of it digitized. It's all on CDs and these big things called records or LPs. His taste was purely 20th century, and basically only the first half of the 20th century, maybe a little beyond. But that was your grandfather," she said with a smile of sweet remembrance.

"This is going to be your schoolroom." There was a desk and chair for Joe. An interactive large data screen on one wall could be written on with a stylus. And various posters on the other walls that graphically and colorfully provided information on geography, geology, history, astronomy, and math. "They tell me you've never been to any school, that your mom was planning to homeschool you, Joey. Well, since we are miles away from any school, that's what I'm going to do. And I daresay, I'm far more qualified than your mother was."

Joey was never quite sure what his Aunt Liz was saying. But he liked this room. And the posters on the wall. He went over and sat at his desk. It felt good. When his mom taught him to read, they sat on the floor, on big pillows. He was so comfortable there he would often fall asleep. He didn't think he could fall asleep at this desk, but he liked that about it.

"Do you like it?" His Aunt Liz asked.

Joey nodded, then said. "Will you read this to me?" He held up the green book.

"I thought you said you could read."

Joe scrunched his eyes together in thought, trying to come up with an answer. "I can read but not everything. I'm only six, you know."

"Yes, I do know that. But I'm not used to six-year-old kids. Or any kids, for that matter. But I guess I'll have to get used to it. Yeah, okay, let me read you the first chapter, then maybe we can talk about why I live in a hole."

~

"This hole is actually a habitat. Do you know what a habitat is, Joey?"

Joey shook his head. He was still sitting in his classroom chair, and Aunt Liz was sitting in the chair where she had sat when she started reading *The Wind in the Willows*.

"Well, a habitat is usually a natural home for an animal. Like a nest for a bird or a hole for a mole. But it can also be a home for people living in an inhospitable environment."

Aunt Liz could see that Little Joey wasn't getting it. Then she got it. You couldn't teach Joey like a college student. She would have to reach for...for...examples, analogies, metaphors, she guessed. Well, wasn't that the way humans always communicated? Of course, it was. "Well, let's say you wanted to live under the ocean."

Joey perked up. "I like the ocean."

"Of course, you do. Because you grew up always around one. Despite my warnings to your mother. But, be that as it may, could you live *under* the ocean?"

"Mommy could swim underwater."

"Yes, but can you live underwater? You can't stay down there forever, can you? You have to come up to breathe."

Little Joey nodded because he knew it was true.

"But what if you could build a home to live in under the ocean? One that didn't let the water in and had air to breathe. Then you could stay underwater. That would be your habitat."

"But this isn't under the water. It's under the ground."

"Yes," Aunt Liz said, "that's true. But this habitat was built for people who want to live on Mars. Do you know what Mars is?"

Joey nodded because he was tired of shaking his head. He was tired of not knowing.

"You do?"

But he couldn't fool his Aunt Liz. Joey reluctantly shook his head.

Aunt Liz did not seem upset, though. "Mars is a planet, like Earth, but out in space. Look, here." She got up and went to a poster showing the solar system. She pointed to the third planet from the Sun. "This is Earth where we live." And then she pointed to the fourth planet. "And this is Mars. And right now, people are preparing to go to Mars; explorers and scientists. But Mars is not like Earth because it has no air to breathe, like being underwater. And it can get very, very hot, and very, very cold. So these explorers and scientists will build on Mars a habitat just like this one so they can live there. Also, on Mars, there's a lot of what's called radiation. Which is something like sunlight but even, well, hotter in a really bad way. They will put the habitat underground, just like this one, because the ground will stop a lot of the radiation. Our habitat here is what is called a prototype, or a test, to see how well it works. It was built by my wife." Aunt Liz paused for a moment. She took in a deep breath, then let it out. "She's dead also. I guess we have a lot of dead people in our life, uh, Joey?"

Little Joey nodded.

"Anyway, my wife, her name was Vivian, she was an architect and an engineer and an inventor and… Well, she was just a very smart woman and knew how to build things. She designed this habitat. And a whole lot of other things. And after she died, I moved in here because it was like still being with her. I don't know if you can understand that, but—" Aunt Liz stopped when memory intruded.

"Are you going to cry?"

"Maybe."

"You gave me all your tissues."

"I did, didn't I? Well, then I guess I better not cry. Anyway, that's why I live in a hole. Is that okay? Are you going to mind living in a hole?"

"Where can I play?"

"Ah. That's a very cogent question. I guess we can set up a playroom in one of the empty rooms."

"I mean, outside. Mommy always sent me outside to play. But I don't like the outside here."

"No, it's not good, is it? Much too hot during the day. And it can get very cold at night. But still, with the proper clothes, which we will have to get for you, we can maybe have some fun after dark. Otherwise…I hadn't thought about this as I never go outside to play…Well, maybe I should take you on some field trips. I'll take you out of the desert, and we'll go visit other places. I suppose that should be part of your education. But for right now, let's go to my bedroom. I've got a tape measure there, and I can measure you."

"Why?"

"Because we have to buy you some new clothes. We'll measure you, then go online and order you a bunch of clothes, and then a big drone will deliver everything tomorrow."

~

Taking the measure of Joseph Charles Smith was a ticklish affair. Aunt Liz had to admonish him to keep still and be quiet as he giggled and squirmed when she ran the cloth measuring tape up and down and around various parts of his little body. Little Joey tried his best to keep still. But he couldn't control his giggles, which soon were as hearty with laughs as his little lungs would allow for, mixed with joyful screams. It was a release, a release he needed, and Aunt Liz soon got it and tolerated it, then couldn't help but join in.

When they were finally finished, both a bit out of breath, they looked at each other deeply. Suddenly, they were for each other, the new face of their lives. At least for now.

~

A pair of Mickey Mouse pajamas, still in their store packaging. A new toothbrush. Two clean pairs of underwear in a package of three, the third pair being worn by Joey. A picture of his mother in a small frame that his mother had placed on his hospital bedside table. And a little stuffed animal, a red dog that he had named Blue. All this was recovered from Joey's bag as Aunt Liz put him to bed after a dinner of cultured hamburger, carrot sticks, and little cups of chocolate pudding. Joey asked his Aunt Liz to read another chapter of *The Wind in the Willows*. She did.

Joey fell asleep in the middle of the reading. Aunt Liz tucked him in and then hesitated to kiss him goodnight. She felt compelled by tradition to do so, but somehow…

~

The next day, Joe was hugely impressed when a drone delivered his new clothes, just as Aunt Liz had said it would. He saw it on the giant curved screen in the living area, in a feed from the outside security cameras.

The clothes were fine, and it became a game trying them all on, then hanging most of them up in the closet, or learning how to fold others for putting in the dresser.

~

That night Aunt Liz had Joey get dressed in his new protective cold weather clothes. She pushed a thick stocking cap on his head and slid mittens on his hands. Then they ascended and walked out of the habitat into a deeply dark desert landscape. Domed overhead was

39

a brilliant, sparkling night sky that seemed to Joey to be both far away yet inches from his face. It made him dizzy as he looked straight up and fell backward into the dusty desert floor.

"Are you alright?" Aunt Liz asked as she knelt beside him and gathered him up, concerned that Little Joey was starting to hyperventilate. She cupped her hand loosely over his mouth and nose and said, "Breathe in slowly through your nose, Joey, into my hand. Slower, come on, you can do it."

Joey did eventually because he had to, so he could ask, "What…?"

"You've never seen this have you?"

Joey shook his head.

"It's the night sky, Joey. It's what it really looks like when you are not surrounded by city lights. This is where we really live, Joey. In the universe."

Little Joey felt as if he was floating or sitting on something floating. Which, of course, he was.

"The ones that twinkle are stars, other suns like ours. The ones that don't—like that one." Aunt Liz pointed to one bright spot among many not as bright. "That's a planet, like our Earth."

"Is that Mars?"

"I don't know. I just know it's a planet. I was a history professor, not astronomy. But I guess I better find out if I'm going to homeschool you. I do know that that big swath of stars up there is an arm of the Milky Way. Which is our galaxy. I'll show you close-up pictures of it later. Are you getting cold?"

"No. I want to look."

"Okay." She stood Joey up and dusted his backside off. "We'll stand here for a little while. But then we'll have to go in. And stay standing, okay? Don't fall down again. And close your mouth. You don't want some night-flying bug popping in and gagging you."

5
FATHER AND SON

Neuro had few childhood memories of Kenya.

He had been taken away from that East African country at the age of five to avoid any harm that may have come to him from his father's enemies. Who, although subtle, could be violent. He was flown to London on a chartered jet with three servants and his mother Afaafa, the youngest of Jaali Kinyanjui's two wives.

The plane ride was exciting, and young Khadambi spent much of the time staring out of a window, looking down at the world below. He saw savannas, mountains, forests, and deserts. And bodies of water that Wokabi, his nurse, called either lakes or seas. He had no idea that the world was so big and diverse in landscapes. But his young life had been sheltered. Both figuratively in the cocoon of family and servants who coddled, hugged, and played with the child as their precious little one. And literally in a walled compound.

When he traveled through Nairobi, where his family lived, it was in an armored SUV with dark tinted windows. But that was okay. For nothing outside of these windows could have intrigued young Khadambi more than the hand-held video game loosely based on the Masai folktale of "The Greatest Warrior of All" that he played with great intensity. He was blissfully unaware of the teeming auto traffic the SUV traveled in. Or the teeming people traffic—African, Arab, Indian, the occasional European, yet all Kenyan—who legged it to here and there and everywhere on the sidewalks, crossing the street, entering markets. He stayed with the adventures of the hare, the jackal, the leopard, the braggart caterpillar, and the brave frog until the SUV pulled into the underground parking lot of The Pinnacle Hass Tower. At seventy floors, it was the tallest building in Africa. Then excitement came from the long elevator ride up to his father's business. When the elevator doors opened upon Kinyanjui Holdings, young Khadambi was set loose to run past the reception and down a hallway and into his father's office, yelling "Baba, Baba, Baba!" all the way.

Young Khadambi's father, having heard the welcome call of his son, had come out from behind his desk and squatted to receive his son as the tall-for-his-age boy flew into his arms. The father's enfolding hug and the young boy's clinging hug were warm and tender, joyful and comfortable. Young Khadambi's older half-brother Yaro Yoshi, son of his father's first wife and his father's apprentice in the business, was also there. He viewed this father-son display with cheerful amusement. It was reminiscent of his own young boy experiences with his "Baba" or "Chichi" that had now been turned into mutual respect and business-like companionship. He might have been jealous, even resentful, but he was too grown to harbor sibling rivalry. Besides, he was as guilty as the rest of the family of cocooning young Khadambi in love, indulgence, play, and protection.

~

Jaali Kinyanjui was a billionaire. Not a Kenyan shilling billionaire, but an American dollar billionaire. It had been a fluke.

Jaali Kinyanjui had been born and orphaned in the Kibera slum of Nairobi and was living mainly on the streets by the age of seven. Then, at nine, he was found and befriended by a young teacher of the newly opened Magoso primary school in the slum. His joyful face, gleeful smile, and energy had attracted the teacher. The school took him in, gave him a home, and educated him. The school was pioneering music therapy to help the children, most of whom were orphans from the streets. Young Jaali had been born deaf in one ear and simply did not appreciate music. But he found his music in math. This got him a scholarship to a fine private Kibera secondary school. There he turned his math passion to computer languages and software. Both schools got most of their funding from Japan, and young Jaali had his choice of scholarships from several Japanese universities. China, which was involving itself in the future of Africa for the influence it would buy, swooped down and snatched Jaali up with the promise of a wholly-free university education in Beijing. And a guaranteed position in a Chinese software concern after graduation.

Jaali, now a young man no less energetic and joyful than he had been at seven, was shocked by the subtle cloud of oppression he found in China. The ancient city of Beijing had become a modern city. It was almost overwhelming for the young slum-raised Jaali. There were suddenly so many glittering new things surrounding him. Slick automobiles, cellphones, designer clothes, extremely tall buildings, luxury accommodations. All hallmarks of the capitalist West that this Communist nation once spurned. But in taking on the hallmarks of the West, of the liberal, democratic West, in taking on these visible stamps on the surface of the West, did not mean taking the more profound inner essence of the West seriously. It was all a frivolous if expensive facade decorating the one-party rule over the lives, movements, and thoughts of the billion-plus individual Chinese humans. Not to mention visiting scholars from foreign lands who China really wanted to impress.

As welcome as the Chinese had made him feel, Jaali could go nowhere outside of Beijing without a minder from the Communist Party. He was discouraged from dating Chinese women, whom he found attractive. He couldn't order books from overseas. He found that his letters and emails back home were routinely censored, edited, or entirely suppressed. The food was good, though. He did like the food.

After receiving his degree, Jaali managed to take a month-long vacation in Japan. He was immediately struck by the hospitality of the Japanese. And their strong sense of community. And the Japanese women were as attractive to him as Chinese women, and the newly rebellious ones found him exotic and handsome. He remembered how much the Japanese had helped his schools in Kibera, and now wondered why he had chosen China over Japan. China, where a guaranteed "dream" job was waiting for him.

Two days before his vacation was to end, he took a train deep into the suburbs of Tokyo to an area rarely visited by tourists. His guide was Sachiko, a young woman he had met in a Roppongi bar. He said he wanted to explore, walk, see Japanese life unfiltered by the mask that Tokyo could present to *gaijin*. Sachiko was happy to be his guide. He was tall and handsome and open, so unlike a *nihonjin* man. It was a pleasure to be with him. Walking along a major *Ōdōri* that cut through the suburb, Sachiko wanted to stop at a Baskin-Robbins 31 Flavors. Sachiko loved all the American food—Kentucky Fried Chicken, Denny's, McDonald's, and others—that had planted themselves in Japan. While inside the ice cream shop, a small five-year-old girl stared at Jaali and reached up to him with one hand. Her mother started to apologize—"Sumimasen, sumimasen." But Jaali bent down to the little girl, smiled, and said, "Konnichiwa," the standard greeting he had learned on his first day in Tokyo. Fascinated by this tall *gaijin,* the little girl gently stroked his black face, possibly to see if any of it would come off. But none did. She spoke with a soft, shy voice. "Anata wa kono-iro desu ka?"

Sachiko giggled.

"What did she say?" Jaali asked.

"She asked if you were that color all over," Sachiko answered.

Jaali was charmed by the little girl's innocent, unfettered curiosity. And at that moment knew what he had to do.

When Jaali got back to Beijing, he went to the Kenyan Embassy. He convinced them to call the founder and headmistress at his Kibera secondary school. Could she get him in contact with one of her Japanese supporters? Could he get sponsorship to stay in Japan, maybe a scholarship for a master's degree, maybe on to a Ph.D.? He didn't want to stay in China. He realized when he looked into the face of the little Japanese girl that he hated China. The headmistress was thrilled. She felt that the prodigal son had returned.

Soon Jaali was studying at the University of Tokyo under Professor Yasuo Otsuka. A genial genius, Otsuka-san specialized in taking *gaijin* post-grad students under his wing as he was fascinated with the world beyond Japan. Not in a superficial way, but deeply. Otsuka-san had a broad face that seemed to have developed to accommodate his wide smile. He could speak passable French, good Chinese, competent Korean, and excellent English through that broad smile. Otsuka picked out Jaali early as a fellow genius, having always subscribed to the old adage, *It takes one to know one.* And he influenced Jaali to focus his studies on Artificial Intelligence, his own specialty.

Even before Jaali had his Ph.D., he and Otsuka-san formed a research corporation. Together, they solved a problem that remade the world. They gave AI human-like intuition, as opposed to fully human intuition. But it was enough intuition to prevent self-driving, self-flying, self-sailing vehicles from getting into accidents caused by the odd, the unusual, the unexpected, the random. With that and other innovations, Otsuka-san and Jaali became billionaires.

Jaali married Sachiko. They were living happily in Tokyo years later when they took a trip to Nairobi. Jaali wanted to visit the headmistresses and teachers from his Kibera schools. Some were now quite elderly, and he wanted to thank them before they were gone. Sachiko was not impressed by Nairobi and had a revulsive reaction to the Kibera slum. She left early to go back home. Jaali stayed on for weeks, reintroducing himself to the slum he grew up in, the city that tolerated the slum, and the country trying to find a solid identity.

Jaali was disturbed to find how deep and pervasive China and its investments had become in the country. The antipathy he had formed for China was aroused. So he decided to create an investment company. He put up much of the funds himself. And persuaded investors from Japan, the United Kingdom, and America to join him, all in competition with China, which did not make him popular with China. Nor with the Kenyans getting rich in liquid and political capital from their association with China.

Sachiko refused to move to Kenya. Jaali took a Kenyan wife, Afaafa. Which was fine. Polygamy was not only customary but legal in Kenya.

Jaali started to remake Nairobi. His investment company funded a process to systematically transform Kibera. He changed it from a cobbled-together sheet metal-and-wood-dwellings-slum to a vast neighborhood of low-cost modular housing. He replaced the trash-infused dirt and mud streets with paved roads with proper drainage. He installed electricity and street lighting. Jaali provided temporary shelter to the displaced families and brought them back once their new homes were ready. He offered thousands of micro-loans to the enterprising, most of them being hard-working women.

And he planted trees. He planted them along the newly-paved roads and in the small but adequate yards of the new homes. Thousands of trees, young but quick to mature trees, would provide green, easy and comfortable on the eye; shade, so lovely to sit under; oxygen, so essential to breathe.

And more trees throughout the city. In old and new parks, foliating around new skyscrapers and old, shading the bustling foot traffic and covering the earth with vibrant, breeze-blown life.

This made Jaali the most popular man in Kenya, a celebrity, an almost mythic character worthy of worship. Natural popularity is always of concern to those in power who have to manufacture popularity. And so, Jaali Kinyanjui became a concern of the Belt and Road Chinese and their Kenyan partners.

Jaali did not care. He delighted in it. He used his power to push for political reform—truly democratic political reform. He wanted authoritarian China and its influence on authoritarian Kenyans out. He was honest about this; he declared it publicly and often. He took gleeful delight in his success.

That there would be threats to his life was inevitable. But he refused to worry about it. He had the money to provide for security.

But when a bomb went off, killing three of his servants while sparing him, Afaafa, and young Khadambi, Jaali decided some pragmatic worry would be appropriate.

Jaali purchased a residence in London, thinking Sachiko would not welcome his "other family" to Tokyo. And he put Afaafa, little Khadambi, and three servants on a chartered jet, saying goodbye with tears, and that he would come and visit as soon as possible.

$\sim$

Little Khadambi was asleep when the chartered jet landed at Heathrow Airport outside London. Between his mother, Afaafa, and his nurse, Wokabi, he was held aloft above English soil until they were through the expedited passport and customs process and safely seated in a limousine. He awoke now and then, his little eyelids opening, his little eyes looking around the airport, his little face questioning what he saw. Then with a tonal moan, he would bury his face back into his mother's shoulder, or that of Wokabi's, and return to sleep.

Barely. Little Khadambi refused to sit up and have the seatbelt put on him in the limousine. So Afaafa and Wokabi held him tight, his head on his mother's lap, his feet at the end of his long legs on Wokabi's lap. And through the pleasant half-sleep and comfort of human contact, he listened to the sounds of the limousine negotiating itself out of the airport, heard intermittent honks, the roar of planes ascending and descending, voices talking and shouting. Then there were the steady rushing white sounds as the car traveled along the motorway into London. And his mother's and Wokabi's quiet voices as they spoke words of relief, worry, and wonderment as they entered London. Then, finally, their voices called to Khadambi to wake up.

Which he did. Fully. He was ready to be inquisitive about this new world his Baba had sent him to.

At the moment, that new world was a secure private parking garage of a large apartment block in Trevor Square, Knightsbridge. A tall, pink-faced man with wispy hair combed straight back greeted his mother. Dressed in a blue suit with a yellow vest and a red flower in his lapel, matching his very bright red tie, he warmly welcomed the new residents. Little Khadambi understood nothing of what he said but felt kindly toward him as the man seemed to want to make his mother happy. The pink-faced man led them to an elevator, taking them up several floors. They exited to a corridor, which led to ornate double doors.

"Welcome to your new home," the pink-faced man said as he opened the doors and revealed shine and polish and gleam, quiet fabric-covered tan walls ahead, and cool blue marble walls to the side. The floor featured large square reflective white marble tiles. Little Khadambi ran in and looked at it all and was immediately drawn to his right to a spiral staircase descending to the lower floor of the residence. He looked down the stairwell and became dizzy at the descent of the curving flow of the stairs.

"Dambi!" his mother called. "Come to me."

But Little Khadambi started to go down the stairs. Wokabi ran after him, caught him in mid-descent, and Afaafa and the pink-faced man soon heard peals of boyish laughter coming up the stairwell.

"You must excuse my son," Afaafa said. "He can become enthusiastic."

The pink-faced man smiled as Wokabi came up the stairs holding little Khadambi, still squirming from her tickling.

"Quite all right, madam. I'm sure this is quite exciting for him. Shall I show you through the residence now?"

~

There were six bedrooms, seven bathrooms, three "amazing" reception rooms overlooking Trevor Square totaling seventy-five feet in length. There was also an "extremely spacious" kitchen/breakfast room.

"I hope you will find this residence adequate, Madam," the pink-faced man said.

Afaafa was a well-educated woman from a middle-class Kenyan family. And although not well-traveled, her voracious reading, not to mention viewing many foreign (to her) films, made her worldly in her way. Worldly enough to be amused by the pink-faced man's understatement.

～

"When will Baba come?" Little Khadambi asked that night as his mother put him to bed.

"He will come when he comes, Dambi. He is an important man with much to do."

"I miss him."

"Already? We have just arrived."

"Why must we live here?"

"Because your Baba wants us too."

"Will Yoshi come?"

"I suppose. But you must not expect it."

"Why not?"

"So you won't be disappointed if he cannot."

"What is 'disappointed'?"

"Disappointed is what I will feel if you do not lay down and go to sleep now."

～

Little Khadambi fell asleep quickly in his large bed in his large bedroom. He awoke in the morning to a beautiful spring day in London.

6
A RUDE AWAKENING CONTINUED

"No, Neuro, please… Oh. Good. You didn't put me to sleep after all."

Actually, I did

"No, you didn't. Not a second passed—

A year has passed.

"A year?" Astro threw off the sheet covering him and stood, this time steady and solid on the ground.

I told you we had more work to do. Before, you woke up too early.

"I'm sorry."

It was not your fault.

Astro looked around. He was still in his loft, as he could now see with a sharp and clear vision. As he could also see clearly his naked body. "I still have no body hair."

Hair is one of the most challenging things to create.

"You have it on my head?"

One of our early efforts. You were always inordinately proud of your head of hair.

"'Were?'"

Are.

"But not so proud of my body which stands here naked before you. Can you please put some clothes on me?"

You have clothes in your armoire.

"Can't you just...snap them on me?"

You are not a paper doll.

"Happy to hear it."

I want you to have as normal a life as possible. You need to dress yourself.

Astro had nothing to say to that. He just padded to the antique French armoire, opened one of the long side doors, pulled out a pair of briefs from a drawer, and slipped them on. They were a deep red. He opened up the double center doors of the armoire and looked in. Shirts and slacks hung neatly, as always, shirts to the right, slacks to the left. And they hung on hangers; they did not float in mid-armoire air. Astro grabbed a long sleeve black shirt and a pair of black slacks and put them on.

"I would love to give my face a splash of cold water."

Give it a try.

Astro walked to the bathroom and turned on the tap. Clear, sparkling water flowed quickly and drained swiftly. He cupped his hands and held them under the flow. The water was wet and cold. He bent to receive a cupped handful onto his face. The result was a disappointment. "I feel nothing on my face. Not wet. Not cold."

We will work on it. For some reason, the palms of the hands are easier to make touch-sensitive.

Astro moved from the bathroom to the triple windows wrapping around one corner of the loft. He lifted the shade of the center one. Below was Fifth and Hill, with Fifth flowing on toward Broadway. He opened the shade to his left. There was the brick building across Hill that had always been there. He opened the shade to his right and saw green Pershing Square across Fifth. Everything was dimensional and textured, and actual. Except for…

"Neuro?"

Yes?

"Nothing's moving."

We are working on it.

"WHAT THE BLOODY BLUE BLAZES IS GOING ON?"

I told you. There was an accident.

"Neuro, did you upload my mind?"

You never believed we could upload minds.

"That doesn't answer the question. Did you and that bastard Carmichael find a way to upload my mind? Am I in some kind of a machine, a computer?"

No, I guarantee you that you, in essence, are not in a machine.

"Not in a machine?"

No.

"Then where am I?"

You are where you are.

"What do you mean I am where I am? What kind of philosophical BS is that? I mean, where am I? Where is my body?"

I don't think we should go into that right now.

"What do you mean we shouldn't go into it right now?"

How important do you think your body is?

"Well, I think it's pretty damn important!"

Be that as it may, for right now, it is not. But you are, my friend. You are important.

7
CARMICHAEL

Brandon Carmichael was once called a *boy genius*. This was appropriate because when he was a boy, he was unusually bright for his age.

After he reached legal age, he was often referred to as *the boyish genius*. As much for his constant enthusiasm (exhausting and annoying to some) as for his unquestioned superior intelligence (exhausting and annoying to some). Not to mention his round face and straight, thin, light brown hair, which always fell forward onto his broad forehead.

Carmichael's body began to square out in middle-age as it does to many men. But his face retained its roundness, so the sobriquet was amended to *boy-faced genius*.

In several discussions with Neuro that centered around Carmichael, Astro amended—or rather altered—that sobriquet to an epithet. He referred to Carmichael as that *snot-faced genius,* acknowledging the quality of his intelligence while questioning its maturity.

"He's so desperate to be religious, to be a true believer, but, of course, he can't be, not believing in anything non-material," Astro once said to Neuro. "He doesn't believe in the immortal soul, so he wants to manufacture immortal souls. He doesn't believe in heaven in the clouds, so he wants to build heaven out of computer clouds. He's scared to death of death, so he wants to craft immortality out of zeros and ones. It's childish, Neuro. Like an ego-centric child—and all children are ego-centric, of course—he has difficulty conceiving of non-existence. Especially his own. But what's existence without non-existence to compare it to? What the hell would a person do with all that spare time? What price immortality? Unending boredom?"

~

Brandon Carmichael was born toward the end of the 20th century and couldn't wait to get the hell out of it. At the age of ten, at the beginning of the 21st century—which he had rightly pointed out for two frustrating years would begin on January 1, 2001, and *not* January 1, 2000—he declared that it would be *his* century. And that he would not only see it all the way through, he also intended to see at least a healthy chunk of the 22nd century. The future was his favorite location, and he hated to think of any of it preceding without him.

Atypical of children of his intellectual abilities, he was not bored being in grades appropriate to his age. He more than understood everything his teachers taught. He read his textbooks with alacrity and speed. He breezed through his homework. All of this left him plenty of time for deep reflections on questions of reality that intrigued him. He reveled in the admiration of his teachers and his parents' pride. He certainly didn't mind the worshipfulness of some of his classmates of good taste. And he simply ignored the jealous discounting of his worth by other classmates of inferior intelligence. So, he never skipped grades as was offered and expected.

He went out of his way to help others with their homework. He assisted teachers. He was able to charm the socially elite kids, commensurate with the socially awkward kids, and show good school spirit by cheering on the physically adept jocks.

Brandon Carmichael graduated from his Illinois high school at eighteen. He declared in his valedictorian speech, "Some of the graduates here are leaving high school knowing a lot about one thing. Some are leaving knowing a little about a lot of things. I am leaving knowing a lot about a lot of things. And I hope to use this mental power for the benefit of all humankind." This outrageous example of solipsistic self-regard received thunderous applause from both teachers and graduates, having been filtered through Brandon's boyish charm.

At the time of Astro's accident and Neuro's call to him, Dr. Brandon Carmichael was sixty-eight, and it was now difficult to call him boyish. His face was still round. But it was a settled round as if it had been a ball bounced too many times. His light brown hair had receded a bit, and no longer fell forward and so had to be pushed. His constant enthusiasm had settled as well. It now was more of a relentless arrogance. This was evidenced by the name he had given the scientific organization he had created, The Foundation for Immortality. The name was a double entendre, although not an indecent one. Although some people would have argued the point. Mostly the same people who had found him exhausting and annoying over the years. Carmichael did not care. He considered such people ill-informed at best and a sub-species to his own at worst.

Neuro had always found Brandon Carmichael amusing. He was undeniably brilliant if obsessed. He had occasional incisive insights into the brain that bordered on Neuro's own research. And his insights never failed to deepen Neuro's thinking. Neuro felt that Carmichael was welcome to his arrogance. Even if it made him an ass on occasion. What would science be; what would all great creative human endeavors be without amusing arrogant asses? A bit dry, he thought.

~

Neuro landed at the Singapore Changi Airport two days after calling Dr. Carmichael. A self-driving Chinese-made taxi took him to the Marina South Pier, and there he boarded the self-piloting ferry to St. John's Island. Less than a square mile, the hilly island had been home to the Tropical Marine Science Institute for years. But five years before, it was moved to a larger facility on the main Singapore island, to a new building built, ironically, five meters above sea level. Its original location on St John's Island was sold to the Foundation for Immortality, which tore down the existing buildings and built a new facility—six meters above sea level.

It was a slick-looking building, leaning very much to the future. And Neuro could not help but be impressed when he arrived at it in a near ancient gas-powered jeep driven by one of the FFI's staff.

Dr. Brandon Carmichael waited at the entrance of the building. He wore khaki pants and boots and a short-sleeved plaid shirt. Carmichael made some notes on a datapad and finished just as the jeep pulled up, and Neuro swung his long legs out of the jeep and planted them on the land. Dr. Carmichael looked up from the datapad, and with a crooked smile that somehow did not seem in sync with his intense staring eyes, he greeted Neuro, "Khadambi! About time we got your ebony butt here!"

It was odd. Dr. Carmichael was no longer boyish, but his voice had never deepened with age. It had remained that of a young man, with traces of enthusiasm wisping around his confident statements.

Neuro looked down on Dr. Carmichael—physically if not metaphorically—and said, "Well, Brandon, you must admit that you are not really in my neighborhood."

"Oh, there are so many ways I could take that statement—but I won't. Being off the beaten track suits me just fine, Khadambi. Geographically *and* intellectually, as you well know."

"Intimately."

"Yes, well, come inside. Let's talk, let's catch up. And do satisfy my curiosity as to why you have finally come after a multitude of my pleadings."

~

Dr. Carmichael led Neuro through his facility. First, he gave him a cursory tour. And then quickly took Neuro to his office, haphazard in its decor and order, demonstrating that it was a working office, not one for show. Unless, of course, that was the show. He gestured Neuro to a couch while sitting in a chair, elevating himself enough to be eye-level with his tall guest. Once settled, Dr. Carmichael looked at Neuro with his piercing, questioning eyes.

Neuro did not hesitate to begin. "You contacted me recently saying you were close to cracking it."

"Cracking what?" Carmichael asked as his crooked smile formed.

"I don't have time for you to be coy, Brandon."

"Do I detect some urgency?"

"You do."

"Interesting? Are you perfectly well?"

"Perfectly."

"Under no medical threat?"

"I would not have said 'perfectly' if I was."

"So, you are asking only for professional reasons?"

"Not entirely."

"Does this concern your brother in Kenya?"

"He is also perfectly healthy as far as I know and has met with no recent...accidents."

"Ah!"

Carmichael suddenly knew by instinct. "It's your diminutive stargazing friend."

"Dr. Joe Smith's stature comes from his intellectual abilities, not from his height. And 'stargazing' as a description of his scientific and teaching endeavors can only be considered an insult."

"Really? Well, I suppose so. But a rather mild one compared to the insults I assume he has hurled at me."

Neuro had to smile. A broad one forming a single *Ha!* "Yes, he is not one of your fans. But he is, at the moment, near death." Neuro's smile faded, and the seriousness of his concern became evident.

It was a seriousness Carmichael decided to honor. "Tell me what happened."

Neuro gave as unemotional an account of Astro's accident as he could. He then described the aftermath, Doctor Chivers' assessment of the damage done, Astro's low prospects for recovery, and his own decision not to follow the doctor's recommendation. "He wanted me to pull the plug, as it is so ungraciously said."

"Ungracious but not as blunt as murder."

Neuro was taken aback by Carmichael's statement. But then, that is what blunt instruments are wielded to do. "Would you consider it murder?"

"I consider all death to be murder."

"Even by natural causes?"

"Natural for now. Just like not being able to fly was once natural."

"Defying gravity is not quite the same thing as defying death."

"Mmm," Carmichael pondered. "Let's not get deeply philosophical here. You said he's near-death?"

"Yes. I have him in a private room at Keck. He is in a BioMed biofoam cocoon which is limiting the trauma his mind is experiencing."

"He is not brain dead, then."

"No, of course not. That would have altered my decision, obviously."

"Obviously."

"So," Neuro said, getting impatient, "back to my original question, how close are you to cracking the uploading of minds?"

"A year or two, I believe. But six months to a year if you join us. I need your expertise in the connectome."

"I see. So, you are still speculating?"

"No. *I* am convinced. We are close to developing a scanner that will give us a complete digital model of a brain down to the molecular level. We are also working on ways to condense that model to take up far less computer storage than we so far have been faced with. With those two tools and others, I believe we will be able to emulate any human brain in a computer, complete with consciousness, memory, and, of course, the sense of self. My dream of immortality—"

"*Digital* immortality."

"Immortality by any other name? Smells just as sweet to me. But, of course, we have to know that what we scan is the complete picture. If we miss even one neuron, will we have the person? This is what I would like you to work on."

"And why do you think you are so close?"

"Testing, Khadambi. Rigorous testing."

"There are rumors out there that your testing has been on animal subjects of some lower levels of consciousness."

Dr. Carmichael answered only with his piercing eyes.

Neuro continued, "Dogs and cats. Chimps and dolphins."

Charmichael's crooked smile framed his next statement. "As politicians and bureaucrats always say, I neither confirm nor deny."

"Appropriate, I suppose. You are one of the most political people I've ever met."

"There's no need to be insulting, Khadambi."

"It's also said that this is the principal reason why you are here in Singapore. The newly authoritarian government allows all animal testing."

Dr. Charmichael stood and walked over to a sideboard with water, soda, and liquor bottles. "I've forgotten my manners. Not, of course, that I ever really had any. Manners are the defense strategy of the mundane. Nevertheless, may I offer you something to drink?"

"A glass of water would be fine."

Carmichael poured two glasses of water and returned to Neuro with them. He sat down, took a sip of water, leaned over to place the glass on the low table between him and Neuro. Then, while still leaning forward, he looked at Neuro and asked, "What's important to you, Khadambi? Joe Smith's survival, or some fucking cats?"

Neuro did not answer but drank his entire glass of water in successive gulps. When finished, he said, "I'm not sure Joe has six months, let alone a year."

"We can solve that problem."

"How?"

"Cryonic embalming of the brain."

"You're kidding."

"We preserve it until we are ready to scan, once confident of success. Khadambi, we have in storage four hundred and fifty cryonically embalmed brains now, with more coming to us every week. To achieve immortality, a great deal of money has been paid by those brains—or rather the selfs contained in those little three-pound masses of spongy fat and protein. When we are ready to go, we are obligated to scan them in the order they have paid. But, Khadambi, if you agree to join us, I will put Dr. Joe Smith at the head of that queue."

"So he will be the head at the head," Neuro stated dryly.

"Yes, well, I hadn't meant to make a pun. I'm not prone to dark humor."

Neuro smiled. Possibly a slightly crooked one. "Are you sure?"

~

Neuro and Dr. Carmichael talked about the details of any arrangement they might come to. Money was not an issue. Neuro had masses of money, especially being a single man with no family. It was conditions, assurances, and Carmichael's actual expectation of success. Neuro listened, asked pointed questions, and offered no indication of what his decision might be.

After they had talked as much as they could about the possibility of a joint future for them—not to mention a single, if not singular, if not singularity one for Astro—Dr. Carmichael had lunch brought in. Not surprisingly, seafood was on the menu. Their talk during lunch centered on gossip revolving around the scientific community, political rumblings, and changes here and there throughout the world. And a few recent books of popular science that Dr. Carmichael took issue with as they took issue with him. Their popularity bothered him. "I've never liked the idea of the exceptional trying to communicate with the mundane."

After lunch, Carmichael suggested a long walk across the island along a trail that cut through a thick forest of massive sea fig trees. They were strange trees with vast high crowns of leafy branches that reached out towards each other and formed a canopy overhead. Each was clothed in many descending aerial roots sprouting from those branches to fall to the ground seeking sustenance, giving the trees plenty of texture to gaze at.

There was much life in and among the fig trees. Mainly heard instead of seen—birds and insects, Neuro assumed. Although a gold-ringed cat snake about seven-feet long did slither quickly across the trail. Carmichael had to stop Neuro, who did not at first see the snake. And who was made quite nervous when he did.

"Is it venomous?" Neuro asked with some concern.

"Mildly."

"Mildy?"

"You won't die, but you would be in for some unpleasant swelling," Dr. Carmichael said with his practiced authority. "Best to stay away from them. They are nervous creatures and tend to strike before asking questions. And they are usually nocturnal. It's kind of rare seeing them out and about during the day."

"Insomnia, perhaps?"

"Well, yes, perhaps. Which would make them even more nervous and irritable, I would think. If you join us at the FFI, I will recommend some good thick high-top boots."

They ended up by the jetty where the ferry had brought Neuro earlier. Carmichael pointed out the elaborate seawall that had been built along the shore, as well as the dike system that would hopefully protect the small, vulnerable island from the continuing sea rise. Then they sat on a bench strategically placed to afford a view of the ocean and Lazarus Island, which was not far to the northeast.

"It seems to me, Brandon, that if you were going to settle on an island of a religious name in this area, Lazarus Island would have been more appropriate."

"Yes, that has been pointed out before," Dr. Carmichael said, displaying some minor irritation.

"Ah. Sorry for not being original in my observation."

"It shows a lack of taking me seriously. But I'm used to it."

"I disagree. Maybe it shows that you are taken very seriously, indeed."

Dr. Carmichael crooked his smile. "So many mundane minds to deal with, to put up with. I didn't use to mind them. They provided an instructive comparison that built my confidence when I was young. But once they became impediments…."

Neuro had nothing to say in response, so he concentrated on the sea. Which was beautiful despite its growing and mindless potential for destruction.

"I came home one day and found my father deeply depressed," Dr. Carmichael broke the silence a few minutes later as he stared out to sea.

"What?"

"He was living with me. This was after my mother died. This was about 2019, I suppose. When he was in his seventies. What's wrong? I asked him. My father was not a man who was often depressed, if ever. He was an easy-going, positive-thinking man. My greatest champion. So, you can imagine, I was a bit disturbed by this sudden change.

"'I just got word that my cousin Carolyn has died,' he told me. I gave him the required condolences but still wondered why he was so down. Carolyn's health had been failing; he had been expecting the news. 'But it's not just that,' he said. And then he named some actors who had just died within the last week, all of them prominent when he was a teenager, all of whom he had been a fan of, all about ten years older than him. And there were more than the mystic group of three this time. There were maybe five or so. He said he felt like he was being battered by death, that it was coming at him from all angles.

"It turned out, though, that what really drove him down was the report of another actor, a very famous one, who was celebrating his one hundred and third birthday. He was an actor known for his vigorous embrace of life. He had been a beautiful specimen of a man. He did a lot of action films and many of his own stunts. But he was also charming, funny, and an excellent actor. I asked dad why this actor celebrating his one hundred and third birthday should depress him. Shouldn't it give him hope? 'Well,' my dad said, 'he's not dead, but he sure looks like death. All withered and wrinkled. One eye droops. His face is covered in liver spots. He had been one handsome guy, I tell you. Now he's so ugly. But his mind is pretty sharp. He still makes jokes. He still tells many scandalous Hollywood stories, which he seems to delight in. Doesn't that just seem wrong to you? To be so alive inside while dying on the outside?'

"It was this question that brought clarity to my genius, Khadambi. My father died three years later. I have never stopped grieving."

Neuro looked directly at Carmichael's round face, which he had turned to him. His piercing eyes tried their best to display some emotion and possibly a request for empathic understanding. It made Neuro want to smile with his own crooked smile.

"I don't respond to melodrama, Brandon."

"But it's true, Khadambi," Carmichael, caught, protested not too earnestly, "it's absolutely true!"

On the way back, besides keeping an eye out for another gold-ringed cat snake, Neuro took time to appreciate the flora.

"I am quite taken with these fig trees. They are like something from a fairy tale."

"Well, they are also known as strangler figs. Because of their aerial roots."

"Yes, I see. They make the trees both beautiful in the complexity of lines—and ominous looking," Neuro said in admiration. "So many different forms that life has taken. It is always fascinating."

"Sure, sure," passed out of Dr. Carmichael's crooked smile. "But try to have a decent conversation with that tree."

8
DAMBI AND FATHER

"Well, Dambi. It seems you are becoming the proper British boy," Jaali Kinyanjui said to his son on one of his frequent visits to his London home.

"No, baba. I am becoming a proper British Commonwealth boy."

"Ah. A good answer." Jaali stood back to take an overall look at his nine-year-old son in his new school uniform. It consisted of gold slacks and a blue jacket—the colors of the British Commonwealth flag—a white dress shirt, of course, and a gold tie with thin blue diagonal stripes spaced broadly along the surface.

The British Commonwealth School was a recently formed institution founded only in 2033. It provided a traditional British public school university preparatory education to children of British Commonwealth countries residing in London. It had been deemed a necessity. British nationalism, now a festering stew of lower-class fear, upper-class snobbery, and good old-fashioned racism, had made daily life for most Commonwealth natives problematic at best and hurtful at worst. Except for those from the Antipodes and Canada.

The Kinyanjuis had not suffered much from this, for they were spectacularly rich. Not to mention as handsome a family as existed anywhere on the planet. Jaali was a striking-looking man with the magnificent head of an African king, or what white Westerners thought of as an African king. He also had natural charisma. That indefinable quality of stopping a room when one entered it, stopping traffic when out and about, and stopping the hearts of women of all ages and possibly a few men. When he talked to you, his eyes seemed to take note of you and dismissed all others in the immediate vicinity. He listened carefully and spoke directly with unerring care for precise meaning.

Afaafa, his wife, was stunning in her beauty, with incandescent ebony skin, intensely dark yet bright eyes, high cheekbones, and a long elegant neck, taking breaths away from both genders of every sexual orientation. But then, this was a matter of aesthetics, not biology. She seemed royal when she was not smiling, a suitable match for kingly Jaali. But when she smiled, she seemed like your best damn friend, the one you most liked to hang out with, the one you confessed everything to. Little Khadambi was, oddly, not as good-looking as his parents. But when very young, he was the essence of cute, cutting thick slices into hearts and filling them with urges to hug.

The attraction of wealth and a wealth of attraction protected them in an England that had closed in on itself. Squeezing out those it felt did not represent their island's long, glorious, if often mythic, past.

But Jaali and Afaafa were keenly aware that others from outside England's geography and history (or, at least, the nice history) were not so protected. Which was sad. For there was much about English culture and learning they revered. They felt it was helpful in the education of any human from any hemisphere, from any point on the compass. As long as it was willingly embraced and not imposed. Just as other cultures had always affected and benefited *this blessed plot, this earth, this realm, this England.* Even if some in *this little world* never took the time to realize it.

Nothing if not a pragmatic couple, Jaali and Afaafa supported the founding of the Commonwealth School and were patrons. They also provided funds for bursaries so Commonwealth students of all classes could attend and mix while gaining a nice patina of British education and culture.

Afaafa's motivation in this was what was best for her child. Jaali joined her in that, of course. But there was the added benefit of keeping his son away from any school partly if not wholly funded by China. Which was a reality of struggling British public schools that had grown almost exponentially since the beginning of the century.

At first, it was just a plethora of students from the recently monied class in the People's Republic of China. They filled beds in British public boarding schools that homegrown parents could no longer afford. Then it was actual investments in and purchases of storied schools by Chinese education corporations. What was the appeal for China? A certain snobbery, of course. But snobbery was often based on undeniable values. The Chinese seemed to appreciate the rigor of a traditional British public school education, especially those who remained more conservative than not. It was a good fit with Chinese elementary education, which was also quite rigorous. But Jaali suspected something more. He wasn't really paranoid about it; he did not believe there was an actual conspiracy of infiltration. Or of Chinese propaganda permeating the well-educated British mindset. But he was sure that the Chinese knew the value of relationships nurtured among the budding young with not yet fully-developed brains. Relationships that often lasted a lifetime, even across international borders. Especially among those with a solid and steady love of authority. Those who liked to follow it; those who wanted to exercise it.

"I am getting good reports about your academics, Dambi," Jalli said to his son, who must have grown two inches since his previous visit and was leaving cute on the floor.

"I have good teachers, baba. And I study hard to make you proud."

"To make me proud? How about your mother?"

"Pride is natural to motherhood."

"And not to fatherhood?"

"Yes, but more demanding. More unforgiving."

"Am I such an ogre?"

"No, baba, I did not mean that I—"

"I demand nothing of you, Dambi, but that you always do your best. And I will never be unforgiving. Do you understand?"

Khadambi nodded.

"I never knew my father. And I barely remember my mother. The adults in my life were all people who saw something in me and encouraged me to do my best—and who gave me space and freedom to do so. That meant much to me. And I am sure I have made them proud on occasion. But that was never my goal. Pride of others is a strange thing, Dambi. There is a certain amount of self-interest in such pride, for are we ever proud of strangers? No. We are only proud of people whose accomplishments somehow reflect well upon us. That makes me suspect the emotion. What I wanted was not to make my supporters proud of me but to simply delight them with my accomplishments. Delight is a much more charming emotion than pride, do you not think?"

Khadambi did not understand, but would not have let his father know that, so he nodded again.

"Good. Now, shall we go to Hyde Park and take a nice walk? Possibly toss around a Frisbee, as I know you like to do?"

"Yes, please, baba."

Jaali, his son, Kahdambi, and three of Jaali's security detail left The British Commonwealth School—once the Hyde Park Hotel on Knightsbridge—and quickly walked to the park at the rear of the building.

~

At three in the morning the day after they arrived in London, a Kahdambi security team member inserted a human cell-based nanotech GPS tracker under Little Kahdambi's skin. He placed it an inch above his posterior hairline. It was a nearly painless procedure, but Kahdambi was so deep in asleep after this long trip that it would have taken a sharp prick to have woken him. Anticipating that kidnapping was not an unrealistic threat given his father's enemies, it was a prudent move.

Kahdambi was never to know that the tracker had been planted. An effort would be made to keep him unaware he was under constant surveillance while living in London. His parents wanted him to have a normal, carefree childhood. Or as normal and carefree as possible, considering his father was an international billionaire and his mother was the Managing Director of Kinyanjui Holdings London, LLC.

They mostly succeeded, for young Kahdambi was a naturally carefree child who seemed most comfortable in his own head. Not that he did not like engaging with others. Others—outside of his parents, half-brother, and his nurse Wokabi—were part of the new landscape he had been brought to. And all of it was stimulating sustenance that fed his active, curious, contemplating, hungry brain.

Possibly it had been the intense visual and aural stimulation that was London, which burst upon him when his mother and Wokabi took him outside for the first time. They had gone down the elevator to the ground floor, then out the front door to face a narrow street, almost an alley. The row of nondescript flat white sides of other buildings perpendicular to theirs were oppressive in their closeness across that narrow street, and little Kahdambi did not like them.

But then his mother said, "Turn around, Dambi, and look at your new home."

Kahdambi turned his head. And Wokabi and his mother, who each held one of his hands, guided his little body to follow. Until he stood facing and looking up at a massive reddish-brown brick and ochre terracotta tile building that was very *descript*, indeed. The red bricks were small, and the ochre terracotta tiles were large and formed broad vertical lines that reached up the building's six stories. The smaller bricks formed substantial spaces in-between. They connected the vertical tile lines and held within them large multi-paned windows reflecting, at that moment, a sky of blue textured with fat patches of white clouds. The windows on the first floor were cathedral windows with curved tops that seemed to Kahdambi to greet him and invite him back in. And there were protrusions, many protrusions jutting out, giving the building a busy if orderly texture for eyes to scan and travel.

"What do you think, Dambi?" His mother asked.

"I want to hug it," the little boy said.

Afaafa and Wokabi laughed. It was such an absurd thing for the five-year-old to say, but endearing and charming despite that. Maybe it was not so much what the boy said as the way he said it, with his child's gentle voice emanating from under his wide-opened, round eyes.

This, of course, was old London, 19-century London, *privileged* 19-century London—solid, imposing, heavy, self-satisfied. But this little five-year-old African boy, sheltered within his own privilege, did not know that. The building to him was just a magnificent manifestation of right, of truth, of what must be the center of the universe.

Would every little five-year-old have thought that? Probably not. But Kahdambi did. As would be apparent later in his life, he had a mind that liked complexity, wanted to see the parts within the whole, and wanted to see how they were connected to form that whole. He hated flat, white, square, smooth, simple, noiseless. He loved curves, corners, indentations, protrusions, the concave, the convex, mountains and valleys, multi-colors, shades, and tones. He loved the big outside buzz of the combined little hums of people talking, shouting, singing; traffic flowing, halting, honking; birds chirping and calling; dog's barking; wind blowing; rain making many little wet slaps against trees, leaves, concrete, asphalt, car roofs, hats, and umbrellas.

He loved quiet only when he was reading. But then words on pages made their own noise and, on occasion, music that reverberated in the hall of his head.

"Come Dambi," Afaafa said to her son, putting herself between his wide eyes and open mouth and the building before him. "We must go. We have things to do today."

"What things, mama?"

"First, Wokabi and I are going to take you to a little park called Trevor Square. This is where you and Wokabi can go at times to be out in the air and sun. Then we will walk to a big store, bigger than any store you've ever been in. It has seven floors of shopping! It is called Harrods, and there we will buy you some clothes."

"Why?"

"Because London is not like Nairobi. The weather can be different. We must buy clothes for that. And we go because it is fun. They have a toy store with many wonderful things, of which I will buy you only one today if it is not something ridiculous."

"What is 'ridiculous'?"

"Oh, like a giant plush lion. You do not need a giant plush lion. You have seen many real lions in Kenya. But they also have toys you can build with or that fly, or that will engage that lovely little mind of yours."

"Do they have books?"

"Oh, yes, many books."

"I want books."

"You shall have them if you behave."

"I always behave."

"Not always," Wokabi said, then laughed.

It was a short walk to the gated garden at Trevor Square. Using a key that the pink-faced man had given them, they entered to find an oblong space of a limited extent. But that, along with the old, tall trees, flowing paths, bushes, hedges, patches of lawn, and a few benches to sit on, gave it a sense of being a world unto itself. Which, of course, was precisely its purpose.

"Lovely," Afaafa said.

"There is nothing to play on," little Khadambi noticed and noted, meaning playground slides and swings and jungle gyms.

"Good!" Wokabi declared. "Nothing to fall off!"

When they walked to Harrods—with hidden friendly eyes following—Kahdambi noticed the pleasant hum of London traffic. So unlike the annoying stalled, stuttering, staccato, strained sounds of

Nairobi traffic he had heard on trips to his father's office.

After shopping, they had lunch at the Indian restaurant in Harrods. Indian food was one of Kahdambi's favorites as they had an Indian cook in Nairobi. The food was not quite as good in Harrods, but still, he liked it.

After they returned home, Wokabi insisted that Khadambi have a nap. Against Wokabi's better judgment, Afaafa had taken them to Godiva's Chocolate Cafe in Harrods after lunch for a treat. The sugar and caffeine had their effect on Khadami's forming brain, and Wokabi knew that slumber was the only antidote if they wanted any momentary peace at all.

~

It was six months after their arrival in London before Jaali Kinyanjui could finally visit his second wife and second son. He had been in Tokyo just before that with his first wife, Sachiko, and his first son, Yaro Yoshi. Yoshi had traveled with him from Nairobi and remained in Tokyo to conclude some business.

In those six months, young Khadambi's world had been limited to his "spacious"—as they say—apartment at 17-22 Trevor Square, where, of course, he had the run of the place. Also, the small and confined Trevor Square Park, where he chased squirrels and birds, and Harrods department store. He spent a lot of time in Harrods, usually with Wokabi, but on occasion with his mother. Indeed, his tiny world could very much have been called Harrods World as the building now known as 17-22 Trevor Square had once been one of the many Harrods depository buildings. It was built in the late 19th-century out of the same reddish-brown bricks as the store. It was almost a smaller version of it. But at the beginning of the 21st-century, it was converted into forty luxury apartments, quickly becoming one of Knightsbridge's most prestigious addresses, a designation it still retained thirty years later.

Harrods World was Khadambi's world for the security it provided. The street in front of 17-22 Trevor Square was short, narrow, and easily watched. The little park was private, and the walk to the store could be tracked closely. As long as they stayed in Harrods World, the invisible security detail had no difficulty keeping a twenty-four-hour watch on Khadambi and his mother each. It was limiting for Afaafa. She understood the necessity, though, and it was easy to run Kinyanjui Holdings London, LLC out of the apartment for the time being.

Upon his father's first visit, Khadambi's world suddenly opened up.

It was as if a million tiny fluttering points of life had burst in his stomach and chest when his father walked through the double door of their apartment. His mother would have wished for some decorum from her son when he greeted his father, but it was not to be. Dambi ran from her side and across the marble floor of the entryway to slide into his baba's arms. Jaali had, of course, squatted to catch his son, which he did, scooping him up into his arms, then up into the air, then back into his arms. The hug was long and tight, and Jaali dropped at least one tear, but he mainly laughed a deep, resonant laugh of relief when his son—for six months but a memory —became flesh again.

Jaali was planning to stay for a couple of weeks in London. He had business to attend to with Afaafa, the MD of Kinyanjui Holdings London, LLC. Parenting needed to be discussed with Afaafa, his son's mother. And the pleasure of intimacies to share with Afaafa, his second wife and lover. But all other time was devoted to his son.

"Dambi, you now live in a great city of great history and great accomplishments. But great is not always good. By great, I mean large, substantial, significant. And in that, there can be many good things. Beauty, art, literature, invention, understanding, even love. But there can also be wrong, sadness, injustice, suffering, and hate."

Dambi looked up at his baba. He thought of his father as a giant —large, substantial, and significant like the building he now lived in, even like Harrods. Baba World.

"But you are only five—

"I am almost six!" Khadambi declared with determined pride.

"Yes, true. You are almost six. But even at such an advanced age, what do you care about beauty or sadness and all the rest? The only thing you need to care about is fun, yes?"

"Yes!"

"Laughter, yes?"

"Yes!"

"And do you know what the quickest way to have fun and laughter is?"

"No."

"To—be—tickled!"

The large, substantial, significant man grabbed his son by the chest. He worked his long fingers rapidly up and down the sides and under the arms of Kadambi, throwing him into laughing screams and

69

screaming laughs as he collapsed onto the floor and gleefully wriggled.

When Jaali stopped, Khadambi begged for more, though breathless and dizzy.

"No, I cannot do this all day. I will become exhausted, and you will laugh your tiny guts out. Your mother would not be happy if your tiny guts came out. So, we will join a few friends of mine, and I am going to show you this great city and find some fun for you. Okay?"

"Okay!"

~

Jaali's "few friends" were his security detail. They were waiting by two identical armored self-driving automobiles in the secure parking garage of 17-22 Trevor Square. They were not SUVs, as might have been expected, but rather plain-looking late-model cars, one a gray four-door Ford sedan and one a white Toyota. The five members of the detail—three men and two women—were not dressed in gray or black suits, as also might have been expected, but in a mix of Western and Kenyan casual clothes. They were uniform only in the baseball caps and jackets, which sported the black, red, and green KBF logo of the Kenyan Basketball Federation that each of them wore. They were all, not surprisingly, tall and fit.

When Jaali and little Kahdambi emerged from the elevator, they all smiled at the father and son. The pair was also wearing KBF caps and jackets. Dambi, as they had all been instructed to call him, was inexpressibly cute in his mini-version of their team look. But they managed to express it nevertheless.

Jaali introduced Dambi to everyone, giving their first names (all aliases). They greeted Dambi with warmth, wit, and immediate affection. Then they got into the two cars; two of the detail took the Ford's front seats while Dambi and father sat in the back seat; the other three in the follow-car.

And off they went—a group of visiting Kenyans out to see the sights.

Agog is not a bad word for Dambi's reaction to his first real view of his new city seen through the crystal-clear bulletproof windows of the car. The vehicle traveled London's well-trafficked streets, turning wide corners now and then, almost making Dambi dizzy. Dambi's eyes darted here and there as he spied buildings old and new, small and large. His head turned right, then left, then back again and

70

again as they passed large green parks; statues of serious men from past centuries; black taxis; and red double-decker buses. And—the most delightful of all the visual delights Dambi saw—colorfully uniformed straight-backed men parading on horseback. The accompanying clop-clop-clops on the pavement a piece of wonderful rhythmic music back-beating the hum of the traffic. He wanted to stop at each new visual delight. But his father gently patted patience into him, telling him that he would not be disappointed when they finally did stop.

And then they were crossing a river over a bridge. Kahdambi had not been aware that there was a river here in London. And it was such a big river, broad and flowing, not like the narrow one his parents had taken him to in Nairobi. There were many boats on the river leaving churning white wakes, and the gray-brown water glistened in the sunshine of the bright spring day.

"Dambi look," Jaali directed his son's view to a stunning sight. It was a giant, spindly, delicate-looking wheel set against the blue sky. A gossamer metal circle held by thin spokes connecting it to some seemingly solid core standing on two skinny legs. Dambi would have been worried that it was all about to collapse if it hadn't given him another impression.

"It looks like an eye, baba."

Jaali smiled then laughed. "Very good, Dambi, very good. That's exactly what they call it, Dambi. The London Eye. And you, and I, and our friends here, are about to become motes in that eye."

～

As the cars approached the London Eye, rising 443 feet above the south bank of the Thames, Dambi could see that it was not fragile at all. But a complex assemblage of metal lines, thin ones and tubular ones, confusing in all the directions they went in, yet making a solid structure of overwhelming logic and coherence.

The cars took a special route to an area close to the base of the Eye, usually reserved for emergency vehicles. When they stopped, they were met by a contingent of staff, who greeted Jaali and his son with smiles and welcomed them. They referred to Jaali only as "Sir" and never addressed him by name. It was eight-thirty in the morning, a full hour and a half before the day's opening of the attraction. The staff escorted "Sir and his party" to the unmoving, deserted Eye. It was a magnificent sight close up with its thirty-two large glass-enclosed ovoidal passenger capsules attached to the exterior circumference of the wheel, like baubles on a bracelet.

"Please, start the wheel," Jaali requested of the staff, "I want my son to see it in motion."

They started the giant Ferris wheel. Dambi, elevated in his father's arms, was fascinated to see the big wheel and its capsules move. It moved slowly, so it did not seem scary at all.

"You see, Dambi, we will ride in one of those capsules and be taken way up in the air and be able to look out over all of the city. Will you like that? You're not scared, are you?"

"No, baba. But we should have gotten on before it started."

"Ah. Always logical and to the point. But sometimes, Dambi, you must look for a second impression. Now, look." Jaali set his son down and pointed him to the lowest capsule. A staff member was opening a door on its nearest end. "It is moving so slow that we can walk right on through the door. Come, now, let's go."

Dambi was delighted. It was magical and thrilling to have his logic refuted in this way.

The capsules were built to hold up to twenty-five people, so there was plenty of room for Jaali, Dambi, and the security detail. The five "friends" positioned themselves to collectively view the shrinking city before them in the full 360 degrees available. And the sky surrounding. Their leader would often drone on about miniature dangers in the sky.

To Dambi, of course, his father's friends were just enjoying the view. As he was. It was amazing. Before him, there seemed to be an explosion of "Harrods" spread out across the land. So many older buildings, even seen in shrinking miniatures, gave a sense of solid strength. And then, jutting upward here and there, were much taller, if simpler in design, buildings. They seemed to be stretching up— triangles, ovals, skinny boxes—as if sprouting up from the concrete land. And the river, the long, living river moving slowly like the wheel, confident in its direction, allowing boats to chop at its flow for their own purposes, at their own speeds, to move them in their own directions. And the bridges, the many bridges that seemed like brackets securely binding the two banks against the river.

Little Kadambi stood on the capsule floor, his forehead pressed upon the curved lower part of the glass wall, his two hands with splayed fingers, gripping a handrail. He thought of tales Wokabi had told him of African birds. She called birds the best of life, the most perfect. One would be lucky and happy to be a bird, Wokabi said, free and high-flying. Dambi felt at this moment like he was a bird, a friend to the air, land, and water.

"Dambi, come here," his father instructed, holding out his arms. Dambi turned and entered them as they enclosed around him, and he was lifted up to his father's height. "I want to show you something." Jaali adjusted his son in his arms, making sure he had a good, secure grip on him. Then he leaned slightly forward, tipping Dambi just a bit downward, directing his view, not to the horizon, but straight down. There, so far below, they could see foot traffic, people moving along the embankment as if in a predetermined mutual purpose. And vehicular traffic rolling as if they were boats along the bridges, but ones leaving no wakes. "Do they look like little siafu ants to you, Dambi?"

Kahdambi took the time to look intensely down at the tiny moving objects, almost just dots on the ground to his view. "No, baba. They look like tiny people and cars."

"They do not look like ants? Everyone always says they look like ants."

"Well—at first, they did. But then I looked for a second impression."

Jaali smiled. "Good, son, good. Keep looking for second impressions and more, and you will grow up smart and knowledgeable."

"And tall, baba?"

"Oh, yes, tall, I think. But that has nothing to do with your impressions but the fact that I impressed your mother." Jaali laughed and gave his son a quick tickle to make him laugh. "Now, look up a little. See that big long building there with the two towers at either end and a smaller one in the middle?"

"Yes."

"Do you like that building?"

"Yes. I like that it is bumpy."

"Bumpy? Why?"

"More to look at."

"Ah. I like the gears of your mind, Dambi. Well, that is the Palace of Westminster."

"Does the King live there?"

"No, he lives somewhere else."

"Can I see the King?"

"Of course, Dambi. His picture is on all their money."

"You know what I mean, baba!"

"Well, maybe someday. But not today. Today is for fun, and Kings are not always fun. But I want you to know that this Palace of Westminster is also called the Houses of Parliament. This is where government happens."

"What is government?"

"Government is something I want you to learn about."

"Why?"

"Because I have decided that it will be important to you. As business in this world is important to your brother Yoshi, the government of nations must be important to you. And someday you will study things that happened in that building over many years, and other buildings in other countries so that you will learn what the good things were, and what the bad things were."

"Oh," Dambi said, as his view was now diverted by the expanding landscape being laid out before him. All the way to the horizon, where it met the blue sky and sat under slowly moving gray-bottomed, white-topped clouds.

"But that is for future days, Dambi," Jaali said as he suddenly lifted his son up high to hang with glee from his father's two strong hands. "For now, we are going to a big park with trees and grass and a lake and ducks!"

"Ducks?" Little Kahdambi's eyes went wide with excitement, almost as wide as his smile.

"Yes, ducks!"

~

There was a method in Jaali's madness of talking to his nearly six-year-old son about government. He wanted a dramatic first impression on little Khadambi's brain to condition him for the role in life Jaali had decided would be his.

The world's condition had changed since Jaali was born in 1980. Which would have been meaningless to Jaali if he had remained an orphaned, insignificant mote of human dust in the Kibera slum in Nairobi. Possibly dying before his adult years. The simple existence of his corporal self would have been his central, perhaps only concern. But chance had been kind to him. He was allowed and encouraged to develop in mind and body into a presence on the earth. Indeed, in the world.

The condition of the world became of utmost importance to him. He feared for the existence of not just himself but for the billions of individuals on the planet and for the freedom, liberty, and self-determination that freedom and liberty provided. Jaali wasn't a romantic. He knew that for most of the billions, their self-determination would be squandered on minor and mundane things. But that did not matter. There would be others, always others, who would thrive in freedom. If they could not create a total paradise on Earth, they would create little pockets of paradise. Hints, intimations, atmospheres of paradise. Some ephemeral, some long-lasting that often benefited those mired in the minor and the mundane.

Seen in the past century as the big, bright, beautiful tomorrow, Jalli feared the 21st-century was becoming a small, dull, ugly today.

Jaali had the instinct to save the world. But he knew he couldn't. So, he decided to concentrate on just a corner of it. He would save Kenya. And his billions, and the billions more he could earn, allowed him to do that.

But Jaali didn't want his efforts to end with him (not that he was planning on going away anytime soon). He would bring up his son Yoshi to learn the business of his investments. To tend that garden with care. As Jaali would continue with his good works to lure—to put it plainly—Kenyans away from what he saw as pernicious foreign influences, especially that of China.

China was a society, a state, a system of stratified places in life. Of control more than freedom. Of authority finding and funding an *author* that the people could love. Or fear. Or both. Jaali's good works were effective. China's influence in Kenya diminished even as it grew in other African states. As did the power of certain Kenyan families who had controlled things in the country for so long.

Jaali's influence grew. He could have become the author of a new authority for Kenya, he could have run for president, he was asked time after time. But he had always refused. Not with modesty, false or otherwise, not like Julius Caesar, but pragmatically. He knew he would make an awful president. Governance is not what he would be good at.

But Dambi? Khadambi Kinyanjui, the beneficiary of what had become a good name. If properly educated and inculcated in effective, efficient, freedom-enhancing governance, might he become the individual to set Kenya on a path to a certain paradise? A refuge, a garden in a world that may become an increasingly dark forest?

~

After this first trip to his London home, Jaali returned for one week each month. Often Yoshi came with him. Despite the twenty-year difference in their ages, a loving bond was built between the brothers.

"Dambi," Yoshi once said to his brother when he was eight, "let's go out for lunch. Let's get some sushi."

"No!" Khadambi answered.

"Why not?"

Dambi, not taking his eyes from the book he was reading, said, "The only thing that should eat a raw fish is another raw fish!"

Yoshi laughed and grabbed Dambi and tickled him like their father had taught him. "Okay, no sushi. Where do you want to go?" Yoshi asked as he let Dambi go.

"Nowhere?"

"Why not?"

"Basketball is coming on. Kenya is playing South Sudan."

"Ah, *sou desu*. Then how about the pizza I have already ordered."

"Yes!" Kahdambi said as he ran to, grabbed, and hugged his big brother.

~

Sachiko, Jaali's first wife, never came to London, and Kahdambi had never met her. But she sent Dambi a birthday present every year. The presents were usually something based on one of the Japanese anime films that Yoshi had introduced Dambi to. Afaafa and Sachiko had much communication over video links as the respective heads of their divisions of Kinyanjui Holdings. Their relationship was businesslike, cordial, and only occasionally lapsed into gossip about Jaali's third wife, whom he had lately married.

No child came from this third marriage. Faraja was the daughter of influential Kenyans, wealthy, politically aligned with power, sophisticated, charming, and free of scandal. Faraja had been sent to the United States for higher learning but learned much of what she needed to know by the state the United States was in. The abuses of power were still subtle, and many Americans had a hard time recognizing them. But Faraja, extremely bright from early childhood, had grown up in Africa, and her eyes were not hooded to them. She came home with an excellent degree in hand and a hatred of politics, and a desire to do what good she could do in the world. As a modern woman, she was not fond of Kenya's state-sanctioned polygamy. Not being a fool, though, when Jaali, almost thirty years her senior, proposed to make her his third wife, she said yes without hesitation. It was not Jaali's good looks and charisma that had won her over, but his good works and influence. She wanted to be an integral participant in his good works. He did better than that. Jaali put her in charge of them.

Little Kahdambi was never told that his father had taken a third wife. He was only barely aware that Sachiko was his father's first wife. She was just his brother's mother who, once a year, sent him something nice from Tokyo. For Dambi, his world centered on his mother, his brother, Wokabi, and, most centrally, his father. That remained the case until he entered The British Commonwealth School at nine. There, his world expanded to include a congregation of children, a troop of teachers, and the rooms and hallways of what once was a grand hotel wherein information was imparted. And when imparted by talented teachers, the information became knowledge.

9
DAMBI AND FATHER CONTINUED

February 2036

J aali entered his son's bedroom. Young Kahdambi was already in bed even though it was only eight in the evening. His long legs formed two ridges under the blankets ending in the peaks that were his feet. There were several textbooks laid out on either side of the ridges. He held another textbook and was focusing intensely on its open pages.

Or so the first impression from Jaali's vantage point told him. But Jaali took the time to form a second impression.

"Is the comic book good?" Jaali asked his son.

"Yes, it is—" Dambi stopped, caught. "How did you know, baba?"

"Print books rarely illuminate a reader's face. Hopefully, their minds, but not their faces."

Kahdambi pulled the digital reader away from the textbook. On its surface was displayed in bright colors a superhero of admirable goodness struggling to overcome a supervillain of shameful ambition. "I only have one more chapter to read in my textbook. I was just taking a break."

"I see."

"Baba?"

"Yes?"

"Why must we read these heavy printed textbooks? We could get them all digitally, and then you would never know what I was reading."

"Maybe that is the reason."

"That's unfair!"

"Yes, I can see that from your perspective. How about this? Maybe because the school finds it hard these days to find digital copies that have unaltered versions of these texts."

"Why would they be altered?"

"The answer to that is possibly too complex for now. But later, you will know. For now, get back to your heavy textbook. Which one is it?"

"It is the history of ancient Rome."

"Ah. And…?"

"It could use more illustrations," young Kahdambi said with a smile. It was the smile his father had come to know as indicating the ironic wit his son had been developing. Where this wit came from, he had no idea.

~

July 2038

Every summer, Jaali ensured that his son would be tutored in great depth on a subject not covered in his regular school year. The summer before it was political philosophies. This summer was the history of Africa. Jaali flew Fatima Maduemezia, a Nigerian professor of African history, to London for the summer to instruct Kahdambi. Her scholarship and research in the history of her continent were funded by grants from the Kinyanjui Foundation. And had won her praise and prizes. She was a particular favorite of Faraja Kinyanjui.

"Baba?" Kahdambi asked for his father's attention during a break when they watched a soccer game in the media room while Fatima Maduemezia was giving a lecture at Oxford. "Why am I studying African history when you will not let me go back to Africa?"

"I suppose I should let you go back to Africa, to home, to Kenya right now."

"Why now?"

"Because you have developed a proper British accent. As nice as it is, it may not help you when you do return home."

"Help me how?"

"To relate to everyday Kenyans."

"Why must I relate to them?"

"You will want their votes."

"Why?"

"To lead them. To protect them. To protect Kenya."

"From what?"

Jaali turned to his son. "Don't you want to watch the half-time show? I know you like this singer, even though she is a girl."

"I'm not sure I want to go back to Africa. I like England." Kahdambi said quietly with his head turned slightly down. Not in shame, but in preparation for admonishment.

But Jaali was not a man who admonished. But he was a pragmatic man who did not equivocate. "That is not a choice you can make. Some are called to relinquish personal freedom to provide it to others."

"Like George Washington?"

Jaali's eyebrows raised in surprise, then lowered in satisfaction. "I see you earned your good marks in American History."

"He would have preferred to be nothing but a farmer. But he fought; he served."

"This is true. Not that Washington was not ambitious. Even egoistic. Not to mention a fine designer of his uniform. But no man is whole cloth, Dambi. We are all patchworks."

~

May 2041

During the Spring break, Jaali and his son took a cruise up the river Thames. They were not alone, of course. Jaali's "friends" came along. But by this time, Kahdambi was well aware that they were his father's security detail. Despite that, despite their professionalism, despite the guns they packed, Kahdambi thought of them as friends.

Now, at the age of sixteen, Kahdambi knew that his father had been grooming him into a political creature. And that he would one day return to Kenya and start a life of public service in various civil and political positions, eventually leading to the Kenyan presidency. He had no objections to this. His love and admiration for his father made him perfectly happy to train his eyes on the political world of good governance, despite a desire to spend more time delving into the why of many aspects of the physical world. His grades in his science courses were outstanding.

"But, father, is there only one way to have good governance?" Khadambi, now over six feet tall, asked Jaali as they lay on the front deck of their private clipper boat. Hands behind their heads, eyes on the sky, which was all blue with the sun slicing through the atmosphere to heat up the land quite a bit more than in years past.

Before he answered, Jaali took off his tee-shirt and used it to wipe his brow, his arms and chest, and his legs of the sweat that had exuded from his pores.

"Well, Dambi, I suppose that depends on what you mean by good. Good can mean competent, efficient, orderly, and the maintaining of order. It can mean a quick response to dangers to the nation. Especially a response that alleviates the danger. All that can be good governance. Government by unquestioned, central, and dictatorial authority can do this easily. But it can also be done by a government of shared authority. Maybe not always so easy, as there are more hands on the tiller. But at the same time, bad governance is just as likely in either system, depending on the players. Depending on who's making the decisions. Depending on honesty. Or dishonesty. Service to the citizens. Or only to the self. It often comes down to individual people, and people are often flawed in one way or another."

"Still," Kahdambi said, thinking of much reading he had done lately. "I cannot imagine why all the people in a dictatorship do not rise up against the dictator. I mean, I know some do, but some don't. I find that confusing."

Jaali sat up, and so did his son. "It is because, Dambi, not one man or woman on this planet would mind living under a dictatorship—"

"But—"

"Let me finish. Not one man or woman on this planet would mind living under a dictatorship—as long as they agreed with the dictator."

Kahdambi thought about this. He realized he had been a bit naive. "Ah. Yes, that seems true. And dictatorship was originally not a bad thing. I mean in ancient Rome."

"But it turned bad."

"Yes, so, power to the people and all that. Democracy seems the only way to truly get good governance."

"Do you really think so, son?"

"Well…"

"I mean, it can be. The greatest asset of democracy is the demos. But then, the greatest liability of democracy is the demos. That, son, is the paradox of democracy."

"So, democracy is both a wave and a stream of particles."

Jaali was impressed by his son's analogy. "You do love your science."

"Blame yourself. I have your mind. Or at least some of it."

"True. And maybe this gives us our final answer about good governance. Whether applied to science or anything at all, the scientific method, despite aberrations now and then, provides objectivity that only freedom of thought can allow for. This method, when applied properly, is the only arbitrator between biases, prejudices, the stubborn human desire to always be right even in the face of counter-evidence. Democracy based on a political system that protects freedom of thought is the only hope for true good governance. That is why it has been so disturbing to see it erode in this century, to see authoritarian governance rise, strengthen, and spread. If this had not been the case, then I would be happy for you to become a scientist. But it is the case. I have prepared you, and you will continue to prepare, to work to make Kenya an oasis of freedom. This possibly has been unfair to you. But it had to be done. Kenya was once a false democracy. Some still honor Daniel Moi. I do not. He murdered many, stole much, denied freedom. But who in the world cared? It was just an African country, a 'shithole' a certain American president I do not need to name once called it along with our fellow African states. Many nations in the world either are—or are in jeopardy of becoming—authoritarian shitholes. Would it not be a most delicious irony for our African nation to become an oasis of true democracy, a spring of freedom?"

Jaali, sweating again, stood and offered his hand to his son so that he might rise up from the deck as well. Kahdambi took it and stood to face his father with no doubt in his mind that he was facing a great man.

~

November 2041

Kahdambi's taste in Japanese cuisine never matured (a term he disputed) to the point where he would eat sushi. He liked Tempura.

And Tonkatsu he liked. But when it came to sushi, he maintained the philosophy he had adopted as a young child. He was not a raw fish; therefore, he would not eat raw fish. He never gave in, even under the loving and gentle prodding of his father, who had been introduced to sushi by his future first wife, Sachiko. Whenever they ordered food for delivery from their favorite Japanese Restaurant in Soho to eat during a casual afternoon watching one of several sporting events they loved, it was well known by the restaurant who would be eating what.

It also became well known by Jaali's enemies.

It had been eleven years since Jaali had moved his second wife Afaafa and his second son Kahdambi to London for their protection. In those eleven years, Jaali's security in Nairobi, Tokyo, London, and wherever he traveled had been efficient, effective, and, obviously, successful. Also, during those years, Jaali came to believe that opposition to his ideas for Kenya's future, and his position as an agent for change, had diminished to a manageable level.

It had not. It had just become quiet and operated with stealth. Certain native Kenyans and particular Chinese authorities continued to find him an irritant. The Kenyans would have liked to do away with Jaali and his influence immediately, as they had once tried and failed. With centuries of patience backing them up, the Chinese bided their time while keeping their determination fresh.

When their agents in London discovered Jaali's favorite Japanese restaurant, they decided to use it to focus that determination. After all, years ago, Jaali had abandoned China for Japan. To use something so fundamentally Japanese was a closing of a circle.

Hinata Tanaka, Japanese by birth, Chinese by indoctrination, a Londoner with a false identity, was placed as a waiter at Tokyo Dreams in Soho in 2037 and was told to wait. Wait for what? For a biotech firm owned by the Chinese Army in Tianjin to develop what they had promised they could create. Hinata was a good waiter, always friendly, and well-liked by the patrons and the staff. Whenever Jaali, with or without Afaffa or Kahdambi, but always with his "friends," dined in at Tokyo Dreams, Hinata made sure to never wait on him. That was his instructions. If he had to suddenly become sick, go to the loo, or take a break for a smoke, he never once waited on Jaali in four years. No words ever passed between them. No pleasantries. He provided no service and received no tips from Jaali. He never inquired about the handsome black man and never expressed any curiosity about him to any other staff. He ignored him and just went about his business.

Until the waiting was over. Hinata Tanaka met his handler on his day off in Soho Square Gardens. She pretended to be his wife, meeting him after a morning of shopping. She showed him her purchases and handed him a gift in a small, beautifully wrapped box.

"It's a hypodermic needle. Next time the target orders sushi for take-out, inject the solution into every piece of fish. Just a little in each, that's all. Do not do this if he is dining in, only a take-out order. Do you understand?"

Hinata nodded.

~

It had been a long week in London for Jaali. He and Afaafa had spent many hours in meetings and discussions over several potential investments and concluded that most were not viable. But two were, and they were satisfied with them. Still, it was exhausting to give deep, serious consideration to peoples' dreams. And wearying to disappoint eager entrepreneurs. But it was exciting to share the joy of those they decided to invest in

But now it was Sunday, his last day before returning to Kenya, a day to relax with his son and the powerful, bruising contacts of American football. It was a sport that they were just getting to know as it played out on the large wall-screen of brilliant digital images.

"Do you think we can go to a live game someday, Father?" Kahdambi asked.

"Yes, we should, shouldn't we? Well, maybe, someday. But I do worry about their heads. So many injuries."

The door to the media room opened, and one of Jaali's "friends" came in with their take-out order from Tokyo Dreams and was invited to join them.

As always, Jaali offered his son one of his tuna nigiri. He held it out to him on the pincer end of his hashi while smiling his large, joking, joyful smile.

Taking his own hashi and capturing a piece of his tonkatsu, Kahdambi presented it to his father with a demeanor of reverence. "And insult the spirit of the lovely pig that died for my pleasure and nourishment? No thank you, Father."

"You do not know what you are missing, son."

"A perfect way to have no regrets, Father."

Jaali laughed a big, open-mouthed laugh, pleased with his son's subtle wit. Then, keeping his mouth open, he lovingly placed the nigiri in his mouth and savored it.

Thirty minutes later, Jaali complained of a headache.

Thirty-five minutes later, Jaali screamed in agony, clutched his head, and collapsed.

One hour later, Jaali was in the imaging center of the National Hospital for Neurology and Neurosurgery in Queen Square.

Two hours later, Afaafa and Kahdambi were told that Jaali was in a coma. And that something was eating away at neurons in his frontal lobe.

Three days later, Jaali came out of the coma. Whatever had been eating away at neurons in his frontal lobe had stopped. The headache had stopped, and he seemed perfectly healthy. But he wasn't Jaali anymore.

Jaali's charismatic smile, which often appeared, was now non-existent. He said he wanted to hit somebody—in the face—he didn't know why he just did. A nurse caught him with his sheets pulled off, masturbating joylessly.

He called Afaafa a slut and his son a fool.

He pretended that he was not African, not black, and certainly not married to three women.

He called his doctor an asshole and demanded to be released from the hospital.

He finally had to be restrained.

Five days later, his headache returned. He was obviously in agony. His brain was immediately scanned and imaged again. The doctors gaped in shock as they watched neurons in his brain shut off or disappear one by one.

Jaali Kinyanjui died that day. Most of his brain had been eaten away.

A thorough autopsy and dissection of Jaali's brain found evidence of a genetically engineered neurotoxin and the nanobots that had delivered it.

Jaali Kinyanjui was given a massive funeral in Nairobi. Masses of Kenyans who had benefited from his good works came out into the street to mourn. His enemies had expected this and hypocritically joined in the mourning, promising that his memory would always be honored. While being quite happy that he was now just that—a memory.

～

Kahdambi's first return to Kenya was to bury his baba and say goodbye to his best friend.

The day after the funeral, there was a family meeting in their compound outside Nairobi.

All three wives were gathered for the first time. But then, this was more than a family meeting. The wives were more than wives. His sons were more than sons. The futures of Kinyanjui Investments, Kinyanjui Holdings, and the Kinyanjui Foundation were on the agenda.

Sachiko was uncomfortable—Kenya was so alien to her.

Afaafa was determined—her husband's vision must move forward.

Faraja was grief-stricken—Jaali had been more mentor than husband, if still a profoundly wonderful lover.

Yoshi took charge. As far as he was concerned, his father's death anointed him.

Kahdambi felt nothing. He tried only to reason. To find a second impression. He thought he should find a way to both preserve the past in a sort of honorable amber. And to cloud it over. He saw nothing of the future. It was black. More than black. No, less than black. He saw no light penetrating whatever the future was.

"We must continue everything," Yoshi said, "everything father was doing. Do you all agree?"

The wives did. Kahdambi stood outside the question.

"Good. This is essential. Or otherwise, our enemies will have won."

"But none of us can be Jaali," Sachiko said. "We are all good soldiers, but his leadership—

"I will do my best, Mother."

"Of course, you will, Yoshi. Our business will be in good hands under you. Unless the other wives have any objections."

"I have always been impressed by Yoshi," Afaffa said. "My only ambition is to stay in London."

"I prefer to spend my time doing the good Jaali wanted to be done. I do not believe I would be good at making money," Faraja said.

"And, meaning no disrespect," Sachiko said, "I do not like Kenya. I can only be happy in Japan. I am satisfied with that. But it is still important to understand that what Jaali was, none of us can be. We can be brilliant in our work. But none of us have that rare quality that was Jaali. So his enemies have won. We cannot deny that."

"I do not want to accept that," Yoshi said. Then he turned to

Kahdami. "What about you, Dambi? You are young yet, but Father had a plan for you. I always thought it might have been a crazy plan. But to honor him, after university, will you come back to be of service to Kenya?"

Kahdambi looked at his family, two of whom he had never met before. Light, slowly intensifying, like the dawn of a new day, kept him quiet for more than a moment until it was strong enough to make clear what he wanted to do.

"No," Kahdambi.

"No?" Yoshi asked aloud as the wives asked with their eyes.

"I admire and honor you all. But Kenya means nothing to me. If it is to become an oasis of democracy, someone else will have to bring it about. I would only have done it for Father. But Father is dead. I do not mean the man who stopped breathing one day in the hospital. But the man who stopped *being* five days before that. What a strange, powerful thing is the human brain that can cradle the self, the person. No, not cradle—give rise to. And yet how weak it is, how tissue-thin the consciousness is that a mere, slight breeze can change it. This fascinates me. How? Why? I must know."

Kahdambi took in a breath of Kenyan air. "I can be true to my father. Or I can be true to myself. I will go to university to study neuroscience."

10
THE EDUCATION OF JOSEPH CHARLES SMITH

When Joey saw the two side-by-side solar flares through his telescope, he said to himself—for there was no one else to say it to in his small observatory— "Wow!" It was not so much an exclamation of surprise as it was an exhalation of wonder. He had seen many solar flares in the six months since his Aunt Liz had had the observatory built for him, but never flares like these. One seemed to be a perfect square or box. The other was a perfect triangle or pyramid.

A PYRAMID ON THE SUN! Screamed a hundred news outlet notifications in millions of texts and email inboxes in his active, fertile, twelve-year-old imagination.

Of course, the flares did not last long in the shapes he first saw. They soon spread themselves into forms geometry could not accommodate. And the geometric shapes he had seen were probably nothing but optical illusions. This was likely caused by his two-dimensional view, his position relative to the sun, the angle he was looking at, and possibly several other factors. Still—it was pretty neat.

No lover of the sun in his everyday human existence—a frail biped standing precariously on a near-deserted desert planetary crust —he loved the sun in this magnified view. To see this burning ball of gas alive with movement as its plasma swirled and exploded here and there into flares; as dark spots appeared then disappeared; as this manifestation of energy deigned to address this mere odd little smudge of life, was to experience a state of consciousness much higher than that needed to just eat, sleep, or even to talk coherently to other odd smudges of life. It was to know joyful fear.

Just like the joyful fear Joey felt his first night in the desert six years before.

~

In taking on her nephew's education, Liz had to re-educate herself. It was not difficult. She had been a history professor and a good one. In studying and teaching history, almost all other disciplines of knowledge are touched on. Philosophy, religions, politics, science, war, daily life, the haves, the have-nots, exploration, exploitation, invention, suppression, art, literature, and a whole bunch of minor etceteras. So she knew a little about much. But to teach each subject in its own vacuum demanded more detailed information. Not right away, not when little Joey was only six, but sooner than one would think.

Well, she thought, *for a woman in her mid-fifties, it will at least keep my mind active.*

Although retired and living in a hole, as Joey had put it, Liz had kept in digital contact with academic colleagues. Not friends. Liz was not big on friends. Vivian, her wife, had been her best and only real friend, but she had died. After that, Liz's big ambition was to grow up to become an old recluse surrounded by books and—more books. When a book disappoints, you do not have to lose a friend. You just set it aside. And you couldn't disappoint books. Books never care for or about you. And yet she did like to communicate with other minds, throwing them up on the giant curved screen in the circular space. She liked to talk out ideas, make inquiries, debate concepts, and commiserate with those of her non-retired colleagues, constantly dealing with censorious interference with their teaching or research or publishing.

So Liz had sources to help her educate her nephew. And she took advantage of them.

Was it fair to keep Joey in this reclusive life in a hole with her? Well, where else was he going to go? Plus, he didn't seem to mind. Especially after his aunt had told him that few other places would afford him the naked-eye view of the night sky that this dry, parched, dirty, dusty, sun-stinging, unfriendly, if not wholly inhospitable patch of the earth did. The hole was fine with Joey. As was his aunt's company.

"Aunt Liz?" Little Joey asked once when he was eight.

"Yes," Liz said as she looked in the freezer to find their dinner.

"I found a funny word in the dictionary."

His aunt had encouraged him to thumb through an old dictionary of her father's whenever he had some time to kill.

"A funny word? What is it, 'clown'?"

"That's not a funny word."

"Well, clowns are supposed to be."

"What are clowns?"

"White-faced, big red-nosed goofs."

"What?"

"Never mind. What's the word you found?"

"*Avuncular*. It means an uncle of kindness and geniality."

"Okay."

"But I can't find a word for an aunt of kindness and geniality."

"Sexism, pure sexism."

"So I'll make up a word."

"Just like that?"

"Sure. It's easy."

"Okay. So let me know—"

"*V-aunt-cular*."

"You got one already?"

"I told you it was easy."

"So you're telling me I am vauntcular?"

"Oh, no, not you. This is only for aunts of kindness and geniality," Joey said as he made a prodigious effort to keep his face straight.

"Why, you, I *outta*…." Liz said as she turned from the refrigerator, a mock villain in a grasping pose. Joey screamed and jumped up from the easy chair he had been sitting in and ran. Aunt Liz chased Joey around in circles in the circular space, then down this corridor, then up, then into another, all while Joey laughed uproariously. When she finally caught him in his bedroom, both of them wheezing out breathy laughs, she tousled his red hair and tickled his belly. "You're a clown," she declared with a smile.

"What's a clown?"

"Look it up," Liz said as she left to return to the circular space to microwave their dinner. "You have a dictionary, don't you?"

~

It wasn't long after Liz took custody of her nephew that she realized that he was a child of exceptional intelligence. Maybe not extraordinary; she didn't allow herself to assume he was a young genius or likely to become an old one. But Joey was certainly well above average. Of course, given the very average intelligence of most humans, it occurred to her that that wasn't saying much. Okay, then, well, *well* above average. Maybe, given that he was only six, kind of cute in his florid face and redheaded way, and diminutive, the best appellation for him was *bright*. Bright with the light of curiosity. Genetics, most likely.

Not genes directly from Joey's mother, who Liz had always referred to as dim, the opposite of bright. His unknown father may have spent his genetic contribution wholly on Joey's pigment and had none left for his intelligence. Her own father, Joey's grandfather, had been a sweet, happy-go-lucky kind of guy but not exceptionally bright. Her mother had been a girly girl, a woman's woman, domestic. While not anti-feminist, she was vibrantly pro-feminine. And although her mother was certainly not dumb, her curiosity was limited. Liz had no knowledge of Joey's paternal grandparents, of course. But she had too much negative bias to give them any credit.

On the other hand, she considered herself intelligent. Which was obvious. It seemed logical to assume that some of her and Joey's shared ancestors of a generation or so ago were to be given credit.

Or maybe it was that first night when Joey was knocked down by the universe, by the vast expanse of it. All that starlight poured down, making Joey bright. A romantic idea, she had to admit. But she kind of liked it.

~

Joey first demonstrated his brightness, crawling up into Liz's lap with a book in hand. She had been quietly sitting in her recliner reading a new translation of Herodotus that the translator, a former colleague, had sent her. Little Joey smuggled himself into a comfortable position and pulled out the book. It was *The Wind in the Willows*, which his aunt had given him just the week before. He opened it to chapter ten, "The Further Adventures of Toad," and began to silently read.

"I thought we had finished that," Liz said.

"Uh-huh," Joey said while not taking his eyes off the pages.

"So why don't we find you a new book to read."

"Uh-uh."

"Why not?"

"I'm trying to figure things out."

"What things?"

"Things that seem silly."

"Such as?"

"Bedclothes."

"Bedclothes?"

"Mr. Toad has a dream that his bedclothes ran away to get warm by a fire. But beds don't have clothes. People have clothes."

"I see. Do you want me to explain it?"

"No."

"You sure?"

"I want to figure it out myself."

"Okay. But can you do me a favor?"

"What?"

"Move a little. Your elbow is sticking in my ribs."

Little Joey moved with his aunt's assistance while still contemplating the mystery of bedclothes. The move was successful, and both were now comfortable, and they settled down to reading their books. It was late afternoon and quiet, and if they had not both been engrossed in their reading, they might have nodded off.

After about half an hour, Joey said, "Yes."

Liz stopped her reading and asked, "Yes to what?"

"Explain it to me."

Having been deep into the account of Croesus's test of the oracles, Liz had forgotten their previous conversation. "Explain what?"

"Bedclothes."

"Oh. Well… What would seem logical? Possibly that they are clothes that a person wears to bed."

"Like jammies?"

"Yes, like jammies."

"Oh, I get it!"

"Good. Can I go back to my book now?"

"Okay."

"Great."

"Wait a minute. The bedclothes would have to get off Mr. Toad first."

"That's true. It might be difficult, then, huh?"

"And if they couldn't and ran away, Mr. Toad would be in them, so he couldn't chase them because he would be in them."

"Is that what happens in the book?"

"No."

"Then I guess I'm wrong."

"Or told a fib."

"Shame on me," Aunt Liz said, going back to her book.

"So—so…" Little Joey furrowed his brow melodramatically to think it all out.

"Maybe it was something else besides Mr. Told wearing the *bedclothes*," Liz offered.

"The bed?"

"Well, what would you call blankets and such?"

"Oh. So, beds do wear clothes!"

"See the benefit of asking questions of your colleagues?"

"You're not my colleague. You're my aunt."

Her nephew's simple statement elicited a feeling in Liz on the border of warmth. "Yes. Yes, Joey. That is what I am all right."

~

After his first night of living in The Hole, as the Vivian Fleming Mars Habitat prototype had now been forever designated, Joey insisted on going outside every night to stare up at the massive number of stars in the black dome above. Desert nights can be cold, and Aunt Liz would bundle Joey up thick and tight. But when she began to hear his teeth chatter, she insisted that he limit his time out under the night sky.

But it was time enough. Time enough to feel unmoored. Time enough to float in his mind up there, leaving down here behind. Time enough to feel insignificant, yet time enough to feel like a god. Not that Joey knew at six years old what a god was. It was a word, not to mention a concept, that had never passed between the lips of either his mother or his aunt. To feel like what then? Not just a little boy with two little feet planted in the desert dust. But something else, some kind of particle part and parcel with the night sky. With the black and the splatter of points of light on it. And the milky swath of illumination intersecting the sky. The vast and the forever.

The feeling stayed with him as he descended back into The Hole. As his Aunt Liz hugged warmth into him, promising him a hot mug of chocolate. And until slumber beckoned.

It wasn't long before this spiritual engagement with the universe became a material one. About a year later, Joey noticed that the sky was not fixed during his time outside. It seemed to move overhead. Of course, he had seen that this was true of the moon, and he liked the moon a lot, but the moon always seemed more here than there. After all, it was the Earth's companion. It was Little Joey to Aunt Liz. An object of affection, not awe.

This was when Joey memorized the main features of the sky within sight of the horizon twice one night. When he first went out. And when he was called in by his aunt. After returning to The Hole, he sketched the night sky as best as he could on a piece of paper while drinking his hot chocolate.

"What are you drawing?" Aunt Liz asked.

"The sky."

"Oh. That's nice. What's that line?"

"The ground."

"And is that a cactus plant on the ground?"

"Yes."

"Just one?"

"One is all I need."

When Joey finished, he immediately started a new sketch.

"Why did you draw the sky again?" Aunt Liz asked after she noticed the second sketch. "You just drew it?"

In answer, Joey picked up his just completed drawing and the one he had done right before, took them over to the recliner chair, and turned on the floor reading lamp. He positioned it to beam straight out like a projector. Then Joey put the two sheets of paper together, edges matching edges. Finally, he held up the papers to the naked light bulb to shine light through the two sheets. Both drawings could now be seen together.

"It moved," little Joey declared.

"What moved?"

"The sky. Look."

Relative to the ground and the one cactus plant, the features of the sky he had drawn had all shifted in concert.

"Wow," Aunt Liz said. "How do you know...I mean, you didn't measure...."

"I don't know. I just know."

"Well," Liz said, impressed, amused, proud, "You are right, of course. But it's not the sky that moved, but the ground."

"Huh?"

"The earth rotates, spins. And we along with it. So, we are moving. But from our point of view, it looks like the sky is moving during the night. And the moon too."

"Oh." Little Joey thought about that. Then he slowly turned

around three hundred and sixty degrees, keeping his eye on the wall of the circular space passing as *it* seemed to travel around him. Then he stopped, thought for a moment, then stated, "Okay. I get it now."

It was Joey's first lesson in astronomy.

~

Liz worried about how she was going to teach her nephew. For most of her career, she had been a university professor, communicating with young adults, not young children. Indeed, she had never cared much for young children—kinetic little screaming animals on two legs with no impulse control. They made her grumpy. But then so did most people of any age. She had not been a popular professor at the university. She had been demanding, challenging, unfriendly, unbending in the giving of grades, not a happy sufferer of fools. But as she was a fascinating lecturer deep into her subject, which she was passionate about, her classes were popular. In student evaluations of her, the main message conveyed by many was that if you wanted to truly educate yourself in History, hers was the class for you. But, "Be prepared to cry if she focuses her wrath on you."

"What a Grumpy Gus you are," Vivian Fleming had declared upon first meeting Liz. Vivian had come to the university to give the famed Phidias Lecture in Architecture as Art. She met Liz at a faculty reception and was immediately attracted to her. But Vivian, twenty-five years older than Liz, couldn't believe that such a relatively young person could sound like a crotchety old bag. Liz bent her ear with complaints about people in general, certain people in particular, and the horrible fact that the world was being overpopulated with them.

"Here's what's really amusing, if appalling," Liz said to Vivian that night. "Every time a new little bundle of joy is born, the parents—in the height of egocentricity—think it's a miracle. Miracle! The damn thing happens four hundred thousand times each and every day. That's hardly a miracle. It's a damn plague."

Vivian laughed. It was a very knowing laugh. "I see why you're a historian. You prefer a world with fewer people in it. Easier to get a handle on it; easier to understand the ebb and flow of events."

Liz was shocked by the insight.

Later that night, after Vivian's lecture, they made stunningly passionate love and, afterward, had a wide-ranging conversation about things profound and trivial, tragic and comic, personal and private.

Liz had been far less grumpy ever since—but still not fond of children.

She was fond of her nephew, though. Joey was different. He was obviously unique—a mind, not just a bag of growing, expanding flesh.

But how to best teach him? Liz couldn't be simple; she couldn't talk down to him. And yet, she couldn't handle him like she had university students. Plus, she needed to teach primary stuff initially, the beginnings of knowledge. He did not have a basis in knowledge to reach higher education as university students were supposed to have. He probably wouldn't like all subjects, and she worried about that. What if he became bored? And worse, what if he began to hate his teacher! Would that make him hate his aunt?

Liz liked being liked by Joey. It was a feeling she had never expected to feel. She would have been sad to give it up.

"You sure love looking up at the sky," Liz said to Joey one night when she came to collect him before he froze to death.

"Uh-huh."

"Would you like to go up there someday?" She was thinking of Vivian, who had hoped to have been able to visit one of her habitats on Mars.

"I am there," Joey said as a matter of fact and a statement of feeling.

"I mean up into space. People go up there all the time."

"Really?"

"Sure."

"Would it get me closer?"

"Closer to what?"

"The stars."

"Well, to the planets at least. But the stars are awfully far away."

"No, just to see?"

"Oh. How stupid of me. I'll be right back."

Liz left and hurriedly got to the elevator, went down into The Hole and to the utility room, grabbed what she came for and a thermal blanket, and rushed back up to Joey. She wrapped the blanket around Joey then handed him her field binoculars. "Look through those."

Joey did so. "Wow!" Then he moved the binoculars to another spot in the sky, then another and another.

"I guess I better bring the hot chocolate up here," Liz said.

~

Astronomy was the key. Liz decided to anchor all her teaching around astronomy. Math was pertinent, of course. And geography was important. Reading was necessary, writing also. Later, of course, chemistry and physics. Even biology. One can't perceive light waves without the eye. And history? Her beloved discipline? She would teach the history of astronomy and wrap all other histories— not to mention myths, legends, religions, and philosophies—around it.

~

"Get the kid a telescope, Liz."

Philip Penko's face, large and looming on the big, curved screen on the circular space wall, broke out into his well-known, slightly goofy smile. It always did when he spoke. He rarely spoke without this smile. Was this due to his face's muscularity? Or was it just his natural emotional demeanor? This was never quantitatively known. He had always been lively, spirited, and enthused about astronomy, so most people's best guess was that it was the latter.

"What the bloody blue blazes for? He seems happy with the binoculars," Liz responded.

"Sure, right now," Dr. Penko, who had sent Liz some basic books on astronomy, and Joey was reading one in his room as they spoke. "But he's going to want to see things better soon. Binoculars are just two little refracting telescopes. They're fine for casual viewing, but you say Joey is really serious, so he needs a reflecting telescope. Plus, I'm sure his little arms get tired holding up the binoculars, and you can't really hold them steadily. And get a reflecting telescope on a tripod. That's what he needs. I'll send you a link to a good basic one."

~

Liz got Joey the telescope for his seventh birthday.

Suddenly Joey's world was the ridges, mountain chains, valleys, and craters of the moon; the double star, Albireo; a cluster consisting of hundreds of thousands of stars within the constellation Hercules (Ah, mythology!); the Ring Nebula and the Whirlpool Galaxy. And, of course, Mars, Venus, Saturn, Jupiter, and other objects in the sky Dr. Penko had directed him toward. It was a world, a universe visited while standing in the dirt of the desert, wearing thermal underwear, bundled up tightly in cold-weather clothes, sustained by a thermos of hot chocolate.

It made Joey giddy. To see these objects so far away, yet get to know them intimately as friends.

~

For Joey's twelfth birthday, Liz had an observatory built onto and entered from the habitat. It was designed by an architect from the firm of Fleming, Sanderson & Lopez, which Vivian had co-founded and Liz as her heir continued to profit from. At the suggestion of Dr. Penko, she outfitted it with a large 25" f/4 Obsession telescope and a computer. And a unique, pneumatic, very comfortable chair Joey could sit in for hours at a time as he peered into the eyepiece at the top of the scope.

The objects in the sky were no longer Joey's friends but phenomena to be observed, pondered, noted. And he did so in comfort and warmth.

~

"What the bloody blue blazes are you saying? A box and a pyramid? Really?" Liz questioned as she and Joey were sitting down to bowls of tuna and macaroni and cheese.

"That's what they looked like," Joey confirmed.

"Did you get a picture of them?"

"No. It was so neat to see that I forgot."

"That's too bad."

"Yeah. Dr. Penko would have liked to have seen it."

"Does it mean there are aliens on the Sun?"

"Don't be silly, Aunt Liz."

"Well, there could be."

"No, there couldn't."

"Well, why the bloody blue blazes not? They could be made of fire."

"No, they couldn't."

"Atomic creatures?"

"We are all atomic creatures. This is because we are made up of atoms."

"Say, you're pretty smart for a kid."

"I'd rather be smart than a smart ass."

It was a routine they had gone through before. A bit of banter to lighten the academic load.

"I don't know," Liz said, suddenly pulling away from the banter. "I wonder if I took your childhood away."

"I am still a child."

"And puberty is just around the corner," Liz quietly said to herself with concern and maybe even fear and loathing.

~

Liz knew that she couldn't confine Joey in The Hole every day, coming out only at night. He was, after all, not a mole, even an anthropomorphic one. Joey was entirely anthro, and anthros needed vitamin D, best obtained by exposure to midday sunlight for ten to fifteen minutes daily. Unfortunately, in the California desert, ten to fifteen minutes of daily exposure to midday sun would quickly turn the kid crisp—even if he hadn't been a redhead. A century ago, this would not have been the case. But now, with a climate crisis not yet totally defended against, the desert, most days, was the fire that had been jumped into from the frying pan. So, she gave her nephew, as she did herself, 600 IU of vitamin D daily.

But vitamins were for the body. What about Joey's mind, his *self?* As much as Liz hated to admit it, she knew her Joey needed exposure to other places and people, both for education and maturation. This could have been done exclusively in The Hole using the massive wall screen in the circular space, the internet, and virtual reality. After all, the brain is easy to fool. But the tactile, the vibrations of proximity, actual reality as opposed to virtual, was called for.

As Liz had realized on Joey's first night but had ignored for years, she needed to arrange field trips.

Liz ordered a self-driving electric RV—very comfortable, air-conditioned of course, satellite-connected—for their first field trip when Joey was ten. She plotted out a route that took them to essential sites in California—mainly museums and universities in San Francisco, Los Angeles, and San Diego. But Joey also got to see redwood forests, or what was left of them, and the damaged California coast. Illuminating if depressing sights. Driving through the agricultural Central Valley of the state bored them, but popping up some mountains didn't. They contemplated going to the Disney theme parks for the fun of a bit of fantasy. But once they looked at some footage of the crowds at the park—which reminded them of a mass of maggots—they both shuddered and decided not to. They did interact with people at the museums, including children of Joey's age, whom he looked upon with some suspicion. And at the universities where they visited some of Liz's colleagues. They enjoyed some intelligent, even delightful chats with a few of these people (even one or two of the children). Driving through the cities getting from here to there, their view of people on the street through the RV's large windows was broad and revealed the passing parade. Although it was not very alluring.

"People ain't my favorite people," Joey often heard his aunt say.

~

After a month, they were happy to return home to The Hole. Despite some good memories of things seen, knowledge acquired, and people of interest met, they found themselves settling back into a deep comfort.

"Home is where you can scratch your ass with perfect abandon," Liz told her nephew.

"You're silly, Aunt Liz," Joey declared.

"I'd rather be silly than a silly ass." Liz laughed at her variation of their old routine.

"We need some green, Aunt Liz," Joey said in a surprising non-sequitur. But then, what non-sequitur isn't?

"Joey, I am not lacking in money."

"No. Plants."

"Plants?"

"That's what I liked best on the field trip. Trees, plants, bushes—green. I think green is my favorite color."

"Well, I'm as much of a fan of chlorophyll as you are but in an underground habitat…."

"We can set up lamps. I read all about it. What this place needs are plants. It will make our air better."

"We have a perfectly fine air filtration system."

"They are nice to look at."

"True."

"Let's get some plants."

"Okay, but you're in charge of taking care of the plants. You'll have to feed them and water them and take them for walks."

"You're silly, Aunt Liz," Joey declared once again.

~

If Liz was silly, it was Joey who made her so. He brought it out of her. Vivian had also been able to do that, mainly to keep Liz off the grumpy path. What was the common denominator? Love, obviously.

And not just love *of*, but love *from*. Both Vivian and Joey showed their love by not always taking Liz, an inherently serious person, seriously. Vivian, because she was twenty-five years older and had already been through her oh-so-serious days, and wanted to spare her new love that waste of time—especially during the world's oh-so-serious days. Joey, because his Aunt Liz was his only playmate. He was a child, and play was forefront in his mind, even if that mind had to be taken seriously. Joey made up imaginative games for them to play, including a word game where they had to come up with new names for animals. Skunks became *scentipeds*; elephants became *trunkatids*; armadillos became *tankyoos*, and rhinos became *hornybastards*. This last one was a coinage of Liz's that Joey did not get until years later. But their favorites were *sicopants* for dogs and *supercilious furballious* for cats. Liz made up a tortuous hop-scotch game utilizing an old oval area rug that featured wild geometric forms. And there were the old standbys: card games, boardgames, hide and seek (particularly fun inside The Hole), and Joey's favorite, simply playing catch with a bean bag.

Joey, of course, did not see all this play as love. He just saw it as play with his fun aunt. It wasn't until Liz had his observatory designed, built, and outfitted when he was twelve that Joey realized he was loved. And what it was to be understood, to be known for the self he knew himself to be. It was immensely satisfying to know this.

Joey began to look upon his aunt differently. Especially as his education became more detailed, requiring more time, thought, and effort. He realized just how much respect she had from her fellow professors in fields, not her own. They admired her efforts to understand their subjects so that she could guide her nephew in acquiring knowledge. Joey began to catch her enthusiasm for her own field, history. Because she taught it with enthusiasm and sometimes found the weird, the silly, and the quirky in the human story so they could have a good laugh.

Joey began to understand that his aunt was not just his play companion, not to mention a great mac & cheese with tuna chef. He realized what smart was, what curiosity was, what the joy of learning was, and how all of that informed his aunt's individual self. He began to understand what love was. Not romantic love, of course. But the deep pleasure it was to be in the company of someone that you found to be almost an extension of yourself without sacrificing their own selves. These were not words that Joey thought at the time, of course. They are but an author's poor attempt to convey what Joey felt.

~

Not all education is academic. Some of it comes from the simple living of a life. Some come from the surrounding culture that life is led within. Joey's daily life was unique. It did not lack love or mental stimulation, or play. But it did lack a surrounding culture, the zeitgeist of the moment; the trends, the fads, the popular in movies, music, sports; political movements, or stagnation, or repression; economic ups and downs. Liz was a scholar of history who shunned the present. She did not stay abreast of current events if she could help it, so Joey certainly did not. Theirs was a comfortable cocoon. But not one culturally infused.

As Liz had predicted, Joey eventually rounded the corner and bumped into his puberty. The carnal aspects of puberty were confusing for Joey, a little traumatic, and boring to report on. But, like the "miracle of birth," which happens hundreds of thousands of times a day, the onset of puberty is nothing unique. Nor is the social reaching out that often accompanies puberty. The embracing of peers and finding one's music (usually the music of your peers, so not actually tough to find). Discovering passions for other arts, clothes, and style, and taking on a mantle that one could call one's own. But the urge to do all this while wrapped in a cocoon was unique.

Joey had nowhere to turn. Until he turned into his grandfather's room, driven by a curiosity born from the stories Liz started telling him about her dad.

Carter Garner had been a sweet, simple man who sold suits. Mainly for men, but also for women. He had a passion for wool and cotton and hated polyester. He knew fine tailoring as intimately as he knew his wives. And Carter Garner never needed a tape measure. He could judge by looking exactly what size any man would need in suits and shirts and what alterations might be required to fit each unique individual.

"Men are not machines, you know. They don't come off an assembly line," Carter Garner would preach to his coworkers, his two wives, his daughter, and anybody else who would listen. He could eye-measure women as well. This truly demonstrated his skill, for there were more facets to a woman's figure than there were to a man's. "In fact, there are more facets to a woman's mind than there are to a man's as well," he often stated. "I wonder if the two are connected?"

"Dad was certainly an admirer of women's minds," Liz told her nephew. "But he was a connoisseur of their figures."

Liz told Joey that her dad always said there were two causes for why the world went to hell in a hand bucket starting in the mid-20th century. Children being allowed to call adults by their first names was one. Adults beginning to dress like teenagers instead of teenagers dressing like adults was the other.

"What does that mean?" Joey asked his aunt.

"You know, I'm not sure I ever really knew."

It was his grandfather's music collection that provided a clue. He started looking at all the old CDs and even older LPs neatly arranged on shelves in the room. And the two very different machines they were played on. Joey had a mind interested in such old mechanics, wondering how they worked. But Joey found something else to attract his mind as well. Or, at least, the part of his mind being recently lubricated by certain hormones. The covers, both small and large, of the music albums. The ones featuring the features of the female form. Especially one that featured the female form foamy with whipped cream.

"Your grandfather was crazy about the 1950s," Aunt Liz said to Joey when he brought a number of the albums to show her and asked if she knew how to run the machines. "And a bit of the 1960s. Not the hippy sixties, you know, the anti-war protests and all that, the tortured political divisions of the time. Or rock music, and love-ins, and certainly nothing psychedelic."

"What is all that?" Joey asked but wasn't sure he really wanted an answer.

"Well, that's a history lesson for later. Let's just concentrate on your grandfather for now. You see, he was a romantic, a bit of a throwback. He liked the early part of the sixties of elegantly dressed men and women because that was his business. And I think he thought his business was under threat from tee-shirts and blue jeans. Dad was constantly chiding me for the inelegant way I dressed. But I told him, 'Dad, elegance and I, that's a twain not destined to meet.'

"Let's see what you got here?" She took several of the albums in both formats from Joey. "Well, look at that, a young nude woman covered in whipped cream. Now that tells you something about the 20th century. Oh, but look here, Julie London. Dad loved Julie London. Look at her in her glittery, low-cut dress folded around her unmistakably sexy woman's figure, well managed flowing thick red hair, and come hither look."

"What's 'come hither'?"

"That's also a lesson for another day. What else is there? Oh, Lola Albright. She was the girlfriend on an old TV show Dad had in his collection. If I remember right, it was about a well-dressed private eye named Peter Gunn. A name so Freudian you wonder how it passed the censors. She was a sexy nightclub singer, never less than elegantly turned out. Oh, and here are a couple of James Bond movie soundtracks. That's James Bond, and he was a spy, and these are what they called his 'Bond Girls.' The sexism makes me shudder. But Dad loved this stuff. I think he wanted to be James Bond packing his peter gun." Liz laughed at her word-wit. "Oh, well, atavistic though it was, Dad would transport himself there through this music and movies of this time and TV and such. And even older stuff of this kind. It made him happy, so how could I complain? You sure you really want to hear this?" Liz asked as she handed back the albums.

Joey took them back and looked deeply at, possibly into, Julie London and Lola Albright and Daniela Bianchi and Ursula Andress. And the anonymous girl covered with whipped cream and with wide eyes that said, "Yes, please."

~

Not all of his grandfather's music featured gorgeous and elegant women on their covers, but all of the music delighted Joey. There was orchestrated suspense, adventure, and danger in John Barry's score for the Bond films. There were the jazzy beats of Henry Mancini's *Peter Gunn* theme and tracks that put Joey in a strange, yearning mood. And he liked the funny music in Mancini's *Pink Panther* but was really drawn to the tracks that put him in a strange, yearning mood. And the cover of Mancini's *Breakfast at Tiffany's* with the most elegant Audrey Hepburn (was there ever a more elegant female neck?) put him in a strange, yearning mood as well. But it wasn't just Mancini. He discovered the fun, slightly askew happy music of Neal Hefti. It introduced him to Batman. He had never even heard of superheroes before. But Hefti's score to the film *How to Murder Your Wife* disturbed him. Not the music, which he liked, but the concept. Murder? Your wife? He had to see the movie. He asked his aunt if she still had his grandfather's movies. She sighed a little and took Joey into a storeroom. There they were, stacks of things she called DeeVeeDees. He found the Bond films from the sixties, a whole set of *Peter Gunn* TV episodes, and a bunch of films from the fifties and the forties, a few from the thirties. All titles he had never heard of, a world of movies he had not known existed. And, yes! *How to Murder Your Wife*. With the funny-looking guy on the cover along with the beautiful blonde woman with cavernous cleavage! (Although cleavage was not even a word Joey knew). Why would anyone, even a funny-looking guy, want to murder her?

"How do you play them?" Joey asked, a little out of breath.

"Well, that's the problem, you see. I got rid of the player and the TV," Liz informed him of the bad news.

"No! What the bloody blue blazes did you do that for?"

They spent a good half day on the internet tracking down a refurbished classic near-antique 19-inch TV with a built-in DVD player. It cost Liz a lot more than she really wanted to pay. But Liz realized she could not disappoint Joey.

The day the TV/DVD combo arrived by a hefty drone, Joey refused to be taught anything about history, math, geography, or even the stars. He only wanted to learn how to operate the machine. They installed it in his bedroom. The DVDs he was interested in he had already taken out of storage and put into a bookcase in his room in alphabetical order.

Once everything was set to go, Joey climbed up onto his bed and made himself comfortable. Then, using the remote control device that cost almost as much as the TV/DVD combo, Joey watched *How to Murder Your Wife*.

Liz left him alone. Soon she heard laughter coming from his bedroom. Joey went into the circular space where Liz was reading when it was all over.

"It's okay. He didn't really murder his wife. It was all a joke. I should have guessed from the words of the song. I feel so stupid."

"Joey, it was just a movie."

"Oh no, Aunt Liz. It was...it was...it was transportation."

~

The worlds that Joey discovered through the moving images and often moving stories on the antique TV screen bore little resemblance to the world he experienced during their field trips. And absolutely no resemblance to the world he and his aunt occupied in The Hole. They were worlds of heroes and villains, lovers and haters, tragic falls from grace, and hilarious falls on faces. There were courageous characters and characters that cowered; simple characters of pleasing personalities and complex characters with perplexing personalities. There was the happy-go-lucky and the unfortunate fools. There were men. And there were women.

Joey studied the men. Never having had a father or a brother or a peer best friend or an influential male teacher or a demanding coach, he'd had no daily male role models. There was Dr. Penko, but he was a gigantic-head source of information on the large curving screen. He played his role, but was not a role model. And there were other of his aunt's male colleagues that participated in his education. But that was his academic education, not his education as a male. Now, though, many fictional men were passing across the small screen in his bedroom. And they somehow seemed more real to Joey than the factual big-headed men on the giant curved screen in the circular space. James Stewart, William Powell, Dick Powell, Humphry Bogart, Cary Grant, Clark Gable, Alan Ladd, James Garner, Paul Newman, Rock Hudson, Craig Stevens, Sean Connery, and Jack Lemon became his favorites. Long-dead men but long-lived images. Characters. Personalities. Selfs. And almost always well dressed and beautifully turned out—elegant.

It seems Joey's grandfather was still selling suits.

Joey did not study the women. He married them. He could no longer remember his mother. And Liz was not a woman; she was just his aunt. (And his teacher, playmate, storyteller, and smart, so smart, she knew everything.) But the females from the thirties, forties, fifties, and early sixties gracing the screen in his bedroom were *women*. Despite being presented in pixels, Joey could feel their flesh and knew that their blood flowed. He took their smiles personally, and their come hither looks. Joey figured out *come hither* on his own, although it came more like a revelation than an evaluation. He wanted each and every one of them—Katharine Hepburn and Myrna Loy; Ginger Rogers and Jean Harlow; Lauren Bacall and Rita Hayworth; Marilyn Monroe (Yes! Yes!) and Grace Kelly (Yes! Yes! Yes!)—to accept his proposal of a lifetime together. Not just because of the flesh he wanted to feel, the flow of blood that would keep them vital and warm, but because of their voices. Their voices spoke their minds. Their minds often displayed wit, smarts, skepticism, low tolerance for nonsense, eagerness—love. And always while they were well dressed, beautifully turned out—elegant.

Joey came to a better understanding of heredity when he realized he had inherited his grandfather's eye for clothes that projected as well as protected.

~

Liz, who was tone deaf, never cared for music. And she found the films her father had liked so divorced from reality, especially historical films, that she had actively ignored them. She was moderately appalled that Joey was now spending most of his free time listening to and viewing these frivolous popular entertainments. But could she begrudge him, having stuck him in a hole? No, Liz could not. But she could kid him without mercy.

"The stars in the heavens must weep, knowing you've replaced them with the stars in Hollywood." Aunt Liz said one Friday evening as they sat down to a meal of chicken-without-the-egg, corn, and mashed potatoes.

"Don't be silly, Aunt Liz," Joey said while tamping down a slight embarrassment to quell a flare of pink in his cheeks.

"I'd rather be silly than a—"

"Too late."

"Oh," Liz grabbed her ample chest. "*A touch, a touch, I do confess't.* But you have to admit, you've been spending less time in the observatory these nights," she pointed out.

"Well…"

"Well…?"

"The stars have been there for millions and billions of years. I don't think they're going away anytime soon."

"But you might miss a comet. You said you wanted to discover a comet." Liz looked at him quite pointedly. "You said you wanted to name it after me."

Joey looked up from his chicken-without-the-egg and at his aunt. He looked at her round face with no makeup but with intense eyes that would at times shine in concentration and other times sparkle in fun. Joey looked at her men's shirt XXL, this one blue and denim and well-worn, her usual mode of dress, along with baggy pants of a comfortable fit. He looked at her graying hair—always short and to the point, the point being not to waste time tending to it—no elegance here.

But oh so much—so much—so much Aunt Liz.

"You're right. I did. I do," Joey admitted.

"Would you like me to make you a thermos of hot chocolate?"

"Yeah, I would. I might have a long night."

Liz got up to make the chocolate.

Joey started to clear the table. "Hey, Aunt Liz?"

"Yeah?"

"Do you have any of Grandfather's old clothes?"

"His old clothes?"

"I mean, he sold suits; he must have worn them too, right?"

"Yes. Dad was a natty dresser, alright."

"So…?"

"Gave them all away. To some charity or other. I don't know, *Homeless Clothes Hounds* or something like that."

"Aunt Liz!"

"Here," Liz said, handing Joey the thermos, "take your hot chocolate and find me my comet."

Joey was disappointed. He really wanted to see his grandfather's suits. Joey wanted to know if they would have fit him. But the sky did not disappoint him that night. Nor did the stars the next day.

11

ANOTHER RUDE AWAKENING PART 1

Okay, Astro, I'm going to wake you up again. Slowly...letting your consciousness dawn...

Astro opened his eyes as awareness dashed around in his brain. The first thing he realized was that he had either disconcertingly grown quite a bit since his last awakening or his bed had shrunk. A glitch? Well—Neuro will have to fix that.

Astro arose and sat on the side of his bed and looked around.

"What the bloody blue blazes!"

Now breathe in, Astro, slowly, take it in.

"Breathe in? Breath in what? Zeros and ones?

If you want to think of it that way.

"Because there really is no air, right?"

Of course, there is. For all your intents and purposes, there is. The point is to stay calm. Where are you?

"Isn't that a question for you to answer?"

Where do you seem to be?

"In my childhood bedroom in The Hole sitting on my small, single bed."

Good.

"The question is, why am I here?"

We're working on expanding the world around your apartment. We can't have you conscious while we are doing that. But I needed you to be conscious to run some tests. So, we moved you over to The Hole. We've just completed its construction.

"Why?"

I thought you might appreciate it.

"Well…" Damn! He felt something there. Some flow of…of…okay, he admitted it, appreciation for what his friend did for him today. "Thank you, Neuro."

You are welcome, Astro.

Astro stood and was met with a surprise. "And I'm not naked."

We're getting good at jammies, as you call them.

"I haven't called them that for years. Nor have I wore them. You couldn't have given me a simple pair of sleep shorts and a tee-shirt?"

Where would be the fun in that?

"Oh. You did it for fun?"

Sure.

"Which is why they're Mickey Mouse 'jammies'?"

Don't you remember?

"Remember what?"

When you were sent to your Aunt Liz, you told me that a new pair of Mickey Mouse pajamas were in the bag they packed for you.

"Oh, yeah, that's right."

Two memories rose in some part of Astro's brain, exciting neurons (or *vice versa*). A memory of the new, crisply folded pajamas in their cellophane package that crinkled like wildfire as Aunt Liz opened it. And a memory of telling Neuro about it when…

～

It must have been in that first year when they both came to USC for their doctorates. They found themselves spending most of their free time together. The second time they met was at the Doheny Jr. Library, which Neuro loved because its exterior reminded him somewhat of his childhood home in London. They were both in the vast high-ceilinged entrance hall. Neuro was admiring the ornate hanging lamps and the three long, narrow stained-glass windows one needed binoculars to truly appreciate. The diminutive astronomer was standing at the counter talking to one of the librarians. Neuro saw Astro first. And he noted that he was wearing a well-cut gray pinstripe double-breasted suit, which, in and of itself, was a sartorial anomaly on campus. But to top it off—literally, it must be said—he wore a dark gray fedora. While Neuro was wearing a comfortable pair of chino slacks and a tee-shirt promoting a British Soccer team. He walked over to Astro and announced himself, asking, "Are you going somewhere special?"

Astro turned to Neuro and looked up at the stately African. "Oh, hello. Have you gotten taller since we met?"

"No, I do not think so."

"Oh. It must have been because we were standing by Tommy Trojan. You seemed much shorter then."

Neuro smiled a very appealing yet knowing smile. "Not likely."

"No, you're right. How is the rarified air up there?"

"Just fine. How is it having a low center of gravity?"

"Keeps me grounded."

Neuro laughed. He liked this man. "But you haven't answered my question."

"1066."

"1066?"

"Didn't you ask me when the Battle of Hastings was?"

"No, I do not believe so. Remember, I went to Oxford. I know when the Battle of Hastings took place."

"No."

"No, what?"

"No, I am not going anywhere special." It was Astro's turn to smile.

"Is that so? I thought since you were dressed up…."

"No, I am just well dressed. I do not need an excuse to be well dressed."

"I see."

"But you could give me one."

"And how might I do that?"

"Why don't we have dinner together tonight?"

"Lovely. Why don't we."

"What kind of food do you like?"

"I have a particular fondness for Indian food."

"Do the Indians make macaroni and cheese?"

"I am afraid not."

"That's okay. I think there's a fine Indian restaurant in Chinatown."

"An Indian restaurant in Chinatown?"

"It's a small world, Neuro."

"So it seems, Astro."

~

111

As Astro did not want to stay in his Mickey Mouse jammies, Neuro directed him to the closet where he found a pair of khaki shorts like some his aunt had once bought him. Also, a tee-shirt with the words MY BRAIN HAS BEEN DRAINED printed on the front. "*Fun-ny*," Astro said, lacing the two syllables together with irony.

It amused me.

Astro picked up the shorts. "Uh, Neuro, this is the size I wore when I was ten."

That's okay. Put them on.

Astro did so and found that they miraculously—or, at least, digitally—fit.

Do you know what "jammy" means in England, Astro?

After slipping on the tee-shirt, Astro said, "Since you're asking me, I assume it doesn't mean pajamas."

Correct.

Astro thought for a moment, then said, "Is it a cute little porcelain pot of jam with King William's face on it?"

Interesting guess, but no.

"Then I am stumped."

It means undeserved luck. Where Americans would say, "He's a lucky bastard," Brits would say, "He's a jammy bastard."

"But in either case, he's a bastard?"

That is correct.

"Is there going to be a test on this later?"

It is just something for you to muse on and make your mind work as we watch it.

"*Now* I feel naked," Astro stated as he marveled at being in his childhood room. There was the bookcase with all of his grandfather's DVDs and CDs. He looked at their spines—there was Barry, Mancini, Hefti, and the big bands of the thirties and forties; there was Bond, Gunn, and Jack Lemon "murdering his wife." Astro took a few out of the bookcase and looked at the covers. They were perfect. The shiny cases, though, felt more like cardboard than plastic. The old TV/DVD combo sat on top of his dresser. There were the posters of astrological marvels on the wall his Aunt Liz had ordered for him. There were galaxies of odd shapes, stunning beautiful clouds of interstellar gas, stars aborning, and stars dying. There was his bed, of course, and a pile of books on his night table. The one on top was *The Wind in the Willows*.

"Neuro, it amazes me how accurate you've made this. How did

you do it? And my apartment as well?"

Well…

"What?"

I had to declare you dead.

"What?"

As your heir, I needed you to be dead to gain access to The Hole. Then I went there and digitally documented everything. And I made certain assumptions from things you told me. I already had a key to your apartment, of course.

"Plus, now you have all my money."

Well, I hardly needed that, but yes.

"So I'm dead?"

Only officially. But you are absolutely alive in reality.

"Death used to be the ultimate reality."

Things change. Times change.

"Change changes. And, being 'dead,' I suppose I have no rights, right?"

Well, I suppose that is true. I mean, with me you do, but not with the world at large because you are no longer at large in the world.

"Except this 'world' you're making for me. So," Astro said, suddenly realizing the implications, "you've become my god?"

If so, Astro, a benevolent one.

"I can't have a god, Neuro; I'm an atheist."

You don't have to believe in me. But, believe me—I'm your friend.

Astro had no doubt about that. What more was there to say?

Astro took another look around. "Is it just my bedroom you've—fashioned?"

No, it is the whole Hole.

"The ho-ho?"

Okay. The complete The Hole. There's no desert surrounding it, though.

"I am grateful for your small mercies."

Although there is…Well, why don't you just explore?

Astro left his bedroom and walked down the corridor to the circular space. It was even more uncanny, the realness of it. There was Aunt Liz's desk with her computer on top, the latest one she had bought just before she did not pass away but died. There was the recliner, looking as worn as ever. Astro—Joey to Aunt Liz—had begged her to get a new one. But she said a new one would be uncomfortable, that this one, after years of supporting her, was molded to her body and hugged her like a mommy. Astro walked over to the kitchen. Everything was as it had been and, "Ha! Nice touch, Neuro."

Thank you.

On the kitchen counter, close to the stove with a pot sitting on a burner ready for use, was a Kraft Macaroni and Cheese box and a tin of tuna.

Astro turned back to the circular space and looked up at the large curved video monitor on the wall. "So, can I get anything on the monitor?

You tell me.

A bar of light popped onto the center of the screen, then spread up and down to a brilliant field of bright white, which then faded into colors, objects in the background, and the huge head of Neuro.

"What the bloody blue blazes!"

"Don't be scared," said Neuro for the first time audibly instead of just mentally, not to mention visually.

"I'm not scared. I'm just shocked. You've got a bunch of gray hair."

"Well, if I do, you gave it to me."

"Me?"

"Do you think it's been easy keeping you alive?"

"Is that what I am? Alive."

"Yes!"

"I wish you would let me panic. I feel like panicking."

"Shut up. And go up the elevator."

"Why? You said there was no desert out there."

"True. But there is something for you to see."

Astro did as his 'god' commanded, rising to the above-ground entry to the habitat. It was as it had always been, including the door to the observatory his aunt had built for him when he was twelve. "Really?"

Yes. Neuro's voice was back in his head.

Astro opened the door. And there beyond was his observatory. Just as it was the last time he saw it. With the large 25-inch f/4 Obsession telescope, his computer, and the unique, pneumatic, very comfortable chair that had molded itself to Astro's compact butt.

The computer monitor lit up, and Neuro's face was soon on it. "You can use the telescope, Astro. It's fully functional."

Astro was confused. "Really? How?"

"In fact, it is more than functional. You can program it to "be" any telescope on the Earth or in Earth orbit. Optical or radio, the whole spectrum, in fact. And you will get that particular telescope's views and data in real-time. Of course, you have to book time on those telescopes, just as you would if—"

"If I was out there with you and the rest of humanity?"

"Yes. But then—you would probably be getting gray as well."

"How?"

"Through the normal process of aging, of course."

"No, how can I tap into all these telescopes?"

"We created a network of all the telescopes, connecting them to yours there."

"You got all those different agencies and universities to cooperate? Why are you—I mean—this is—" Astro felt himself to be on the edge of the feelings he would have usually felt: amazement, disbelief, deep gratitude, and love of a particular kind.

"Don't try to cry. We haven't programmed tears yet."

~

When Astro returned to the circular space, he flopped on the couch and stared up at the giant head of Neuro on the curved screen. He could see a wall behind his friend against which a bank of computers hummed. Neuro was smiling. "You will be able to continue your work, Astro. More powerfully than ever before."

"But you had me declared dead. Can a dead man publish research papers?"

"A little joke on my part."

"A little joke?"

"Don't you remember? You had given me your Power of Attorney."

"Of course. Of course, I did. After Aunt Liz died and I dealt with her probate and estate, we both became worried about such things. You had your brother, but I had—"

"No one but me—brother."

"But still… How have you…? I mean… You said I wasn't in a machine, but you never really answered me on uploading, did you? Maybe I'm in something different, maybe…? Look, is Carmichael there? Is that bastard just off-camera smirking with his damn crooked smile? Come on, Neuro, answer me."

On-screen, Neuro suddenly looked to his left as if he had been called. Somebody was talking to him; Astro could see that Neuro was obviously taking in important information by the concentration on his face. Finally, he turned back to "face" Astro, expressing some concern. "Let me get back to you on that," he said as the screen went dark.

Astro stood from the couch. "Neuro? Neuro! What the bloody blue blazes!"

12
BLOWHARD AT THE BOVARD

Neuro and Astro first met Brandon Carmichael in 2050 during their second year as Ph.D. candidates at USC. He made an early evening appearance at Bovard Auditorium on the USC campus, scheduled to give his famous, well-paid speech on *Extending life into Eternity*. Many thinkers in the 21st-Century had vied to become the grand guru of Transhumanism. Some of them just wanted to uplift *Homo sapiens* via mechanical adaptations to human biology, extending individual life for hundreds, possibly thousands of years. Others wanted to do it by divorcing human consciousness from anything biological or substantially mechanical— except the information mechanics of the universe—thereby making eternity no longer the undiscovered country. As the title of Carmichael's speech indicated, he was among the latter and, at that time, the most famous of the latter.

This was not so much because of the force of his ideas or personality, as it was that several previously favorite grand gurus of Transhumanism leftover from the Twentieth-century had succumbed to the oh-so-human habit of dying.

Astro accompanied Neuro to the lecture under protest, as he did not think much of Brandon Carmichael—or any *true believer* in scientist's clothing, for that matter. But Neuro had insisted. It was his

Friday night to choose an activity, and this was his choice. Why in the bloody blue blazes, Astro had no clue. Maybe it was just for the amusement value. Maybe Neuro didn't want to go off-campus until later, when the horrendous traffic on the roads would be lighter. Or maybe, just perhaps… No, Astro did not think Neuro took this stuff seriously. He was too immersed into the complexity of the dance of brain and body to ever… At least Astro hoped so.

They sat in the third row of the ornate auditorium with the two sweeping balconies. And the dark wood beams in the heavenly ceiling, the cathedral windows, and the plush red seats with plenty of legroom keeping their footed limbs stretched and relaxed and their fleshy bi-caramel posteriors comfy. The white noise buzz of the audience that filled most of the 1,235 seats had that anticipatory energy that was usual in such gatherings of shared purpose. Astro and Neuro added to it by chatting about the last lovely lady—a rather interesting historian of medieval music—Astro had dated. He told Neuro that they (Astro and the historian) were thinking of starting an elegance movement.

"You should see how she carries herself, with such grace—" Astro said as the lights came down. And Brandon Carmichael, sans any formal introduction, took the stage.

The still boyish-faced (despite his fifty-nine years) guru of eternal life was dressed all in black. Except for bright red running shoes and a matching bright red tie and glasses with brilliant red frames accenting his shiny ebony suit and slightly less ebony shirt.

"Hello, all you pathetic, putrid meat machines!" Carmichael shouted out in greeting, soliciting much applause for this line he was well-known for. "For that is what you are, decaying dabs of flesh and organs heading downwards, ever downwards. I don't care how much you keep yourself fit with exercise and vitamins. Or meditation and good thoughts, or so-called healthy living. You all had mothers who, to paraphrase Samuel Beckett, gave birth to you astride a grave."

Astro turned to Neuro and whispered, "For someone who hates his decaying dab of flesh, he sure takes care to adorn it with style. A godawful style, but a definite style nevertheless."

"And after this funereal birth," Carmichael continued all alone upon the stage, "Beckett perfectly describes human life—your life. '…the light gleams an instant, then it's night once more.'

"I am a warrior against the night!"

Applause from the audience; a loud snort from Astro; a "hush!" from Neuro.

Carmichael's speech lasted one hour and fifteen minutes. He updated the audience on his current progress in designing effective emulations of whole brains. He assured the audience that this would allow him to transfer minds, personalities, memories, and individual "selfs" to an ever-upgradeable computer. This would not just stave off death but conquer it. He ended the speech basking in warm applause and returning the appreciation with a practiced grateful smile, oddly crooked, as he left the stage.

The audience rose as if one entity, ready to vacate. Except for Astro, who always hated mixing with a crowd determined to crowd the exits. And Neuro, who was used to this and sat patiently next to his friend.

"Well," Astro said when he finally stood and watched the last of the audience leaving, "let's go get some dinner. This meat machine is hungry."

"Not just yet," Neuro said.

"What?"

"We have got to go backstage."

"What the bloody blue blazes for?"

"Well—don't get too upset now—I was invited by Carmichael to meet him after the lecture."

"You're kidding."

"He has read my research on the connectome. He wants to meet me. Come on, it should be interesting."

"Why must I go?"

"Because it is Friday night."

That seemed to be answer enough, and Astro followed his tall friend out of the auditorium and around it to the Artists Entrance and the Green Room, where Brandon Carmichael waited for them.

As post-performance Green Rooms have always been, this Green Room was a comfortable lounge-like space with platters of decimated foodstuff. Only bits and pieces of fruit and cheese and crackers, some scattered sliced meats, and a few little sandwiches were left on the platters. There were also two near-empty bowls of M&Ms, one holding plain and one holding peanut. Depending on the celebrity of the performer, the quality of the performance, and possibly even the sexual or intellectual appeal of the performer, a milling crowd of people congratulating, glad-handing, worshiping, or skeptically assessing the live-in-person-ness of the performer would usually fill a Green Room post-performance.

This Green Room on this night was crowded with the president and several members of the Student Transhumanism Society, which had sponsored Carmichael's lecture. And Carmichael's publisher, who was prepping his latest book *Immortality is a Right,* which was supposed to have been out by this speaking date but, well…. Several staff members of Carmichael's Foundation for Immortality were also there, and some USC faculty members and students. And, of course, more than a few run-of-the-mill true-believing star-fuckers.

The room buzzed with congratulations for another well-delivered presentation, some quick chats on fine philosophical points of mind uploading, some technical talk of technical difficulties, and even a mention of the USC Trojan football team's recent glorious victory over UCLA.

Standing in the middle of all this, basking in the attention with marvelous calm, was the man-of-the-hour—or at least the next fifteen minutes or so—Brandon Carmichael.

Neuro and Astro, late to the party, walked into this maelstrom of attention-seeking and stood by the entrance observing, neither wanting to just dive in. But Brandon Carmichael, despite being surrounded by the crowd, caught sight of them. Or at least, of Neuro.

With charming rudeness, Carmichael broke from the crowd and walked over to Neuro with arm extended and hand out. "And, you, of course, must be Khadambi Kinyanjui. Goodness, you are the tallest person I have ever met. You obviously stand head and shoulders above everyone in the room. But even if you were as short as this guy," Carmichael said, giving Astro a glancing acknowledgment of his existence. "You, in my estimation, would stand head and shoulders above everyone in neuroscience."

"That's an odd thing to say," Astro said with his head slightly bent to one side to even out Carmichael's crooked smile, "seeing how you want to take everyone's heads from their shoulders."

Carmichael now gave Astro a thorough look and extended his crooked smile, saying after a bit of staccato laugh, "Clever. And almost funny. Who might you be?"

Neuro declared from on high, utilizing his stature's natural authority to claim control, "This is my good friend, Joe Smith. He is a fine astronomer."

"An astronomer, huh?" Carmichael questioned. "Got your head in the stars, then?"

"No, I've got my head firmly planted on my shoulders—where it belongs."

Carmichael crooked his smile once again as a form of gracious surrender. "Well, Joe, I hope you don't mind my taking Khadambi here off to dinner. I want to talk to him about the future. If you will excuse us." Carmichael began to lead Neuro out, taking him by his elbow.

But Astro took Carmichael's elbow and stopped him. "Oh no, *I* don't mind. But my *mind* minds. Where he goes, I go."

"What are you, his *minder*?"

"I really think," Neuro exerted control again. "That we all three can enjoy a nice, quiet dinner together to discuss futures, or the past, or even this most palpable present. Now, Dr. Carmichael, what kind of food would you prefer?"

"I have absolutely no preference for food. I try not to think about food. Food to me is just pre-atavistic sustenance. It's something I look forward to doing away with. But until then, I'll eat anything. Shall we go?"

Carmichael led Neuro and Astro out of the Green Room, leaving behind a disappointed crowd who could only find solace in the remains on the food platters.

As they followed Carmichael, Astro whispered up to Neuro, "I wonder if he eats shit?"

Neuro suppressed a laugh into a subtle chuckle. "Please be on your best behavior, Astro."

"You're asking me to censor myself?"

"Oh no, my friend. Just the opposite," Neuro said with his broad, open-mouth smile, which was very much on the level.

～

Neuro called forth his self-driving car, the precursor to Gathii, and it pulled up in front of Carmichael, its doors opening to greet him.

"Wow! What a car," Carmichael said as he entered, followed by Astro and Neuro. "Very posh," he said as he fastened his seatbelt, impressed, which showed on his face. As did a question.

"He's filthy rich," Astro answered, having guessed the question.

"Is he? I did not know that."

Astro was quite sure that Carmichael had been aware of it. But said nothing as he gave the car instructions to drive them to his and Neuro's favorite Indian restaurant in Chinatown.

"A good choice," Neuro said.

"I'm sure it will be fine," Carmichael said, although his opinion had not been solicited.

~

Before the three sat at a centrally placed round table in the restaurant, Astro excused himself to visit the men's room. On his way, he stopped by the kitchen.

"Hey, Banjeet!" he called out to the chef.

"Hello, Joe!"

"Come here a second, will you?"

Banjeet came to the door, and Astro pointed out Carmichael sitting at their table in a spirited discussion with Neuro. "Whatever he orders—he's going to want it super hot. That's just the kind of guy he is."

"Suggest then that he should order Phaal Curry. I'll put in a little extra chili."

"What kind?"

"Well, there's ten altogether, so I have much to choose from."

~

When Astro returned to the table, Neuro was just saying, "Well, it is an interesting offer."

"What's he trying to sell you, Neuro?"

"Neuro?" Carmichael questioned.

"That is Joe's name for me. Because I am a neuroscientist, you see."

"And I suppose you call him—what?—Starboy?"

"Not at all. I call him Astro."

Carmichael sat back in his chair. "Oh." He thought he had figured it out. "Endearing pet names."

"*Mr.* Smith!"

A young, attractive woman had walked up to the table and stood there in an assertive yet charming pose.

Astro, who had not yet sat, turned around. "*Ms.* Crick."

"Round two?" The woman was several inches taller than Astro, had long black hair that she had obviously spent a long time preparing for the evening, and was dressed in a distinctive if simple and serious style that still emphasized the glories of her gender.

"I sent you a note today with such a request," Astro said to Ms. Crick.

"Really? I received nothing."

"Nothing digital. Except in the fact that I used the digits of my hands in its composition. It should come tomorrow by way of our beleaguered postal system."

Ms. Crick parted her red lips in delight and said, "You are a class act, Mr. Smith."

"And you are the essence of class, Ms. Crick."

"Later then?"

"Well, it certainly can't be earlier."

Ms. Crick placed her hand on Astro's cheek for a touch of the future.

"I guess I was wrong," Carmichael said more or less to himself.

"What?" Neuro had heard him.

"Nothing."

Before leaving, Ms. Crick turned to Neuro and greeted him. "Khadambi."

"Francis," Neuro returned the greeting.

As Astro sat, Carmichael, who usually tried not to be gobsmacked by mundane human information minutia, said, "Her name is *Francis Crick?*"

"Yes," Astro and Neuro said in tandem.

"And she's a rather fine geneticist," Astro was delighted to declare.

~

"What do you recommend?" Carmichael asked as they looked at the menu.

"Phaal Curry," Astro suggested before Neuro, the true expert in Indian cuisine, could speak.

"Really?" Neuro questioned Astro and elaborated on it with a look.

"Khadambi, do you concur?" Carmichael asked.

"Well, it's one of my favorites."

"Okay then."

Upon his first bite of the Phaal Curry, Carmichael's face flared up to a red almost as bright as his tie.

"Try not to think about *that* food, Dr. Carmichael," Astro said.

Neuro grabbed the attention of a passing waiter and asked, "Can you quickly bring our friend here a glass of sweet lassi?"

Astro had been hoping for a bit of comedy shtick, maybe Carmichael spitting out the lovingly prepared curry or jumping up and hopping around and fanning his hands by his open mouth with its tongue hanging out in a vain effort to cool the inferno inside. But

Carmichael, being a quick-thinking genius and thus more intelligent than the average victim of a prank, was not about to give Astro the satisfaction. He sat still, although with every muscle in his body contracted. A couple of tears made a glistening appearance as Carmichael smiled, chewed, and eventually swallowed. He was going to say something (but found that he couldn't) just as the waiter brought him the tall, cold glass of sweet white lassi that Neuro had ordered. With much gratitude but in complete control of his movements, Carmichael took the yogurt drink and, as casually as he could manage, brought it to his lips and began to swallow. He did not stop until he had drained the glass.

When he could finally talk, Carmichael said, with a slightly altered voice. "Well, whew! Thank you for that experience."

"One you'll not soon forget?" Astro asked.

"Unlikely."

"Life is full of them," Astro stated. "Experiences you'll not forget for both positive and negative reasons. One might say that they are the seasoning of the big meal that is life. Good times, bad times. Moments of fear or fun or delight or love, or sometimes, sadly, of hate. Moments of guilty pleasures, petty pleasures, hopefully, some profound pleasures. Certainly, my friend Ms. Crick has provided me with some profound pleasures—and not all of them were intellectual. So, I have to wonder, Dr. Carmichael, if you finally succeed in uploading a mind, the consciousness of a person into a computer— and I don't for one moment think you ever will succeed—what experiences will that person then have? Outside of thinking about whatever the hell it wants to think about, what will this uploaded person experience? I mean, will it ever sit and shit and shave and shower?"

Carmichael was preparing to give his standard answer—which had been well patted down through the years into a compact yet dense explanation—when Astro's last question took him aback. "I'm sorry?"

"Well, it's so essentially mammalian, isn't it? So animal-of-flesh-and-organs. I, like billions of my fellow *Homo sapiens,* after my morning meal and in preparation for the coming day, sit and shit. A necessity, you'll agree, to finish off the process of sustenance you seem to disdain. An almost mechanical process. And yet, seriously, who doesn't like a good dump? It feels good to rid yourself of what your body couldn't use, even if the waste is a dirty, stinky object of revulsion. And then to shave and shower, to make one's face as neat

124

as it can be, and to cleanse one's body. Now that is a profound pleasure. Of course, many men, and most women, don't shave their faces, but that's not the point. The point is grooming. To keep us healthy. To present ourselves in the best possible light to the world. And to give us a certain pride of self. *Of self.* And then what do we do? We humans, at least? You, obviously, the least of them all." Astro indicated Carmichael's black and red with a brief gesture of his hand. "We adorn ourselves. An act not just of aesthetics but of communication. Now, you may say all this is just the mundaneness of our animal selves, our *meaty* selves, to be jettisoned in your uploaded future. But I, for one, would miss all this essentially animal mundaneness. What will be the equivalent experiences for your uploaded minds, Dr. Carmichael? Polishing our ones and zeros? Preening while we process information? Spic and spanning our silicon-based hosts? Will our silicon hosts ever allow us to be silly, to pull stupid pranks? Dr. Carmichael, will our uploaded minds ever enjoy a fine meal with good friends? Will they ever give those friends nicknames—or 'pet names' for that matter?"

Carmichael looked directly at Astro's small face, which featured a few freckles, light reddish eyebrows, clear blue eyes, and an almost cliché pugilistic Irish demeanor. It was the kind of face Carmichael felt should always be pushed in.

"You are a quirky little man, aren't you?"

"Yes!" Astro shouted out, surprising Carmichael with this reaction and grabbing the attention of some of the other diners. "That's my point. Will your uploaded minds ever be quirky?"

"Why would you ever want them to be?"

"Because it's the quirky that makes life interesting. The odd ducks, the offbeat, the unusual, the unique, the crazy bastards! And aren't all of us quirky in one way or another? From the hardly perceptible to the outrageous? And yet you call us nothing but meat machines, reducing us down to rather unattractive lumps of matter."

"Well, like it or not, Mr. Smith, that's all our bodies really are. Machines of meat mass-produced on our genome's assembly line."

"I agree. If you prick us, do we not bleed? But I also agree with Jacob Bronowski, who said, 'Man is a machine at birth but a *self* by experience.' So, I come back to my question. What experiences will your uploaded minds ever have to continue shaping their individual, quirky selves?"

There was a hint of pity in Carmichael's face as he asked Astro, "Do you really want to die, Mr. Smith?"

"Not today," Astro answered with no hesitation. "Which is why I didn't order the Phaal Curry. And not anytime soon. But if you are asking me if I fear the deep, dark void of non-existence? No, I do not, Dr. Carmichael. I can happily stand on the edge of that void, stare deep into it, and feel nothing because I am too busy feeling life. And the thrill of discovery, the excitement of new ideas, the smooth bodies of consenting females, the pleasure of their personalities, not to mention the warm charm of Neuro's companionship. Even feeling some not-so-happy feelings. Because life isn't always a bed of roses. Still, it's the bed I've got, and I'm more than willing to lay in it."

Not using his hands to eat his pushed-aside meal, Carmichael brought them together and intertwined his fingers as a display of his fully-integrated composure and control. "What a stirring, if comic, defense of meat while you sit there eating your lamb tikka, Mr. Smith. At least you didn't try to browbeat me with that awful cliché argument that it's only death that makes life precious."

"I agree, that would have been awful. Because it's not true. It's not death; it's the fact that life seems to be so odd, unusual, and rare that makes it precious."

"So you're not one of those astronomers who believe the universe with a hundred million galaxies or more, each with a hundred million stars or more has to be littered with life? Including intelligent life?"

"No astronomer who's a good scientist *believes* any such thing. Some may think it's likely, but they know that there is not a shred of evidence. We have not contacted them. They have not contacted us. There could be many reasons why not, but the most compelling is that the conditions for life, the odds for life, are far worse than any casino in Vegas gives to win."

"Yes, yes, the Cinderella zone and all that."

"Oh, so much more than that. The right amount of energy, complex chemistry, a magnetic field, or something else to protect against UV radiation, and it goes on. Not to mention life ever developing a mind, self-awareness, and consciousness both creative and intelligent. The crapshoot of crapshoots."

"Do you like Las Vegas, Mr. Smith?"

"Hell, no. I grew up in the desert; I hate anything in the desert, but let's not get off the point."

"A point," Carmichael said, "I happen to agree with. It would not surprise me in the least to discover that life has begun here on Earth and only here. And so recently, too. I believe there has been no life anywhere for most of the universe's existence. I believe life is nothing but an anomaly of matter. A sudden mixture of chemicals, proteins, and elements gave rise to a prolific, if an extremely fragile, form of matter. So fragile that it can only exist under the dome of our thin atmosphere. And yet we yearn to leave, to jump out of our protective dome and roam the throughways and byways of space, as some bad sci-fi writer must have put it. Why? Why would we ever leave what's comfortable and life-sustaining for what's dangerous and deadly?"

"Well, most animals don't. They migrate only for food to survive."

"Exactly, Mr. Smith. Sit and shit and shave and shower? Actually, all most life wants to do, or better said can do, is hunt and eat and sleep and copulate—over and over and over until they—die. But humans, Mr. Smith, humans want so much more than that. Thus, we, in a ridiculously short amount of time, have gone from hunter-gatherers on the savannas of Africa to an inquiring, questing, yearning species. Who wants so much more than just to hunt our food and eat it, lay our heads down in slumber, and fuck to generate either fun or family. And certainly, so much more than just to sit and shit and shave and shower. Why Mr. Smith? Why should that be so?"

"Curiosity, Dr. Carmichael. A great desire to know what's over the next hill."

"Well, for some members of our species in the past, maybe. But most of humanity went over the next hill—just like all their meaty animal cousins—for food. Hunger in the belly is a far more powerful motivator than the hunger of the mind, Mr. Smith."

"You seem to be contradicting yourself."

"No, Joe—can I call you Joe? We are getting to be so intimate."

"Sure, Brandon. Unless you want to call me Astro, and I can call you Trans."

"No, I think Joe and Brandon will suffice," Carmichael said as he caught the eye of a passing waiter, who came over. "Might I have a simple bowl of rice, please, plain and unadorned?"

Neuro and Astro both looked at Carmichael with a certain irony.

"I am still meat," Carmichael addressed their faces. "And meat must be fed."

"You were defending your contradiction," Neuro reminded him.

"It was a contradiction only if you believe all humans to be created equal, which they manifestly are not, despite political documents, rallies, and campaigns. Look, here's what I don't tell the audiences who come to my lecture, the people who read my books. But you two—yes, even you, Joe—I consider part of the Elect and —"

127

"The Elect?" Astro, astonished, questioned.

"It's a perfectly apt if old-fashioned word. You both have expansive minds. And it was the few expansive minds with expanding consciousnesses that went over the hill for reasons far more important than just to find the next—bowl of rice." Carmichael said this just as the waiter placed before him his ordered rice. He then proceeded to partake of it, as greedily as he could without being unseemly about it.

Neuro and Astro respected Carmichael's need to feed and remained quiet, taking sips of their now warm Indian beers and finishing off what was left on their plates. Finally, satisfied, Carmichael began speaking again.

"I rail against meat because it is holding us back. It's fragile. Slings and arrows can do grievous harm. It survives only, as we agree, within the thin smudge of the atmosphere around our globe. Meat is just not conducive to the rest of the universe. But consciousness, both simple and complex, is. My eventual goal, far beyond just the uploading of minds of our conscious selves into computers or some other substrate, which will just be waystations, so to speak, will be the joining of human, or rather transhuman consciousness, to the universal consciousness that surrounds us."

"Oh, bloody blue blazes, you buy into that panpsychism crap, don't you?"

Carmichael sighed and turned to Neuro. "Your friend is rather rude, isn't he?"

"Well...," Neuro raised his head up and set it at an angle, and focused his eyes somewhere far off where the answer might lie. "Some might say so. But I prefer to think that he is blunt in a not always charming way."

"I was hoping to have a serious conversation with you, Khadambi, about your future, our future, and the future of the intelligent and creative minds on this planet."

"What about the not-so-intelligent and not-so-creative minds on this planet?" Astro, who had not been addressed, spoke up anyway. "Will you not upload them? Will they not eventually join with the universal mind in a "paradise" of right and good and virtuous calculations?"

"I'm done speaking with you," Carmichael said, turning to Astro. Then he pulled the cloth napkin that had rested on his lap from it and folded it neatly. He placed it on the table next to his now-empty bowl of rice as he slowly stood, gently pushing his chair back. Then, extricating himself from the table, Carmichael began to leave.

"Dr. Carmichael," Neuro said, standing. "Would you like us to drive you back to your hotel?"

"No, thank you. I will call for an autoride service."

"Well, let's keep in touch. I am not sure about your goals, but I have found your consciousness research invaluable."

"And I yours, Dr. Kinyanjui."

"I am not a doctor yet."

"Your work is such that I think I'm safe in conferring the honor on you early. Goodnight, Dr. Kinyanjui."

After Carmichael left, Neuro sighed as he sat, which surprised Astro.

"He's a nut-job, you know. He's quite a few planets short of a solar system," Astro said.

"He does have a bit of an arrogant fool about him. And yet…"

"What?"

"Well, it is not just meat that is fragile, Astro. Consciousness—is it anything more than a thin, gossamer fabric easily blown this way or that? And yet, it is us. You. Me. Our waiter. Ms. Crick. Each one of us, right now, vibrant, happy or not, loving, loved, possibly loathed. But real. Existing. And meaningful in some regard. A flame is hot. Then suddenly, it is not when extinguished. Do not even you, Astro, find a deep sadness in this?"

"I'm sorry. You mentioned Ms. Crick, and my mind went immediately to her smooth and sensuous flesh. What was your question?"

Neuro smiled at his friend. "You know what the question was. You just refuse to entertain it."

"Maybe because I don't find it very entertaining. So, next Friday, I'm taking you to the Hollywood Bowl for a classical concert of Mancini music. Now that's entertainment!"

13
THE TALL AND SHORT OF IT

Khadambi Kinyanjui's first impression of Joe Smith on that hot August day in 2049, in the shadow of Tommy Trojan, was that he was the oddest, most unique, most eccentric person he had ever met. And this was after growing up in London and attending Oxford, where the odd, unique, and eccentric were not unknown. It was not just that Joe stood there under the bare-chested, bare-legged statue, under the hot August sun, dressed quite nattily in a perfectly-pressed full suit, crisp white dress shirt with links at the cuffs, and a tightly cinched tie, whereas Khadambi was reveling in being able to wear shorts and a tee-shirt (bespoke though it may have been). A much more appropriate L.A., not to mention Nairobi, mode of dress. London and Oxford had seen warmer temperatures of late, of course, but his family and academic positions had demanded only an occasional breach of the appropriate well-financed dress expected of him. And so he was pleased, once he had landed on the Angeleno shore, to liberate his wardrobe. Khadambi had bought into the still-potent idea of Los Angeles as the true land of freedom. *Personal* freedom to qualify it. A wide-open, relaxed, calm, and casual (or laid-back, as they used to say) culture of reinvention, innovation, self-expression, and hot, sandy beaches. A culture where the only expectations you had to meet were your own. Late in his Oxford studies, it had occurred to Khadambi that he did not have to stay in England to get his Ph.D. Or go back to Kenya to his family-endowed Nairobi New University of Science and Technology, even though it had become as fine an institution as any in the world. But that he could become a delighted stranger in a delightfully strange land and embrace a new life under no one's watchful eyes. And so, that is what he did.

Khadambi had not expected that the first person he would meet in L.A. would be a diminutive fashion plate male. Especially one with a blunt directness and an odd way of taking you at face value while looking directly into your face. Even when your face was a foot higher than his. But so it had been.

This first impression Khadambi had of Joe came from more than just this brief encounter and the words they exchanged. It must have been something more chemical, like a low dose of cortisol, adrenaline, and dopamine, leading not to sexual desire or romantic love but an attraction nevertheless. Without being able to explain this, Khadambi knew it to be true. As he walked away, looking at the campus map Joe had given him to find the Dornsife Neuroscience Imaging Center, he felt immediate regret. This brief encounter would probably be his only one with Joe Smith (or Astro as Neuro had just dubbed him). Because that's how these things often happen. Ships slipping past each other in the night; self-driving vehicles veering off in opposite directions. A pity, he thought. But he had so many other things to think about at the time.

So Neuro grinned broadly when he encountered Astro for the second time in the Doheny Library. And Astro's suggestion of dinner together that night very much pleased him.

"You will dress up a little for it, won't you?" Astro asked quite commandingly.

"What is wrong with the way I am dressed?"

"I worry that your tee-shirt has the word *Arsenal* blazoned across it."

"It is a British Soccer team."

"Really. That's odd. To be named after a collection of weapons and military equipment."

"Yes, well, their nickname *is* The Gunners."

"Logical. Although still disturbing."

"I suppose you would like me to wear a suit."

"Well, if I had my druthers…."

"What is this word, *druthers?*"

"It's an old American word. It means—"

"I think context defines it for me. Do you know how hard it is to fit a man of my size with a suit?"

"Nonsense. Do you know how hard it is to fit a man of *my* size with a suit? I'm sure you have a tailor. I do."

Neuro did not want to take this further. It was bordering on the subject of money and one's access to it, which was a conversation he was sensitive about. "It is predicted to still be in the thirties tonight. But—"

"Thirties?"

"Sorry, I am still thinking Celsius. I guess here it would be—"

"The nineties."

Yes. of course. In either case, it is still bloody hot. But I do have with me the light linen suit I wear when I visit home."

"England? I assume it's gotten hotter there, but—"

"No, Kenya. Nairobi."

"Ah. Is the suit white?"

"No. Why?"

"Well, it would really bring out your fabulous ebony color, wouldn't it?"

"Is that a compliment or racism?"

"What does race have to do with clothes? Unless you know of a race that is always nude."

Neuro smiled and made a note of Astro's interesting turn of mind. "Well, it is a nice light gray, will that do?"

Astro thought for a second. "Sure. And I bet you look great in it."

~

Neuro, who was particular about Indian food, was quite impressed with Astro's restaurant in Chinatown. They both had a fine meal. Even the cultured lamb meat did not distract. It was indistinguishable from slaughtered meat, not that either had eaten slaughtered meat for quite a while.

"How did you hear about this place?" Neuro asked Astro.

"Before leaving home, I researched all the best restaurants in Los Angeles. I grew up eating my Aunt Liz's cooking, which was not anywhere near gourmet. Although I'm already missing the way she made mac & cheese."

"In England, they call it cheesy pasta."

"Really? Thus, the difference between these two nations. Anyway, I was determined, once on my own, to eat well and fine and to develop a demanding palate for the best in cuisine."

"Why?"

"Because I always liked the portrayal of gourmets in old movies. I mean from the last century. They always seemed so elegant, not just in their tastes but in their whole approach to life. A handful of nuts and berries can feed the body, but a well-thought-out mixture of tastes and textures can feed the—I hesitate using the word soul, but you know what I mean?"

"Something beyond nature red and raw in tooth and claw?"

"Exactly!" Astro declared excitedly.

~

After they had ordered their meals, their conversation started where most long, relaxed first conversational evenings started, with biographical sketches.

Astro was fascinated by Neuro's experience as an African growing up in England. There had been many British movies from the 1930s to the 1960s in his grandfather's collection of DVDs. They gave Astro a taste for things English, especially accents and eccentricities. His Aunt Liz, who was not a great lover of films, said she always could tell when her father, and later Joe, were watching an old English film.

"How?" Young Joey had asked her.

"Because you can always hear seagulls on the soundtrack." An exaggeration, surely, but possibly not too much of one.

Neuro was fascinated by Astro's experience growing up in a hole. "That must have been very strange," he said.

"No. The Hole was my normal. It was everything above ground that I found strange. Or, rather, not really strange. Just different. We took a lot of what Aunt Liz called field trips, and they were always fun and exciting. But after a while, an overload. And yet, I found that once back home and comfortable in The Hole, contemplations of my memories of the field trips were certainly worth entertaining myself with."

"I would think that...well...."

"What?"

Neuro took a moment to understand what was churning in his head before bringing it out. "I was going to say that I would have thought the lack of social interaction, especially with peers, would have been detrimental to your youth. But then envy crept into my thinking on this."

"Really? Would you like to have grown up in a hole?"

"No, I rather think not. But less interaction with peers I might have enjoyed."

Astro looked at Neuro, this tall man with an elegant head, who looked very much like he could be an inspirational leader of men, but... "You're shy," Astro declared what was now apparent to him.

"Yes. I always have been. Except with my family, of course."

"Because you're so tall."

"Such a horrible cliché of a reason. But, yes, this is what many have assumed."

"But you were also a black man in a country that relishes its white history. A wildly intelligent man elevating you among the masses in a non-physical way. And, I think…." Astro roamed his eyes around Neuro's elegant head, penetrating it. "Yes. I get it. You are a lover of solitude. You know how to entertain yourself with your own thoughts. You like being alone."

"You are spot on, I'm afraid." Neuro was impressed with Astro's perception. Impressed and grateful. "And yet I hate being lonely."

"Two different things, really."

"Exactly."

"So, how have you dealt with it?"

"That is a good question? Have I? Well, yes, I suppose when I do, it is through sports."

"Sorry to hear that."

"Why?"

"I hate sports."

It was now Neuro's turn to take in his dinner companion's head and wonder what went on there. "You hate sports? I have never met anyone who hates sports."

"You have now."

"Why?"

"I just don't find any pleasure in following the movements of sweaty, ball-chasing and smacking people trying to best other sweaty, ball-chasing and smacking people."

"Not all sports have balls."

"It's the beating that's the key to my objections."

"There is such a thing as 'your personal best.' Not to mention rising to the challenge."

"Those are hardly exclusive to sports. And they don't demand the beating down of the other guy."

"Ah, but there is in competition something so elemental, so

human in the striving of opposing forces."

"The only thing I hate more than sports is intellectualizing it. It's war, plain and simple. But then, we all know how attractive war can be."

Neuro smiled. Not in agreement, but in response to the charm and humor of Astro's querulous declarations. "Well, I think I will rise to the challenge."

"What's that?"

"Seducing you over to the dark side of sports. I will have you cheering with bloodlust for your team like a madman in no time."

Astro laughed at the concept. "Well, if you must. But when you lose, please don't take your ball and go home."

~

Toward the end of dinner, they decided to form a club of two and meet for dinner every week. And as this dinner took place on a Friday evening, Neuro proposed that Friday of each week be the day for their club dinners. Astro balked at the idea.

"What is wrong with Fridays?" Neuro asked.

"Well, now that I'm out in the world, besides sartorial excellence and a gourmet sensibility, I was hoping to enjoy the company of females. Other than my Aunt Liz and certain beloved movie stars of the last century."

"Why would our Friday dinners upset that plan?"

"Well, Friday is a traditional date night, isn't it?"

"Saturday, I think would be better," Neuro said. "But I am hardly an expert."

"Shy with women too, huh?" Astro gave him a small smile of understanding.

"Yes, I might well be. If I could find the time to consider them. Not to mention finding women who at least approach my height."

"Physical or intellectual?"

"Well, certainly physical. I had not thought about the intellectual. Is that your criteria?"

"Desire more than criteria," Astro said immediately, indicating this was a thought he had thought about often. "I mean the meeting of bodies, so I understand, is a really *wonderful* experience. But I can't imagine it without a meeting of minds to go along with it."

"A curious idea?"

"Really?"

"As one in the biological sciences, I suppose I have been

concentrating on the question of procreation. My family certainly has."

Neuro then began to talk about his family. His mother was still in London. She was a powerful individual in business with a strong reputation for acumen, vision, and fairness in negotiations. And yet, she still yearned to become a "gogo," as some Kenyans affectionately call their grandmothers. His half-Japanese half-brother Yoshi headed up Kinyanjui Investments and Kinyanjui Holdings. He had increased the Kinyanjui fortune beyond what even their father might have imagined. And like their father, he used much of it to benefit Kenya as a counterweight to China's influence. And, since Khadambi had turned away from politics and governance, Yoshi was doing double-duty, serving as a senator in the parliament of Kenya. And a pain in the ass to the current president.

"Wait a minute," Astro stopped Neuro. "It sounds like your family is rich."

"I suppose that is correct."

"You suppose?"

"I prefer not to talk about it."

"Your shyness? Or have you picked up a British reserve?"

"Yes. Shy Kenyan-British reserve."

"Do you get any of this money?"

"Shy Kenyan-British reserve."

"Oh, don't think I give bloody blue blazes whether you do or not. It's just curiosity."

"I see. Misplaced, you have all of the heavens to be curious about?"

"Absolutely! But then, that's why it kills the cat."

Neuro had not said much about his father. Astro wondered why.

"It is late," Neuro said as he gave his mouth a last wipe with the cloth napkin he had brought up from his lap. "There is not enough time for me to tell you about my father and do him justice. I suggest we continue this next week. In the meantime—dinner is on me."

"Really? What did you spill on yourself?"

"I did not spill anything on my—"

"It's *a joke, son, a joke!*" Astro declared, changing his voice to an echo from a long-gone comedy past.

~

Astro and Neuro opted for French cuisine the following Friday, finding a restaurant on Melrose Avenue. Astro was determined to try escargot and have a bottle of excellent French wine. It was an intimate storefront restaurant, and they were happy to be shown to a quiet table in a back corner.

After ordering and receiving their meals, they chatted about insubstantial subjects. Settling in at USC and L.A. was the first subject. Then Neuro talked about his soon-to-be-delivered self-driving Tesla. Astro expressed his desire to learn to swim. Neuro immediately offered to teach him. But while they started their second bottle of wine, Astro got Neuro to talk about his father.

Astro immediately perceived a change in Neuro's demeanor. Neuro usually seemed to most of his colleagues a standard-bearer for seriousness, monosyllabic unless he really had something to say, and precise and business-like in what he did say. But this night, Astro solicited a more talkative, open person with sly humor along the edges. The Neuro he now sat across from relaxed into a warm, blood-flowing calm of reflection that emerged out of a loving and lovely smile.

Jaali Kinyanjui had been his son's hero. That was evident from Neuro's first words as he began to speak about the man. "I have always been aware of my great fortune in having a father worthy of worship. I am fully aware that I may feel that way because my father was not a daily presence in my life. So I never grew tired of him and his authority over my life. A power that might have been natural to rebel against. I was also greatly influenced in my view by my mother's propaganda, if I may call it that, on my father's behalf. But my mother is nothing if not a clear-eyed woman, not gullible, not prone to fancy or fantasy. And she was always adamant that Jaali Kinyanjui was an exceptional man of wisdom, compassion, creative intelligence, and a passion for the truth. He also had quite a passion for women. He was fortunate that Kenyan tradition and law allowed him to have several wives. All of whom he loved and all of whom he kept happy by dividing them among continents. But that always seemed natural to me. I did not know of any other way a man could be a husband. And by the time I learned of Western monogamy, it was far too late to be prejudiced.

"But it was my time with him when we could be together that meant everything to me. It was not just what my mother or my brother, a dutiful and respectful son, would preach to me about my father. It was being in his presence that confirmed my love for him. Certainly, it is natural for sons to love their fathers, even if rebelling and contending, even if competition becomes a part of their relationship. But I believe my case is different. My father was all as my mother preached. But to me, he also was more. He was a kind man and as kind to me, as he was to all. But his kindness to me was, I have always been convinced, of a different sort. Part of his kindness was his acknowledgment that I was not just his son, a reflection of him, but a unique individual. He made an effort to know me intimately despite our time away from each other. He showed great appreciation for me as—me. Now it is true that he designed a future for me in the politics of Kenya because he saw in me something that he was convinced would have made me successful in that. And had he lived, I would have followed this path he laid out for me without hesitation. I have no doubt I would have delighted him with my success."

Here Neuro's lovely and loving smile faded, and his mouth fell into something more like the slash of a wound. "But he died. At the hands of enemies. Who took *him* away from me even before his body expired. I was devastated, distraught, angered, and thrown into a deep grief that my mother thought I might not recover from. But what she did not understand is that it was not just grief for the loss of my father, but deep grief for the fragility of one's essential self. One's mind and consciousness. For lack of a better word, one's *I*, and, no, a better word is not *soul*. We are tissue-thin and can be crumpled so easily while assuming we are immortal against all rational evidence. After the death of Jaali Kinyanjui, my father, the man who knew me better than anyone, I could not think of Kenya and its future. I could only think of understanding the why of our fragility and finding a way to combat it. To strengthen the tissue if not into steel, at least into something substantially more resilient."

∼

After that second dinner, Astro realized that Neuro—or rather Khadambi Kinyanjui–was a far more interesting person than he was. He, Joe Smith, was just a red-headed mole lately out of a hole who was anthropomorphizing himself via old movies and music of the past century. But Neuro? Neuro had had such an interesting life. It had been one of mixing clashing cultures, danger, and a global perspective. This was the extreme opposite of a hole perspective that can never be a whole perspective. Neuro's had been a life of intense family relationships bathed in expectations moderated by nurturing love. Of several triumphs. Of one overwhelming tragedy.

And of sadness. A sadness that Astro could see in Neuro's eyes

138

only when Neuro allowed it. A sadness deeper than normal grief, something understanding the more complex situation of not just the death of a single man or woman, even a beloved one, but of the loss of some essentialness that all humans shared. Something common to all yet, in each instance, blazingly unique.

Astro had retained only a little memory of his own sadness when his mother had died—not "passed away" but died, his Aunt Liz had insisted. He remembered crying, profuse moisture of several consistencies spilling from his face, the warm comfort (consolation?) of his aunt's more-than-ample bosom. But that was it. After that, sadness was just never a part of his life. His Aunt Liz saw to that. She did not believe in sadness, hated the feeling, felt it was of little benefit. Instead, Aunt Liz liked to tickle in word or deed to solicit laughter and joy. If you are going to live in a hole, she had felt, it was the only way. Otherwise, your hole might as well be a grave.

~

After dinner and after they had parted, Astro was filled with the desire to take Neuro's sadness away. It was a strange feeling. The dictionary in his mind found *compassion* to be the most appropriate way to define the feeling. But it was absurd. Not that he should feel something for his new-found friend, but that he would want to take away from him that which may well be the driving force of his intellectual journey. He didn't mind feeling the feeling. It just wasn't practical. How could he take Neuro's sadness away? He could not change the event in the past that had brought it on. He would not want to change the thing in Neuro's mind. For what was there had expanded that sadness beyond the particular event to a more universal consideration resulting in sound science, in deep understanding. What could he do? He thought, not having any particular sadness of his own, he could just be a non-sad presence in Neuro's life. Not being shy, he could be a non-shy presence in Neuro's life. Not being tall, he could be a non-tall presence in Neuro's life. And desiring to become a connoisseur of the ins and outs of women (or more accurately stated, the inner and outer essences of women) surely, he could find a potential mate for Neuro. One of the proper height—and depth—to suit both Neuro and his mother, not to mention Astro himself.

~

139

Neuro had never spoken of his father to anyone in such detail and feelings as he had to Astro. Not to his mother or his brother, not to professors or tutors, certainly not to any fellow Oxfordians or fellow lovers of various sports. It is something he had always kept to himself, locked up as you would a precious gem. What key did this little red-headed young man have that opened the lock? Neuro did not know and did not care. He had not been embarrassed to reveal this about himself to Astro. Nor had he been relieved. He had not been waiting for a confessor. It had just seemed a natural thing to do. Somehow, Astro was one-of-a-kind in a world of standard-issued people. But was that fair to everyone else? Was the world filled with nearly ten billion one-of-a-kinds? It was hard to imagine, but, in some respect, it must be so. Maybe each one of us is attracted to a particular one-of-a-kind? Thus, deep friendships, often unfathomable ones to others. Therefore love—often incomprehensible to others as well.

~

Both Neuro and Astro completed their Ph.D. research and dissertations in record time. They were both bright lights in the USC firmament. And, knowing how many competing institutions were vying for them, the university had striven mightily to keep them by offering them much money. The money did not impress either Neuro or Astro. Still, they had developed a loyalty to the near-naked Tommy Trojan, a stalwart metaphor for their friendship. And they shared a desire not to be separated by taking jobs in two far-flung locations. So, they stayed at USC.

In conducting their research and writing their dissertations, they had been each other's sounding boards and read and critiqued each other's dissertations

"You know what hits me?" Astro once said to Neuro while relaxing at Neuro's home.

"No, what?" Neuro responded.

"Between the two of us, we cover all the bases."

They were sitting in Neuro's living room quietly reading, and Neuro looked up from his book, astonished. "Astro—I am shocked."

"What?"

"You just made a sports analogy."

"Did I?"

"'Cover all the bases,' you said."

"Oh, what the bloody blue blazes! That's a common saying. Its life has long surpassed being just a sports analogy."

"Do not try to intellectualize your way out of it. Do you have a secret desire to go to a baseball game?"

"No! Not at all. Although I wouldn't mind some popcorn right now. Do you have any?"

"Africans do not eat popcorn."

"Sure they do."

"How would you know?"

"Everybody eats popcorn."

"You have the statistics to prove that assertion?"

"No. Just a magnificent, rational intelligence."

"Computer?" Neuro called out to the house computer.

Yes, Khadambi Kinyanjui?

"Why haven't you given your computer a name?" Astro asked.

"Why should I? It is a computer."

Yes, Khadambi Kinyanjui? The computer asked again.

"I call mine Doug."

"Doug?"

"Yes."

Yes, Khadambi Kinyanjui?

"Why?"

"It just seemed like a Doug."

"Have you known many Dougs?"

"Not a one."

"Then you have no bases to—"

Yes, Khadambi Kinyanjui?

"Sorry, Computer. Do Africans eat popcorn?"

Once widely associated with the now-archaic projection of films in theaters, popcorn is a favorite snack in Africa. Although it did not originate in Africa, it is quite common on the continent.

"Ah-ha!" Astro declared in triumph.

"I now have a name for the computer."

"And what is that?"

"Computer?"

Yes, Khadambi Kinyanjui?

"Your name is now Guy Fawkes."

"But it's an American computer," Astro protested.

"Guy Fawkes?"

Yes, Khadambi Kinyanjui?

"Your name is now Benedict Arnold."

"And then again, what computer can actually be tied to one

nationality? What with its parts coming from all over the world? Possibly something more universal."

"Benedict Arnold?"

Yes, Khadambi Kinyanjui?

"Your name is now Brutus."

"Now that I like! And speaking of the universal, that was my point."

"What point?"

"About us covering all the bases. I study the macro-universe we all live in, and you study the micro-universe that lives in all of us. So we cover all the bases of reality."

"Are you sure about that? What is reality?"

"Oh, please, let's not get into silly philosophy. Reality for all intents and purposes, how's that?"

"Acceptable. Now, about that popcorn."

"Yes?"

"You will find a jar of it in the pantry."

~

When Neuro and Astro began their new positions at USC, Neuro was required to teach little. It was part of his deal. Time for research was more valuable to him than money. Astro took on a decent load of teaching, including an undergraduate course in the history of astronomy. Astro had found that he liked teaching. He enjoyed an audience, and, strangely, he liked the students. Neuro did not like being in front of an audience. His shyness did not allow for a strong presence in front of the classroom. Many students complained about the soft voice of this tall, substantial man when he lectured. It was surreal. He should have had a commanding voice. The students were told to rely on Neuro's class notes.

"I wish you could teach your students with the same passion you show me in our conversations," Astro said to Neuro after visiting his class once.

"It is easy with you alone. It is not so easy with all those eyes staring at me."

"They're not staring, Neuro; they're just looking at you, paying attention. Would you rather they ignore you?"

"That would be fine."

"Well, that's hardly the mission of education."

"I think I am a truly selfish fellow," Neuro said with an apologetic smile. "I only care about educating myself."

Astro thought about that for a second. "I don't know if that is sad or admirable."

"All I know is that it is true."

"Well, in any case, how would you like to go down a hole with me this weekend?"

"To your home in your dreaded desert?"

"Yep. I owe Aunt Liz a visit. Plus, I want to ask her something. And I'd like you to meet her. And then, of course, there is the raw, naked night sky of the desert. I miss it. And I would like to share it."

They took a self-piloting passenger drone early the following Saturday. They arrived before the sun was slapping the hell out of the landscape. They were greeted by Aunt Liz in the entranceway before the elevator. Now in her seventies and fully gray-haired, but with no perceivable lack of energy, she wore some baggy pants and a plaid men's shirt unbuttoned over a plain white tee-shirt. For the occasion, she had put on a bra.

"Well, if it isn't Dapper Dan's and Beau Brummel's love child!" Aunt Liz declared, referring to her nephew's light gray, well-cut suit with a plastic boutonniere prominent on his left lapel. "Surely, you're not going to dress like that all weekend?"

"Why not?"

"Because I won't be able to relax around you."

"I've never known you not to be relaxed, Aunt Liz. I like this suit. I may even go for a walk outside around noon."

"Don't be stupid, Joey."

"Seriously. Here, feel." Astro offered his sleeve to his aunt, and she touched it.

"It's cool," she reported with some astonishment.

Astro unbuttoned his coat and opened it wide. "Feel inside the coat."

She did. "Even cooler," she declared with widening eyes.

"It's a prototype. It has nanotech air conditioning. This boutonniere is the control knob. I'm testing it out for my tech-tailor. Neat, huh?"

"I would say, 'what will they think of next,' but that would just make me feel old. And we have ignored your friend for far too long." Aunt Liz looked up at Neuro as she offered her hand. "And speaking of far too long, are you really that tall, or do you have on some radical elevator shoes? Don't answer. I'm Liz Fleming, but you can call me Aunt Liz if you want."

Neuro was delighted to shake the offered warm and soft hand. "I am Khadambi Kinyanjui, but you can call me Neuro if you want."

"I think not. I like Khadambi. Khadambi has texture!" Aunt Liz released Neuro's hand. "Well, you're just in time for breakfast. I have bagels, I have cream cheese, I have lovely pork sausage from my favorite meat farm lab and some nice Quaker Oats!"

~

After breakfast, the aunt and her nephew took Neuro for a "grand tour" of The Hole. It was a horribly traditional thing to do with a virgin guest to a home, but this was too rare of an occasion to buck tradition. Plus, Liz was proud of this creation of her late wife.

"There are three like this—much larger, of course—in full operation on Mars right now, two American and one Chinese. And three under construction for commercial interests."

"Aunt Liz?" Astro called for his aunt's attention.

"Yes, Joey."

"We have a lot of spare rooms in The Hole."

"Sure. I've set one up as a guest room for Khadambi. You guys weren't planning to bunk together, were you?"

"No, but that's not why I asked. Would it be okay to set up the other spare rooms as guest rooms? Except for Grandfather's, of course?"

"What the bloody blue blazes for?"

"Oh, I see where you get that!" Neuro delighted in the revelation.

"Because I have an idea to bring my undergrad students here for weekends. I want to show them the real night sky. So few of them have had that experience. And we can use the observatory to augment my lessons."

"You want to turn The Hole into a field trip?" Aunt Liz was more than slightly appalled.

"Sure."

"Upsetting my solitude? Bringing lots of people here? You know that people ain't my favorite people, especially young people."

"Don't play the old curmudgeon with me, Aunt Liz."

"It has nothing to do with being old. Hell, I didn't like young people even when I was a young person."

Neuro, amused, said, "I notice, Aunt Liz, you said nothing about not being a curmudgeon."

"Why should I? Do you want to see my badge of honor? I have it

144

around here somewhere."

Neuro laughed, and Astro chuckled.

"But I suppose if you must, you must," Aunt Liz said in capitulation. "But you don't expect me to cook for them?"

"Oh, good grief, no." It was Astro's turn to be more than slightly appalled. "The weekend meals will be catered."

"Catered?"

"Drones from restaurants all around Southern California will litter our sky with culinary delights!"

"You've grown up to be kind of weird, Joey," his aunt said with a practiced straight face.

"But do you love me any less?"

"Hell, no, you weirdo!" Aunt Liz grabbed Joey and crushed him in a tight hug.

Neuro was moved by this with distinct emotion. And wondered what neurons were firing, what chemicals were flowing in his brain to account for it.

~

That afternoon Astro played some Mancini, Barry, and Hefti film scores for Neuro then reached back to the 1930s and 40s and played Miller and Goodman and Ellington and Shaw big band music. Neuro was not impressed, although he kept that to himself. In his childhood home in London, his mother played almost exclusively African pop music, much of it Kenyan-based. Heavy with guitars, rich in rhythms, domestic and imported, slow and fast, folk-inspired, jazz-infused, sometimes reflecting techno-reggae, sometimes classic hip-hop. In school, in and around London, on the telly, at Oxford, whatever was currently popular in music was constantly flowing in the air and making its communal impressions. So, obviously, that is what Neuro liked, was nostalgic about, and moved naturally in rhythm to. He understood this. And he knew that his lack of appreciation for Mancini, Barry, and Hefti film scores, and Miller, Goodman, Ellington, and Shaw big band music, was not a criticism of such music. It was merely a reflection of the musical history of his brain.

"This is the only music you listened to as a child?" Neuro asked Astro, not imagining that the answer would be Yes.

"Well, I had no other. Aunt Liz is not musically inclined or adept, so she has none of her own."

"So, this is what was imprinted on your brain, built itself up in your consciousness, and now offers continuing drug-like highs?"

145

"Drug-like highs?" Astro questioned in protest.

"Well, comfort then."

"I just like it, Neuro. There's elegance there, and romance, adventure, and romantic adventure. And sometimes humor, chilling suspense, all coming at you from a myriad of instruments orchestrated and working in concert. Like little pocket universes with their own set of physical laws. Do you have to analyze it?"

"And this big band music?"

"Well, that's just happy stuff, Neuro. It makes me happy to listen to it. But, as I said, why do you have to analyze it?"

"Do you analyze different frequencies of waves from space?"

"Does a squirrel crack nuts in the old oak tree?"

"Precisely!"

~

That night Astro introduced Neuro to the desert night sky.

"You've got to admit," Astro said, his eyes delighting in the display, "That's a damn magnificent sight." There were so many stars in the sky that they were almost oppressive. The Milky Way took the center position, an overlord seemingly in command.

"Yes," Neuro said, scanning the sky. "I have always enjoyed the night skies like this."

Astro did not have to bring his eyes down much to stare at Neuro. "What do you mean? You grew up in London."

"I am an African."

"What, you have special aboriginal eyes that can cut through a city's light pollution?"

"That would be nice if it was true. Maybe I should have qualified it as the *African* night sky."

"But your family in Kenya lives in Nairobi. A city. With light pollution, I assume."

"Yes. And much more than there used to be, partly thanks to my family's construction of skyscrapers. But still not as much as London or L.A."

"Well, sure, but still…"

"There is more country than big cities in Kenya. Do you not have any understanding of African geography?"

"My eyes have been on the stars, not hills and valleys."

"So, my friend, your wide view of the universe is somewhat narrow."

"Crap!"

"Yes?"

"It is. I need to correct that."

"That would be advisable."

"But if you have seen many great night skies full of stars, and if you have been intimate with the Milky Way, why didn't you tell me? Why did you let me go on like a madman about how this view," Astro swept the sky with his arm. "Would knock you for a loop, blow your mind, and fundamentally alter you?"

"And disappoint you? Oh, my goodness, no, I could never have done that."

Astro laughed. At the situation and at himself. "Well, thank you for that."

"And, quite frankly, I knew it would not be seeing the night sky that would be new for me. It would be seeing it through your eyes."

Neuro's eyes, Astro's eyes, returned to the night sky, and the two became quiet in their shared awe. If they had been lovers, they probably would have held hands.

~

After an hour of naked-eye star gazing, Astro took Neuro into his observatory and showed him many fine things through his telescope. Neuro had, of course, seen pictures of telescopic views of astronomical phenomena. Planets and moons, star clusters, galaxies, nebulae, great clouds of interstellar dust, even black holes, but this— this was different. Digital photos of such phenomena were higher in definition and more brilliant in color, bringing one closer to each phenomenon. But this peering, peeping, peeking at the things themselves, even if through the mists of time, was somehow palpable, reachable, touchable. It was something about your eye—*your* eye gathering up the magnified waves at this exact moment. Neuro was not shy in his exclamations of awe. Astro was delighted.

~

As they both yawned and knew they were ready for bed, Neuro said, "Astro?"

"Yes?"

"This summer…" Neuro hesitated to continue.

"Will surely follow the spring," Astro said to not leave the thought hanging.

"No," Neuro started again. "This summer, I want to take you to

147

Kenya."

"Really? What for?"

"A geography lesson. The African night sky. You can sample African cuisine and music."

"Are you trying to round out my education?"

"You could use it."

"No doubt. But—"

"I want you to meet a woman."

"Oh. Well, I haven't meant all the women in L.A. yet."

"She is not for you."

"Then why would I want to meet her? Unless she is an astronomer of some talent."

"My mother and brother have picked her out to be my wife."

"You're kidding. The last joke before bed."

"I am earnest. More importantly, my mother and brother are earnest."

"Do you *have* to get married?"

"I would prefer not to, not for my sake, but for hers. I would not want to be married to me. But, I have disappointed my family before."

"What? You're on your way to being the most important neuroscientist in a generation."

"They are not impressed."

"Family! I'm glad Aunt Liz is my only family."

"Thank you!" Aunt Liz, who had been listening, said. "Makes for cheap family reunions if nothing else."

"I want you to assess the woman. You know women. If you think I should marry her, I will."

"What the bloody blue blazes, Neuro! Why would you want to give me that responsibility?"

"Oh, go ahead," Aunt Liz said. "Sounds like fun."

"I will put you up in a luxury hotel with a fine restaurant with a Michelin starred chef," Neuro continued. "And introduce you to the most elegant people in Nairobi."

"Do you know the elegant people of Nairobi?"

"Not really. But my brother can call them forth."

"Call them forth?"

"The attraction of billions."

"And we will still get to view the African night sky?"

"Of course."

"But you won't try to get me to watch football or soccer or

whatever you call it?"

Neuro smiled, made no commitment, and went to his room.

14
ASTRO AND WOMEN

Neuro chose Astro to be his "second" in the upcoming duel with his family because he knew that Astro understood the mechanics of women. The way he—to the extent that Neuro did—understood the mechanics of the human brain. Whether the duel would be with his mother, with his brother as her second. Or the flip of that—his brother taking aim and his mother enumerating the paces—was debatable but inconsequential. Neuro was sure they were of one mind about this. The Kinyanjui family had become an international institution. But one that was based in Kenya and very proud to be so. For the honor of the family, of Kenya, and for Africa, they needed to continue to grow. They needed to show the world their family-fueled power. Khadambi might never participate, but they might have a chance with his children.

Neuro would have loved to accommodate his family and was willing, if not obligated, to do so. But if he did, would the outcome for him and this woman-of-his-family's-choice be something warm and nurturing or cold and malignant? Neuro would be delighted with the former—who wouldn't be?—but dreaded the latter. He was willing to accept tepid and benign, if that was the only choice, for his family's sake. But might that not actually be worse than cold and malignant? He had no answers, so he decided to rely on Astro because Astro was his best friend and would guide him well in the dark.

Astro loved women. He did not believe in the equality of the sexes. He felt women were, on average, superior to men in both common and uncommon sense, genuine compassion, natural empathy, and tenderness. But also toughness of a uniquely feminine kind when called for. Even if most women were a bit quirky in all this and had a tendency to overuse the word "cute," Astro *loved* women. But then, he grew up with his Aunt Liz—and Kathryn Hepburn and Rosalind Russell and Bette Davis. And Myrna Loy! Myrna Loy! If Astro had believed in God and if God were a woman, God would be Myrna Loy!

In the mid-21st century, Astro's knowledge of women was quite esoteric. Like the secret knowledge of some ancient organization with rites and symbols and special handshakes. It made him powerful in an opaque way and attractive to women, although they never quite understood why. When Astro came to USC, it was his first extended stay among a myriad of fellow *Homo sapiens,* especially a society of creatively conscious mammals. He immediately worked to integrate and ingratiate himself. He joined any student organization where he thought he would meet interesting women. These included a student theater company (he wanted to meet real actors). Both a liberal and a conservative student political organization (might as well get both facets of how to govern). A group that promoted interdisciplinary knowledge (they might have a potpourri of women of different turns-of-mind). And, of course, a group dedicated to stars (nuclear fueled, not Hollywood created).

And he did find many engaging women in these groups. His bias was toward those women who did not uniform themselves in the cliché and mundane clothes of the day. Women who displayed some sense of style in their dress and manner, women who stood out in their declarations of self—like Kathryn Hepburn and Rosalind Russell and Bette Davis. And Myrna Loy! Myrna Loy!

And those women—almost to a man—took immediate note of Astro. His height in the ordinary course of gene-generated events might have caused them to look past him. But this lack-of-manly-stature he finely and neatly clothed. Dressed thus, he moved confidently with a straight back, and head held high. And so, despite not being able to stand tall, Astro stood out. As had always been his intention.

Of course, Astro did have some non-sartorial attributes. There was his red hair, full and thick and well tamed. His face was pugnaciously Irish but with the highlight of twinkling blue eyes that did not just look but saw. And his lilting voice, which was easy on the ears. His voice would have been even better if it had had a "cute" Irish accent, but he grew up in a hole in the American desert, so, alack and alas, it did not.

The best of all these attributes was definitely his twinkling blue eyes that did not just look but saw. When he focused them on a woman, she felt she was being understood—as if her *being* was being understood. But that was only the beginning. Whenever Astro became attracted to one of the USC women he met, he took the time to find out something about her field of study, whether it be microbiology or literature or history or political science or medicine or art or music or urban design, anything at all but sports. Astro would embark on a brief but intense study of the field, enough to ask intelligent questions upon their second meeting. He would then suggest a coffee or a drink or dinner and a movie or an exhibition of art or science, whatever seemed a good fit for the woman's personality and interests.

Most of the women were intrigued by his offer and said yes. Some, of course, were not and did not. Many later regretted it, as Astro often later learned. Not to a manly satisfaction but to a human sadness over what might have been.

Having grown up alone with his aunt, having little contact with other people, and most of that being digital, Astro was fascinated by individual life stories. And the aspirations those individuals had for the continuation of their stories. This made him a good listener who asked questions that made his companion a good talker for the moment (not that most of them weren't already good talkers). As talking about oneself is most people's favorite pastime, it made for lovely evenings.

Which often ended in sex.

But not always.

Astro's goal was never to "get laid," therefore he was never disappointed. But he was often pleasantly surprised.

His first surprise came the evening he lost his virginity at the hands, and other such fleshy physical attributes, of Kimberly. Despite Astro's lack of experience, Kimberly had no idea that she had deflowered him—if that term can be applied to a man. For Astro was book smart on sex, especially since the books were abundantly illustrated. Astro paid much attention to the cause and effect of tactile explorations at various locations along and within Kimberly's body. And he was pleased by the pleasure she expressed unreservedly. Afterward, Kimberly, an economics major who hated statistics and had been fretting about whether she should change her major, had her best night of sleep in six weeks.

Astro did not sleep at all. He just laid next to Kimberly, his head propped on his hand, admiring her sleeping body. The hills and valleys; the smooth, soft skin; her slightly upturned nose; her curly light brown hair now just a little matted with sweat at the top of her forehead. When he had finished surveying and cataloging all these lovely features, he laid his head back down on the pillow. He reran several times his climatic pleasure as best as his faulty human memory allowed.

~

After Kimberly, Astro got to know a steady stream of women mentally, physically, and delightfully. Not a raging torrent, just a steady stream. He found each one fascinating, but then he seemed to have a nose (or some such appendage) for the riveting in women. Each one had a positive sense of self, which they displayed not only in their actions but also in their physical presentation. Each one was attractive, if not always classically beautiful. Each one fell a little in love with Astro, but not one fell deeply enough to foresee a future life with him. They were, after all, young women of impressive accomplishments with obvious potential to continue to accomplish and impress as they matured. All of which would take time, focus, and dedication. Of course, some of these women during Astro's years at USC did branch off and acquire steady boyfriends, which occasionally led to marriage. But then, biology will have its way. Astro, though, always seemed to appeal more to the conscious manifestations of their biology than their instinctual ones. Their time with Astro was no less lovely because of this, or their sex (if that was part of their relationship) any less passionate and satisfying. Indeed, it made it precious and gem-like, which a long-term relationship might have found the flaw in.

Neuro was amazed by his friend's relationships with women. And envious, possibly a little jealous. But he also admired Astro for this accomplishment. Neuro had acquired a few girlfriends during his USC years, but none lasted long. They resented Neuro forgetting their dates. And, worse, his obliviousness to their existence outside of the dates he did remember. And his reluctance to be romantic. So, they left the field, often without Neuro noticing. If they had known how rich he was, some of his girlfriends might have stuck around and tried harder. Wealth was not an unknown replacement for true love or even comfortable affection. But his wealth was a secret kept obsessively by Neuro and faithfully by Astro. Neuro might have tried harder in these relationships if Astro had competitively boasted to Neuro about his sexual "conquests." If he had racked up the numbers like an ace listing many enemy planes shot out of the sky. But that was not Astro. He had not been raised that way by 20th century Hollywood movies, at least those before the sexual revolution of the 1960s. Astro fancied himself a gentleman. Neuro knew there was nothing fanciful about it. And he counted himself lucky to have such a uniquely anachronistic friend.

Neuro asked Astro to come with him to Africa to meet and assess the woman his family had picked out for him, as he might have consulted with Astro on the purchase of a new suit.

15
ASTRO IN AFRICA

Neuro and Astro took the nearly twenty-hour flight to Nairobi in the Kinyanjui Holdings corporate plane. They were not the only passengers. Neuro offered seats, free-of-charge, to native Kenyan college and high school students from around L.A. traveling home for the summer. They all had a good time in the cabin that featured a transparent dome held together by a bionic structure that mimicked the efficiency of bird bones. It looked fragile and worrisome. But once you spent time watching the brilliant blue sky directly above, the landscape of clouds, oddly substantial-looking in their ephemeral existence, and the occasional island-in-a-cloud peak of a mountain, your awe overtook any apprehension. And when they flew into the night, and the cabin lights dimmed, you were suddenly flying among the stars.

Astro was utterly astonished by this view of the stars despite his long experience of the desert night sky and magnified views of magnificent cosmic structures. Those stars off on their own, and oh so many gathered in the stream of the Milky Way. They burned with different intensities, different histories, and different vitalities. Here at this time, they were not just illuminated dots in the sky but proper bodies in space, occupying dimensions. It may well have been because he could feel the plane's movement, whereas he never had, of course, felt the movement of the Earth. Somehow that made for a wholly different experience. But Astro did not want to analyze it; he just wanted to take delight in it.

They landed at the new Jomo Kenyatta International Airport in the Embakasi suburb of Nairobi. If there were any other choices, they would not have landed here, for this airport was a sore point for the Kinyanjui family. It had been built over the deconstructed bones of what had been the Jaali Kinyanjui International Airport. Named for their patriarch after his tragic assassination in honor of his many good works for Kenya. But then that Kinyanjui airport had initially been the Jomo Kenyatta International Airport, named after the so-called Father of the Nation, the first president of the Republic of Kenya after breaking away from British rule in 1963. But Kenyatta was no George Washington. Washington hated the idea of political parties. Kenyatta also hated political parties—except his own. Washington was happy to give up power after eight years in office. Only death would remove Kenyatta after nearly fifteen years in power. Fifteen years as a one-party dictator. Not that what he dictated was all bad, but what was bad was bad enough to be loathed by the Kinyanjui family. The new airport was built with money, material, and manpower from China. Being a one-party state, China thought it only proper for the gateway to East Africa to be named once again for a man of Kenyan historical stature. And of like-mindedness with the People's Republic. Another reason the Kinyanjuis loathed the airport.

But where else could they land their corporate plane?

"My brother Yoshi is constantly talking about building a landing strip right by the family compound, but the government will not give him the permits to do so. There are questions of emigration control, worries over smuggling, and other matters. Yoshi believes they could be answered satisfactorily if the government wanted to listen. But it doesn't. And my father's third wife, Faraja, is against it for the noise and the impact the construction of it would have on the local environment. And while her voice is soft, Yoshi tells me it is quite powerful. So, we land at the Jomo Kenyatta International Airport and will have to walk by innumerable grand portraits of Kenyatta done in the cult-of-personality art style so loved by the Chinese. By all authoritarians, for that matter."

~

Astro's first impression of Nairobi proper was of color. Or rather, colors, a multitude of melodious colors—pink and blue and yellow and fuchsia and orange and turquoise and green. Although much of the green was on the urban foliage. Trees of height and shade danced and sang with breezes. Many of these colors were on display on the clothes of the people of Nairobi, sometimes in solid and plain statements, but more often than not in loud. No. Verbose? No. Garrulous? No. Elegant, soaring, and poetic declarations of self? Yes! In sometimes swirling, sometimes geometric patterns that commanded eyes to not just glance, but stay a while. Delightful! Astro thought as he stared at the people of Nairobi walking the streets, sitting at outdoor cafes, shopping, whizzing by on motorcycles as colorful as they, talking, laughing, thinking, musing. And the buses! The Matatu, Neuro corrected. Mini-buses carrying folk here and there, each painted as a unique rolling work of art with portraits, symbols, bright fields of African colors, words of meaning. And each blaring out music pied-piping to the youth who preferred this mode of transportation.

Neuro and Astro were picked up at the airport by a Kinyanjui Holdings self-driving limo. When they got in, Neuro gave the intuitive AI instructions of where it should take them and the route it should use. There were places he wanted to show Astro, one area in particular.

"This is Kibera, where my father was born," Neuro told Astro as the limo drove slowly up and down the paved streets of houses similar in design but diverse in owner-applied accouterments. And the commercial streets bustling with foot traffic patronizing shops and cafes and services.

"It looks nice," Astro said.

"It did not when my father was born. It was the largest urban slum in Africa. People lived in cobbled-together sheet metal and wood homes with no plumbing or electricity. The streets were just dirt, often mud. Trash was everywhere. Sewage ran in filthy streams behind the houses. And sometimes, sadly, down the streets. All the people were impoverished. Many had HIV. They did what they had to, to live."

"Hard to imagine," Astro said, not knowing what else to say.

"My father did not have to imagine it. He lived it. He was orphaned young and grew up in the streets until he was rescued by a Japanese-funded school. The headmistress saw something in him and changed his life."

"And he got out?"

"Yes. But that is not the story. The story is that my father came back. After he made his billions, he came back to get rid of the slum and build what you see here."

"With his own money?"

"Certainly. The government had, off and on, cleared parts of the slums. And built some apartment blocks for the people. But that process moved quite slowly. My father was not a patient man. So he took care of the problem himself."

"It must have been a monumental undertaking."

"Yes and no. As they say, all it takes is money. Money and good planning. First, he bought a vast amount of land outside of the city. And there he erected a tent city to move all the people into—close to a million people."

"A million people? Living in tents?"

"They were high-tech tents. They had running water and electricity and wi-fi connections. They were designed to give comfort even in our rainy seasons. Then my father told the government he intended to level the slum and build a new community, and if they tried to stop him, he would focus his attention on defeating certain politicians at the polls."

"Why would they want to stop him?"

"Oh—for various reasons. But the government decided to let him have his way. He built modular, low-cost housing. But very smart technically. He built shops, community halls, and schools. He put in a sewage system and paved the roads. And he planted many, many trees. My father loved trees. For workers, he hired as many people from Kibera as he could and paid them a decent wage, giving many of them on-the-job training. He brought them in every morning from the tent city and sent them home by a fleet of matatus at the end of every day. It was the most joyful two-times a day procession. When New Kibera was done, he moved everyone back."

"Did they get the new homes for free?"

"No, they had to make mortgage payments to own. Or rent if they didn't want to own. But my father offered micro-loans to people to create businesses that would fill the shops he built, serve the community, offer employment, and build a local economy. And the first mortgage and rent payments were not due until five years after occupancy to give people time to 'Learn, earn, and save,' as he put it."

"It sounds incredible."

"My father made it very credible. It was all done by one of his non-profit NGOs. The tents have subsequently been sent to many areas worldwide to house those made homeless from natural and man-made disasters. His third wife, Faraja, handles all that now."

"Wow," Astro exclaimed in a whisper. "Your father was—"

"A good man, Astro. Simply a good man. A genius, yes. A husband to three wives. A father. But mainly, simply, a good man."

"You must miss him."

"That is a term wholly inadequate to my yearning to have my father back."

As the trip around New Kibera ended, there was silence in the car. Neuro had no more to say, and Astro did not know what more he could say. Neuro had submerged somewhere deep inside himself, and Astro did not want to disturb him. But when the electric intuitive AI self-driving limo hummed its way out of New Kibera and headed toward the center of Nairobi, Neuro seemed to awaken brightly. With a big smile, he said, "Now it is time to get you to the luxury hotel I promised you and, of course, a gourmet meal for lunch."

～

The Karibu Tower Hotel sat in the center of Nairobi and dominated the skyline. At one hundred floors, it provided spectacular views of the city and, off in the distance to the south, the Nairobi National Wildlife Park. Especially from its observation deck on the ninety-ninth floor. There were special, powerful digital telescopes there through which people could actually see the movement of herds within the park. But the highlight for the Kinyanjui family was that to the southwest, they could look down on the seventy-story Pinnacle Towers where Jaali Kinyanjui once had an office. Then, the Chinese-built building had been the pride of Nairobi. But now, the Karibu Tower Hotel eclipsed it.

All this Neuro explained to Astro as they drove toward the building. The intuitive AI self-driving limo's roof, having gone transparent, they could look up and take in the full extent of the building, a circular tower of smart, intuitive AI-infused glass.

"Let me guess—your family owns this hotel," Astro confidently stated.

"You would be wrong in that guess."

"Oh?"

Kinyanjui Holdings did the design and constructed it, though."

"Ah."

159

"They sold it to the Mandarin Oriental Hotel Group for quite a profit. Part of the price was the Hyde Park Hotel in London which was then deeded to The British Commonwealth School where I received my proper British education."

"The Mandarin Oriental, Neuro? From what you tell me, your family are not fans of—"

"It is a British company, not Chinese. We are not sure the Chinese government has ever recognized the irony. Or, if they did, appreciated it."

Neuro's lips parted and widened into a pleasing smile, and his eyes twinkled. He had amused himself with his last words but was also happily excited to announce, "We are here!"

"Wonderful!" Astro said as the limo doors parted and they exited the vehicle. "By the way, what does karibu mean?"

"It is Swahili for 'welcome.' So, karibu, my friend, karibu."

~

The lobby of the Karibu Tower Hotel was massive and open and surrounded by five stories of terraces, along which were shops, restaurants, a barbershop, and a beauty salon. There was also a business center on the third terrace. On the fifth, a health center and gym with a circular swimming pool ran the circular hotel's entire circumference. There was a shallow area for children and seven lifeguards at stations along the circle.

As they entered the lobby and moved toward the registration desk, Astro was taken by the African art and design throughout. It hung on the walls, was weaved into the upholstery of chairs and couches, decorated posters of information about the hotel's services and events, and graced tables. Not just Kenyan art and design, but the whole of the continent was represented. Contemporary, historical, and ancient. The colors and patterns were as intense as the streetwear Astro had seen. And spoke of both the celebrations and the tragedies of life. Astro could not take it all in, in his sweeping glances as they walked through, so he decided he would have to come here later to spend some time to just look and look.

As they moved toward the registration desk, many staff members of the hotel passing by greeted Neuro:

"Karibu, Doctor Kinyanjui"—

"Hello, Doctor Kinyanjui"—

"Good to see you again, Doctor Kinyanjui."

And, of course, the registration desk clerk said, "So very happy to see you again, Doctor Kinyanjui!"

"Asante sana," Neuro thanked the clerk in Swahili.

"Doctor Smith's suite is prepared and ready for him. Please offer your handprint to the register, Doctor Smith."

As Astro laid his right hand on the glass platen of the register scanner, Neuro whispered to him, "My brother obviously sent a memo."

"Why do you say that?"

"This is my first trip back since receiving my Ph.D. This is his way to congratulate me without having to get emotional about it when we meet."

~

They settled Astro into his suite, which was the Kinyanjui Family Suite reserved at all times for guests—business, charitable, personal —of the Kinyanjuis. Unsurprisingly, it was opulent. And large.

"What the bloody blue blazes! I'm going to get lost in here!"

"I will give you a map," Neuro said.

"A map? How about a guide?"

"Use your GPS if you cannot find your way to the bathroom."

Then they went to lunch at the signature restaurant in the hotel that carouseled on the 100th floor, giving guests a moving 360-degree look at Nairobi. They ordered and enjoyed rainbow trout fresh from a lake on Mt. Kenya. After which, Neuro announced, "And now I must leave and report to the family."

"Report?"

"A little joke?"

"Little, but revealing?"

"Is it not common knowledge that family feeling is not a pure elixir?"

"I wouldn't know. All I've got is Aunt Liz, and she is hardly an elixir. More of—let's see?—more of a hot mug of chocolate laced now and then with whiskey."

"Well, be that as it may, to the family compound, I must go. There is to be a big family meeting tonight in preparation for the meeting tomorrow night of my hoped-for-intended. You will be there tomorrow night, and you will need to be very observant and mentally awake. Therefore, I suggest you get some rest."

"Are you kidding? After a twenty-hour flight and radical change in time zone, rest? I—" Astro pretended to suddenly fall asleep at his seat.

~

Astro awoke in the Kinyanjui Family Suite's master bedroom's masterly large bed—which Astro dubbed the Serengeti Plain—six hours later. He had intended to just "rest his eyes." Or at the most "nap." But he fell into a deep sleep. Dreamed a weird nonsensical dream. (But then, what dream isn't?) And awoke refreshed and ready to explore deepest, darkest, yet superbly well-lit downtown Nairobi.

On his way out, he stopped at the concierge desk and asked for suggestions of what to see and where to eat. The lovely, smiling, friendly woman behind the desk gave Astro a small digital tablet with a digital map of the local area with a list of restaurants and nightlife establishments. She instructed Astro that if he wandered far and did not feel like walking back to the hotel, he only had to tap a button at the bottom of the screen. Then, a hotel self-driving car would be sent to pick him up. Then she said, "All of the establishments on the tablet are quite fine. But adventurous visitors will not ignore street vendors for food or smaller entertainment establishments that may not be listed. If you have any questions about these places—because some are, regrettably, very low in quality—you have but to scan their front with the tablet. A rating, or warning, will appear to guide your choice."

Astro thanked the helpful woman and left the hotel, various staff members wishing him a pleasant evening on his way out.

And, indeed, Astro found a peasant evening outside as he began a ramble into the heart of downtown Nairobi. It had just gone into twilight. The lights from the surrounding skyscrapers—many of them less than twenty-years-old—were beginning to make their presence known. And would soon dominate as natural solar illumination receded west. He walked along the street, looking forward and up and over to the sides. He observed and noted and wondered. Then he stopped and questioned whether a perception he was receiving was real or an illusion. No. It was real. There was a vibration—how he defined it to himself—a vibration coming from his surroundings. Was it coming from the tall strutting structures around him? Certainly. Because of their attack on the heavens? Possibly. But really, it wasn't their scraping of the sky; it was their feet planted firmly on the earth. Their solid bases were occupied at the ground level with shops, markets, restaurants, music clubs of various kinds, with various kinds of music flowing into the street in friendly waves. And it was the patrons of these establishments milling about, passing through, stopping to chat, bending over and rising up in laughter, involved with others or determined to go it alone. There were the purposeful and the purposeless, some brightly dressed, some in gray business attire rushing home to become brightly dressed. And the traffic, almost all self-driving (except for the legion of Boda Boda motorcycle taxis), heavy with people going home or going out. There were individual pods containing a few seeds of humanity and many matatus, both visually and aurally loud, filled to capacity with sentient seeds. All this life and the right-now living it was where the vibrations came from. Astro had seen many old movies that took place in New York City as he sat in The Hole growing up. This is how he had imagined it must have felt to have actually been there. But he probably was wrong. It was probably different. A vibration, yes, but wasn't it usually defined as a pulse in New York? A steady forward-moving beat? Was this here different? Not something that drove you forward, but something that permeated you whether you were standing or moving, alone or with others. Something that kept you awake, aware, astonished to be alive. Was it uniquely African? Kenyan? Or focused on Nairobi? Astro looked around. So many consciousnesses enclosed mainly in black bodies. But there were also lighter-skinned Indians here and there. And some pale minds with like bodies probably down from doing business in the towers ascending. And then him, red-headed, slightly freckled Joe Smith. Talk about standing out in a crowd!

Talk about standing out in a crowd and suddenly being hungry. Astro looked to the building he was standing by and to the building across the street and counted four nearby restaurants—Indian, Chinese, meat-heavy, swimming with fish.

But adventurous visitors will not ignore street vendors for food.

He was adventurous. Of course, he was! When you grow up in a hole, every move above ground is an adventure. He walked up to a friendly-looking man nodding his head to the beat of music shouting out of a speaker nearby. "Excuse me?" Astro asked for attention.

"Hello! How are you?" The man said with a smile.

"I'm good."

"Good is good. Is your red hair natural?"

"Oh, yes, indeed."

"I like it!"

"Thank you. I grew it myself."

"Ha!" The man laughed as the excellent thought sunk in, "Ha-ha-ha!"

"I was wondering," Astro said. "How far would I have to go to find some street food vendors?"

"Not far. A couple of blocks. Around a couple of corners. Here, let me show you."

"I don't want to trouble you, just directions—"

"No trouble, man. Happy to do it. I know a place with fine nyama choma."

"Okay, thank you," Astro said as the man began to lead him down the street.

"I am Francis," the man introduced himself.

"Good to meet you. I'm Joe."

"I was named after a saint!"

"Really? And are you saintly, Francis?"

"Ha-Ha! No! But I am no devil, either! So what were you named after?"

This is something Astro had never thought about. "Joe? I don't know. A cup of coffee, maybe."

"Ha-Ha!"

Francis walked with long strides and quickly took Astro a little way out of the central core where the skyscrapers were, to a section of older commercial buildings, most under ten stories. He stopped at the entrance to a small street, maybe it was a large alley, between the backs of several of these buildings. A mixture of enticing smells intrigued Astro as echoes of people talking provided a soundtrack.

"This is wafanyikazi wa ofisi row," Francis said.

"What does that mean?"

"Like, office workers row. This is where the non-executives from all those office buildings come for lunch or dinner while they wait for the traffic to die down. All kinds of Kenyan street food here. Come, come, meet my friend Cosmos."

The street was lined with stalls. Some had small openings fronting a tiny hot kitchen where you ordered and received food. Some were large enough to seat customers with maybe three to five tables under a canvas canopy. Francis took him to one of the latter.

"Cosmos, my friend, meet Coffee Joe from America!"

"How did you know I was from America?"

"I know all English accents," Francis offered the fact as an obvious one.

Cosmos, who had been grilling slabs of meat—beef, pork, lamb, chicken—over dancing flames, the meat resting on a cast-iron grid, came over to them wiping his hands of juice and grease to offer one to Joe. "Hello, Coffee Joe. Welcome! Are you hungry?"

"Very," Astro said, not at all reluctant to take Cosmos's hand.

"What meat do you like?"

"Do you have lamb? Real lamb?"

"I've got Red Maasai lamb, raised with love by my Maasai brothers. The best! Succulent! No finer meat in Nairobi! You will never be able to eat meat anyplace else than Nairobi after this. You will have to move here!"

"Well, I'll take that chance."

"Good, good, Coffee Joe. You sit down. Lamb, with kachumbari salad and ugali! Have a beer while you wait, maybe two. I do not rush making nayama choma!"

Astro asked Francis if he would like to join him, but Francis said, "No, thank you, Coffee Joe, I am taking my lady love to dinner, and I better not be late."

Astro thanked him again for his kindness. Francis instructed Astro to enjoy Nairobi, his city, which he was obviously proud of, then they parted. Astro sat at an empty table, and Cosmo brought him a cold Tusker Beer, which Astro enjoyed while he waited. He drank and watched people passing by on the street. Listened to the sizzling of all the meats on the grid of the grill and luxuriated in the scents emanating from them. He felt deeply satisfied to be here in his smallish red-headed body at this time and this place.

When Cosmos delivered his plate of lamb, kachumbari salad consisting of chopped tomato and onions with a bit of avocado, and the cornmeal mush ugali, Astro was disconcerted that Cosmos left no flatware. He was about to say something when three young women sitting at another table caught his attention. Through gestures, they informed him that this meal is eaten with your fingers, as all food once was. They were so delightful in their own hand-to-mouth eating of their meals that Astro felt no hesitation to dig in with his digits. It was one of the best meals of his life, and he was not shy about saying so to Cosmos and anyone else who would listen, including people passing by on the street. The three young women took great joy in this and invited Astro to their table.

The three young women were named Duni, Zera, and Nafula, and all were strikingly beautiful. They held various mid-level positions in a giant insurance company. They were roommates in a lovely apartment just three blocks away. They were fascinated by his red hair and more than fascinated when he said he was an astronomer. Duni asked how large his telescope was, and all three started giggling before he could answer. Then Astro did what he did best and solicited a deeply personal passion for something from each. For Duni, it was travel. She wanted to visit every country on the African continent and then move on to Europe. For Zera, it was art. She was saving to open a small gallery. For Nafula, it was flying. She had just gotten her pilot's license and was vice-president of the Nairobi Flying Club, whose new motto was, AIs Need Not Apply.

The women were all brightly dressed in nightlife clothes and planning to go to their favorite dance club.

"You will come with us," Zera said, "because you are too funny to say goodbye to."

"Funny?" Astro asked. He was not aware of having been humorous.

"She means fun," Duni said. "She grew up in the country, and her English is not as good as ours."

"No, I mean funny." Zera was adamant.

"You mean amusing," Nafula suggested.

"Yes! A better word."

"Charming. I find Joe charming," Nafula said, grabbing Astor's hand and stroking the back of it. Then she laughed. "Look how red he is becoming!"

Astro was blushing to a sunburn finish. "Well, um, I would love to come with you, but to be honest, I can't dance."

"Everybody can dance," Nafula said. "They just may not have yet informed their feet. We will talk to your feet."

~

The club they took Astro to was called Ngoma Nights. A ngoma, Zera explained, was an East African drum. It was a vast, high-ceiling venue on the ground floor of one of the city's newest skyscrapers. The sidewalk before it was crowded with people waiting to get in. Or milling around just listening to the music coming from within. The music was muted until the door was opened to let one or two or ten people in at a time, then the waiting and milling crowd would whoop in acknowledgment. Three young women as attractive as Astro's companions had no trouble getting in, dragging Astro with them.

Ngoma Nights was a "disco." An atavistic appellation. DJs and their turntables and stacks of vinyl discs had long been replaced by intuitive AI music machines. These "DJs" somehow always knew the moods of the patrons and so chose wisely the numbers to play and mix.

Mix was a good word to describe the interior. A mix of lights of many colors. Of loud music beating out a stream of blaring instruments and sharp attacks on vibrating strings. Of the whirring drone of human voices. There was the constant movement of bodies that, en masse, seemed one living entity quivering and undulating in some coordinated method for some unfathomable purpose. The colored lights swirled and flew and flashed and seemed to join in the dancing. The music pulled all the strings attached to all the limbs. The human voices coming out of the quivering and undulating mass articulated no thoughts, only the elevating emotion of joy.

The three young women glowed in this atmosphere. They grabbed Astro by his arms, pulled him onto the dance floor, surrounded him, and began dancing out their delights, saying, "Come on, Joe, watch us, watch our feet." But it wasn't their feet that took Astro's attention; it was their sensual explosions of movements celebrating the fact that they could feel. Feel the music, feel the vibrations, feel their bodies, feel young and vital, feel a part of everyone there, feel the fancies flowing in their heads.

"Come on, Joe! Come on Joe!"

Astro tried his best, but his best was pretty damn awful, which made Duni, Zera, and Nafula laugh. Not at him but with him and his valiant efforts. With joy, they took his hands and guided him to sync with the music, whether it be classic hip hop or reggae, soul, or soukous, zouk, rock, funk, or the latest in Europop.

Then there was a break, a time for people to sit and breathe, recharge and—most importantly—order new drinks. Astro and the women crowded around a small table and slowed their breaths, passing them through smiles.

After their drinks had been ordered and arrived. Astro said, "Thank you for not letting me embarrass myself too much."

"No, just enough," Duni said, and they all laughed.

"My feet and other extremities have never moved in such a variety of ways before. So, to thank you, I can teach you a very simple dance where you hardly move your feet at all. And your body in just one simple movement."

The young women were intrigued and game. "What is it called, this dance?" Nafula asked.

"The Twist. And it was very popular in America in the early 1960s. But I will have to see if I can get access to the music machine." Astro took out his small PQC, his personal quantum companion, from his pocket and spoke to it. "Doug?"

Yes, Joe Smith? The PQC responded.

"Can you access the closest AI music machine?"

Certainly, Joe Smith.

"Good. Don't do it yet," Astro commanded, then turned to the women. "I suppose we should ask permission?"

Fortunately, Duni knew the club owner well. He was happy to let the red-headed visitor to Nairobi add a little variety to the evening. He made a big announcement to everyone in the club that a visitor from America would teach them all an American dance from the 20th century.

Astro looked at his music library in the PQC with all his grandfather's music that he had digitized. He soon found what he wanted and sent one track to the music machine. "Okay," he said. "This dance is called the Twist, and it was started by some early rock and roll guys, but this is from an old movie called The Pink Panther and—"

The crowd laughed at the idea of a pink panther.

"Yeah, I know, that sounds weird. But the movie was a comedy. Anyway, the music is by Henry Mancini, and it's called 'The Tiber Twist.' And this is it, and I'll show you the dance." He tapped a spot on the display of the PQC, and out of the club's speaker came horn blasts, accordion squeezing, trumpet solos, all backed by an agitating beat. Astro twisted his torso side to side to that beat while his feet on the floor began a duel metronomic tick-tocking. He was concentrating so much on the dance that he made it look more like twisting tightly rather than the twisting loosely it should have been. The crowd, at first, was unsure about this, but Duni jumped in and joined Astro and made the dance look a lot more attractive as she twisted her lovely body with abandon. Seeing the potential, Zera and Nafula joined Astro and Duni, and soon the dance floor was crowded with human agitators protesting their delight. Astro was thrilled to see this and shouted out, "MAN-CI-NI!"

MAN-CI-NI! The dancers repeated, and even spectators at tables shouted out MAN-CI-NI!

When the music ended, and the dancers were laughing through their breaths, Astro yelled out, "Try this! A mambo!" And he threw into the music machine "Mambo Parisienne." Another Mancini from another movie with, oddly, a cowbell beating a call to dance, move, and jump, which the crowd did, inspiring Astro to heights of dancing skill he had never reached before, not to mention heights of joy.

MAN-CI-NI! MAN-CI-NI! MAN-CI-NI! MAN-CI-NI! Astro

and others kept shouting while jumping in an improvisational competition until the track was done. All were nearly crazed with exhaustion.

But it was enough mid-20th-century movie music magic for this crowd, and they went back to classic hip-hop or reggae, soul, or soukous, zouk, rock, funk, and the latest in Europop.

The night ended with Astro and the young women exchanging contact numbers and vowing to keep in touch despite future distances. Then, declaring himself a gentleman, Astro insisted on walking the three back to their apartment building. He said goodnight to them at the entrance to their building, and all three gave him a sweet kiss goodbye.

Were any of them disappointed that none had suggested carrying sweet kisses forward to other sweet somethings? Who knows? But Duni did have the thought that before she traveled to all the African nations, she might just see if there was anything interesting to discover in Los Angeles.

~

Astro spent the next day quietly in his suite. He ordered breakfast from room service, and while waiting for it, he spent time at one of the suite's large windows taking in the view of Nairobi. After that, he read for a time until his scheduled video chat with Aunt Liz on his PQC. Then he went off to explore the hotel, ending at one of its fine restaurants for lunch, which he savored.

As Neuro would not arrive until four for the ride to the Kinyanjui compound, he took a long swim and a relaxing lounge by the pool after lunch. Feeling refreshed, he went back up to the suite to shower and dress at three.

Neuro was on time, and when they were settled in the limo and on the road, he asked Astro how he had spent last evening. Astro gave him the details, and Neuro said, "So you are here less than forty-eight hours, and already you know more Kenyan women than I do."

"Talent is talent, my friend. And it shall not be denied."

"But can it be taught?"

"That's a good question. Possibly. But surely only to a willing student."

"Ah. Being a neuroscientist, I may have my doubts about free will."

"Well, hell, you're stinking rich, Neuro. Buy some will!"

Neuro chuckled at the thought. Then he began to point out

interesting features in the landscape.

After they drove through the large security gate at the entrance to the compound, Neuro pointed out a complex of buildings on a hill. "Castle Kinyanjui," he said in a slightly mocking tone. "But before we go there, we will take a detour to visit an old love."

This was curious, Astro thought as the intuitive AI veered the limo to the left, putting it on another road, the endpoint of which seemed to be a large grove of trees. Neuro had never mentioned an old love before. What was also curious was the trees in the vast grove ahead, all looking like open umbrellas, spaced so as not to interfere with each other.

"Acacia umbrella trees," Neuro said, perceiving half of Astro's curiosity.

"Aptly named," Astro said.

"Yes. The national tree of Kenya. Usually, you do not see these trees gathered together. They often stand alone and lonely in the grasslands, food for giraffes. But, as you say, the Kinyanjui family is quite wealthy."

"I said it was stinking rich."

"Rich can come from finding buried treasure; from winning the lottery. Wealth comes from effort."

"And a split hair is still just a hair."

"Well—be that as it may," Neuro said as the limo pulled into and stopped at the grove's center, "This is also where the family has decided to bury our dead. And, of course, that makes it a political statement."

"How so?"

"That will take too long to explain. Come on."

The double doors to the limo opened, and Neuro led Astro down a path through the trees that ended in a fork. "To the left is my father's grave. But I visited that yesterday. So today we go to the right."

When Neuro stopped, it was before a gravesite within a square fence of small pickets. The tombstone said simply WOKABI—Rest Now Your Loving Arms.

"My nurse when I was a child."

"You had a nurse?"

"Of course."

"Do you miss her?"

"Of course."

"Didn't you bring flowers for her grave?"

"No."

"Why not?"

"She had horrible allergies."

"Ah. That's very considerate of you."

After a few moments of silence, Neuro turned and led Astro back to the car. On the way, Astro said, "Can I ask you a question?"

"Of course."

"Were you a spoiled brat as a kid?"

"Not at all."

"Why?"

"Wokabi."

"Ah."

~

When they pulled up to the complex's main building, a statuesque woman smartly yet comfortably dressed was waiting to greet them.

"Mother," Neuro said, "I'd like you to meet my friend, Dr. Joe Smith."

Afaafa Kinyanjui's deep ebony face rose with a gracious smile as she offered her hand. "Dr. Smith."

Astro took her hand, which was smooth, soft, warm, and which she closed onto his with a firm grip. "Mrs. Kinyanjui. It is good to meet you."

"Are you going to say that my son has told you much about me?"

"Not much. A little. Certainly not enough."

Afaafa Kinyanjui was one of the most impressive people Astro had ever met. Just in her presence alone. He was smitten.

"Yes, my son is a reticent individual."

"Your son is a man with an always active mind. He usually speaks only when he has something potentially unique, even revelatory, to offer. I'm sure the given—such as his deep love for his mother—is something he feels does not need to be stated."

Afaffa's smile broadened, and she said, "I have always enjoyed Irish charm. Or do they still call it blarney?"

"Well, actually, I have no idea if I'm Irish. I never knew my father, nor even who he was."

"Have you not had your DNA tested?"

"No, only my intelligence. As it tested quite high, what else did I need to know?"

"I like you, Dr. Joe Smith," Afaffa said sincerely.

"Then you must call me Joe. Or, better yet, Joey."

"And you can call me Afaffa," she said, then turned to her son. "Dambi, your brother would like to see you both. You will find him in his office.

~

"Are you two gay lovers?" Senator Yaro Yoshi Khadambi asked without preamble as they entered his office.

Neuro laughed, not in nervousness but over the absurdity. "What?"

"It is quite okay if you are, of course. I introduced the bill that decriminalized homosexuality in Kenya. And I am now pushing through a bill to sanction same-sex marriage in Kenya. So, I have no objection. I just need to know if this meeting we have arranged for tonight is a waste of time."

"Well, Yoshi, it may well be a waste of time, but not for that reason. My good friend Joe here spent most of last night in the presence of three stunningly beautiful young Kenyan women who I do not doubt are now all in love with him."

"Did you have sexual relations with one of them, Joe?"

"Well, Senator—Yoshi—sir, I did not."

"Why not?"

"I couldn't make up my mind between them."

"Could you not have had all three together?"

"Ah, well, sir, as you can see, I am a man of below-average height. Had I had all three together, I probably would have been smothered to death."

"Ah, so desu ne," Yoshi said, calling on his Japanese half. "Okay, good! I did not want Zawadi and her mother to be embarrassed. I still don't quite understand why you wanted Dr. Smith to be here, Dambi."

"Well, brother, if this meeting tonight leads to marriage, Joe would be my best man."

"That does not explain it."

"Well, that is the best explanation you will get."

"Then I will have to accept it, I suppose." Having settled the matter, even if not satisfactorily, Yoshi returned to standard courtesy. "Welcome to Kenya, Dr. Smith."

"Thank you, Senator. May I ask a question?"

"Certainly."

"Your bill on legalizing same-sex marriage, will it include more than one spouse?"

172

"No. Only one spouse at a time."

"But I understand that polygamy is the norm and legal in Kenya."

"True, Dr. Smith. But polygamy is defined as one man and as many wives as he wishes, or can afford—or who will have him. It does not allow a woman to have multiple husbands. Or many wives. Or a man with many husbands. You see our dilemma?"

"I would not want your job, Senator."

"Nor did Dambi. Which is why I am here. And which is also why, on occasion, he should accede to my wishes."

~

An elaborate dinner was put on that evening for the Kinyanjui guests. Astro, of course, but most importantly, Senator Henna Mital and her daughter Zawadi Mital. But first, Yoshi's three children by his one and only wife, Nyokabi, were brought out to meet the guests and be put on display. There were two boys, ages thirteen and ten, and a six-year-old girl. They had just enough Japanese to give them unique coloring and interestingly attractive faces. Astro was quite sure the boys would grow up to be handsome, and the girl would be a beauty. Their mother Nyokabi was, as her name indicated, of the Maasai people and was a proud looking woman. He thought he was safe in assuming that it was not a false pride. The children were well-behaved and polite, with only the girl breaking form to ask if she could touch Astro's red hair. He obliged willingly, and Yoshi suddenly flashed on a story his father liked to tell.

As they sat down to dinner, Astro spent time, while the polite conversation flowed over the meal, to look over Neuro's family.

Yoshi, Neuro's half-brother, was a middle-aged man who had begun to widen out with added flesh in body and face. It was not fat, just a bulk that took away his youth without condemning him yet to old age. He was serious in demeanor. This may have come from his Japanese half or from his dual responsibilities of overseeing the family enterprises and being an active—occasionally agitating—legislator. Or was it that his youth had been taken away? In any case, he did not seem now to be the demonstrative, loving, kidding brother Neuro had told him about.

Afaafa, Neuro's mother and his father's second wife, still resided in London and oversaw all Kinyanjui Holdings business in Europe. She was the hostess, lightly keeping the conversation going and exuding a friendly openness.

Sachiko, Neuro's father's first wife, now a handsome woman in her sixties, was also of a serious demeanor. But what Astro really observed was her handling of the silver fork and knife she used to eat her food. It was such an ordinary activity, yet she brought grace in the movement she gave to the fork in her left hand and the knife in her right. As meat was cut, rice was gathered, the Indian naan bread was sliced—against all Indian traditions—into strips; it was like a ballet. More aesthetic than pragmatic and yet still accomplishing the primary purpose.

And then there was Faraja, Neuro's father's third wife. Whereas everyone else was dressed in what might be called Western clothes, Faraja wore an elegant purple Kitenge patterned dress and a light orange headwrap. And traditional African earrings and other jewelry. If Astro had wanted to be rude, he would not have taken his eyes off her during dinner. Faraja never remarried after the death of Jaali Kinyanjui, and they had not had children. Instead, she dedicated herself entirely to the good works started by her husband and had expanded beyond them. Her dedication to the betterment of Kenya was unquestioned, which made her loved by some and hated by others. But she counted herself safe within the Kinyanjui family, especially with Yoshi as her protector.

Including Yoshi's wife, Nyokabi, Astro found this a most interesting family. But then, having grown up in a hole in the desert with only Aunt Liz as his family, Astro found most families interesting. This family, though, he was sure, was uniquely interesting. And he was delighted to be sitting at the table with them.

The cuisine that evening was Indian not only to mark the visit of Dambi, who loved the food, but to honor their guests. Senator Henna Mital was a fifth-generation Indian. Her daughter Zawadi was half Indian, her father having been a revered African soccer star.

Senator Mital was an ally of Yoshi's, and they had worked on many legislative initiatives together. She was a woman most in her party admired and most in the opposition feared, although not liked by many of either party. Yoshi, though, not only liked her but found her amusing. She was loud, opinionated, smarter than most everyone else, and a subtle political strategist. And she was a fierce patriot. Which is why Yoshi liked her. She always proudly wore two pins on suit and jacket lapels or blouses. One was the Kenyan flag, a not unusual adornment on politicians. The other was a large, solid gold pin in the shape of the numeral 44. It signified her pride in being Indian-Kenyan. In being a member of the 44th tribe of Kenya, as the government had declared them in 2017. Which was only after almost a century and a quarter of a significant Indian population in Kenya. As a team, Yoshi and Henna had achieved much good.

But tonight, Henna Mital was not a senator but a mother. And not always a happy one. "I often ask myself, what am I to do with my girl? She is bright. She is beautiful. She is a combination and the best of two great people. She could achieve so much in business or politics. So she wants to go to university to study what? Humanities! For what reason? To get a job as a human? You are already a human, I tell her. And not only that, she wanted to study in America just because Harvard offered her a scholarship. Which she applied for unbeknown to me! I told her I was a Kenyan senator and proud to be one. I am an Indian-Kenyan who fights every day to be seen fully as just a Kenyan. No child of mine will run off to America to go to university and insult her native—I emphasize native—land. So, I forbid it. Our University of Nairobi is first-class, top-drawer, as good as any old dusty ivy-covered American university. And the University of Nairobi has a fine department of Diplomacy and International Studies. Yoshi, do you not think Zawadi would make a fine diplomat representing Kenya?"

Yoshi began to answer, but—

"Never mind. I think Zawadi would. But she refuses to go to university here. Instead, she says she will study on her own, she says. She says she will be an automated student, she says."

"Autodidact, mother," Zawadi, speaking for the first time, corrected her mother.

"I know that child. It was a joke. That is another thing. Zawadi has no sense of humor at all. So I told her, 'You better make a good marriage, my child, some nice rich man who wants a professional human as a wife.'"

With all eyes on the senator, while she talked, Astro trained his on Zawadi. He guessed she was about nineteen and displayed all the benefits of being that young. She had short, straight black hair that shone under the dining room chandelier. Her skin was colored slightly darker than her mother's and was clear of any imperfections, smooth and vibrant with life. It would have been easy to call her exotic-looking, but Astro avoided that. And yet it was undeniable that her beauty was unique. Her eyes were almond-shaped yet wide, giving her an air of fully observing her surroundings but not necessarily accepting them. Her lips were full and soft, and Astro was desperate to see her part those lips in a smile. Her beauty would really shine then, he thought. But she had not yet done so, and dessert was about to be served.

Astro wondered what Neuro was thinking about Zawadi. He did not once catch him giving her any but short, polite glances, concentrating mainly on showing rapt attention to her mother. Who seemed to be addressing Neuro most of the time.

After dessert and coffee and brandy, the evening ended with the parting of the Mitals. All the Kinyanjuis, and Astro, escorted them to the front door.

"You two!" Senator Mital exclaimed to her daughter and Neuro. "I think you should go to a nice quiet dinner tomorrow night. Get to know each other without family and politics and me dominating the night."

"That's a fine idea, Senator," Neuro said. "But, unfortunately, I have arranged for Dr. Smith and me to take a group of astronomy students from the New University of Science and Technology out tomorrow night. For a special safari in the wildlife park."

"A photo safari at night?"

"Well, in a way. But we are not looking for animals but stars. I have arranged for a large raised platform with tents to be constructed for us to spend the night. And I've had them equipped with some fine quantum telescopes. Dr. Smith will lecture and point us to interesting astronomical phenomena."

"The next night then," the Senator said.

"Ah, well, we have a flight to L.A. very early the next day. How about lunch that day?"

"Yes," Zawadi said quickly, surprising everyone that she had spoken again. "I would like that."

Astro immediately assessed that maybe Neuro's offer and Zawadi's quick acceptance was just a way for both of them to avoid something more potentially romantic, such as an evening meal in a fine restaurant. Lunch? What was that? A congenial breaking of bread amid the hubbub of daily activity. Not a potential field of—well, not battle of course, but possibly of dreams? But was this assessment true? He couldn't tell if they were attracted to each other. Or just trying to quickly and painlessly get a little family duty done. Astro saw that nothing this way was going to get resolved. And he liked resolutions.

"I've got an idea, Zawadi. Why don't you come with us tomorrow night? I'm sure there's room. It is a co-ed venture. And Khadambi tells me we will have plenty of delicious food."

"This is an excellent idea!" Henna Mital, senator, and mother, said.

"Zawadi, you will spend some time with our fine Kenyan university students. You are a bright little man, Dr. Smith!"

~

The next day a small caravan of Land Rovers took off about two in the afternoon for a rolling plain in the middle of Nairobi National Park. It wasn't a long trek, as the forty-five square mile national park started just a few miles south of the city.

The day before, a small contingent of workers from the Kinyanjui construction company, a few members from Kinyanjui Security armed with tranquilizer guns, and several senior park rangers had traveled to this location. They quickly raised a beautifully designed and solidly planted large twenty-foot-high platform. Upon it, they set up eight two-person tents, tables and chairs, portable toilets, a small canvas-covered portable kitchen (both supplied with a reservoir of water), and four state-of-art-quantum telescopes.

In the Land Rovers were Neuro and Astro, three male and two female astronomy majors from the New University of Science and Technology, and Zawadi Mital, who the three males were quickly falling in love with. And the two females were happy to have aboard to even the numbers.

They arrived at the location in the late afternoon and were in awe over their accommodations. The Kinyanjui crew and rangers had spent the night protecting what Neuro dubbed Astro City and greeted the company of stargazers. Sitting next to Astro City was a scissor truck with an elevating platform large enough to elevate the stargazers up to their home for the night. It was a short but fun lift, and all reacted with that tickling kind of delight usually reserved for childhood.

Once the stargazers were settled, the Kinyanjui crew and rangers left for their camp, which they had set up a quarter of a mile away. The two groups would stay in touch via their PQCs.

The local wildlife, whose home, after all, this was, had all moved away from the area the day before during the noisy activity of the construction. Not so much frightened as annoyed. What the hell were these damn two-leggers doing now? The wildlife might have wondered, if they had the capacity to wonder. And who's to say they didn't? But their capacity to be annoyed was unquestioned. And yet, in the relative quiet of the next day, which was now waning, they had returned, possibly curious, possibly looking for opportunities. In either case, they allowed for the first item on the stargazers' agenda.

Training the telescopes on the fauna on the ground while there was still light. Before training them on the stars in the sky. Off in the distance were zebras and giraffes, which could hardly be missed, and the occasional lion, which took time and concentration to find. Other members of the East African menagerie were spotted and honored with breaths taken away and compliments on their beauty.

At the same time, two of the students, one from each gender, assisted Astro in putting together the evening's meal. It had been pre-prepared with clear instructions on how to cook, if cooking was required, or laid out, if not.

There were laughs and chatter and reveling in the companionship and the sense of something special being experienced. The food was good, and libations were consumed as darkness fell and the stars came out to play.

Astro had prepared a short lecture and declared himself as much a student as they. For part of his thrill being here was the opportunity to train a telescope on Supernova2050C. It could not be seen in the Northern Hemisphere, where he lived, but was beautifully visible here in the Southern Hemisphere—even with the naked eye. It was a type 1a supernova—like Kepler's in 1604—that had surprised the world when the evidence of its explosion some 22,000 years before had finally reached the Earth. Not that Earth was its intended destination, of course. It was just evidence passing in the night. The peak of its brightness happened the previous year (thus its discovery), and now it was fading. But it was still brighter than anything else in the East African sky.

And something to see with the naked eye. But something even more fascinating to view when the extension of sight provided by an AI-assisted quantum telescope had its way with the captured photons. Peering through the eyepiece, a reality was presented that reached out and touched you—allowing you to feel it in return.

As the students and Neuro and Zawadi took turns peering, Astro said, "It is easy to romanticize that you are looking directly at the past. That you are looking back in time. Traveling back in time to 22,000 years ago. And as neat a thought as that is, not to mention as cliché a thought as it is, it is no more true than if you were looking at early documentary film footage from the end of the 19th-century, say of a street scene in New York. No, what you are observing is a record of something etched in light, a record containing data, not the thing itself. In the latter case, you are observing and noting the urban modes of transportation and dress in 1895. In the other, what elements were present at the explosion of a star and its aftermath 22,000 years ago. And then you make of it what you will as you apply dispassionate thought to it. As scientists, this is what you must become "romantic" about, not a general feeling of awe that is nothing but awe for awe's sake. But data that helps you search for rational truth."

~

It was a fine evening. And as busy as Astro was with the students, he kept an eye on the beautiful Zawadi and the tall Neuro. Although, while observing, he did think of his friend as Khadambi, African born, London raised, L.A. living, neuroscience obsessed. Astro especially noted their interactions. He was pleased to see Khadambi consciously paying attention to Zawadi. Before leaving the Kinyanjui Compound, he had played the gracious host and introduced her to all the students. He made sure she rode in the same Land Rover as himself. As the scissor platform started its elevation with a jerk, he made sure she was comfortable and felt secure. Even holding her by the elbow to keep her steady.

During all this, Zawadi responded pleasantly, if with few words. And Astro noticed that she kept her eyes down most of the time, lifting them only briefly when she had to address Khadambi. Modesty? Shyness? Apprehension? Zawadi was not a short woman. She was a statuesque five foot nine, which greatly impressed the students. But next to six foot five Khadambi, she was a statue in a shadow. Did this mute her? During dinner, Khadambi seemed happy to let the students dominate any conversation with Zawadi. And she did seem a little livlier with them. But not as lively as the students themselves. Was she intimidated that they were all in university and she was not? Or suspicious of their attention because of her beauty? It is rare for a beautiful person not to know they are beautiful. And not to perceive the effect that beauty had on people. Whose assessment stopped at the skin's surface, the body's aesthetic appeal, the precise proportional alignment of the face's components, the charm of the smile, the excitement of bright eyes. The beautiful might assume that observers loaded with all this may have no time or interest in anything happening within. In the mind, the self, the interior delights, or even the deep pains. Which the observers would not believe existed in any case.

Or maybe she was just shy.

Like Khadambi was shy?

Zawadi paid polite attention to Astro's lecture and looked into her assigned telescope when it was her turn, and expressed the proper amount of awe. But as the students and Astro were engaged in some technical astronomical discussions, and Khadambi engaged himself in cleaning up the dining table and kitchen, Astro noticed Zawadi sitting off to the side by the polished wood railing. She was not looking out onto the dark African plain. As one might have expected. Possibly wishing she were home or just dreaming dreams. Instead, she examined that railing with some concentration, running her fingers lightly over it, deep in some thought.

They were all up late, knowing that they were participating in a unique moment, wanting to stretch it. Eventually, exhaustion took hold of them all, and "Good Nights" were offered, and all retired to their tents.

∼

Astro woke around five in the morning and heard some light scratching and the occasional dry flutter. He wondered what small creature might have climbed up the twenty feet to their platform. Or what kind of bird might have landed. He wondered if he should satisfy his curiosity or, for once, tell his curiosity to go back to sleep. But curiosity is a child, and children never like going back to sleep. Gingerly so as not to wake up Neuro, his tent companion, Astro unzipped the tent's flap and peered outside. He saw Zawadi sitting in one of the dining table chairs by the railing she had been sitting by before. She was scratching a pencil across the page of a notebook by the light of her PQC. Astro quietly left his tent and, in bare feet, padded across the deck to stand close enough to see the page upon which Zawadi wrote. Then, softly so as not to startle her, he said, "Hi. Couldn't you sleep?"

Not startled at all, Zawadi looked up at Astro and said as she closed her notebook on her pencil, "Hello, Dr. Smith. No, I couldn't, so I thought I would sit out here until I got sleepy again."

"And write?"

"Oh, just a little. Some notes to remind me to, uh—"

"Notes? In lines of approximately equal length arranged in stanzas?"

Caught, Zawadi smiled her confession.

"I'm a scientist. We are good at observing," Astro said, then walked over to the dining table, grabbed one of its folding chairs, and brought it back. He placed it next to Zawadi and sat. "What's the poem about? If I'm not intruding on the creative act."

Zawadi looked directly at Astro and seemed to be examining him as if she needed to know if he might understand or, at the very least, could be trusted. Then she turned to the railing and focused her PQC light on it as she gently stroked a few inches along it with two fingers. "This wood," she answered.

"The wood?"

"The grain. The patterns of the grain. See. Look. It's beautiful."

Astro looked as he followed her fingers. "Yes, I suppose it is."

"I like to find beauty in small things. Or the little beauties in things. Ordinary things. Do you? I don't think most people do. But I do. Even in cement."

"Cement?"

"Tiles of cement making up a walkway, maybe, or in blocks forming a wall. The texture, the grayness, the corners coming together. Not the whole, but the parts. Everyday things. Useful things people pass by or live with without notice. Do you know how beautiful the folds of a rumpled blanket are? They form flow, peaks and valleys, hidden spots, exposed worlds of thin threads coordinated into spreads of comfort, of warmth. I want to notice this. I want to word it into other people's notice."

"Is everything worthy of notice?"

"Of course," she said with no uncertainty in her voice. "Everything that exists has a presence. And a continuity. Like this wood. We call it wood. But it was once a tree. Part of one. Life flowed among these grains. I was thinking about that. About the possible history of the tree. What it might have witnessed. My thoughts fell into lines. Writing them down was unavoidable."

"This is what you want to be—a poet?"

"This is what I am."

"Does your mother know?"

"She thinks of it as a hobby."

"So you wanted to study the Humanities because—"

"That's just an excuse to stop being forced to study large things."

"Large things?

"The world, politics, the universe, governments, even science—or the sky. Sorry."

"Nothing to be sorry about."

"Mother likes a big stage. The better to strut upon. I like to be still and see the small, even the mundane, the ordinary. Possibly boring to most. I want to see the essence of them, the beauties within. Then I want to capture that in words. I love words that travel."

All this time, Zawadi kept her focus on the grain of the wood, but now she looked at Astro. "I wanted to go to Harvard not because it is such a fancy university, but simply because it was thousands of miles away from my mother."

"Is she that awful?"

"No. Mama is actually quite wonderful. And loving. But she is too much herself to understand me. Her fruitless expectations are a burden upon me."

"And now she wants you to marry, but you don't want to marry."

"No, that is wrong. I very much want to marry. I want children. I want to be simply domestic, everyday, normal, and find the beauty in all that. I want to reveal the wonders of all that in poetry. Wonders that maybe others have not noticed. I want to know if love can rise above the biological, the genetic. I want to know if humans can really merge into—a joint entity without losing individuality. I want to find small things in domestic life that make it more."

"More what?"

"That is what I want to discover. Mother wants me to only discover tolerable affection for a rich man. And then she says I can have fun with my hobby."

"And so, you are trotted out to meet Khadambi. What do you think of him?"

"He is nice. Handsome in a way. Pleasant. He does not seem like a rich man."

"Well, he is. But it means nothing to him. Only his work means anything to him."

"I find that appealing."

"You shouldn't. Khadambi will never offer you inspiration for poetry. Certainly not poetry of the domestic. He will always be nice and pleasant and certainly can provide. But he will not really participate in domestic life. He cares only to understand and see a rather large thing—the whole truth of human consciousness. He cares very little about the small. Even if he were to love you, which he might, he would never realize the effort love takes and so cannot be expected to put in that effort. He will forget to come home to dinner, and your birthday, and whether you like roses or lilies. If he ever looks deep into your eyes, he will wonder about the synapses beyond them and not their incredible beauty. He will intellectually understand what is unique about the "you" that your brain projects, but will never emotionally be delighted by it. It is not so much that he is a cold fish but a fish that is never comfortable outside of his pond. He's not the husband for you."

"Are you and Khadambi gay lovers?"

"No!"

Zawadi was a little surprised by Astro's quick and adamant reaction. "I was just wondering because—"

"I am his friend. His only friend. Because I ask nothing of him and have an instinctual understanding of him. As he understands me. I applied that understanding of him to the advice I have just given you."

"I did not ask for advice," Zawadi said, stating a plain fact.

Chagrin slapped Astro's cheeks and warmed them.

"But I am truly grateful to have received it. I hope someday to have a friend as good as you are to Khadambi."

With relief, Astro said, "And I hope that friend is your husband."

Zawadi smiled. "Are you sleepy? You should go back to bed if you are."

"No, not at all. I thought—well, how often does a little boy from California get to see the sunrise over an African plain?"

"Or a little girl from Kenya, for that matter. I am usually asleep."

"Okay, good. How about I make us some coffee. And as the sun comes up, will you read me your poem?"

"Oh, I don't know. I'm a bit shy about—"

"Never be shy about your art. You can be shy about love, sex, or matters of the toilet, but never be shy about your art."

"Okay, then. It will be my pleasure."

~

On their way home, Neuro and Astro sat alone under the cabin dome of the Kinyanjui corporate plane.

"How did your lunch with Zawadi go?" Astro asked.

Neuro, who was just thanking the attendant who had brought them two cold beers, said, "It was fine. A good meal at the hotel. Zawadi is a pleasant girl. Once she gets over her shyness. She was more lively than she had been. She had no problem holding up her end of the conversation."

"That must have been good for you."

"Yes. I was able to practice my listening, that is for sure. Did you know Zawadi is a poet?"

"Really?"

"Unpublished as of yet. But she seems quite determined to be

183

one."

"Do you think she'll be any good?"

"I don't know. Poetry baffles me."

"Nothing baffling about her beauty."

"That is true. I wish she had longer hair, though."

"Well, you could always ask her to grow it out. I mean, if the two of you—"

"Oh, no, we had a big laugh over that—our families trying to matchmake. Absurd."

"Oh, so you agreed—"

"That we weren't right for each other? Yes. Zawadi made a perfectly reasonable argument of why it would not work. If she ever gets married, she said, it will be to a man less, well, dedicated to his work, whatever that may be. She seemed to have a very clear understanding of how important my work is. It is first in my heart, she said."

"Your heart? I would have said, your brain."

"She is a romantic. You know, a poet."

"And yet, she can make a perfectly reasonable argument."

"Yes. Yes, she can. In this instance, at least." Neuro lifted his glass of beer to Astro. "Thanks to you, my friend. Cheers!"

Neuro downed his beer with a satisfied smile as Astro realized that any protest he could make would be a protest too much.

PART TWO

16
ANOTHER RUDE AWAKENING PART 2

"But still… How have you…? I mean… You said I wasn't in a machine, but you never really answered me on uploading, did you? Maybe I'm in something different, maybe…? Look, is Carmichael there? Is that bastard just off-camera smirking with his damn crooked smile? Come on, Neuro, answer me."

On-screen, Neuro suddenly looked to his left as if he had been called. Somebody was talking to him; Astro saw that he was obviously taking in information by the concentration on Neuro's face. Finally, he turned back to "face" Astro expressing some concern. "Let me get back to you on that," he said as the screen went dark.

Astro stood from the couch. "Neuro? Neuro! What the bloody blue blazes!" Astro said as he ran to the circular screen. "Damn it, Neuro, come on back! What the—"

Neuro was back. "Sorry, Astro, but—"

"Stop!" Astro commanded. "What the bloody blue blazes. You've been gone only seconds, but you changed your clothes?"

"It has not been seconds. It has been three months."

"Three months?"

"We lost power, which digitally froze you."

"Well, why didn't you unfreeze me?"

"I just did. Now go sit down, Astro."

Astro was in no mood to do as he was told. He wanted some answers; answers now! Whatever the hell "now" was. "I don't want to sit down—what the hell!"

Having no patience, Neuro took over Astro's motor responses and turned him around and walked him back to the couch, and sat him down. It was the strangest thing Astro had ever felt.

Once plopped back onto the couch, Astro said, "What am I? Your puppet now?"

"I can stop your vocal cords from working, so you might as—"

"What vocal cords? I'm not real! I have no—"

"There was an assassination attempt on my brother, Yoshi."

That stopped Astro. Such godawful, non-digital, blood and thunder reality.

"What?"

"One of my assistants had just caught my attention to let me know. Then the power went out."

"Your brother? Like your father?"

"Yes."

Astro noted the quick inhalation of breath that Neuro took in.

"Except Yoshi survived," Neuro said.

"Why did they—?"

"He is currently Kenya's president."

"What year is it?"

"2070. Yoshi had won reelection to his second term just before the assassination attempt."

"Bloody blue blazes."

"It's been a rather busy three months."

"Stop with your British-infused understatement. It must have been hell."

"Yes. You are, of course, right. Unfortunately, the assassination attempt was quickly followed by chaos fermented by Yoshi's enemies, probably aided by a foreign nation."

"Which foreign nation?"

"They suspect China."

"Well, at least it wasn't the U.S."

"It might have been?"

"What?"

"Astro—in the eleven years since your accident, the world has been on a political teeter-totter between democratically sanctioned governance and authoritarian governance. For a short time, the U.S. teetered very close to authoritarianism. As it had in the past. And during that time, it was no friend of Kenya's. Or, at least the Kenya my brother dreamed of."

"So, what has been going on for the past three months?"

"Yoshi fought for his life and won. As the Kenyan people fought for their democratic life and won. Inspired by Yoshi and his struggle. And Henna Mital. You remember Henna Mital?"

"Like it was only seven years ago."

"Well, she's our deputy president."

"Is she running things now?"

"Not any longer. Yoshi has fully recovered and is back in office. He has bestowed on Henna the honor of Chief of the Order of the Golden Heart of Kenya."

"So you have a Kenyan/Japanese and a Kenyan/Indian in the two highest offices."

"True. And enemies have exploited this among the more tribal of our citizens."

"But everything is back to normal now?"

"Well, my friend. Democracy in both your nation and mine is ascendant at the moment. But I cannot say as much for the rest of the world."

"That's scary," Astro saids and meant it. "I wish I was hungry."

"Hungry? What for?"

"I feel…. Or, rather, actually, I guess you would say, I think—intellectually, you understand—that I would really like, or maybe need, some comfort food. And I keep staring at that box of mac & cheese and that can of tuna you placed on the counter in the kitchen."

"Ah. Well. Almost easier done than said. Let me just…."

Astro could see on the large screen Neuro divert his attention to another place, and he could hear rapid inputs on a keyboard, and then—

"Oh, no, too much!" Astro yelled. "I'm starving to death!" Astro doubled-up in hunger pains.

"Sorry. We are refining now."

Soon Astro was no longer starving to death but felt just a little peckish. Although there were lingering mental reverberations of having felt severe starvation. "Whew!"

"Better?"

"Don't let me go through that again, will ya?"

Astro got up from the couch and walked over to the kitchen. The box of Kraft Macaroni & Cheese, the can of tuna, and the pan to make it were all still there. "Couldn't you have just made it up already prepared and full of warm comfort?"

Neuro appeared on a small screen in the kitchen. "No. I cannot do everything for you."

"Really? You seem to be doing a pretty good job."

"What I mean is, you need to do things for yourself. So you can *feel* yourself."

"What are you, my Big Brother?"

"No. Just your much taller brother."

Astro chuckled as he opened the box of mac & cheese.

"And your loving one," Neuro added quietly.

17
A LETTER FROM HOME

"Kahdambi, you know how I hate to use clichés."

"You do?" Neuro asked as he wondered where this *non sequitur* had come from. He and Dr. Carmichael had been discussing a fine point about a fine point in the connectome of a bonobo's brain. There had been a pause as each man looked out over the ocean toward Lazarus Island, but still one would have expected the next words from either of them to be at the very least another fine point.

"You know I do."

"I do?"

Dr. Carmichael shifted his position on the jetty bench to face Neuro directly. "Khadambi, I am famous for hating clichés."

"You are?"

Dr. Brandon Carmichael's idea of the extent and particulars of his fame was highly influenced by his never-less-than-active self-regard. Especially the fine points thereof. Neuro was sure that the fame Dr. Carmichael believed his hate of clichés enjoyed was not much in the minds of the ten billion inhabitants of the planet. Or even the few thousand scientists who may have any interest in the work, philosophy, and character of Dr. Brandon Carmichael. Nevertheless, Dr. Carmichael continued.

"Absolutely. And I bring it up only as a preface to and an apology for the fact that I am about to use a horrid old cliché."

"Apology accepted," Neuro said, assuming it was not only the right thing to do but the required one.

"Okay. Here goes. It seems the world is going to hell in a handbasket."

"Oh," Neuro said. Then he breathed in some fine ocean air. It had been a year since he had accepted Dr. Carmichael's offer to come and conduct research at the Foundation for Immortality. He was now quite used to his evening walks with Carmichael along a trail cut through the thick forest of massive sea fig trees. Their destination was always the St. John's Island jetty and the bench they now sat on. It was a time for Neuro to relax, get the ocean view in his head, sometimes discuss essential ideas with Carmichael, and, on occasion, entertain frivolous thoughts.

"I wonder, though," Neuro said. "Is the statement a cliché? Or is the cliché the thought? I think people have thought this ever since the first man burnt his fingers in the first fire."

"The climate crises," Dr. Carmichael said by way of answer.

"You do not think the world has it in hand?"

"In *hand*, maybe. But to rein it in, don't you think that takes two hands on the reins? With the democratic nations constantly knocking heads with authoritarian nations, the world can't seem to get heads together to finish what needs to be done."

"And what needs to be done?"

"One political system needs to dominate the planet."

"Are you placing any bets?" Neuro asked.

"I somewhat like the efficiency of authoritarian states."

"I somewhat like the creativity and innovation of democratic states."

"Ah."

"Ah."

"Hell in a handbasket. So, we must, Kahdambi, we absolutely must preserve the best of us. We must offer them immortality, and design a future based on the rational direction of intelligent energy, the essence of humanity purified into something beyond. Otherwise, ours will be but a quick blip in the history of the universe. It motivates me. It stokes me. It fires me up."

192

"Dr. Carmichael, I think you do not want to prevent the world from going to hell in a handbasket. On the contrary, I think you look forward to it."

"That, Kahdambi, would be inhuman of me. I just think it is inevitable. But with our hard work, possibly not total."

~

Neither spoke as the two men walked through the sea fig trees back to the Foundation for Immortality. As they walked, the sound of the ocean faded, and the sounds of the forest—breeze through trees, birds in flight, something falling or landing onto the forest floor—ascended. Astro gave a side glance to his companion, who was at home in his thoughts.

He is quite mad, Astro thought. *Where have I found myself? On the Island of Doctor Moreau?*

As melodramatic a thought as it was, it did not mean it was entirely fantastical. The irony of having brought Astro here struck Neuro. It was an irony reflexively expressed in the bastard child of a laugh and a snort.

"I'm sorry, did you say something?" Dr. Carmichael, leaving home, asked.

"No. I did not," Astro said. "Just an old memory surfacing."

"Aren't all memories old? Even ones from yesterday? The present leaves the past behind so quickly," Carmichael said, then retreated back home into his thoughts, obviously not expecting an answer.

But what else could I have done? Neuro was going to die.

Carmichael's exclusive technology combining BioMed cocoons with cryonic embalming of the brain settled the matter for Astro. He accepted Carmichael's offer for him to do his research at the Foundation for Immortality and had the cocooned Astro shipped to St. John's Island, where he now "resided" in a specially equipped room next to Neuro's

It had been a year since the accident, and Neuro was still grieving. If grieving was the word. Maybe just deeply missing explained it better? No. It was grief. Neuro—Khadambi Kinyanjui—knew grief. Grief had penetrated his being when he was a young man. And being a young man of fresh flesh, the grief for his father had saturated and stained, and he could feel it to this day. But he had managed it. His adult years allowed him to do that. Still, it was ever-present. And then Astor's accident. And the stain darkened.

Someone had once told him—he couldn't remember who or

when—that the worst of grief passes in eighteen months. Why eighteen months? A whole year, and then half a year. But those were measurements, not the actual change of molecules and atoms and particles—and minds. Still—eighteen months. *In six months, will all of this seem wrong? Frivolous? Silly? Will I "pull the plug" and say that it is finally time for Astro to rest in peace? What rest? What peace? What stupid old notions! Astro did not believe in the soul, and neither do I. But if we go by ancient mythologies that some still believe in, what rest? What peace? Scorching by fire and brimstone? Or a place so eternally peaceful it becomes nothing more than the emotional equivalent of white noise? No, dead is just dead, and grief hurts. It is the living left behind that need to rest in peace, not the dead.*

But he missed Astro so much. His voice, his wit, his damn determination to always be well-dressed. Astro *knew* Neuro. And never brought Neuro down to his short stature but always rose to Neuro's well above average height. Metaphorically speaking, of course. Neuro was going to miss this. Their knowledge of each other had formed a constantly active loop transporting and transforming information. And knowledge, quirks, laughs, concerns, wonder, disgust, amusement, bemusement, awe, aw-shucks, and ontological anomalies. In essence, Being. Neuro liked being a "being" with Astro. But with the loop broken…

~

When Neuro returned to his room at the Foundation, he found a message from his brother Yoshi waiting for him on his desktop PQC.

Dambi, my brother. Do you remember Zawadi, Senator Mital's daughter? We had dinner with them when you visited with your friend Joe Smith. I hope it is not a bad memory because of our intrusive matchmaking. For we, I mean our family, have become quite proud of Zawadi as she has published her first book of poetry. Why should our family be proud of her? That is a story I may never have thought to tell you. Possibly knowing you might not care. But, as you are a member of this family, however long distanced and rarely communicated with, I thought I would share now…

(Neuro thought they communicated quite often enough. But close relatives traffic in relativity, as many far from the nest will attest.)

…our pride and the reason for it.

Shortly after you went back to America, Henna came to my office to commiserate over our failure to make a match between you and Zawadi. I have known Henna for years and have always valued her creative political advice, instincts, and wisdom. But as a mother, she is truly a walking cliché…

(There was that word again.)

194

...going on and on about how she didn't know what to do with her disobedient daughter. She was, of course, seeking my advice, which I normally would have been quite at a loss to give in a situation like this. Luckily, I had in hand a note sent to me by your friend, Joe. It seems he spent some time talking to Zawadi on that little outing you all went on and wanted to share with me some insights into the reason for her stubbornness. And to plead a case for leaving things alone and not continue to push you or Zawadi in directions you did not want to go. At first, as I read the note, I thought Joe was overstepping his bounds, possibly because of jealousy. I was still not convinced that you two were not gay. But, of course, you both lived in America. Far, in your case, from African eyes. Which are still not wholly tolerant. So why wouldn't you be open about it?

As I continued to read Joe's note, I understood that he was just reporting facts. Reporting facts and conveying a concern built upon his friendship with you and empathy for Zawadi. A concern that a mistake at this time could lead to unhappiness for two and possibly more people we all cared about. I found wisdom in the note and was happy to pass it on to Henna.

"The only thing to do," I told Henna, "is to let Zawadi accept the scholarship to Harvard.

"What!" Henna screeched. And I do mean screeched. But when she calmed down, I made my case based on Joe's wisdom and sealed the deal by saying, "After all. My father was grooming Dambi to be a political creature as he groomed me for the business. But Dambi knew his own mind better. The wisest thing this family has ever done was not insist on him fulfilling our father's wishes. And look how proud Dambi has made us. How promising he is in the field he loves. And consider this, Henna, if Dambi had gone the political route, I would not be here now, your political partner in affairs essential to this nation. I'm sure if you let Zawadi go her own way, she will make you proud of her, even if you may not completely understand why."

I also told Henna that the family, especially Faraja, who runs the family foundation, has always been impressed by Zawadi. So, if she does well in her undergraduate studies, I was sure Faraja would be supportive of a grant to continue her education.

Zawadi did, and we have, and this is why we have a right to be proud of her. Dr. Zawadi Mital is now teaching the humanities at our New University of Science and Technology. She could have taught just about anywhere, but she wanted to come home to Kenya. And to her mother, I am happy to say. She also feels that teaching the humanities to budding scientists and engineers is a mission. Exactly why, I am not sure.

This first collection of her poetry is receiving a positive critical reaction. And I thought you would like to have a copy of it. I have attached the ebook to this message for you to download. You might find the poem on page 26 of particular interest.

I hope this finds you well on your little island. I still cannot pretend to understand what you do or what you pursue, but I wish you well in all of it.

Yoshi

Neuro downloaded the volume of poetry and opened it. The cover was simple, ochre in color with the title, SEEING, in a handwritten dark blue script at the top. POEMS 2050-2060 floating in the middle, and ZAWADI MITAL resting comfortably at the bottom in the same script. Neuro advanced the digital copy to page 26 and found a poem entitled, "On Visiting Harrods Department Store in London for the First Time." Neuro read the beginning.

Man
Puts his hand
To the raw
And refines
Making practical
Without realizing
Making beauty…

The poem continued detailing nothing in the interior of the famous department store that Neuro knew well from his childhood. There was no poetic consideration of the renowned luxury goods, dry and edible, that were still prized by the elite, dreamed about by others. Although also scoffed at or not even thought about by so many. Zawadi's words did not acknowledge the purpose of the place, nor its history, changing hands more than a few times, several being non-British holding up this most British institution. No. The poem put a close eye, a concentrated consideration only on the terracotta blocks that covered the facade of the building, ochre in color, plain, smooth, retaining the beauty of the earth, the clay it once was before….

Purposeful man
Snatched heat from fire
To bake the mire.

Creating a versatile and durable building material, doubly practical in the Edwardian time of its application for its resistance to the smoke-filled atmosphere of London….

Not allowing
One hand of man
To desecrate the work
Of the other hand

Zawadi then puts into words the color and texture of the blocks seen by the eye. The smoothness of the surface felt by the fingers. The shape the mind appreciates. And the beauty of a manifest musical repetition of block upon block ascending, a community of like, with subtle variations of light and dark in the color.

But how, Neuro smiled as he questioned, did Zawadi get this personal, up-close view of the ochre terracotta mind-loving, finger-stroking, eye-pleasing blocks, one after another, after another, after another? These blocks, this part of Harrods' facade, was not at ground level. They started one floor up and ascended beyond the reach of anyone in the street. Did she take a scissor truck with an elevating platform—like the one they used in Kenya that night—to raise herself up to the height needed to reach out and touch, to be near for a sharp look? Did she use binoculars? Suitable for looking, but not so good for feeling. Was it just poetic imagination? No. Neuro knew. She got the experience to inform her poem at Neuro's old home. He was sure of that. Once a depository for Harrods, the building on Trevor Square was built with much of the same materials.

The materials here, especially the tiles, came down to street level. Having been taken under the wing of the family foundation, Zawadi must have been invited to stay with Neuro's mother on a visit to London. Neuro could see Zawadi—this surprised him—standing close to his London home. Running her fingers among the tiles and over one individual one. Focusing her eyes on the ascendance of this community of tiles, the soul of the facade (if he could briefly be poetic). His mother was there, urging Zawadi to hurry up as she wanted to take her to tea at Harrods. What an image! This beautiful African princess with her nose not to the grindstone but to the tile. Finding a world there as the world outside awaited—

Wait a minute.

Beautiful?

Princess?

A while ago, he was contemplating grief. Now he was…

Neuro sat still for moments he would never count. Then he turned to his computer and opened a new document, and typed:

Dear Zawadi—I don't know if you remember me…

18
THE HIGH TEA

Neuro and his team at the New University of Science and Technology in Nairobi had made vast improvements to Astro's world. He now had his choice of where he wanted to be. Either in his condo in the Title Guarantee Building, across the street from Pershing Square in downtown Los Angeles. Or The Hole, originally in the middle of a California desert but now in the middle of...where? Space? Nothingness? Negative space? A circuit board? The micro-ist microchip in all of creation? Or a nano quantum computer with that slime residue of a slug called Brandon Carmichael at the keyboard? Or a gigantic quantum computer to match Carmichael's self-regard?

Neuro had yet to inform Astro. He kept saying that Astro was not yet ready to know the full extent and particulars of this existence he was leading. Or was the existence leading him?

Oh, what the bloody blue blazes. I think, therefore, I am. I am home in my condo. And it's about time I did some house cleaning.

Neuro felt it was important for Astro to do things for himself, like having to make his own mac & cheese. Even though Neuro could have programmed fully prepared warm and cuddly mac & cheese. Or the total lack of dust. Or a command that plates and books and media center remotes and chairs had their places and must automatically return to them once they were no longer being utilized by the hand of Astro.

Neuro wanted to make this surreal world of Astro's more real than real.

But he hadn't gotten to the surrounding landscape yet. Astro could not leave his condo, take the elevator down, exit the building, and call up a self-driving car to take him out to the desert and The Hole. No, he simply stated his desire to be in The Hole, and The Hole seemed to come to him, surrounding him while supplanting his condo. One might think that was damn convenient. And it was, in a way. But where was the journey supposed to be more important than the destination? Actually, Astro would have just settled for a stroll up 5th Street to Pershing Square or the Central Library.

Neuro knew this. Neuro and his team were working on it. And one other thing.

One day. Relatively speaking. Astro didn't really have days "...rounded with a sleep." Instead, he had periods rounded with non-existence. Sometimes for maintenance (which does sound like sleep), sometimes for corrections or upgrades (which sounds like anesthetization during surgery). But be that as it may...

A buzzer sounded.

It was a sound he had not heard in years, and it took him a moment to place it. Oh, yes. It came from his vintage intercom unit, connected with the building's security/doorman in the lobby. Astro moved to it and cautiously said, "Hello?"

"Mr. Smith, there is a Dr. Kinyanjui down here to see you. Should I send him up?"

"What's your name again?" Astro asked. He had a memory that it should be Roberto. But it really didn't sound like Roberto. In fact, it didn't sound human at all. "Hello? Are you there?"

Then a very familiar voice came on. "You have not given him a name yet. Or an existence, for that matter."

"Neuro?"

"Yes. I am in the lobby."

"What lobby?"

"The lobby of your building."

"And *you* are in it?"

"In a manner of speaking. Can I come up?"

"How?"

"By the elevator, of course?"

"I have an elevator?"

"You do now."

"But, how?"

"I am coming up."

The doorbell rang. Fear jumped from Astro's guts to his throat. But that did not prevent him from going to the door and opening it.

There stood Neuro. Tall Neuro. Older Neuro. But no older than his image on the video monitors had been. And well-dressed Neuro in a nice suit. He was smiling a self-satisfied smile combined with a smile of joy. Astro's mouth was agape.

"Astro, I would tell you to close your mouth before a fly flies in— but we have not programmed flies."

Astro closed his mouth only to then use it to say, "What the bloody blue blazes are you doing here?"

"That is not the pleased-to-see-you reception I was expecting."

"Well, what do you expect in your expecting?"

"You were never shocked before when I appeared at your door."

"Not "here" my door, "here" in this, whatever this is that you've got me in!"

"Speaking of in—may I?"

"What?"

"Come in."

"Oh, sure," Astro said as he moved aside and gestured Neuro in. "Welcome to my world. Or your world, as the case may be."

Neuro walked in and looked around, now with just the rumor of a smile on his lips. "Very impressive. To see it in all dimensions; to be among it." Neuro walked over to Astro's desk and knocked on its surface, and was gratified at the sound resonance caused. "So much better than just seeing all this on a screen."

"I'm happy you're happy. But that brings up a cogent point. Why aren't you on my video monitor?"

"Little by little, my team has been perfecting this world and our access to it?"

"So, you are, what? An avatar?"

"No. That is both an antiquated and inadequate word. I prefer to just think of me—this me—as a projection of the real, or rather, other me sitting in a very comfortable recliner chair in my lab connected to—something—and being monitored by my team." Neuro turned to Astro. "Are you hungry?"

"No," Astro said. Then said, "Wait. Yes, yes, I am. Suddenly peckish indeed."

"Fine. Let us walk over to the Biltmore Hotel. They serve a fine Afternoon British tea."

"We can walk over?"

"Yes. That is what I came to tell you, among other things. Nice suit, by the way," Neuro said, looking over the black and white large houndstooth three-piece suit that Astro was wearing.

"Thanks. I just suddenly felt compelled to put this suit on."

"Really?" Neuro went to the door and opened it. "How interesting. Shall we go to our tea?"

~

When the elevator doors opened onto the lobby, it was as if the doors opened onto a new world. Although it was nothing more than the lobby of Astor's building as he remembered it. The same one he had passed through many times before, bidding goodbye to the security person at the lobby desk—whether it be Roberto or Carlos or Rigo. Or hello or some other exchange of pleasantries. But his life of late—or better said, his intermittent existence—had been confined to his condo. And The Hole. And Astro had gotten used to thinking of it as the whole of the universe. Or at least his universe. There was that other universe Neuro had gifted him by setting up the telescope at The Hole to gather light and report to Astro. But, at this moment, Astro wasn't thinking of that universe. Although in reality, if this was reality, he was rarely *not* thinking of that universe. But at this moment, he was thinking only of his own digital skin and its immediate surroundings.

And his surroundings right now were the lobby as it had been when this 1930 building housed commercial enterprises. It had fallen into disrepair, as buildings of extended use often do. But was refurbished and maintained beautifully for years since it had become a building of living spaces. The lobby was walled in beautiful marble, dark and light, and had a marble floor set down in patterns. And there, look up! There were the Hugo Ballin murals, beautiful and vibrant in color. All four elevators were doored with Art Deco geometric shapes, brass in material and gold in thought.

"Amazing," Astro said. "It's just—"

"As you remember it?"

"Yes."

"The team did good work."

At the security desk was an asexual individual. With the trunk and appendages of a typical human, but so nondescript, looking like no one yet looking like everyone.

It was painfully disconcerting for Astro, and he turned to Neuro, saying, "The security—"

"I know. Just concentrate on it for a moment."

"It?"

"Look at it. Look closely."

Astro did so. And in a few moments, the individual, the *Homo thing*, turned toward Astro and Neuro while vibrating as if experiencing a personal earthquake. By the end of its turn, the *Homo thing* had coalesced into—

"Roberto?"

"Yes, Dr. Smith. Is there something I can do for you?" Roberto asked. He was a stocky man with a thick full head of hair, a handsome Hispanic face, and one of the best smiles on any person Astro's had met. Roberto had always worked the noon-to-eight shift. He was the one who greeted Astro's female companions, who came to pick him up for an evening out. Or spend some quality time (evening to morning) with Astro at home. Roberto had always been very impressed. To Astro's amusement, he had dubbed Astro an honorary Latin Lover.

"Uh, no, Roberto. I just wanted to say that I'll be out for a little while if anyone else comes."

"Okay, Dr. Smith. Enjoy your afternoon."

~

They exited the building and stood for a moment on 5th Street. There was bustle from humans walking on the sidewalks, humming from the self-driving electric cars rolling along the street, bird sounds in the air, and the far-off sounds of construction somewhere.

The cars were of particular makes and lacked no fine details. Astro looked up but saw nothing flying.

"We haven't added the birds yet," Neuro said. "Just the sounds. But how often do you actually see birds? It is not disturbing, is it?

No, it wasn't. But the humans were. Like Roberto, before he became Roberto, all the bipedal whatevers walking here and there along the street were asexual nondescripts, *Homo things*.

Neuro knew exactly what Astro was feeling. "Just concentrate on them for a moment. One by one or *en masse*, it doesn't matter. In your lifetime, you have seen thousands of people. Directly or on video monitors or in the old movies you love so much. Two sexes, more or less, many ages, many types, many sizes, shapes, weights, attractive, not so attractive. Concentrate, and you can populate this world."

The challenge was exciting. And amusing. And finally, delightful as the asexual nondescript bipeds vibrated into real people, a cross-section of faces and bodies that have passed by Astro's vision at least once in his life. Soon the solidity of reality was Astro's impression, especially as he suddenly realized that he could feel the sun on his face.

"Let's walk up to the Biltmore," Neuro said as he guided Astro to the right to stroll the one long block, passing Pershing Square across Fifth to Olive Street.

Astro was still in the strange state of feeling that everything was simultaneously familiar and yet new and undiscovered. But this did not stop him from being suspicious.

Why were they going to tea?

Yes, the afternoon tea at the Biltmore was justifiably famous in L.A. Yes, Neuro and Astro had indulged before, many times. It might even be said that it had become a semi-tradition of theirs. But if Neuro had something to tell him, why not in his home? Because there was going to be a third party at the tea? Someone Neuro wasn't going to show up at Astro's door with? Carmichael! Damn Dr. Brandon Carmichael! Of course. He is there, in the lab, in another recliner, ready to appear and gloat!

"And there the bloody blue blazes he is!" Astro shouted, startling Neuro. They had gotten to Olive Street. They had turned left and crossed Fifth to go the half block to enter the Biltmore directly into the Rendezvous Court where the tea was held each afternoon. Astro had stopped and pointed to a person exiting the Biltmore. "You should have told me I would be breaking scones with dopy Doctor Carmichael, Neuro. You should have given me a choice to say no. So, he has been involved all along. Why would you hide that from—"

"That's not Carmichael."

"Sure it is." The person was heading in their direction. "Look at that self-satisfied crooked smile. I think I'll go wipe it off his face!"

Astro started to move, but Neuro grabbed him and pulled him back. "That's not Carmichael. You must have been thinking of him. Think of somebody else. Think of that guy who played James Bond in the Sixties movies.

"What?"

"Think of him."

Astro thought of him. And in a moment, a ridiculously young and handsome Sean Connery passed them, and Carmichael was nowhere to be seen.

"What the—"

"Why were you thinking of Carmichael?"

"Why wouldn't I, Neuro?" Astro asked as he turned and looked up at his best friend. A best friend who had betrayed him? "You've kept me in the dark about Carmichael's involvement because you know what I think of him. But am I so fragile I have to be protected from the truth?"

"Brandon Carmichael is not involved in any of this. I assure you of that. He has had no hand in it."

Astro was glad to hear it but wasn't sure he believed it. "He hasn't? Why?"

"Because Brandon Carmichael is dead."

∼

Astro remembered the last time he saw Brandon Carmichael. It was 2053, a year after his and Neuro's trip to Kenya. Astro had dropped by Neuro's office on campus one day to invite him on another trip out to The Hole to visit Aunt Liz. She was not feeling all that well, and Astro felt she needed cheering up.

He walked into Neuro's office and found not Neuro but Carmichael.

"What the bloody blue blazes are you doing here?"

Carmichael sat on the office couch, reading that week's copy of *The Daily Trojan*. He looked up at Astro, seemingly unperturbed. "One, I do not know what a blue blaze is, bloody or not. Two, what I am doing here is my business, and I intend to keep it that way."

"No, you don't," Astro said as he fully entered the office, went to Neuro's desk, and sat in Neuro's chair. It was, of course, the act of a mammal claiming his territory.

"What?"

"You're dying to tell me what you're doing here."

Carmichael smiled his crooked smile. "I am not dying, Dr. Smith. Nor do I have any plans to. But, yes, I actually don't mind telling you. I have come to report to Dr. Kinyanjui about my Foundation for Immortality's exciting move both scientifically and geographically."

"You're moving to the moon? Perfect."

"Not the moon. Nor Mars, so don't ask. To a small island off Singapore where we can conduct our research and experiments in peace."

"In peace?" Astro questioned the concept.

"That's right."

"You mean, without government interference?"

Carmichael answered only by extending his crooked smile.

"Are you going to invite Neuro to join you on this island paradise?" Astro asked.

"Of course."

"He'll turn you down. As he always has in the past."

"It's an open invitation with no expiration date. In the meantime, we share research and communicate like the genial colleagues we are."

"Humph," Astro expelled quietly as he swiveled 180 degrees in Neuro's chair to look out the window onto a green space featuring trees he was fond of.

The moments of quiet that ensued needed the tick of an old clock to mark. Unfortunately, all time-keeping in the office was digital.

Finally, Carmichael said to Astro's back. "Kahdambi's work on the connectome has been invaluable to me."

"Glad to hear it," Astro said insincerely while remaining still, his eyes on his trees.

"His work is helping us to move closer to the day—"

"Dr. Carmichael," Astro said, his back still to the man. "Why are you so determined to nip us in the bud?"

"In the bud?"

"The first great city was Uruk. Founded 4500 to 3500 BCE. Let's say 3500."

"Why are we saying anything at all about it?"

"It was the beginning of human civilization, wouldn't you say?" Astro posed the question as he swung back around to face Carmichael.

Carmichael answered only with a look half of impatience and half of irritation.

"My Aunt Liz, who was an historian, loved the city of Uruk."

"Is that why she lived in the middle of a desert? Oh, yes, I know about The Hole."

Had Neuro been talking about him to Carmichael? Astro wondered briefly, then put it aside to remain in homeostasis. "An interesting thought, but no. But she did love Uruk as the beginning of human civilization, the start of a, relatively speaking, rapid ascendency to where we are today. If we consider a generation as one hundred years—that's not a social or family generation. Aunt Liz called it a historical generation. But if we do that, then there have only been fifty-five generations of human civilization. Fifty-five. A ridiculously small number. Can't you and your rabid transhumanists and uploading fanatics give us at least one hundred generations to enjoy our civilization before dissipating us into zeros and ones?"

"Dr. Smith, you are like a blind man so enamored by dark and touch and sounds that you are afraid of light and color."

"Am I?"

"Yes. Sadly, you lack vision, but there it is. What has human civilization been, but striving for perfection? All I strive for is the most perfect of perfection. As long as we remain meat, continued frailty will be our destiny."

"But I love human frailty."

"Then you are a fool."

"Possibly. But without human frailty, there would be no comedy. And I love a good comedy. So when we are all immortal minds floating in some Carmichael computer, will there be comedy? Will there be any art and culture? Or will it just be calculations? All calculations and no contemplations?"

"You're an idiot, Dr. Smith."

"And you're an egocentric piece of shit desperate to be a godhead if not an actual god."

"Dr. Smith!" Carmichael jumped off the couch, flaring red in his face, and approached Neuro's desk.

"Dr. Carmichael!" Astro stood, thankful that there was a desk between him and the angry man before him.

The office door opened, and Neuro walked into an atmosphere thick and heavy. He looked at Astro and Carmichael, who couldn't take their stabbing eyes off each other. "Why do I feel," Neuro said cautiously, "like I just walked into a classroom of misbehaving students?"

~

"Dead?" Astro queried as they settled down to their high tea at the Biltmore. "Mr. Immortality himself?"

"Yes. He did not reach his life goal of everlasting life."

"When did he die?"

"2065."

"And what year is this again?"

"2070."

"So I'm—forty-five."

"Yes. As I am."

"But you look it."

"Do you want to be aged? Bulked out a little, some lines on your face. Just a distinguished touch of gray?"

Astro was contemplating Neuro's question when a waiter brought to the table a three-tier dessert stand filled with lovely indulgences and a highly polished antique silver teapot. Astro picked up the teapot, heavy with brewing Earl Gray, and used its mirrored if distorted surface to view his thirty-four-year-old face. He liked it. Youth was still apparent yet was melded with experiences lived. He looked over at Neuro. He didn't look all that much older, except for the gray crowding the temples. And yet, there was no hint of youth, as if it had been a creme Neuro no longer applied. Neuro's face now had that bulk that comes in middle age, and his eyes were those of a man who had seen a lot pass by—not all of it pleasant.

"I'll stick with what I have for the moment," Astro said.

"You can stick with it forever if you wish."

"And let you become 'old man wise' to my beamish boy. No, thank you. Just let me catch up with you slowly."

"Of course."

"Right. Now, I'm still hungry, so let's have our tea and treats, and then you can tell me what the occasion is, why you are here, and what it means."

"I thought this would be a comfortable place, a pleasant time, to finally tell you exactly what has happened to you."

"Oh." A cold stone filled Astro's stomach. "I don't think I'm hungry anymore." Just how unnerving, horrifying was Neuro's information going to be?

"No. First eat, drink."

"And be merry?"

"That I cannot predict."

～

The pleasure of the tea was not diminished by the anticipation of strange news. In fact, Neuro and Astro fell into talk of old times. Of visiting Astro's Aunt Liz and of missing her. Of women that they had known and of Neuro teaching Astro to swim. And of an African night full of stars.

"Do you remember Zawadi Mital?" Neuro asked as the waiter was taking away their dishes and the empty dessert stand after refilling the teapot.

"Sure. Like it was just seven years ago."

"We are married now."

"What?"

"She is an accomplished poet. Well-regarded and has won several literary awards. She is also a professor of humanities here in Kenya."

"Here in Kenya? Where, supposedly, I really am?"

"Yes."

"So you met again when you came back to Kenya?"

"No. We met again before that. On an island."

"An island?" Astro didn't understand. An island? Where? How did — "Damn it! You went to Carmichael's damn island!"

"Yes, but… Let me explain. Let me explain everything."

19
IN A JAR

❝ You were a mangled mess. It was only the barest chance that you were even alive. Your head was not injured, nor was your spinal cord. But to fix the rest of you, the doctors told me, would be so traumatic that it was unlikely you would survive the surgeries. The only thing keeping you alive was the induced coma and the BioMed cocoon. It was state-of-the-art. No one had perfected biofoam like the BioMed company. But it would not maintain you forever. Only for months. Six maybe. Maybe less. It was suggested that I, you know, pull the plug. The only merciful thing to do.

"But I could not. You, you diminutive, red-headed, life-loving, passionate, sensual bag of meat carrying around a deep intelligence, got under my skin. No one had meant so much to me since my father. I could not lose you. I would not lose you. Not while I knew that you were in there among that mangled mess.

"So, yes, I called Brandon Carmichael. And I went to see him on St. John's Island. No—don't say anything. Let me continue.

"Carmichael had a way to—preserve you. He offered me a deal beneficial to both of us. Or rather all three of us, I suppose you could say. If I joined his Foundation for Immortality and did my research into the connectome there. He needed the results of my research to complete his experiments, to fulfill his dreams. In my mind, it was an equitable arrangement.

"But I also consulted with my brother Yoshi about an investment I wanted to make. He helped me make a deal with the BioMed company. I would fund a push to extend their BioMed biofoam cocoon's ability to not only maintain life but, specifically, the life of the brain. I wanted something that would completely connect with the brain in various ways. Obviously, my research and findings on the connectome were invaluable to them. I knew nothing would be developed in time to help you—I was counting on Carmichael for that. But I was thinking of the future. Of other accidents and other victims in need. Of other friends and families. It is certainly something my father would have done. The investment turned out to be the best decision I have ever made.

"Although we were both making progress, after a year with Carmichael, it was not as much as either had hoped for. And I started to become somewhat concerned over Carmichael's reaction to what was happening outside of our tiny island. The world situation, I suppose you would call it. There was, of course, the continuing and not always successful effort to control the climate crisis. And then there was the debate over the funds spent on Mars exploration. Which was surprisingly international. Even Kenya had contributed scientists to the effort. One of them was one of the students with us that night under the stars. Yoshi has made her a national hero."

Neuro stopped to take a sip of digital tea.

"But the most significant international problem," Neuro continued, "was this constant comparison and conflict between democratic forms of politics and governance and concentrated power, authoritarian power, within individual nations. And among nations. The United States had been vacillating for years but had returned as the beacon of democracy. China had only strengthened itself as the very model of efficient, if ruthless, top-down governance. Russia, as you know, continued to be a mess. But a dangerous mess. Europe, as ever, seemed split between the two poles. India was fully authoritarian and relatively stable. After the genocide of their Muslim population. Which many in the world condemned. But not as many as should have.

"I really did not want to care about any of this. I was focused on what I was doing. I suppose I am the worst of citizens because I had left politics behind and did not want to think about these issues. But Yoshi would not let me. He sent me reports on all the problems facing this world that he thought I should be concerned with. I assumed it was my punishment for forcing him to fulfill my father's dream for me. Which was fair, I suppose. So I dutifully read the reports and thanked him. I have a deep respect for Yoshi. He has put Kenya fully in the democratic camp.

"What concerned me about Carmichael was specific comments he would make that convinced me he would happily have resided in the authoritarian camp. As long as the authority left him alone. I had a growing fear that if he succeeded with mind-uploading, he would be —shall we say—very selective as to what minds would be uploaded.

"No! I know what you want to say, Astro, but drink your tea.

"Outside of that concern, I was becoming lonely on this little island. Carmichael was a strange companion. I am sure you are not surprised by that. The other people there were talented, intelligent, professional, but not that companionable. At least with me. And you, whose continued existence was the focus of my day, ironically did not exist at that time to be the companion I most wanted to break bread with. Or mac & cheese.

"Then I received a letter from Yoshi about Zawadi. She had become, as I said, a poet. And she was teaching at the New University in Kenya. She had done well. And my family had helped her. He sent me her poems. I have never much cared for poetry. But hers…" Neuro did not have the words he needed. So, he moved on.

"I wrote to her. Suggested possibly that we could meet up somewhere when next she had a break from the university. Some island of repose.

"No, not St John's Island. I needed a break from there. She suggested Lamu, right off the coast of Kenya. Her mother has a house there. We met. We were both stupidly shy. But after a day, after a sunset sail around the island in a dhow, after a chaste night of conversation, we were shy no more. We spent seven more nights on this island. None of them were chaste. At the end of our stay, I asked her, 'Do you think it would be possible, practical, if we were to be married?' Zawadi burst into laughter. It must have been a full five minutes before she stopped. It was the worst minutes of my life outside of my father's death and your accident. When she finally stopped, she said. 'Practical? No. Possible? Yes.' Then we flew to Nairobi and made her mother a very happy woman.

"Then I returned to you and—do not give me that look, Astro. You know I did not mean in a romantic way. Possibly I should have suppressed your sense of humor.

"Let me continue. In the two weeks I had been away, Carmichael had a breakthrough. Everyone was excited. Then the excitement was quelled when several scans of living animal brains did not result in those brains' hoped-for integrated and functioning emulation. The animals had, of course, unwillingly sacrificed their lives.

"The staff, true believers all, was depressed. But not Carmichael. He thought valuable data was achieved in the experiment. I was not so sure.

"But I continued to concentrate on my work. And to miss you. But I now had Zawadi. We vid-communicated daily on our PQCs. Not about wedding plans. Her mother and Yoshi had all that in hand. Nor about how much we loved each other. Neither of us, I am happy to say, have mushy personalities. We talked about you. Zawadi grew concerned about you. At first, on Lamu, when I explained to her what I had done; what I was doing, she was—appalled is too strong of a word, as is repulsed. But she certainly was not accepting of the idea. But when I began to talk about you, and knowing you, and things we had done, meals we had had, our sharing of ideas occurring to us in our own fields, that time you had ordered very spicy Indian food for Carmichael. Well, I think she began to understand. She got to know you through me, through signals beaming back and forth between our PQCs.

"But Zawadi did wonder—she put it in gentle yet unequivocal words—if I might have been too obsessed with your recovery. I would have fought the suggestion from anyone else, from my brother or even my mother. But Zawadi, besides being beautiful—do you remember how beautiful she was that night? But, of course, you do, don't you? Well, besides that, she has a wisdom that—this may sound strange—it is a wisdom that seems to be part of her skin. She did not even hint that I should stop anything I was doing; she knew what it meant to me, she came to accept that. But she said that I needed to, as she put it, open a compartment in my head for other things.

"She suggested—strongly, yet seductively—that I take her online course in the humanities. 'You think of the mind and its connections,' she said, 'and its computations. But the minds of people are also creative. There is culture to consider, not just neurons in individual brains. But group, social culture, Dambi.'

"Well, Astro, you know me. My taste in music has always been quite rudimentary. I have never much cared to read fiction. I had been much too concerned with finding realities to bother with unrealities. And I have never been able to understand musical theater.

213

Without knowing where the music is coming from, it always seemed a strange dimension for characters to occupy. And art? I went to art museums with you mainly to enjoy your enjoyment. Even clothes, for me, were just utilitarian objects of modesty and climate control. To you, they were always self-expressing adornments. I never really fully understood that. I'm sorry.

"I was reluctant to be my fiancé's student. But once Zawadi started talking about the myths and legends of Africa in her first lesson—some of them I remembered my beloved Wokabi having told me when I was very young—she filled that compartment in my head—my mind—with... Well, I can only call it a most revealing view of humanity. How stupid I had been. I had been nothing but a mechanic trying to understand and repair and extend the life of a machine. Even though my original mission in science was to understand how the fragile self in our heads, this gossamer ephemeral entity, can be existent in this universe of matter, I somehow turned that being, that self, into nothing but an operation.

"My wife's course taught me that the brain, the mind within, is not just a thinking machine that thinks itself into a *self*. A self that desires only to survive. That it was not only essential to find out why and how we think, despite us being a mere puff of existence. But why and how we think creatively—despite being a mere puff of existence. Why do we respond to beauty? And create beauty? Why do we tell stories of our past and ourselves, real, not real, and surreal? Why do we study our own existence and find both terror and joy? And often respond by making art; creating cultures. Why are we not just survival machines clinging to life? But creative selves projecting, enhancing, even, you might say, gilding life.

"Now, if I would let you speak, I know you would ask me, 'But, Neuro, did you not already know all of this?' And I would have to answer, 'No, I did not.' I, as a human, had been *informed* of this data, of course. Culture informs us of this. But I did not *know* it."

Neuro stopped to take a sip of tea while holding up a "muzzling" hand to prevent Astro from speaking. It was not necessary. Astro, by this time, had become a willing listener.

"I was thinking the other day," Neuro continued, "of that crazy early 1960s music you love. Mancini, was it?—is it? And music from your spy films. I knew you loved it only because that was the only music you were exposed to in The Hole. Your grandfather's music. And so, the only music to be imprinted on your young, developing brain. An operation of neurons. But I discovered that it still was not any less of a love. Love—a feeling, not an operation. An indication of a sort of flourishing toward a state of pleasure.

"During her next break from University, Zawadi did come to visit me on St John's Island. Carmichael was nothing but a gracious and, I must say, charming host. Nevertheless, Zawadi responded to him as you always have. Stop looking so triumphant, or I'll have them change your clothes to torn blue jeans and a dirty white tee-shirt.

"We took many walks around the island, Zawadi and I. She wrote poetry, and I agonized over a decision. A life or death decision. Zawadi encouraged me to debate myself on the best way forward. She did not debate with me, just allowed the proper atmosphere for me to debate the question plaguing me. The debate remained a draw. And Zawadi returned to Kenya.

"Yes, the debate was whether to pull the plug on you, my friend. You, who I must tell you now, were locked into your cryogenically frozen brain. Which was all that was left of you. You were housed at the Foundation for Immortality, waiting for Dr. Brandon Carmichael to perfect a process of mind uploading. So that you, Joe Smith, would reawaken to float around in your new digitally (quantumly?) emulated brain and be my existing friend once more.

"But a year after Zawadi visited St John's, Carmichael was no closer to that perfection than he had been. And Zawadi was waiting for me in Kenya."

Neuro, who had not always looked at Astro as he told his story, sometimes looking at his hands, sometimes looking around the room, now looked at him strangely. Astro noticed and wondered why. What was there on his friend's face? Sadness? Apology?

"I could no longer avoid the full pounding of grief," Neuro said.

Ah, a little bit of both, Astro decided.

"Carmichael, ever confident, said he would maintain your brain, that I did not have to pull the plug just yet. Give him more time, he asked. But I knew you would not want to be left in Carmichael's care. But just before my leaving, just before I would have… Well, I got a message, a most welcome positive message from BioMed.

"And you are now with me in Kenya. I was able to transport you here using the prototype of the BioMed brain cocoon they had created. Unfrozen but still in a deep coma. I did not know what I was going to do with you. Keep you in that state? Just in case Carmichael finally succeeded and was still willing to give you 'immortal life.' The BioMed brain cocoon and its newly formulated biofoam would have protected and nourished you for years. Or would I eventually give you up? Bid a final farewell. Retain only my memories of you. Damn good memories.

"But here you are. No! Again, I tell you, you have not been uploaded to your emulated brain into a computer. You are still your own brain in all its spongy biological matter glory.

"How? Why? Well, that's another story. And I am quite tired from telling this one. But to answer what you have wanted to know and what I have promised to tell you when I thought you were ready. You, Astro, my friend, are in your brain. Your brain is in a special integrated BioMed brain cocoon connected to you as finely as your body once was. And which resides in a special tempered glass container, the walls of which are three-feet thick."

Astro, who had no problem being quiet for the last minutes of Neuro's story, now opened his mouth wide as his red eyebrows descended. Yet with one side of his right eyebrow rising. He stared with this altered face at Neuro for a moment or two, then said:

"What the...what the blo...what the bloody blu...what the bloody blue blaz...what the...oh what the fuck! I'M A BRAIN IN A JAR?"

20
LETTER FROM A STRANGER

Neuro returned to Kenya in 2062 and was welcomed not only by his family but by the New University of Science and Technology, which granted him a tenured professorship and a fully-equipped lab. He installed the BioMed brain cocoon encased in thick tempered glass connected to a unique monitoring computer within that lab. It had pride of place in the lab. It was considered strange, freaky, macabre, and somewhat off-putting by his lab assistants for only a short time. For they got used to it quickly and came to think of Astro as the lab mascot. Early on, one assistant found a photo of Dr. Joseph Smith of USC on the internet, printed it, and taped it to the outside of the thick tempered glass. He was warned by the others that Dr. Kinyanjui might not appreciate it and might take it as a joke. But he did not think so. When Neuro came into the lab that day, it took him a while to notice the picture. When he did, he walked over to it. He gently ran his fingers across this captured and stilled moment in Astro's life. It was a color photograph of Astro in one of his favorite three-piece suits. It was shockingly green and set off his vibrant red hair. There wasn't a twinkle in one of Astro's eyes, but it didn't take much imagination to see one there.

Neuro asked the assembled nervous lab assistants, "Who put this up?"

Feye Naeku, a promising doctoral candidate, usually shy and quiet, did not hesitate to come forward and say, "I did, Dr. Kinyanjui."

Neuro looked at the young man. He was average-looking with a medium-sized nose and lips, a smooth face cleanly shaved, and a hairline destined to recede. He looked straight at Neuro with the most sensitive eyes. "You are Feye, correct?"

"I am."

"Well, Feye, you will be in charge of monitoring the cocoon."

"Doesn't the computer do that, Doctor?"

"Yes. But I'm quite sure the computer does not care about who it is monitoring."

"Then it will be my pleasure, Doctor."

"I don't know how much of a pleasure it will be. But it will be appreciated by me. And you may call me...." Neuro was going to say *Neuro*, but then he thought, No. "Call me Dambi. It is what my family calls me. And," he looked to all the assistants, "if we do not become a family in this lab, then I will have done something wrong."

∼

Neuro and Zawadi would have loved to have avoided a big wedding. But with Senator Henna Mital as the mother-of-the-bride and Senator Yaro Yoshi Kinyanjui as the brother-of-the-groom, a big wedding was not only inevitable but an opportunity for brilliant, non-controversial political theater destined to build solid political capital for the two legislators and their faction in the Senate. Given that, the big wedding was unavoidable.

Neuro knew he owed it to his brother.

Zawadi knew she owed it to her mother.

The wedding was carried on Kenyan television. Making "Dambi & Zawadi" celebrities. Much to their amusement. But neither being stupid, they realized it also gave them capital to spend. Neuro spent it on behalf of science and, with his brother's strong support, an ambitious build-up of the Kenyan space program. Zawadi spent hers securing funding for the arts, such as literary festivals emphasizing the international spread of African literature and a history project tracing the contributions of various nationalities to Kenya.

Neuro and Zawadi settled into a gated community (mother and brother demanded they have security) and life at the university. And life as a couple—as intellectual companions, emotional pals, physical lovers, and simply as two humans who almost seamlessly interlocked. Their marriage was many things, but most prominently, it was comfortable. Comfort accented by many smiles and not a few sighs of contentment.

Astro rested unconsciously in his BioMed brain cocoon encased in thick tempered glass, monitored by the unique computer, which was monitored by Feye Naeku. Meaning the brain that had resided in the skull of the head once connected to the body of Dr. Joseph Smith. But now it was just a thing by itself, spongy and wet with neurons still active if muted, with potential for a future, if only…

If only…

~

Late one night, Neuro was in his lab alone. Zawadi taught an evening class every Wednesday. Neuro always took the opportunity for quiet time in the lab to go over notes and electronic communications, delete unnecessary "stuff" on his PQC, and quiet reflection. Which is what he was doing that night.

He was reflecting on nothing in particular. Possibly it was something to do with his favorite virtual soccer team's game coming up this weekend and the family time it meant spending with Yoshi. Or perhaps the letter he received that day from his old university, USC, inviting him to deliver an address on a subject of his choosing. But nothing of any true significance. The simple act of reflecting itself was such a cozy berth wherein the outside universe seemed to fade away. Or possibly it was consumed within. In either case, it made the act of reflecting its own justification.

As Neuro reflected on nothing in particular, a man walked into the lab unannounced.

He was Caucasian, not short, not tall, not young, not old. He was neatly dressed in a gray business suit with a tightly knotted tie. He stood still with his arms resting at his sides. In his right hand was a white envelope, the letter-size kind that once was used for physical mailing.

"Excuse me, how did you get in here?" Neuro asked, thinking of Yoshi's security man, always posted outside.

"My employer," the man said in an even, pleasant voice, "has taught me ways to gain entrance into any supposedly secure facility. Not that I have many occasions to use the skills. Although it was amusing to divert the attention of the security man outside, he-he-he."

219

"You are an American?"

"That's true. I have flown in from Los Angeles."

"For what purpose?"

"To deliver this letter." The man held up the envelope. It was not addressed.

"To whom?"

"Why to you, of course, he-he-he." It was a breathy little laugh, more punctuation than an indication of found amusement. "You are Dr. Khadambi Kinyanjui." It was not a question; it was a statement.

"I am aware of this."

"Called Dambi by family and colleagues. Except for Dr. Joe Smith, who calls you Neuro."

It was not meant to be a poignant remark, but it pricked, just the same. "Used to. Astro used to call me Neuro."

"And may well again. This is why my employer has sent me to deliver this letter."

"And who is your employer?"

"I cannot say. No one knows who he is, really."

"Then who are you?"

"My name is Macbeth."

"Really?"

"First name is Roger. My father, Norton, was my employer's business manager for years. Currently, I handle all my employer's business affairs. He is very rich."

"So am I."

"He is aware of that. May I give you his letter?"

"As long as there is not a bomb in it."

"I assure you if there was, I would not be hand-delivering it, he-he-he."

Neuro took the letter from Macbeth and opened it, withdrew the single sheet of expensive-looking stationery, unfolded it, and read:

Dear Dr. Kinyanjui:

I would like you to please come to Los Angeles accompanied by the bearer of this letter, Mr. Roger Macbeth. I wish to speak with you and offer you something of great value.

I know of your efforts to save the life of your friend,

THE DEFINITION OF LUCK

Astro—if I may call him that. I also know you have left St. John's Island and Carmichael's Foundation for Immortality. That was a good move. However, I understand that it was partly made because any hope you attached to Carmichael's efforts had dwindled to an unsustainable point. I believe that what I have to offer will revive that hope.

If you think this is an effort to kidnap you (I applaud your brother's rational security concerns), I suggest you fly to Los Angeles in the Kinyanjui Holdings plane, allowing Mr. Macbeth a seat. Once you arrive in Los Angeles, he will take you to my residence by any form of transportation that you arrange.

Sorry to be so mysterious. But it has been my stock in trade.

Sincerely,

The Fixxer

"The Fixxer?" Neuro looked up at Roger Macbeth and questioned.

"Yes, I know. A bit of outdated melodrama. But that is the only name anyone has known him by for, oh, certainly seventy years or so."

"Seventy?"

"Yes."

"How old is your employer?"

"One hundred and three. He's quite frail now. May not have long to live. I suggest if you accept his invitation, we should leave as early in the morning tomorrow as possible, he-he-he."

∼

Hope, Neuro thought as he laid next to a sleeping Zawadi that night. *Hope is often crazy. They say it springs eternal, but nothing is eternal, is it? Still—*

Still, Neuro immediately called Yoshi to see if the plane was available. It was. He asked to use it. Yoshi asked why. Neuro made up some story to do with USC, which required his immediate and physical presence. He was sure Yoshi did not believe him, but he arranged for Neuro to be flown to Los Angeles in the morning nevertheless. After making sure that Mr. Roger Macbeth had accommodation for the night, Neuro went home and explained to Zawadi what he was about to do. She saw nothing wrong with Neuro going off on a mysterious adventure. But then, her secret reading vice was mysteries and thrillers.

~

It was a long flight to Los Angeles. Yoshi insisted that Neuro take one of his security detail with him. Roger Macbeth, on behalf of his employer, had no objections. Macbeth and Odongo Njoroge discovered that they shared a passion for gardening and spent much of the time talking about plants, flowers, and fertilizers. A slight dereliction of duty on Odongo's part, but Neuro did not care. The six-foot-five, well-muscled Odongo could certainly subdue the middling-sized Macbeth if he suddenly became a threat. And why would he? What would this Fixxer gain by harming Neuro? If there actually was such a person?

In the long hours of flight, Neuro questioned this action. Was it rash? Yes. Was it intriguing? Certainly. Could it lead to disappointment? Of course, everything in life could lead to disappointment. But it could also just as well lead to…?

Will he hear Astro's "voice" again? Will he talk to, joke with, share with Astro again? Why? Why had he ever thought he could? Or would? Or should?

Neuro was like a man in the dark holding onto an ember until he could get to a combustible to reawaken flame. But embers die. It is inevitable.

"Movie?"

It was Odongo standing over him.

"What?"

"Mr. Macbeth and I wondered if you wanted to join us in watching a movie before we go to sleep."

"Depends on the movie, I think."

"A comedy. It would justify Mr. Macbeth's constant he-he-he's."

"Do we have popcorn in the galley?"

"We usually do."

"Well, if we have popcorn, then yes."

~

The plane had a shower, and all three men were refreshed when it landed at LAX in Los Angeles. Odongo ordered a self-driving limo to take them to the address Macbeth gave them. It was a building on Wilshire Boulevard in Westwood just east of Beverly Glen. It once must have been one of the few high-rise condominium buildings that dotted this section of Wilshire. But now, it seemed a squat building compared to the recently built super high-rise residences flowing up and down Wilshire.

"The Fixxer used to own a floor in this building," Macbeth said as they came up to it. "But when they announced they wanted to tear it down to build one of these massive ones, he bought the building. It's a throwback to the 20th century, and many people would love to live here. You know, like people in the 20th century wanting to live in 19th-century buildings. But they can't. No one lives here now but Fixxer in the penthouse."

"What are the other floors used for?" Neuro asked.

"That I cannot reveal."

Not willing to entertain any more questions, Macbeth instructed the car to enter the underground parking once he opened the gate with a remote device. Both Neuro and Odongo were fascinated to discover the garage filled with classic internal-combustion autos from the past century. Some were obviously expensive in their day, some luxurious, some sporty. But there were also just standard vehicles, middle-class transports. Some were well maintained, and some were junky. Macbeth noticed Neuro and Odongo's interest in them.

"None are used today, of course. Once they were well-used by The Fixxer in his various endeavors, though."

"Why does he keep the cars?" Odongo asked.

"He's a sentimental man. No one he had dealings with in the past would have guessed that. But my dad knew. And a few others."

They traveled up an elevator to the penthouse, and Macbeth led them into a large bedroom. The curtains were closed. The interior lighting was muted. At one end of the room was a king-size bed. A very old man lay under covers in the center of the bed. He was propped up against a group of pillows. His head rested back on the pillows, his eyes were closed, and his breathing was regular. However, he was not asleep, as his exposed right hand was keeping time with the jaunty ancient-sounding music that seemed to come from everywhere in the room.

"Fletcher Henderson, Dr. Kinyanjui," said the old man, who Neuro assumed was The Fixxer. "Early 20th century jazz. I find it joyful. Life-affirming, some might say. I don't know about that. But certainly lively, don't you think?" He opened his eyes and moved his head up to look at his guests. "Odongo Njoroge, would you like to search my bedding and person to make sure I have nothing that could harm Dr. Kinyanjui?"

"That is not necessary," Neuro said.

"Please, let the man do his job," The Fixxer said.

Odongo looked to Neuro, and Neuro gave his ascent. Odongo then did his job and declared that he found nothing that could harm.

"Thank you, Odongo Njoroge. Are you hungry? Of course, you are. Macbeth will take you to our dining room and feed you. Don't worry. There is a monitor there, and you will be able to watch Dr. Kinyanjui and me as we have our talk."

Neuro gave another ascent, and Odongo and Macbeth left the room.

"Now, Neuro—May I call you, Neuro?" I have a particular fondness for nicknames."

"If I have to call you The Fixxer, you might as well call me Neuro."

"Good. Pull up that chair, and let me tell you why you are here."

As old as he was, The Fixxer still had a full head of hair, white enough to glow in the low light. His face, as wrinkled as one would expect in a man of a hundred and three years, retained some evidence that he had been a handsome man in his youth. It was clean-shaven and still had color. His hands, one of which he waved in an arch, turning off Fletcher Henderson, were withered. But they must once have been strong. His eyes were as clear as his mind obviously was.

After Neuro had moved a chair close to the bed and sat, The Fixxer began.

"I spent many years in this city exploiting certain aspects of Hollywood for my benefit. Meaning, of course, the entertainment industry, not a geographically contained area. The aspects were overheated egos and overweening hubris of both talented and non-talented individuals. If you assume, I was a con artist, that is not true. Rather, I was true to my name. You see, overheated egos and overweening hubris often lead to unfortunate situations that need to be fixed. Now Hollywood, indeed many areas of life, especially commercial and political life, have always had individuals paid outrageous sums to fix these situations. And so were referred to as fixers. But no fixer, past or present, ever had the skills and success I had. So I became known as *The Fixxer*. It is spelled with two Xs, by the way. Not overheated ego and overweening hubris, just a tiny conceit. But an earned one. And the powers of Hollywood loved it, as they always loved a pre-sold brand.

"I made a lot of money fixing these situations. With the advice of Roger's father, I made many wise investments with that money. Including investment in BioMed. Which is how I came to learn about you and your situation."

"My situation?"

"You have placed your friend in limbo, possibly a purgatory, not that I mean anything Dantesque by those terms. Does he exist, locked in his brain, which you have unfortunately separated from his body—"

"There was no other choice," Neuro said, reacting to the statement as an accusation. Which it may well have been. "His body was—"

"I know exactly what condition his body was in," The Fixxer said in such a way that Neuro did not doubt him. "You did at least save his brainstem. I applaud you for that. Life is, after all, not an old horror movie. But, of course, you tossed out the rest of his nervous system that his brain was the—shall we say—head of? I know there was no practical way to preserve it. In any case, does your friend exist in this brain and brainstem? Or does he not exist? Is that brain you've got cocooned in Kenya nothing but a little over three-pound mass of eighty-five billion neurons, nerve fibers, and nothing else? Nothing you could call a mind, a personality, a self? Is Astro already dead? And if so, why haven't you buried him?"

"I—"

"You don't know. But you thought that if the long-sought dream of Carmichael and others ever came true, you would at least have the chance to find out. And maybe retrieve your friend."

"I—"

"Ego and hubris on your part? You must be asking yourself that. A little. You must admit to a little. You are, after all, human. But I choose not to think overheated and overweening. Or otherwise, I would not have contacted you.

"Few of us are lucky to even have one friend close enough to share the center of the universe with. I had one. His name was Roee. He was gay. I am not. He was a devout Israeli Jew. I profess no nationality, no religion, no ethnic identity. And yet, we found comfort together in the center of the universe. You had—or possibly still have —Astro. You both entered the world by two very different doors. And yet, were you not quite comfortable with him in the center of the universe?"

Neuro had to smile. For various reasons. "Astro would have found your way of explaining it somewhat—"

"Bizarre?"

"No. Amusing. As the universe does not really have a center."

"Or it has as many centers as there are people on this planet."

Neuro thought about that for a moment before concluding that it was true.

"But all this philosophizing is meaningless," The Fixxer said as he adjusted himself in his bed, pushing himself up slightly. "Unless I have something to offer that's more pragmatic than philosophical. Well, I may have. But it's going to entail a lot of work on your part."

Neuro had nothing to say to this. He knew this aged man would not have brought him to Los Angeles if he had not been sure that Neuro was willing to work. He sat in silence, waiting to hear what The Fixxer had to offer.

"In the nineties, when I was well established in my chosen occupation of extricating the foolish from personal crises, I saved the world from tyranny. A tyranny so deep and vast that it would have lasted well beyond the next millennium. Not as surprising as you might think. Hollywood intersects with many aspects of society, including the manipulations of minds. Indeed, it might be stated that Hollywood is all about the manipulations of minds. For the essentially benign purpose of amusement, of course. But it is still manipulation."

"This all seems fairly—melodramatic."

"And a brain in a jar isn't?" The Fixxer smiled. That smile and a certain depth to the penetrating look he gave Neuro amounted to an odd compassion. "At first," The Fixxer continued, "the job was fixing a minor problem a film director had in stealing an idea for a screenplay. He assumed that this idea was so good that he wanted full credit for it as he thought it would propel him into the pantheon of great filmmakers. Of course, his crude mind and stunning lack of talent would have prevented that no matter how good the idea was, but he was, as the job requires, blissfully unaware of that fact.

"This idea for a screenplay turned out to be based on the work of a young genius at Caltech. Through hardware and software, he developed a way to connect with a human brain and completely take over its operation and its view of reality. He called it Veritas. Truth. Small minds thought he was creating a new form of virtual reality. But there was nothing virtual about his invention. The brain takes in many exterior and interior signals and assembles them into the reality you live through. Where you are, how you're feeling, what you're seeing. Veritas replaces those signals with ones of its own designs. It presents whatever reality it's programmed to. This genius, a young and arrogant little shit, but a genius nevertheless, was creating Veritas mainly for the challenge. He thought little of the consequences of his work. Although he admitted that it had applications for the blind, stroke victims, the sufferers of paralysis, or just people bored with their lives.

"I say he thought little of the consequences. But he did amuse himself in coming up with a movie idea of how the nefarious could use his Veritas to control the minds of masses of people. And give them not just experiences—but opinions. The opinions whoever controlled Veritas wanted them to have. I think you can see the dangers this might engender.

"A childhood friend of the genius, a budding screenwriter, part of a virtual plague of them at that time, stole the movie idea from him and presented it to a few people in the industry as his own. This was the idea that the director was trying to steal with my help. Although in a more or less legal manner. Unfortunately for the director, the genius, and the budding screenwriter, a film executive with pretensions to power beyond Hollywood became aware of the idea. And of the potentially brutal reality of Veritas. Many deaths followed, including the genius and his friend. The film executive got his hands on the hardware and the software. Then was disappointed to find that the genius had not yet perfected Veritas. It was full of glitches. He then became determined to get a perfected version. More deaths followed.

"As I bore some responsibility for these sad events, I opposed and eventually defeated this film executive and buried Veritas and any hint of its reality forever."

"Forever?"

The Fixxer smiled again. "Well, there were two prototypes of the Veritas system made. The first one came into my possession. After the events I have just outlined, I gave it to a trusted colleague. It was returned to me upon his death. The second, an improved but not yet perfect one, was stolen from the genius by agents of the film executive during an attack on Caltech that—"

"The Science Kills terrorist attack sometime in the 1990s!"

"You know of it?"

"I took several History of Science courses. It is legendary."

"Well, it is certainly mostly legend. They were not terrorists. It was a ruse to break into the young genius' office and steal the prototype and his notes. They both wound up at the bottom of Lake Arrowhead. I retrieved the hardware later. Not that it's ever been useful."

"Why didn't you just leave it in the lake?"

The Fixxer took a moment to muse upon the question. "I suppose I should have. The potential for misuse of this technology is quite frightening. Especially in this teeter-totter world we live in. But the potential for good is heartening, given the right reasons for its use. And that the right minds are allowed to take it in hand to try to perfect it. I believe I have found those minds."

"Minds?"

"Yours, of course. And your brother Yoshi's."

Neuro stood. He needed to move. He walked around the large bedroom as he tried to settle on whether he was amused, bemused, intrigued, or incredulous.

"I'm hungry," Neuro finally said.

"Then you should eat. I can provide a fine meal."

"Well, you've provided a fine story. But—"

"But is it just a story? A simple demonstration of Veritas will suffice, I think, to answer that question."

~

When Neuro came back from a damn fine if slightly flawed ancient Athens, from a dungeon in a castle in 14th-century France, and from a 1990s SciFi view of a 2026 underwater oceanographic institute, he was convinced of the power and potential of Veritas.

The Veritas hardware had been brought into The Fixxer's bedroom by Roger Macbeth. First, he asked Neuro to sit in a recliner chair. Then he handed a pair of glasses with two dark opaque lenses to Neuro and asked him to put them on.

"You can see nothing, of course," The Fixxer said from his bed, "because those are not real glasses. One lens receives an infrared beam sent from the Veritas hardware. The other sends an infrared beam back to the hardware. This creates a loop of information going to and from your brain. There are contact points in the bows of the glasses."

Macbeth then gently pushed a key on the hardware's keyboard, and Neuro was sent to ancient Athens.

When Macbeth later removed the glasses from Neuro's face, Neuro turned his head to The Fixxer and, with an open mouth of wonder, listened to The Fixxer explain.

"Veritas puts you into a state of dream paralysis. Then it inhibits all neuro activity, all communication, in effect, to and from your central nervous system—the brain, the brainstem, and what have you. It replaces the signals you would have gotten from the nerves throughout your body. All the signals mapping your exterior and interior conditions and stimuli. Cold or hot, hungry or satiated, in pain or feeling pleasure, seeing the beautiful or the ugly. It replaces them with its own designed signals. Effectively, Veritas gives you a manufactured reality. Or a curated dream. It causes you to think you are living the life of a person in ancient Athens. Or that you are a prisoner in a Medieval French castle. Or a scientist in an underwater lab. Or it could just be you climbing Mt. Everest, flying like a superhero, or making love to the latest screen goddess. It is not a virtual reality to watch, to take in only through your optical and auditory nerves, but a truth you live in the center of. You will have noticed the glitches, though. People with faces with no details, for example. And incongruous items and people from your own memories popping up.

"If those glitches can be fixed. And the power of the system is enhanced by connecting it to the BioMed brain cocoon. The one that your investment spurred the creation of. Then you might be able to offer your friend Astro a life. Assuming he's still there."

It was undeniable. It was a viable potential. It was hope.

But…

"Where to begin?" Neuro asked. "Without the notes—

"Yes, they did not survive the dunking in Lake Arrowhead. But an investigation I undertook discovered that our arrogant young genius, not trusting digital storage, put his trust in a bank. He stored hard copies of his notes in a safe deposit box. I extricated them through extralegal means."

"Why? If you were worried over the potential for abuse, which I admit is great."

"Instinct. Pure instinct. Somehow I knew or hoped that if I

turned over Veritas and the notes to you, and if you could perfect it, you would use it to recover your friend. But I was also quite sure you would use it for general humanitarian purposes. Assuming there is time."

"Time?"

"The world is on a dangerous precipice."

"It seems lately that it always is?"

"Well," The Fixxer gave consideration, "maybe it is a matter of how close we are to the edge, then. Always, I suppose, a debatable point. But be that as it may, I admired your father. I believe his sons inherited the best of him. I can think of no one else to entrust Veritas to."

Neuro's head felt heavy. Whether from being under the dictates of Veritas, the responsibility The Fixxer was handing him, or the complex difficulties ahead if he took on that responsibility, it did not matter. Neuro stood, rising up to his six-foot-five height, putting the bulk and strength of his body under his head, giving it the full support it needed. He walked over to the hardware, looked at it, and fingered it softly with his right hand. He looked at a binder containing the notes. He thought of the task ahead.

"Do you accept my offer?" The Fixxer asked.

"I must," Neuro said. "Gladly, I think. Or, at least, with no hesitation."

"Good. Now let's eat. I don't know how much longer I will be here to enjoy a fine meal of roast lamb."

21
A LETTER FROM ST. JOHN'S ISLAND

May 12, 2065
FROM: Dr. Jonathan Redfern, The Institute of Immortality,
St. Johns Island

TO: Dr. Khadambi Kinyanjui, New University of Science & Technology,
Nairobi, Kenya

Dear Dr. Kinyanjui:

I regret to inform you that Dr. Carmichael is dead. At least we think he is dead. It was his request, his last actually, that no matter the outcome of the attempt to upload his mind, you be informed immediately. Your research and findings were of extreme importance to what he hoped would be the final breakthrough in his long-sought goal.

On April 30 of this year, after years of research, experimentation, and computer enhancements, Dr. Carmichael became convinced that we now had the ability to scan a mammalian brain in full high-resolution detail, fully accounting for all the neuronal connections, etc. The data from the scan could then be the foundation for a whole-brain emulation in a unique quantum computer space controlled by an intuitive AI program. The latest version of the one your father helped develop.

As a test, we scanned the brain of a mature bonobo of twenty years on May 2. It was fascinating to watch the computer reconstruct the brain and provide a rendered image showing all the billions of neurons, synapses, axons, dendrites, etc. The program can enlarge any section of the WBE to an HR detailed degree. That way, we could track the release of transmitters. What we saw in the WBE of the bonobo was an active brain, a functioning brain. We sent specific signals to the WBE, and it responded in the way Dr. Carmichael predicted. We were elated. Our only frustration was that the WBE, being that of a non-verbal mammal, could not be adequately communicated with. But Dr. Carmichael was convinced that we were now ready to scan and emulate a human brain.

Each member of the staff immediately volunteered, but Dr. Carmichael would not hear of it. He said he could not ethically ask anyone except himself to submit to the scan, even though there would be little chance of a destructive outcome to the subject.

On May 5, Dr. Carmichael had us scan his brain. It took little time for the quantum computer to emulate his brain. It was suddenly there. In the computer, if I may say so, in its full glory. Dr. Carmichael took a few moments to contemplate that there was another him in the computer space. Another Dr. Brandon Carmichael, with all the same memories, thoughts, intelligence, and even tastes in food. "Or lack thereof," Dr. Carmichael joked.

Dr. Carmichael was about to try to communicate with his WBE when he suddenly felt that to do so was beyond surreal. He assigned me to make the first communication with what we assumed at the time to be his other self.

The program allows us to communicate by typing questions on a keyboard and receiving responses in written form. I sat at the keyboard and typed. "Hello. Dr. Carmichael? Are you there?" In answer, we received this --

dookwyiklmfjkwoqovnvmeopf[ecjuydyeruiewjcd7489 d n c v s c m a , l ; v j f ; s l j i o ; c k ! ! ! $ ~ %

$Ybvsmxkalckldvjklsddfkqweotprgid;lcsklcdmkf;fkwop fiueovmdklcmdkblfhwiropervmkszjlbdjklbkosa'sxjsuigj krofeopgkrfasjidodekgojidsfks'.....;;.;;;;;.

And then nothing. All neuronal activity in the WBE ceased. It was effectively dead.

The disappointment for all of us was, as you can imagine, deep. But Dr. Carmichael was nearly devastated. He retired to his office and did not come out for two days.

On May 7, he called me into his office. He was standing at his desk, the top of which was clear except for one envelope. "Jon," he said to me. "It is evident that the scan was incomplete, that not all the connections made it to the WBE. It is my opinion that it is going to take years to finally be able to scan a living brain thoroughly. Therefore, I've decided that we must slice a brain into very fine sections, each section to be preserved in resin. Then each section can be scanned thoroughly. The computer and AI will then take the data from the scanned sections and reconstruct the brain. That should, I believe—no, I know—will give us a functioning WBE— a true uploaded mind."

"Should we take one of the bonobos and...." I started to say.

"No. We will take a human brain."

"One of our clients in cryo-storage?"

"Of course not, Jon? That would be against our contract with them until we have evidence that it will work. It would also be wholly unethical."

"Well, then, who...."

Dr. Carmichael raised his right hand. In it was a small pistol. He shot himself in the heart.

The shock was intense. Others of the staff came running and found me nearly paralyzed over the sudden change in the world. Our world. My world.

Someone—I forget who—ran to Dr. Carmichael and found him to be dead. The small-caliber bullet had pierced his heart cleanly with little other damage to the rest of his body. As his heart had stopped immediately, there was very little blood. But that also meant that blood was not being transported to the brain.

I then made the most momentous decision of my life. I ordered the others to immediately take Dr. Carmichael to the surgical lab, remove his brain, and finely section it. I was, quite frankly, surprised that they did as I asked.

I opened the envelope on his desk. In it were his will and his instructions. I had anticipated his wishes correctly. He wanted his brain to be finely sectioned, each section preserved in resin, to be scanned and uploaded to the computer for WBE. After his instruction to report all this to you, he ended by writing, "I will be back with you soon."

We did everything as Dr. Carmichael instructed. The WBE of his brain was a wonder to view and contemplate. It was obviously a very alive and active brain in there. But it was not without trepidation that I sat down to type what I hoped would be the first of ongoing communication.

"Hello, Dr. Carmichael. Are you there? How are you feeling?"

Why did I ask how he was feeling? I don't know. Feelings were no part of what we needed to know. In any case, this is the response we got—

wkodjewoifjerfae7634789rpjewkpo'fwl;nlvadjk'kko;jl
hj,l;k;nhuMNSIDOFHEIOFKLFGJIOKJOjidofudy478563
4 9 j s c m s i o s d v n b n b n b n s w a d j i s o j i o j ~
$^cmsilanjklsnsndsskl;sk;aewk2y78othji5l;ym,lt;'bno0-
df9e90fsklcmsvldcxlap['jaiopfeoglr,klv;ashjufreyt84fnj
ksxmzfjesolfdu5690-m,l;'/scdx----,,,.........

And then -- I swear this to you, Dr. Kinyanjui -- I thought I heard a scream of terror and confusion. Impossible, of course. But in my mind, it was there.

Part of Dr. Carmichael's instructions was the story he constructed for us to tell the Singaporean authorities in the "unlikely event of my demise." The story held, and there will be no repercussions for the staff.

In his will, Dr. Carmichael tasked me with becoming the director of the Institute for Immortality to carry on the work. As you know, we are funded by a foundation. However, with the absence of Dr. Carmichael, I anticipate that future donations to that foundation will not continue at the pace he had established. That being the case, it would be remiss of me not to ask if the Kinyanjui Family Foundation might consider a donation.

But, far more importantly, I must ask if you have advanced your research into the connectome. Are there any data you now have that you have not previously shared with Dr. Carmichael?

Obviously, something was missing in the WBE of Dr. Carmichael. We are determined to discover what and complete the doctor's life-long work. So that we might, quite frankly, bring Dr. Carmichael back to the non-biological life he dreamed of.

~

Neuro read Dr. Redfern's letter, which had been sent to his PQC twice. He was shocked over the circumstances of Carmichael's death but not surprised over the outcome of the attempt to upload his mind. After two years of studying Veritas and marshaling the brightest minds in neurobiology, neurology, anatomy, computer science and computer graphics, nano-technology, and nano-engineering at the New University to perfect it, he felt confident to write—

May 12, 2065
FROM: Dr. Khadambi Kinyanjui, New University of Science & Technology,
Nairobi, Kenya

TO: Dr. Jonathan Redfern, The Institute of Immortality,
St. Johns Island

Dear Dr. Redfern:

I send the most heartfelt condolences to you and the staff of The Institute of Immortality over the loss of Dr. Carmichael. I considered him a brilliant and most interesting colleague, and I always appreciated his support of my work.

I am sorry to report that I have no recent data from my research into the connectome to offer. For the past two years, I have been engaged in a different research project that has taken all my professional time.

I am afraid the Kinyanjui Family Foundation would not be able to make a donation to The Institute for Immortality. Its focus is purely Kenyan based at this time on science, the arts, social justice, and the promotion of democracy.

It is with deep regret that I read your account of Dr. Carmichael's last days. I'm assuming you conveyed this to me in confidence. Rest assured that I will keep that confidence.

After Neuro hit SEND on his PQC, he looked to the BioMed Brain Cocoon in the lab, specifically to the picture of Astro—of Dr. Joe Smith—taped there.

"Well, my friend," he addressed the photo, "Am I just a variation on Dr. Carmichael? When the day comes when I will try to communicate with you, will you respond with nothing but gobbledygook? Are you still there? Or are you long gone?"

It was late on a Wednesday night, and Neuro was alone in the lab. The quiet and stillness allowed his words, thoughts, and concerns to resonate. But there was no one in the forest to hear them but himself.

237

"Baba," Neuro said quietly, not knowing why.

22
EXISTENTIAL HYGIENE

On the long flight home from Los Angeles, Neuro studied the Veritas notes of Jim Skinner. Skinner was the young Caltech scientist who had invented the flawed Veritas program. And who had been endeavoring to perfect it when he was killed by a sniper's bullet in a mock anti-science terrorist attack on the campus. So that a motion picture executive with delusions of ultimate power could achieve his dream.

"Whatever your dream is, if you just work hard enough, you can achieve it," millions of parents have told their kids for years. What a damn dangerous idea to plant in an impressionable young mind. Especially in this pulp fiction world Neuro had just come from.

Or had he? Or was he logged into some kind of dream? A fever dream, perhaps, born from the elevated temperature of an obsession?

No. This was real. That mysterious character, The Fixxer, was real. As real as the plane he was encased in, that kept him from falling to his death by exploiting a basic understanding of physics. As real as those stars up above his head. Which he could see through the transparent dome of the plane's cabin, secured by a bionic structure that some engineer, some excellent manipulator of forces and materials, has fashioned.

But were the stars real? Nothing but points of light to him. Long-traveled, long-lived (if that was not ironic) points of light, projecting what was real millions and billions of years ago. But can reality last that long?

The stars. Astro's stars. Illusions of what once was? The brain. Astro's brain. An illusion in Neuro's mind of what once was?

Skinner's notes. The Fixxer's simple explanation of how Veritas worked was accurate but merely hinted at what Skinner's notes revealed. The human brain gave rise to intelligence but was not intelligent itself. It could so easily be fooled. Well, we knew that. Booze, drugs, patterns, past experiences, future desires, a stroke, plaque build-up, and an iron rod could all fool the brain. We don't like to think about it. That who we are—John or Joannie; Antonin or Antoinette; Fadhili or Fatima—are who we are only moment-to-moment. And any old odd moment can quickly derail us from our arrogant sense of selfhood. So thin ourselves under the protection of such a thin atmosphere. We don't like to think that, so people usually don't. Unless your profession, your passion is not just to think about it but also to strive to know it deeply. Even if it pushes you to the brink of despair. An uncomfortable place. Don't go there without packing some comfort. Friendship, love, delights, awe, wonder, and many little packets of funny. Pack them all with your toothbrush. Existential hygiene to go with oral hygiene.

"Popcorn?"

Odongo Njoroge, Neuro's bodyguard companion on this strange trip, held out a bowl of fresh and nicely warm exploded kernels of corn.

"Oh," Neuro said. "I thought I smelled something pleasing. But I thought it was just an illusion."

"You want to take a break from all that reading and see a movie?"

"A real illusion."

"What?"

"No, Odongo, I think I'll keep reading. But do leave the popcorn."

~

Veritas could only work with a living person, a living brain. In reading Skinner's notes, Neuro became convinced of that. It would not work paired with a whole-brain emulation. For it exploited the actual function of the brain. Not just to think, not just to be aware of what's in front of its nose. But to be a second-by-second cartographer of a living body. Mapping what it is experiencing, sensing, and feeling, allowing it to navigate away from discomfort and pain and toward comfort and pleasure. To stand firmly, walk securely, not trip, not fall. To survive. Hopefully, to thrive. And with much good fortune, to know.

Neuro ate the last exploded kernel of corn in the bowl, knowing that Veritas might well give him back his best friend. The knowledge made him drunk and giddy. He felt he could fly. Or, at least, float. Or was he re-experiencing being in the London Eye, in one of the glass-enclosed ovoidal passenger capsules with his father, rising above it all for a clear, long view of the reality before him.

"Baba," Neuro said quietly, knowing why.

23
ON A PEDESTAL

"I'M A BRAIN IN A JAR?"

Astro's shouted question weirdly echoed throughout the Rendezvous Court.

BRAIN IN A JAR—BRAIN IN A JAR—BRAIN IN A JAR—BRAIN IN A JAR—BRAIN IN A JAR.

It was an ample space with a high ceiling, but no sound within it should have echoed like this no matter how loud. The other patrons enjoying afternoon tea at the Biltmore hotel were not bothered. None of them were programmed to hear, except if they happened to be addressed by Astro. They were just part of the atmosphere, the scene, and the surroundings to give verisimilitude to Veritas. And that included their chatter, which never stopped even as the echo bounced from here to there and back again. Nevertheless, it was not right.

Neuro looked off to where he really was and said, "Bring down the reverb, please, Feye. This is a hotel, not the Shimoni Slave Caves."

Unintended though it was, the echo intensified and made poignant Astro's shock born of surprise. His umbrage was blown up to anger. He was made too afraid to suspend his disbelief.

"A brain in a jar," Neuro said, returning his attention to Astro, "is a much too simple way to think of it."

"Is it?"

"Yes."

"Tell me—am I now understanding right?—it's not my whole body that's in your improved BioMed cocoon, small though it is. Or even just my charming red-haired and fairly attractive head. But nothing but my raw, naked, kind of yucky-to-look-at brain?"

"And the brain stem, of course."

"And that's encased in three-feet thick glass?"

"Tempered glass."

Astro threw up his hands and said, "Glass by any other name…." Then he stared at his hands, suddenly mesmerized by them. "So the only digits I have are purely digital digits? And I'm suddenly a tragic character in a bad 1950s black and white sci-fi flick!"

"This is science, Astro, not popular culture." Neuro smiled. Even though he had waited to reveal the truth to his friend, and Astro seemed comfortable in his new reality, Neuro had anticipated this not-happy reaction. But "not happy" he could live with. It was "traumatic" he had strived to avoid.

"I had thought," Astro said, still trying to understand, "That when you said BioMed Brain cocoon, it was like the first cocoon I was in. But only with an emphasis on keeping my brain functioning."

"I told you, your body was a mangled mess. It couldn't be saved."

"It? That 'it' was me, buddy! Not just throw away parts. Or if you had to throw them away, couldn't you have given me a robot body? I might have liked that, outside of the danger of rust."

Neuro was still smiling. "You have retained your humor, Astro. You are you. There is nothing about you that could be tragic. You are just you, the you I have always known. You, in this illusion as good as the illusion of reality your brain provided for thirty-four years before the accident. But you are right. Your body—your torso, arms, legs, organs within and without, nose, ears, eyes, and even your red hair—was also you. Or part of you. Members of the orchestra, that was you. Although that may be a bit of a tortured metaphor. But in any case, we have organized a new orchestra for you."

"Your tortured metaphor is torturing me. Are you saying my brain is just a conductor making music with my body?"

"Yes," Neuro agreed to what the torture was. "You are right, that is not quite the correct metaphor. You see the deficit my lack of understanding music brings. But you like jazz. How many times have you preached improvisation to me? Maybe your brain and body are just members of a jazz band, improvising not individually but as a

243

whole unit—putting out, taking in, responding to each other. And yet, as you have often told me, there is usually a leader, even in the smallest bands?"

The PA system in the Rendezvous Court had been playing Vivaldi in the background but now sent out "Just in Time" by the Gerry Mulligan Quartet.

"Ah," Neuro said. "You can thank Feye for that."

"Who is Feye?"

"He is your guardian angel. He watches over your cocoon in the lab. And he is, I think, making a suggestion. Would you like to go to our lab? So that you can see you."

"I don't know. I have an image of my brain floating in some solution inside a jar."

"Well, get that image out of your head."

"What head?"

The Rendezvous Court began to melt. The Moorish-carved wood ceiling, arching in sections above, seemed to drip down, as did the walls and pillars with all the gold-leaf accents. The rose marble fountain in the middle of the space lost its stature, shrinking as its four streams of water dissipated away. And the famous Baroque stairwell at the back of the court flowed away into nothing as nothing began to surround.

Neuro and Astro remained. Even as their table and the chairs they sat on disappeared. And even as they were involuntarily straightened out and placed in standing positions as a solid illusion of Neuro's lab with its clean white walls, doors made of musheragi hardwood, work areas littered with laptops, and connecting rooms with cylinder imagining machines sprung up around them. It was disorienting for a second or two, then seemed a completely natural environment.

The only other person in the lab was Dr. Feye Naeku. A medium-sized man—somewhere between Neuro and Astro in height—with a deep ebony complexion, especially along his domed hairless head, came forward eagerly. He outstretched his hand toward Astro. "I am so very pleased to meet you, Dr. Smith," he said as Astro's hand filled his and both applied the proper pressure.

"This is marvelous," Feye said with an excited grin. "I can feel your skin; I can touch." He turned and put a hand on a wall. "Nothing here, Dhambi."

"Tactile walls were not, I think, a great priority in constructing this digital scene, Feye. But I am sure the team can get to it. But how often will Dr. Smith want to come here?"

"I don't know," Astro said. "What do you serve?"

"More Indian food than I care to ingest," Feye said, then laughed, the joke being on Neuro.

"Come," Neuro said. "We are not here to ingest."

Neuro led them into a small square room, at the center of which, resting on a block of polished musheragi hardwood, sat a cube of tempered glass. There was another cube of dull white biofoam within. It was the BioMed brain cocoon encasing Astro's brain. On each side of the glass cube, three thick wires were attached. All emanated from connections to a bank of quantum computers placed along three of the room's walls. Within the glass cube, hundreds of bright silver filaments extended out from the inside walls of the glass cube, and their other ends were embedded into the biofoam of the BioMed brain cocoon. Everything—the room, the computers, the glass cube, the cube of biofoam—seemed clean, polished, slick, and antiseptic. The only thing that seemed out of place was a slighted faded with two bent corners photo of Dr. Joe Smith.

Astro stared at the cube within the cube, imagining his raw, naked, kind of yucky-to-look-at brain within. It was a weird tale. An amazing story. Not a fantasy and not science fiction. But the hard analog base of a digital reality of illusion. He was feeling something. But he had no idea what it was. For he had no reference to inform him, no real grasp on the fact that he was standing there—"there" being but a construct—staring at a reality that was more surreal than real. So he pulled back his imagination from within the cocoon to think only of the cubes. Their surfaces, the dull white, bubble pockmarked surface of the brain cocoon, the shiny, slick, brightly reflective surface of the tempered glass cocoon. The cubes resting on a block of polished musheragi hardwood (Zawadi's influence?). And, of course, the picture that seemed to float on the glass at eye level, the image of him, short-in-stature him, red-headed him in a favorite suit, smiling his Irish smile of charm.

"Well, Neuro," Astro said after this time of contemplation. "I always knew you liked me, maybe even loved me as a boon companion, but did you really have to put me on a pedestal?"

24
THE TRUTH OF VERITAS

"The computer on the right wall holds and maintains your WBE," Neuro said.

"What the bloody blue blazes! You said I wasn't in a WBE. I thought my spongey self was in that cocoon?"

Neuro chuckled. Astro had never seen Neuro chuckle. Smile, yes. Laugh happily, yes. Even guffaw. But never chuckle. Neuro had always been either slightly amused or struck in the gut with the comic. But he had never just chuckled. And the worst of it was, he chuckled delightfully.

"I thought that would get you," Neuro said, coming out of the chuckle. "In that computer is not a Whole Brain Emulation, but a Whole *Body* Emulation. We took your DNA, many photos and videos of you, and just general human anatomy and constructed a digital body for you. Which is manifested in—well, in the body you seem to be standing in right now."

"So it's just an illusion to fool me?"

"No. It is much more than an illusion. It is a body, truly a *whole* body. Interior and exterior organs, nerves and nerve endings, hormones, proteins, cells, DNA, RNA, bacteria, even hair. And not just on your head. Did you notice this morning that you finally have hair on your chest?"

Astro opened up his shirt, saw the chest hair, and then looked up at Neuro. "Today, I am a man," he declared with a couple layers of meaning.

"It was our final touch."

"But why, Neuro? Why so detailed? Hell, you could have made me nothing but a stick figure, and as long as I had my mind in my spongey brain, as long as I was me, it would have been okay, wouldn't it?"

"No. That is our big discovery. Or rather, confirmation of the theories and hypotheses of others who came before. To find your mind, your subjective self, we had to reconnect your brain with your body. As we no longer had your body, we had to build a facsimile that could fool your brain."

"Fool it?"

"Yes. The brain, especially the human brain, is a marvelous thing. But it is easy to influence, manipulate, and fool. Well, you know that. You have been drunk often enough, my friend. The brain lives, so to speak, to monitor and manage. To map the body's functions. And its interior and exterior environments. To respond to signals from the nervous system. And to signal back appropriately. All to achieve homeostasis. To, hopefully, move away from pain and to move toward pleasure. Or maybe well-being would be the better way to put it. In any case, simple terms for something actually more complex, but they suffice. In the higher beings on this planet, what the brain does creates minds. In us, consciousness arises, a subjective sense of self. The you that you think of as you—your thoughts, your desires, your loves, your hate, your attractions, your fears—do not exist in some vacuum we used to call a soul. And which some now call consciousness. And certainly not as some 'program' your brain has written and which can be uploaded to a computer, pure and unadulterated by bodily functions. Your mind, your consciousness, and your *self*, cannot exist without your body because it is an inseparable part of your body. We had to return your brain to a body for it to fulfill its function and allow you to be you again."

"Well, it's good to know that the late and lamented, by some, I'm sure, Brandon Carmichael was always wrong, and I was always right."

"Does that please you?"

"Not particularly. My position was not really scientific, was it? It was just a sentiment of rationality."

"True."

"But wait a minute. If you can make a whole body emulation, why not a whole-brain emulation and pair the two."

"The brain is so complex. If it can be done, it will not be for years."

"And what would be the point?"

"Well, what did Brandon really want?"

"Not to be meat, it seems. And not to be meat forever."

"Yes. But he was also hoping, I believe, for an instant exponential growth in intelligence."

"What's the fun in that? I'd rather strive for knowledge than have it handed to me."

"Well, that's probably all we can hope for anyway."

Feye, who had quietly listened to Neuro and Astro's dialog, entered the discussion. "Why does that sound sad?"

"Because people are idiots for perfection," Astro said. "They're always looking for a paradise. They want to snuggle in the bosom of a god, or find perfect goodness, or complete knowledge of everything, instead of negotiating as best possible Shakespeare's slings and arrows."

"Evolution has brought us forth as very contradictory beings, don't you think?" Neuro put forth. "To survive, we sometimes harm others. But also, at times, we find that cooperating with others secures survival. Trying to understand why, especially in the days when we understood so little, led to the false classifications we called evil and good. Facing our capacity to do both—harm and cooperate—tends to confuse us. As did so much else in the past. Life is wonderful. What a great gift! But then why does it have to be mean, brutish, and short? We feel ourselves to be so real, so solid, so substantial. And yet a sharp piercing shaft can destroy us. A submicroscopic nonliving complex molecule can infect us and cause us to shut off. To just shut down, lights off. A drug can cause our—to us—immutable subjective self to suddenly become someone else. A breath of air rearranging a gossamer web. I cannot blame Carmichael for pursuing perfection, even immortality."

"You don't have to," Astro said with a laugh, "I've always been perfectly capable of doing it myself."

"Yes, well—Brandon is gone now."

"Ever to return?" Astro asked, oblivious to the slight sadness with which Neuro had spoken.

"*You* think not. So why should I answer?"

Was it a rebuke? Astro took it as such. Neuro's intellectual flirtation with Carmichael had always made Astro intellectually jealous. Not that, until this very moment, had he ever understood that. He was just being judgemental and gleefully prejudiced—thoroughly human emotions. While never realizing—again, until just this moment—that Neuro had always been empathetic, even compassionate toward Carmichael and his deep desire to live, be, exist, and not give up the ghost forever. Also, a human emotion. But, well, gee, Astro thought, how was he to know? Neuro had never been one to openly express his feelings. It was probably all the tee shirts he wore when they first met. Tee-shirts do not have enough sleeves to wear your emotions on. So how does he address all of this now? He, Astro, a three-pound spongy mass connected to a digital body. Manifested as his thirty-four year old self when, if there had been no crash, he would be a fleshy forty-five. He wasn't sure. But there was always the option of avoidance.

"So, um, there are two other computers in the room. What do they do?"

"Feye?" Neuro said, giving his colleague a chance to contribute.

"Oh, well, Dr. Smith—"

"Call me Joe."

"Okay. Thank you. I have tended to think of you as Joe."

"Joe in the jar?"

"Astro!" Was it another rebuke from Neuro?

"Uh…" Feye needed to cut through the atmosphere with just a rendition of the facts. "The computer against the back wall holds all the digital scene simulations our graphics team has created. Your home, The Hole, now the Biltmore, or at least the Rendezvous Court. And there's more coming."

"Really? What?"

"Later," Neuro said, putting him off.

Feye continued. "And the computer on the left monitors and manages all the facsimile neuro connections between uh, your, um —"

"Yucky brain."

"Astro!"

"Yes," Feye continued, "your brain and your WBE and all the digital environments."

"Essentially, Astro, this computer fools your brain into believing —if that word applies—that it is receiving all the regular neuro inputs it received—"

"When it was in my gorgeous red-haired head."

"Well, my friend, red-haired, at least," Neuro smiled, enjoying the banter. "This computer, linked with the other two, allows your brain to do its job, mapping the millisecond by millisecond condition of your body within and the environment without. And to respond appropriately to what that mapping tells it. It allows you to see, hear, and touch. It is told that your "organs" are functioning as they should with no ill effects. Although, if you wish we could give you the pain of an oversized gallstone, or the nausea of eating and drinking too much."

"No, thank you."

"This computer, coordinating all of this, frees up your imagination, memories, and creativity, allowing you to contribute to the loop."

"Putting faces on those walking dummies on the street, right?"

"Exactly. Faces and, eventually, when you interact with them, personalities of a kind. But then, most people we deal with superficially or intimately are just characters in our story, are they not? Do we not 'assign' them their roles? Do we ever know anyone as deeply as we know ourselves?"

"But outside of that," Feye added, "you will have your full intellectual and imaginative capabilities to do your work in astronomy, with all the inspiration you can call forth."

"So, I have a life?"

"Yes. You are alive."

"In my own little pocket universe."

"Well, yes," Neuro said. "That is true."

"And you guys, you and Feye, right now, are visiting my pocket universe."

"We are?"

"But where are you really?"

"We are both in another part of the lab, reclining in special chairs, connected to the Veritas system."

"Veritas? Cute. Truth. And where did it come from? Did you invent it, Neuro? You and your team?"

"No. Where it came from is a hell of a story. One for some other time. But we put together Veritas and developed it from a flawed base. We improved it and brought it to this level of function."

"All to give me—little old me—life in a pocket universe, otherwise known as a glass jar? All the time, all the money spent, all the effort put out, just so Dr. Joe Smith, a perfectly nice guy, a fairly competent scientist, on occasion a charming companion—but of no special value beyond any other poor schmuck on Earth—just so Dr. Joe Smith can continue to exist? Now, how the fuck do you expect me to live this digital life knowing that? I wasn't raised Catholic, but I probably am part Irish, so why would you want to kick in my genetic propensity for guilt like that?"

Neuro took a moment. Then said, "Feye, please return Joe and me to the Rendezvous Court."

As Neuro's lab began to melt to be replaced by the Rendezvous Court, Feye, fading away, said, "It's been a pleasure to meet you, Dr. Smith."

Then Astro and Neuro were sitting at their table in the Rendezvous Court. The other patrons were happily going about having their high tea, their indecipherable chatter the only sound until Astro said, "That guy needs to get a life."

25
LIFE IN A JAR

"Astro, you have nothing to feel guilty about."

"Why did you do it, Neuro? Why?"

"Well," Neuro said, then took his eyes off of Astro, raised his head, and stared a little off to the left, up to the curve of the ornate ceiling. "That is a question."

"Yes, that is a question, isn't it? Which I'm sure was made plain by the tone of my voice, by the way I said it, striving to punctuate it with an almost visible question mark. But the real question is, what the bloody blue blazes are you ignoring it for?"

"I am not ignoring it, Astro. I am trying to form an answer."

"You shouldn't have to form it. It should be right there, ready to leap off your tongue!"

"And yet..."

"Neuro!"

"I—I couldn't let you die."

"Was that your choice?"

"It was in my power."

"But everything else—nature, fate or a random accident, that doctor, hell, for all I know, the universe itself said, 'Hey, this guy is a mangled mess, better toss him away.' I wouldn't have known the difference. I would have been okay with it."

"There is a contradiction in what you just—"

"Don't get technical."

Neuro now looked down to the white table cloth, the china cup, the last drops of tea in the cup. "Feye, return us to Dr. Smith's home."

A fading melt, a quick reformation, and they sat at Astro's dining table in his apartment. It was quiet. Astro, fully acclimated to the malleability of his digital world, had not jerked in surprise or expelled a startled breath. He just sat still, focused on this representation of his old friend, and thickened the atmosphere with anticipation.

Neuro stood, rising to tower over. But not for effect, nor did it affect. He moved away from the table and began to pace. After several steps, he began to talk.

"I suppose it was because I harbored an atavistic, residual, certainly subconscious belief in the soul. Your soul, Astro. Usually, people believe in souls because of their subjective experience of themselves. You know, I think therefore I am. I am whole, complete unto myself, individual, unique unto myself. That never impressed me personally. Or wouldn't have if I had ever thought about it. And when my father was attacked, they attacked, physically, his brain. To stop his mind. Being shocked over the fragility of both brain and mind led me to study neurobiology."

"Would you stop pacing, Neuro? You're wearing a groove in my digital floor."

Neuro stopped with a question on his face.

"Sit in the easy chair," Astro gently commanded. "I'll go sit on the couch."

Both men moved to their respective corners. Then Neuro continued.

"As you know, I had a…. A sheltered childhood, I suppose one would say. Certainly a protected one. Surrounded mainly by family. Later in school, the other students were all of the same cloth to me. That none of them became close friends is evident by the fact that I have never cared to keep in touch with them. At Oxford, I was intense in my studies. Friends would have been a distraction. And then I came to USC and met you. A little red-headed mole, newly above ground and blossoming into this most unique character. This singular self. At first, you amused me. Then you impressed me. You were a nut."

"Hey!"

"No, I do not mean crazy or silly. I mean a seed in a hard shell. A most charming personality in a most well-defined outer, shall we say, garment."

"Shall we say, stylish garment?"

Neuro laughed a quick and loud laugh. "Yes. We shall."

"But was my garment a reflection of me? Or was I a reflection of my garment?"

"Ah, my friend, you are always quick to understand. I was believing, unconsciously, the former, when all my studies, my whole career was focused on the latter."

"So when my garment was mangled into a mess ...."

"Yes. I thought it was easily discarded. As long as you, Astro, the seed inside the garment, survived. My friend. My most unique friend. Who made my life richer by his presence."

"I didn't know you were so damn sentimental."

"Neither did I."

"I...," Astro began but could not finish what probably no longer needed to be said. He said instead, "I'm hungry."

"Feye can solve that with a quick—"

"No! I want to eat. I want to masticate. I want to chew foodstuff between my teeth. I want texture in my mouth. I want to know I am alive."

"Mac and cheese and tuna?"

"No, my friend—Indian."

～

The chicken tikka masala, the crisp papadum, the lamb vindaloo, the kofta, and, of course, the lassi had long been created by Dahmbi's team in a quantum space just waiting for the day Neuro might ask for the meal while digitally visiting Astro. While Neuro and Astro were enjoying the food, its tastes, textures, heat, and coolness, Neuro knew it was just an illusion. In his brain and body in the special recliner chair in his lab. But he also knew that it was more than an illusion for Astro. For the elements of such a meal that, in reality, flooded a body once ingested—the vitamins, the proteins, the starch—had been recreated in Veritas as information. Information sent to Astro's whole body emulation. Which Astro's brain happily monitored, fooling the quantum/digital body that didn't actually require nutrition, that it had just been nourished. Then those pertinent areas of the WBE happily reported the nourishment to Astro's brain. Both brain and WBE were happily pleased with the well-being being felt.

~

After some moments of quietly enjoying the satisfaction of the meal, Astro said, "But why shouldn't I feel guilty?"

"What," Neuro said, leaning back in the easy chair, his long legs extending out straight. He had just been on the verge of nodding off.

"You said I had no reason to feel guilty. Money, resources, time, people's intelligent efforts all spent just for little ol' me? What the bloody blue blazes! Of course, I feel guilty."

Neuro sat straight, planting his feet flat on the floor. "That is because you are ill-informed about the great spinoffs in data, knowledge, and even practical applications that have come from our efforts to perfect Veritas and connect it to you."

"Oh." Astro could not let it go, could not bypass a moment to poke at his friend. Not in anger or dismay or umbrage. But in that kind of kidding affection that good friends often practiced. Practiced until they got it right. "So, I'm just a lab rat, am I?"

"Well, you reside in the lab, and you have a nickname. And some on my team think you are cute. But have you ever seen a rat with red hair?"

"A mutant rat from Mars?"

"No. A space program."

"What kind of a non sequitur is that?"

"Think about it—*Astro*—think about it."

~

Much like in real life, an existence most people have no choice but to live, Astro settled down into this manufactured and manipulated existence. Trusting in Neuro and his team to look out for him, to collaborate with his desires and needs. Which real-life did not always do. He was one up on the universe, and he supposed that was good.

~

Now that he could, Astro began to take walks in his neighborhood. Something he had always enjoyed doing in his spare moments. But now, it was almost an obligation. Neuro's team had put out such effort to recreate it that it would have been rude not to enjoy it. And he did, although in a different way than he had before. It was fun watching the *Homo things* pop into familiarity as they walked by. Becoming other people—men and boys; women and girls, generally speaking, young and old and often somewhere between. They walked, they rushed, they stood in groups and talked and laughed. They entered stores and restaurants and exited. Any good urban person usually passes others without acknowledging them with eye contact or a smile. As Astro himself had typically done. But here, in his own little world, he made eye contact and smiled at others to satisfy a slight ache. At first, the others passing in the street ignored this. But soon, Astro's imagination, running the loop between his brain, his WBE, and Veritas, churned out responses from the others. And they began to smile back, then wave, then greet with age-old articulations—*Hello! Hi! Good Day! Your servant! Salutations! Cheers! Howdy! Nice to see you! How are you!*—as they walked on by. Then they began to stop and address him by name—*Dr. Smith. What'cha know, Joe? Professor*—and waited for Astro to answer.

When he did, each of the others became individualized. And often recognizable as colleagues, actors from film and TV, people he had met on his childhood field trips with Aunt Liz. And once, quite freakily, Aunt Liz herself. That was too much, too weird, too… He wiped her away with a gesture of his hand and began to cry. To cry? Crying? Among his tears, he found himself saying, "My Aunt Liz has passed away."

Joey, I died. I am dead. Happens to people every day. I didn't just pass away or fade from the scene. I died.

It was Aunt Liz's voice. The tears were wet. He could feel the wet. He inhaled in a reflex, and Veritas told his brain that precious air was flowing into his lungs and told his WBE to be revived by it. And his brain was happy that all was functioning normally.

~

Time is relative. Everyone knows that. Or have been informed of it. Or have, on occasion, felt it. Even if they hold on to seconds, minutes, and hours; days, weeks, and months; years and decades. But for Astro, time was more relative than not in his Veritas world. He would work in his observatory at The Hole. Observing, noting, shifting data, analyzing, wondering, hypothesizing, concluding, for what an outside observer would count as far too many hours, several days at a time, often more than a week, before deciding to stop. He did not really need to sleep. But his brain did. Veritas would inform his brain once a day that it had slept for eight hours, and his brain believed it. Astro would only feel sleepy and crawl in bed when Neuro's team needed to install upgrades or do maintenance. Which was a good thing, as there was an absolute pleasure in waking up and feeling rested.

~

Neuro was on the big screen in The Hole, and he asked Astro, "Would you like to climb Mt. Everest?"

"What the bloody blue blazes for?" Astro responded between bites of his peanut butter and pickle sandwich.

"The adventure, the challenge."

"Don't be ridiculous. I'm on the cusp of some exciting astronomical observations. That's adventure enough for me."

"Yes. But my team has just finished creating Mt. Everest in Veritas, and they would like to know how good it is."

"You want the lab rat to run up the mountain?"

"They hope the exhilaration will create a flood of endorphins in your brain. And they want to study that."

"No, thank you. Sounds like a lot of effort, all that climbing. Hell, I don't even like climbing stairs. If nature wanted us to climb, it wouldn't have given us the capacity to invent escalators."

"Astro, please. Can they at least put you on the top of the mountain and see how your brain reacts? I understand the view is stunning."

Astro blew out a breath of acquiescence. "Oh, okay."

Then Astro, in a complete mountain climbing, body heat-retaining outfit with a fur-lined hoodie, was standing at the very summit of Mt. Everest. He looked around at the knobbly white field of mountain peaks popping out of cloud cover that seemed to extend into infinity. "Very nice," he said. "Now can I get back to my peanut butter and pickle sandwich, please?"

~

"Hello, guess what?" Neuro said as he walked into Astro's observatory.

"What the!" Astro looked up as he gasped a nice startled breath. "Crap! You scared the crap out of me." He had for two, relatively speaking, non-stop weeks been deep into studying readouts of observations of a newly found binary black hole. His mind had definitely been somewhere else.

"I've been in The Hole making you lunch."

"Lunch? Me? Making it?"

"Mac and cheese. I used Aunt Liz's recipe."

"Well, it's hardly a recipe. Just add no milk but a lot of butter."

"Still, I thought it would be appropriate as we celebrate."

Astro was reluctant to leave the data, but he was suddenly hungry. Probably thanks to Feye twiddling with some dial. "What are we celebrating? The fact that I'm starting to get some gray hairs."

"Feye just wanted to add some verisimilitude."

"Well, that's kind of him."

"You are no longer a beamish boy."

"I'm no longer a—"

"Let us go. The mac and cheese is getting cold."

They walked out of the observatory into the reception area, then into the large elevator. Astro asked, "So what are we celebrating?" as they descended into The Hole.

"I've established a collaborative relationship with the observatory at the International Mars Colony. I thought you might enjoy talking to the people there."

As they sat down to two hot bowls of macaroni and cheese, Astro was struck by a feeling he had not previously known. "You know what? I think I would. I think that would be fun. To talk to people on another planet. What's their focus at their observatory?"

"I have no idea. I only know their telescope is in orbit around Mars. But here is the best part of it. I've arranged for your contact there to be Makena Wafula."

"Who?"

"You don't remember Makena Wafula?"

"Hey, I'm just a brain in a jar. Cut me some slack. This is good, by the way. You made good mac and cheese. Thanks!"

"You are more than welcome. Makuna Wafula was with us on our night under the star's trip."

"Oh, yes. You said one of the students got to go to Mars."

"Correct. Makena is the one. And she is very excited to be your contact."

"Excited? Or weirdly curious?"

~

When the link was made between the International Mars Colony and Veritas in Neuro's lab, and thus with Astro, an introductory meet was arranged. Astro sat in his aunt's old easy chair (or rather the quite reasonable facsimile thereof), looking up at the large curved screen on the wall. As he waited for it to come alive, he thought about this two hundred plus million-mile communication. Once a technological marvel, it was now a mostly mundane occurrence. Astro guessed he was the technological marvel now. Or rather everything surrounding his spongy self in the jar.

The screen lit up, and there was the attractive face of Dr. Makena Wafula, big-eyed and wide smile, both beaming across the two hundred million plus miles.

"Hello, Dr. Smith!"

"Please, Dr. Wafula, call me Joe."

"Okay. And I am, of course, Makena."

"Done. Old pals already."

Neuro had sent Astro several documents on Dr. Wafula. Her CV, her official International Mars Colony bio, several papers she had authored or co-authored, and some press she had received. He found the scope of her mind that they revealed fascinating. But he was struck by how often she mentioned their night under the stars in the articles. She called it an essential inspiration for her. Especially in her development as an astronomer. It gave him pause—assuming there was such a thing as a pause in his personal relativity-of-time. But then it really wasn

t a pause. It was more of being—yes—moved. Even as a teacher, he had never thought of his effect on anyone, positive or negative. He had always done what he had done for pure selfish joy, even if he bored his students. So this sudden revelation that his doing was not always attended by collateral narcoleptic damage, but possibly something like the opposite, moved him in his little glass jar. "Hey," he said to himself, "I'm Mr. Chips in a jar!"

Was he also James Bond in a jar? Even though he was impressed by this woman's breadth and depth of mind, intelligence, and analytical abilities, she was still a woman. An attractive woman of bright ebony skin, high cheekbones, liquid eyes, a ready smile, a melodious voice, and a certain sensual quality not diminished, it seemed, by being two hundred million plus miles away.

Astro hadn't thought of women for quite a while. Was that Neuro's doing? Or Feye's? Had they digitally blocked, or not even programed in, raw hormonal responses to the idea of sex? Maybe they thought it would be merciful to do so, given that he was…

But he was thinking about sex now. Even though he should have just been having a pleasant conversation with a new colleague.

"Ah, so, Makena, tell me about your work there on Mars. I mean, why is there even a telescope orbiting Mars? I thought you guys were just interested in planetary research and the possibility of terraforming. Not to mention mining and what-have-you."

"Well, Joe, we are a colony, not just a research station. We are looking to the future, to have every capability that earth has to satisfy our own curiosity. That is why I am here."

"But can't you just get the info and data from Earth? I mean, I can't be the only fellow astronomer you are in contact with."

"Certainly. But would you be happy with just receiving data and not looking for yourself?"

"No, that's true."

"Plus, Earth may not always be there."

Astro was shocked to hear such words. "Makena, I didn't know you were such a pessimist."

"Not a pessimist. Just pragmatic."

~

Most of the conversations between Astro and Makena focused on astronomy and their work and the technical and scientific questions they had for each other. The communications lag time between Earth and Mars being an average of twelve and a half minutes, didn't really allow for anything more chit-chatting or chewing-of-the-fat. But eventually, the planets were both on the same side of the sun and were closer to each other. Which brought the lag time down to a little over three minutes. Makena took advantage of this to ask if she could ask a personal question.

"No, I'm not seeing anyone right now," Astro quickly and flippantly said.

"That is not what I meant," a smiling Makena responded three minutes-plus later. "I am just curious as to how your life goes. You are the ultimate pioneer, living an existence, unlike anyone ever has. I know that Dr. Kinyanjui and his team have strived to make your life as normal as possible, but still...."

"Well, Makena, whatever this existence is, I have gotten used to it. It is the relativity of time that I had to really adjust to. Neuro—you know I call Dr. Kinyanjui Neuro, right? University nickname. Well, in any case, Neuro tells me I will sometimes work weeks on end without a break. Then he forces me to sleep. I don't perceive the time at all. It's just the work—data inputs, analysis, deep thinking—that I perceive. It wasn't until we started our conversations, you and me, that I realized that I needed to round out my life. Even though we talk about our work, and I usually work during the lag times, I have found a certain relaxation in our conversations. Sometimes, during the lag times, I do nothing. Just sit and—well, not even think, I think. I mean, sure, I think, but not in any structured way. Random thoughts, memories, feelings even. I have looked for some other, uh, activities to engage in for, um, you know, fun and relaxation. But you know what I really miss? Books. In the original Hole—you know about The Hole, right? Of course, you do. I know that the first buildings in your colony were all Vivian Fleming Mars Habitats. Do you know that Vivian Fleming was my Aunt Liz's wife, and The Hole was the original Vivian Fleming Mars Habitat prototype? Well, yes, you probably do. But my point here is that in the original Hole, we had a library of books that was my grandfather's and Aunt Liz's. Neuro and his people have done a wonderful job recreating The Hole. But when I went to the library to get a book, they were nothing but digital facades. My hand went right through them; you couldn't pull one out, much less hold it and read it. I keep meaning to ask Neuro about it, but I keep forgetting. So many other things to think about. This has all been a long-winded way of saying that I would love to just sit in a chair and read a book. Fiction mainly, I think. You know, the original virtual reality."

When the large, curved screen lit up with Makena's face three minutes-plus later, her smile was broader than usual, and her eyes just beamed. "I have the solution to your problem, Joe!"

"What problem?" Joe asked, having, in the three minutes, forgotten what he had been talking about.

"Books, Joe! I can get you any book you want."

"Really? How in the bloody blue blazes can you do that?"

"When I was nominated to be the Kenyan member of the colony, part of the requirements was to bring something to the colony besides our core skills or profession. Some ideas, talent, or food recipes. Even something odd, they said. Something roundly human, they requested. I did not know what that should be; what had I to offer besides my learning and passion for astronomy? It was Dr. Kinyanjui's wife, Dr. Zawadi Mital, who came up with the idea.

"You know, she has little interest in space exploration. She is very, shall we say, Earth-bound? Have you read her poetry? It is about small human experiences as we exist on a very material planet. That's not an original thought. It was in a blurb on one of her books. I like her poetry. For one always looking out millions and billions of miles, it can be a nice, uh, mind-shift, I guess, to focus on something small and constrained. No! Not constrained, just contained. I'm not getting to the point, am I? Sorry. What I mean to tell you is that she proposed that my contribution should be a digital library of world literature, art, music, dance, film, and theater. She said that humans should not go off to other planets without taking our humanity with us. As you might expect from a humanities professor. But, of course, she was right. A few colony leaders thought the idea was irrelevant to the mission, but they were overruled.

"Everybody here in the colony can call up any book in its original language or translated into one of the major languages. Well, not any, but a good many, millions of them, in all genres. I think it would not be a problem to allow you a colony library card to download any book you want. It will take some time to download, but, as you said, time is more than relative for you. So, Joe, would you like a card for the Bradbury Library?"

Why didn't Neuro think of something like this? Astro wondered. But then Astro hadn't complained about not having books to Neuro. And Neuro's first thoughts rarely went towards artistic endeavors, even being married to Zawadi. Digital copies of the world's great art? Why not? But did he have to go to Mars to get them? Why not? Being a repository for another planet, maybe it was more inclusive and exhaustive than any such digital library on Earth.

"Makena, do you have *The Wind in the Willows*? If you have that, then yes, please sign me up. I guess they named it the Bradbury Library because of *The Martian Chronicles?*"

"No, not really," Makena answered three-plus minutes later. "It's because of an old book from the 1960s that Dr. Mital found in a London bookshop. *If the Sun Dies* by Oriana Fallaci. She was an Italian journalist fascinated by the nascent U.S. space program. However, she was trying to answer her father's question about why we should bother with space when there were still so many problems on Earth. So she went to America to interview people involved in the program. But the first person she went to see was Ray Bradbury because he was known as a cheerleader for the space program. And he said something like, If the sun dies, and, of course, the Earth, then Shakespeare dies, you know, and Homer, and I think he mentions Da Vinci and Einstein and Galileo. No Africans, of course, but that's not surprising. His point was made. Of course, we know now that the sun will not die for billions of years. But the Earth? So, Dr. Mital said, don't just save humans, save the humanities. She was, of course, somewhat biased, but, again, a strong point was made.

Don't you think so?"

~

Astro found he looked forward to his video talks with Makena, interrupted by dead air (or vacuum, if you will) though they were. It began to make time for him a little less relative as the talks had to be scheduled. Feye was his timekeeper, counting down for Astro the time remaining—weeks, days, hours, minutes—when the next one would be. This punctuated his time, demarcated it, and he came to call it his Makena Clock.

Makena was, of course, extremely intelligent, knowledgeable in her research area, creative in her work, and in responding to Astro's. Each talk was illuminating, often challenging, and always, finally, delightful, even if it was a talk that cosmologically stuttered.

Makena became a valued colleague.

But Astro never stopped seeing her as a woman. For she was a beautiful one. And he always had a great appreciation for beautiful women. A purely biological response. He knew that. And in his past, the lack of it when communicating professionally or frivolously with women not beautiful by specific community standards never deterred him from appreciating their other attributes. Intelligence, charm, wit, professional passion, and basic humanity. And no beauty less than a compassionate human, a bright mind, a person of good humor or— in an antiquated sense—good bodily humors, would he allow to waste his time.

Astro felt no guilt when he noted and admired her physical beauty in the middle of the scholarly communications between him and Makena.

He also noted that she wore make-up. Which seemed odd. An astronomer on Mars, living and working in a pioneering colony, applying vanity to her face? He didn't think pioneer women in America's westward expansion wore make-up. He wanted to ask her about it. He almost did several times but found he just couldn't. It certainly wasn't relative to any of their discussions. But then, on Makena's birthday, Astro scheduled a call to wish her a happy one. He found her relaxed and comfortable. And pleased that the colonists had baked her a cake.

"Makena, can I ask you a personal question? Something I've been curious about. I'm not going to wait for your answer; I'm just going to assume I can. I notice you wear make-up. In a way, I've always been fascinated by make-up on women. Especially women who don't really need it. You know, natural beauties, like you are. Of course, I'm speaking quite objectively here. Anyway, you are on Mars, in a colony, trying to survive in a hostile environment. Is make-up a resource you really need?"

There was at this time an eight-minute communications lag between Mars and Earth, and Astro spent the bulk of it regretting that he had asked such a stupid question. But when Mekena appeared once again on the giant curved screen in The Hole, she was laughing.

"You know, Joe, my mother always said that she never felt completely herself until 'I put my face on in the morning.' I am definitely her daughter. I guess it's a simple fact that men strive always to put their best foot forward. And women strive to put their best face forward. And as to my living here in a hostile environment where other things should take precedence... Well, Joe, everybody on Earth is living in the hostile environment of the solar system, the galaxy. If you think about it, the universe really doesn't want us around, does it? Maybe make-up for a woman is the brave face she presents to the universe. All I know is, I can't be me, every one of the MEs that I am, without my 'face.' And, as long as it's not a false face, what's the harm? And thank you for the compliment. You are one of the sweetest men I've ever known. Even if you are just a 'brain in a jar,' as you like to put it."

∼

A brain in a jar. Astro contemplated this after his birthday conversation with Makena. Well, they always said sex was more mental than physical. But it was the physical he was thinking of. And touch. And hugging, especially hugging. He suddenly realized he missed hugging. And, of course, other things. Did Neuro and Feye have anything to do with this? Did they turn the dial up? Or was it just a testament to the whole body emulation they built for him? Was his WBE ready for copulation, if not replication? It didn't really matter. Besides his mind focused on the mysteries of the universe, he now had a great desire for the physical companionship of women.

He took a day off—not that he really knew what a day was anymore—and walked around his neighborhood in his digital downtown L.A. He noticed that almost all of the *Homo things* passing by were women. But then, that was what was on his mind. Soon though, they became "real" women of his past acquaintance, even if that acquaintance was via antique filmed entertainment. *Myrna!*

Also Susan, Lysee, Donna, Trudy, a biologist, a political scientist, a professor of engineering, a drama professor. And Zoey, the bartender who was also a civic activist. And Maude, old-fashioned, not just in name. And Iris, the florist (you're kidding?), was as delicate as a petal but as insistent as a perennial.

And Kimberly! Kimberly, the economist who believed in the *tickle* down theory and gave him his first taste of the pleasures of the flesh.

Pleasures of the flesh? This is absurd, Astro thought as all these women walked by and smiled at him. What flesh? What pleasure? The joy of the zeros? The thrill of the ones? Digital sex when you really didn't have any digits to touch tender flesh with, be tender with, have the tactile signal satisfaction to the brain.

"But, Joe, sex is really all mental."

It was Kimberly. Kimberly came up to him, looked him in the eyes, smiled, then took his hand—so damn tactile!

"It doesn't feel that way," Joe said.

"Feel this way," Kimberly countered as she kissed him. "Now walk this way," she said, leading him back to this condo.

It was like the first time all over again.

And they did it over again and over again and over again.

Astro was beginning to appreciate the attributes of Veritas.

But there was also, besides sexual behavior, cognitive behavior—talk, conversation, communication, ideas imparted and understood, arguments, agreements, meetings of the minds. But, most importantly, laughter.

And hugging. Just that. Hugging. Clinging together in an uncertain universe. A universe, as Makena said, that didn't really want us around.

26
NOT IN OUR STARS, BUT IN OURSELVES

Did Astro have a good life? Being a brain in a glass jar wrapped in the illusion that he had a flesh and blood body? Was this actually a life, much less a good life?

He experienced more well-being than pain, which is undoubtedly what a good life should be.

His intellectual pursuits bore fruit and excited, satisfied, and led to new knowledge.

He was extending his knowledge of the carnal, despite not being carnal, except for his spongy self of organic matter. This certainly added to his well-being. And where should knowledge of anything reside but in his spongy self?

He truly enjoyed masticating various foods, believing texture to be as important as taste. Even though he knew he wasn't really ingesting them. And that his nourishment was under the control of Neuro and his team. Which they delivered as information to his whole body emulation via Veritas. Which then was noted by his spongy self. And his spongy self received actual nourishing stuff via the beauties of the BioMed biofoam cocoon.

He enjoyed digital visits from Neuro, his best friend. They ate together, had long conversations, and often looked at pictures of Neuro and Zawadi's three children. Often because the children kept getting older, taller, growing away from childhood toward adulthood.

He continued to enjoy his collaboration with Makena Wafula. They published papers together; went to virtual conferences together.

Astro reveled in the beautiful fact that he did not have to do strenuous physical exercises to remain fit and healthy. His WBE just had to be informed that he had. This was a significant advantage in being but a brain in a jar!

Neuro and his team offered him entertainment and diversions— travel, lectures, theater, movies. But he was judicious in accepting them, not wanting to take time away from his work, sex, reading, and eating. Which was an emotional decision only as time was not really a problem for him as it was for everyone else.

And he continued to listen with great joy and satisfaction to the music of Henry Mancini. He was possibly the last human entity left on Earth that did. But he hoped not. How could the world possibly be fine without the Pink Panther?

It was a good life.

A very good life.

So, of course, something had to upset it.

∼

In 2090, Neuro, now entirely gray, suddenly appeared in Astro's home. He had not knocked on Astro's door as he usually did to maintain a sense of the normal. But just appeared, out of thin digital air, startling Astro, who was relaxing with a good book.

"What the bloody blue blazes!"

"I am sorry, my friend," Neuro said calmly but with a peculiar catch in his voice.

"What's wrong?" Astro was struck with fear for his friend. "Zawadi? The children?"

Neuro walked over to Astro and sat in one of the easy chairs. "They are fine. The problem is a bit more...global."

"What problem isn't?"

"Too true," Neuro acknowledged, then slumped into himself, taking a moment to hide from the world. Astro knew to respect the moment and did not press Neuro to continue. Then Neuro looked up and faced Astro with the facts. "The world seems to be on the brink of war."

"What?"

"Things are getting out of hand. Madness is prevailing. The majority of humanity will probably soon be annihilated."

"Soon?"

"Well, it could be years. We are hoping for years, of course. But not that many."

"But...you've...I mean...why wasn't I told?"

"We saw no reason to worry you. We did not believe it, really. How often in this century have we been on the 'brink of war' as the world teeter-tottered between authoritarian states and democracies? It started in the twenties. Then once, sometimes twice a decade. A basic instinct to survive rescued us each time. No one is confident that is going to happen again."

"But it could, couldn't? I mean, it is a powerful instinct."

"It could. But many of us have concluded that we should assume it will not, and we should prepare. Those that can are trying to buy their way into colonies on Mars. Offering much-needed supplies, equipment, the latest technology that applies, and promising to bring it with them to expand the colonies."

"And, well, is that happening?"

"In some cases, it looks promising for them. But other options for the colonies are being proposed."

"By whom?"

Neuro smiled.

"Your brother's involved, right?"

"The whole situation is so complex that I prefer we just deal with you at the moment."

Astro understood. "But what about people who don't want to go to Mars?"

"We've heard that some are literally digging in, building underground habitats here on Earth."

"Following Aunt Liz's lead," Astro said with a not jolly chuckle. "What are you going to do? You and Kenya?"

"This will be a war between Europe, Asia, and America. The bombs will fall there. Africa will probably see none of that. But—"

"The fallout."

"Yes, the fallout. We have done intense research at the New University for years, trying to find protection against radiation. Something simple and fully effective. A shot or something."

"Any luck?"

"Luck, my friend, at least the good kind, has fled."

"Plus, nuclear winter compounding the damage already done by the climate crises."

"Yes. This is true."

"Are you all going to Mars, then?"

"No. My brother says he is too old. Says he gave his life to Kenya and will not abandon it."

"And you? The family?"

"We have made a decision not to. If the world does move back from the brink, it still will be changed. If we survive this, there will be much to do. The Kinyanjuis will have much to offer. We will stay. But I do have a plan for you."

"Me? I don't want to go to Mars."

"Not Mars, my friend. But how about the stars?"

～

Astro found Neuro's plan for him somewhere between ridiculous and outrageous, probably landing on crazy. He said as much to Makena Wafula, who answered the accusation six minutes later.

"I disagree with deep respect for you, my old friend and colleague. Khadambi and I worked on the plan together. It is perfectly reasonable and, may I say, necessary."

This is why Neuro encouraged him to talk with Makena. It was a conspiracy of two. Which is all it took for a conspiracy. And, of course, because it was Makena. Neuro knew what a vital friend she had become to Astro. She was a beauty not just in body but also in consciousness and in her whole self. A physical beauty still, partly because of her African heritage, partly from less sag from the lower gravity (compared to Earth's) that she had lived under for more than twenty years. The beauty of her whole self? She was born with certain positive propensities combined with a lifetime of purpose that excited her each day, which made her beautiful. Neuro knew this because Astro had often told him how much he admired Makena for these qualities.

"You worked with him on this plan? This crazy idea to send me on this, this, what would you call it? This grand tour of the solar system?"

"You will be anything but a tourist. Although I hope you take the time to see and feel the wonder out there. We are asking you to shift your focus as an astronomer from far distant phenomena to our immediate neighborhood. I am asking you to become a planetary scientist. Because it's never been so vital for us to know what we are

269

living in—what we can survive in. Did Kahdambi tell you about the probe ship being built for you?"

"He gave me blueprints. I don't like blueprints. They're stupid, bones without flesh. Plus, why should I care what it looks like? From what Neuro said, my environment wouldn't change. Just the focus of my science."

"Joe, give Kahdambi some consideration. He is justifiably proud of what his New University and Kinyanjui Enterprises engineers and designers have come up with. You will be housed in a probe-ship that will travel throughout the solar system in a trip finely plotted out using a combination of electric propulsion and solar sails. And gravity assists, of course, especially to get you from Jupiter to Saturn when they are aligned in their orbits. That's why you have to go this year when they are aligned. For they are only every twelve years. And we—we may not have another twelve years."

Mekena cracked, just slightly. Astro, watching her six minutes in the past, could see it. And hear it in her voice. The full weight of humanity's potential demise, a weight she must have been carrying for years, suddenly pushed down on her harder, despite being in thirty-eight percent of Earth gravity. But grave is grave when it comes to mass graves, no matter the percentage. Mekena wiped a small trickle of a tear while turning away with slight embarrassment. The scientist, the rational being, the beauty, and the beautiful self, moved to at least one tear. Makena once said that the universe really didn't want us around. Obviously, then, the universe would be shedding no tears when most of humanity ceases to exist. But Makena will.

"So," Astro said, "what will I need to do up there? What am I looking for? What must I discover?"

～

Neuro and Makena had worked on their plan for Astro for years. Neuro might have preferred to concentrate only on his research into the brain, consciousness, and the creation of self. He certainly would have preferred to have concern only for his family and not the whole human family. And, of course, there was the ongoing task and duty (and joy) to maintain and enhance Astro's life. But As oblivious as Neuro might have wanted to be, Yoshi had never let him. He was more than aware of the trials and tribulations, crises and conflicts, threats and terrors that humanity was going through while huddled under the thin smear of Earth's fragile atmosphere. Gossamer

270

consciousnesses under a flimsy sky. And Makena, now fully a Martian, still had a great love for her birth planet. If not for all of the denizens that walked upon it.

The constant conflicts between nations, mainly in the Northern Hemisphere, often spilled over to countries in the Southern Hemisphere. This battle to settle on the proper management of masses of people ironically did not allow for competent management. Strict, top-down authority taking on the burden of decision-making for everyone had the advantage of getting things done quickly with no questions permitted to be asked. Until corruption set in, which it always did. And greed. And vain egos. Bottom-up democracy (at least that was the ideal), where there were many inputs into decision-making from the local level to the national, had the advantage of the freedom of conscience, spirited innovation, and good lives lived. Until corruption set in, which it always did. And greed. And vain egos. But corruption, greed, and egos never set in so solidly in a democracy that only violence could root them out. The advantage for general well-being, then, went to freedom. But that did not guarantee success.

The tussle between unquestioned authority and participatory freedom used to be local. Each city-state, territory, nation coming to its own conclusions throughout history. But the world had long become global. It was as if the whole Earth demanded humanity, which benefited from its bounty, make up its damn mind! Or leave, expire, off yourself, give up the ghost, wither away, and leave the Earth to heal itself and move on.

When it became clear to Yoshi, Neuro, and Makena that the latter was now more likely than the former, they felt deep sadness over the coming massive loss of humanity. And possibly of all the culture and civilization humanity had created. No big deal on a universal scale. But who measured things on a universal scale? All measurements are local.

Their plan for Astro was part of a much larger plan put into effect by Yoshi Kinyanjui. He was no longer president of Kenya but had become a respected elder statesman, especially on the African continent. His influence and his powers of persuasion were massive. And he was, of course, head of one of the wealthiest families in the world. The escalating ills of Earth—the climate crises still not conquered, the pandemic contagions of micro viruses, the far too macro contagions of myths, lies, and profoundly arrogant ignorance, to name but three—now were deemed unstoppable. They might have

271

been stopped not so long ago if the world had learned to cooperate. But the major nations were too busy debating—often bloodily—ideological supremacy to cooperate. The world was destined for another extinction event. Self-made; hand-crafted by humanity.

Yoshi concluded that whatever else the rest of the world might choose to do, Africa, the cradle of humanity, would not go to the grave without a mighty striving against the dying of the light.

Yoshi organized a Pan-African effort to support the colonies on Mars, the only possible last refuge for humanity. A terrible fate for this barely out-of-the-womb example of creative intelligence. Maybe the only example in the universe.

"But that," Yoshi once said to Neuro, "is the reality of the situation. The real truth, not your Veritas truth." Mars had to be supported—and prepared for what future may come.

The colonies on Mars had worked incessantly to make themselves self-sustaining. They were close, but had not yet succeeded. They were still corded to Earth for certain supplies and materials, not to mention fresh colonists. But the prominent nations in the Northern Hemisphere who had first driven humanity into space and onto Mars had turned inward in their dangerous visions. And so had lessened their commitments to the red planet.

A small tribe of trillionaires contacted the Martian colonies. They offered much in takeover bids to build sanctuaries for themselves and their nearest and dearest. Yoshi found this frightening. What such people buy, they tend to want unquestioned authority over. Why export what he knew had been the bane of humanity for millennia? The Martian colonies had been founded by the rational; why introduce the irrational?

Using much of the Kinyanjui trillions and funds from the African nations he had helped move toward strong forms of democracy, Yoshi reset the priority of the Kenyan Space Program. It would now work to strengthen the survivability of the Mars colonies. He demanded no authority and played no favorites. Each colony would receive equal support and an equal surplus of supplies, materials, and technology. They would receive the latest Otsuka-Kinyanjui AI Intuition software that would be self-sustaining. It was designed to create and install its own upgrades as needed. It was a head-spinning undertaking that looked not just to the moment but to the next several hundred years. Colonists were recruited. Many with practical skills for the extension of the colonies and working toward self-sustaining status. More scientists signed up not just to study Mars but also to continue studying our soon-to-be-an-endangered species. Many teachers in all subjects were chosen, but also chroniclers, spinners of tales with words, dramatic performances, and digital moving images. Visual artists in several mediums were invited, and even comics and humorists. Laughs, all agreed, were going to be needed if most of humanity dies and the Martians are left very much alone. The first humorist recruited dubbed her new unearthly form of entertainment, Existential Vaudeville.

Despite Mars becoming the last small island of humanity tenuously hanging on, the study of the unfriendly universe would not be abandoned. Everyone agreed—humanity would not fold itself into a cowering creature. "Expire we might, but until then, aspire we will," said a colonist scientist who considered herself quite wise.

Probes were designed and built by the Kenyan Astronomical Union in collaboration with a Martian team headed up by Makena. They would be sent to Mars via Kenyan Jaali rockets. And would be placed into "storage" in Mars orbit until they were ready for use after their missions were decided. Small reusable rocket boosters were designed with Mars gravity in mind. Hundreds were to be built in Earth orbit and then sent onto Mars to land in the newly named Spaceport Ares.

There was much research, experimentation, and design of mining techniques and equipment for Mars and beyond. One team worked on the creation and engineering of drone mining ships and the software to support them for a hoped-for future of mining asteroids, moons, and possibly Venus and Mercury. New synthesizing technologies were being developed to allow for more efficient creation of beneficial organic compounds from the raw materials of Mars, such as CO, methane, methanol, and ethanol. From those precursors, they would be able to make more significant amounts of plastics, lubricants, and fertilizers. New 3D printers, so much faster than the first ones decades ago, were being designed for Mars. They would manufacture many valuable things from building materials to highly nutritious meat.

It was a plan much larger and more logical than any other trillionaires were offering. But the limited scope of the others could be accomplished much quicker. Yoshi's project would take longer. Was there the time? That was the gamble each colony had to decide whether to accept. A majority agreed to risk it. Some small colonies set up by commercial enterprises decided not to. Instead, they decided to find comfort in the arms of the trillionaires. They would soon, Yoshi was convinced, be living under dictatorships. He remembered something his father once told him. "Not one man or woman on this planet would mind living under a dictatorship—as long as they agreed with the dictator." He was pleased this thought did not apply to most on this new human-occupied planet. But Yoshi worried about those it did apply to. Would they be a problem in the future? That was a question for other people at another time. Yoshi could only do what he could do now.

~

Astro had never wanted to go into space. That first night living in The Hole, when six-year-old Joey was taken outside by his Aunt Liz to see the desert sky; that first moment (the first of many) when he became dizzy with the expanse of the universe, when he was overawed by the glittering points of light coming to him after long travels; when Joey felt both small and yet large; unmoored and yet rooted; floating and yet held in the embrace of the desert's floor— that first night he did not see what he saw as something separate. He did not see space above and the Earth below. Joey did not see a far-off territory. Instead, somehow, his instincts saw himself and the planet he rode on as part of the above, or, better said, part of the surroundings. Joey did not see himself as part of something larger than himself (as so many have been so facile to state), for he did not separate himself from what he saw. He felt he was it, and it was him.

He felt awe—not wonder, but awe. He was not surprised by this brilliant night sky as something unimaginable and strange. Instead, he accepted it with reverence as something natural and right. He did not admire the sky. He just simply wanted to know it better. And, oddly, he wanted it to know him. Although his six-year-old self would not have known how to express that. Indeed, he could never explain that thought to himself and had always kept it to himself.

Nor had he ever felt that particular wonder that came with the extraordinary adventures of science fiction literature and film. His Aunt Liz, being a historian planted firmly in the past and on Earth, had no love of the future or far off planets. Her library, the books that flowed into young Joey, did not take him there. The wind was in the willows. His grandfather's collection of films included no speculation about, nor the wonder of, anything alien to the lives and loves, dramas, and comedies of men and women on terra firma. And space travel was so well established, it never seemed to Joey as anything different or less mundane than sailing upon the ocean.

274

Which he also had no interest in.

Astro was never interested in being a final frontiersman. He always thought it would be a terribly uncomfortable way to live.

But he was interested in knowing his surroundings, penetrating the strange phenomena of the universe until they became explained and not so strange. His nickname, then, was both ironic and accurate. A little bit of complexity he had no problem with.

No, Astro had never wanted to go into space. And yet, here he was, soon to be Astro the astronaut. What the bloody blue blazes!

$\sim$

Aunt Liz had often said, "People ain't my favorite people." Astro, himself, had always been non-committal about people in general. Individually, he took each face at the value that face put forth. He had a bias toward aesthetically pleasing faces; he admitted that. But he also had preferences toward intellectually fine minds, and terrifically fine talents, especially in the arts. And kind people, happy people, and people who gifted him with smiles he found fitted him quite nicely. The rest of humanity? Well, he was certainly not a species self-loather who looked upon his own kind as creeping two-legged vermin or a virus plague infecting dear Mother Gaia. Nor was he what one might call a *Homo sapiens* chauvinist, who touted his species as the ultimate expression of biological evolution. He was, he supposed, an agnostic regarding his species, its value, and worth. Humans were well-evolved mammals, that's true, but so were bats in caves, whales in oceans, and sloths in trees. But if we can worry about bats, whales, and sloths going extinct, shouldn't we have at least some concern for humans? Intellectually he agreed. But Astro never found that he could get all worked up about this. After all, it might just be the inevitable outcome of this strange creative consciousness humans developed. If it was inevitable, it was inevitable, and so be it.

"You don't really believe that," Neuro had said to Astro as he chastised him for this attitude.

"Sure, I do."

"No, you do not."

"Sure, I do."

"No, you do not."

"Prove it!"

"Your hate for Brandon Carmichael."

"Well, he was loathsome."

"You always hated his ideas. You hated anything that would

275

transform humans into transhumans, so you must love humans as they are."

"Well…"

"Ah-ha!"

"Humans are still children. You know how I've never really liked children. Except yours, of course."

"You don't really know my children."

"Must be why I like them."

"You want humans to grow up."

"That's it!"

"So, don't you find it sad if most of humanity is cut down in its childhood?"

"Well, unfortunate, certainly, but…."

And Makena upbraided him. "You're such a phony."

"How could I be anything else but? I've got a digital body. I eat digital food. I have digital sex."

"Your brain is entirely organic. It is the seat of your emotions, and I know you are sad about what may happen."

"What the bloody blue blazes! Why does everybody think they know me better than I know me?"

"Think of it. No one left to listen to Henry Mancini's music."

"No one listens to him anymore but me, anyway."

"Why do you want to be so damn unfeeling?"

"I call it being objective. As scientists, isn't that the way we are supposed to be? Besides, as you know—I was raised by a hermit."

"You're just being a poseur. You enjoy being a contrarian."

"But you still love me, right?" Astro said as he broadened his lips into a smile, and his eyes danced in hope.

"Yes, I still love you," Makena admitted.

"Well, then. All's right with the world."

~

Despite Astro's lack of existential dread over the near certainty of humanity's more than potential complete extinction, he took his new task seriously. He began a deep study of planetary science. Aided by Veritas, which could implant vast packets of information into his brain and ignite the data and suppositions as if they had been a part of Astro's intellectual memory for years. It was disconcerting at first, but he got used to it quickly. It was a forced-fed fascination with our solar system that he found ironically gave him a great sense of comfort. It was like a man looking for the exotic, leaving his constraining, mundane, ordinary, close-minded, hick hometown, and becoming a world traveler. Only to discover that Dorothy was right. There is no place like home. It was much too pat and even cute, but he was stuck with it. And it was necessary for his new task.

∾

"You know," Astro said to Neuro during one of Neuro's digital visits. "A question has occurred to me. And I don't know why I haven't asked it before."

"What is that?" Neuro asked.

"Am I immortal?"

"Immortal?"

"You know, like what Carmichael was trying for. This, whatever you have made me, is it so, so...so something that I'll live forever?"

"No. But the technology of the BioMed biofoam cocoon, even without the destruction of our world, will allow you to outlive me by many years. A hundred, at least, maybe more."

"So, I'm going to be tooling around the solar system for a century or more?"

"Unless your batteries give out prematurely."

"And you will be gone, and eventually Makena will be gone… What the bloody blue blazes! *Now* I'm sad!"

∾

Astro spent every moment of two months contemplating the solar system, a system, of course, not of space but of matter. For without the matter, what would matter? Every moment meaning just that—every second of every hour of every week of the two months. 86,400 ticks when they weren't tocks dedicated to bringing forth the information Veritas had planted in his spongy self. Understanding it, comparing it with other data, musing on it, finding surprising suppositions, leaping to conclusions, and often changing his very packed mind, shifting his rapid-fire thoughts, and allowing himself to be amazed. Sometimes he would forgo the ease of traversing this implanted info and sit down to read books to gather information. Of course, the information could probably have been found in what Veritas had planted. But Astro wanted the old-fashioned comfort of dancing his eyes among white floors of words.

After the two months, he stopped as he felt he had a good grasp of all the most current and relevant information about our solar system. Information, not knowledge. Information derived from the knowledge of others derived from their experiences and observations. Not knowledge he had discovered on his own. But information that made him anxious to get out there and see, simply put, for himself. He became hungry for it. As Makena knew he would.

He was also hungry for mac & cheese and tuna! After all, he had not eaten for two months.

He was in The Hole making himself a large pot of the Krafty stuff when a video message from Mekena from seven minutes in the past came on.

"Hi, Joe! Sorry I wasn't here when you called. I was taking a break to ramble up top outside. You know, our landscape here is rather stunning. I sometimes forget that, having my head both underground and in the stars."

"I just wanted to check in," Astro responded. "I've been a bit in my own head, so to speak, for a couple of months." He then dug into the mac & cheese while waiting for her response.

"I'm assuming it was time well spent. We have been busy here designing your mission. It's not set in stone, and I would welcome your input now that you are an expert on the solar system. I'll send it in the next day or two."

"Can you give me the basics? But, let me guess. Are you sending me out to look for potential habitats for humanity? You know, that's a mission that's likely to fail, don't you? As far as I can see, you're currently on the only viable one. And it's none too kind to frail flesh and blood. Maybe the moon, but only as, what, a mining town? Maybe you could have some research communities there, but for what real purpose? After all, if Earth blows itself up, you won't have it as a wealth generator to pay for all the elaborate engineering needed to make, I don't know, Venus and Europa livable. I mean, seriously, you guys will be stuck hunkering down on Mars, cut off from the resources for system expansion. But still, I'm going, I guess, so whatever you want, I am yours to command. Although I'm still unclear why you guys want to send me out there. You'll have plenty of probes to send out without the burden of maintaining a living entity."

Astro finished his macaroni and cheese. Then washed his dishes, immersing his hands in hot, soapy water, feeling the benefits of heat that comforts instead of cooks.

"Joe…"

Makena was back. Astro dried his hands quickly, went over to the easy chair, and sat.

"Do you really want to know why Khadambi and I have insisted on sending you out there? Of course, you do, or you wouldn't have asked. Well, the core of our decision, I suppose, is emotional. It seems to be oddly easier for us to accept the demise of most of humanity than it is to accept yours. Isn't that weird? Especially given your unique existence. Which provides us with an opportunity. Otherwise, the answer is because of all you brought up. Despite what Khadambi and his family and my African brothers and sisters are providing to help us become truly independent colonies. We will just be survivors clinging onto a raft for hundreds, maybe thousands of years. Or maybe better said, we will be the monks cloistered in our monasteries hoarding and protecting what we can of human culture. It's sad, Joe, it's damn sad. We won't have time to expand our species beyond Mars for a long, long time—if ever. But that doesn't mean we won't be thinking about it, planning for it, researching ways. If only on paper. So yes, all our probes, including you, will be gathering data that may provide clues on how best to do that. And if by some slim chance humanity dodges extinction, then we will be renewed in relief and ready to get our little black, brown, and white butts beyond Earth and Mars. Think how glorious that will be. But, yes, we don't really need to send you along. However, your immediacy to the planets and moons you'll be visiting may give you a perspective that will be helpful. Who knows?

"But you have a more critical role to play. Extinction being more likely than not, you are our only chance to send a human out there—to be there. To simply be there. To provide your warm presence in the cold regions of space. To—let me be melodramatic—plant humanity's flag. You will become a symbol, an inspiration to us and our prodigy clinging onto this raft. Khadambi and I are shamelessly using you for this because we think it is essential. In the long run—although a long run is not certain—it may be that you will be the beacon keeping some human hope alive. To give us a reason to continue doing what humans are supposed to do. To survive. And to quest for knowledge. What do you think of that?"

"What the bloody blue blazes?" Astro questioned. Not as an exclamation. But quietly. Introspectively. And yet it reverberated throughout his spongy self.

~

279

Neuro came to dinner at Astro's downtown L.A. condo. They had neither Indian cuisine nor macaroni and cheese. Instead, they had porterhouse steaks, fat baked potatoes, green beans, a salad, and a peach cobbler for dessert. The steaks didn't even have to be lab-grown meat because they were just digital representations of fine cuts. But they tasted terrific. And satisfied completely.

As he was about to put the last bite of the steak in his mouth, Astro was stopped by a thought. "Holy shit!"

"What?"

"I just realized something."

"Nice to know your mind is active."

"Seriously, it was like being slapped."

"What are you talking about?"

"About what I just realized."

"Which is?"

Astro looked down at his plate to see the juicy evidence of the steak-that-was, the empty shell of the potato, the last two green beans and shook his head to order his thoughts. "That this meal is the classic last meal of a condemned man."

Neuro laughed. A big one for him. "You watch too many old movies."

"You laugh at my existential angst?"

"Better to laugh at it than to give in to it."

"True," Astro had to admit. "True, my friend, true. I suppose I'm being selfish given that—"

"So many of us are condemned?"

"Do you really believe that, Neuro? I mean, really?"

"It has nothing to do with belief. Only probability."

"Of course, of course, but still—"

"Have I accepted it emotionally, as opposed to intellectually?"

"Yes, exactly! Because I certainly haven't," Astro admitted

"A survival technique? So as not to go mad?"

Astro took the last bite of his steak, waiting patiently impaled on his fork, and put it in his mouth and masticated it as he mused. Then, after swallowing, he said. "Yes. I think that's right. Although, of course, we are all mad. But we certainly don't want to go mad."

It was not the last meal of a condemned man—or species, for that matter—but it was a meal to mark an occasion. The space probe ship that would carry Astro beyond Earth was completed. The next day, they would install into it the new microcomputers containing his WBE, the Veritas program, and all the other hardware and software supporting Astro's living being. Neuro had come to dinner to celebrate that and ask Astro a question.

"What would you like to name your ship?"

"Why do I have to name it?"

"It is your prerogative to do so."

"Really?"

"Yes."

"Well… How about, *The Last Gasp*."

"Astro…?"

"*The Titanic?*"

"You try my patience."

"Really? You'll have to try mine someday."

"An old movie?"

"You know it."

"Please, my friend."

"Okay, okay. How about *Shoeless Joe?*"

"*Shoeless Joe?*"

"Because I'm shoeless. And footless. And legless. And—"

"Okay, *Shoeless Joe*, it is."

"No, Neuro, I was only kidding."

"Too late. It is decided."

Astro felt panic as his petard blew him upward. "Wouldn't you prefer something inspirational?"

"Obviously. But—"

"Okay. I'm sorry."

Astro truly was. Neuro could feel that. Even Feye, in the lab monitoring all of this, could feel it.

"What are you trying to ignore, Astro?"

Astro stood up and walked to the kitchen area and grabbed a bottle of brandy and two glasses. He returned and set it all down. "What the hell have you burdened me with?"

"Burdened you with?"

"The hope of all Mankind! Miniscule as it's about to become."

"Oh. Do you not want to be the hope of all Mankind?"

"I…."

"Yes?"

"I'm feeling it."

"What?"

"A big blast of self-importance."

"Oh."

"I like it. But I don't like liking it."

281

"Turn it into something else then."

"What?"

"Something mundane. Duty. Purpose."

"Are those mundane?"

"If you take ego out of them."

"I've always been a bit of a selfish person."

"I know. But not in a virulent way. Oddly, in sort of a charming way."

"Thank you."

"You are welcome."

"This is important, this task you and Makena have given me, isn't it?"

"Yes. But not self-important."

"That's going to take some getting used to."

Neuro smiled a particular smile he had. Not a broad one, but an encompassing one. One containing—and dispensing—joy. "I think you are well on your way."

Astro saw the smile and heard the words. And he was ready.

∼

The *Shoeless Joe* was ready for GO. It had been placed on top of the powerful Jaali rocket. The launch crew was at their stations in mission control. They were men and women and others that came from several of the nations of Africa, Europe, Asia, the Americas, the Middle East, and India. The Kinyanjui family was gathered in a special room overlooking mission control. They were joined by representatives of the Pan-African nations Yoshi had organized to realize this day and support the Mars colonies.

The world's press was not in attendance. They were taken up with matters of more immediate concern and unwilling to devote their dwindling resources to what most considered a grandstanding move by fanciful dreamers. They would not, this time, be the first writers of history. But then, they didn't believe there would be much history left to write.

Astro was asked to take a nap while his "jar" was disconnected from Neuro's lab's power source and computers. It was then taken to the *Shoeless Joe* to be installed. First, it was connected to the ship's power source. Then plugged into the micro quantum computers that now housed Veritas, Astro's whole body emulation, and a unique Otsuka-Kinyanjui AI Intuition software program. It would monitor everything and would be able to respond to Astro's needs and requests. Of course, it would never have Feye's long devotion to Astro as an emotion. And it would certainly never act out of compassion for Astro. But the job would get done nevertheless.

Once Astro was fully installed and mounted on top of the Jaali rocket, he was awoken and introduced to the AI he had decided to name Aloysius Ignatius. And then, he conducted the first test on the launch schedule.

"Aloysius Ignatius?"

Yes, Shoeless Joe.

"You can just call me Joe."

Okay, Joe.

"Aloysius Ignatius, connect me with Makena Wafula on Mars."

I'll be happy to, Joe.

"You're very polite, Aloysius Ignatius."

Don't blame me. I was programmed this way. You are now connected with Makena Wafula on Mars.

Makena would be Astro's only link with humanity. Even while still relatively close to Earth, he would never again be able to speak to or see Neuro. It was Astro's choice. On Neuro's end, the connection may not be operable for long, and Astro did not want to face the moment when he called, and Neuro did not answer.

Neuro had asked him, "But if it becomes clear that we put off self-extinction once again by some miracle, don't you want to know?"

"No. Because how long will it be put off? You wouldn't let me die alone the first time. You're not letting me die alongside you this time. You've forced me into this new reality. I might as well commit to it one hundred percent. Besides, just because I'm supposed to be a symbol of hope doesn't mean I have to have any myself. I'll just do my job."

When Makena responded, she was, at first, just doing her job. Astro was in The Hole and looked up at Makena's face on the large, curved screen on the wall as she said, "Okay, the connection is good. The signal is strong. Eventually, there will be a considerable lag time between our conversations. And—and eventually, I will not be around, of course. So I have begun to take on some young assistants, and on occasion, you may get a response from them. Be kind to them, Joe. They are in awe of you. As, um, you know, as am I. I guess. I mean... You see, I had a funny feeling the other day. I had this tremendous urge to kiss you. But where? You have no lips. Or cheeks. Or even an ass, for that matter. And I certainly would not kiss your spongy self if I could even get to it. So how can I kiss you?

283

Blow you a kiss over thousands, millions of miles? This will embarrass you, won't it, Dr. Joe Smith? Well, that is unfortunate for you, but I guess I needed to express it. Had it been another time, another place... Oh, well, don't think about this as we go forward. We're both too old to add to our population anyway. I guess I should have recorded this before I sent it out. Then I could have erased it. Well, bon voyage. Or *safari nzuri*, as we say in Swahili."

"What the bloody blue blazes!" Astro exclaimed to himself. "How am I going to respond to that?"

When he responded, Astro said, "Makena, if some random force or even fate is determined to eradicate humanity, they would be dissuaded from it if they could but meet you. *Unafanya maisha yafae kuishi.*"

Makena laughed at Astro's pronunciation. But she teared up over the meaning. "You make life worth living," Astro had said in Swahili.

∽

The countdown began. There was nothing for Astro to do. He had not even had to suit up, wear a helmet, or strap into a reclining seat. He did not have to be a Rocket Man. Instead, he went about his day as he always did in his digitally created curated environment, whether at his downtown L.A. condo or The Hole in the desert. As the countdown began, he was in his condo, staring out the window at the passing parade below. He saw *Homo things* walking east and west, north and south. Automatic autos of no design beyond those he knew thirty-some years ago effortlessly rolled up streets and down. Birds, which Neuro's crew had finally added, flew by. Flight. High-flying. Well, it was going to happen to him. But would he ever feel it? Not that he really wanted to. All that damn pressure on his body as the rocket accelerated. All that vomit when hit by zero G. Uncomfortable and messy. This way, he could casually just sit and eat his breakfast.

There was a knock on the door. It could only be Neuro, of course, and it was.

"Come to say goodbye?" Astro greeted his friend.

"Of course," Neuro said as he walked in.

"I knew you would."

"How could I not?"

They both sat.

"Let's not get maudlin, though. Okay?" Astro said.

"Agreed."

"Danm!"

"What?"

"I am going to miss you, Neuro."

"You can see me whenever you want. Just think of me, and one of the *Homo things* will—"

"Won't be the same. It will be the Neuro I think I know, not the Neuro who often surprises me."

"That is so."

"If I do it, though, I think I'll make you shorter."

"Why don't you make yourself taller."

"No. I tried that once. It was weird. I got vertigo."

"Best you leave things as they are, then."

"Yes. I think so."

Neuro gave Astro one of his big, broad smiles on the edge of a laugh. "I brought you a present."

"Why? It isn't my birthday."

"Well, it is in a way, I suppose."

"Let's not get all meaningful here."

"Okay," Neuro said, then sat still and in silence.

"But let's not *not* give me my present, either." Curiosity had gotten to Astro.

"Of Course," Neuro said, then addressed someone else. "Aloysius Ignatius?"

Are you ready, Dr. Kinyanjui?

"We are."

The condo crumbled, and Astro and Neuro were, in an instant, on the twenty-foot-high platform in the middle of the Nairobi National Wildlife Park, deep into the night and the thick dark. Astro fell back in his wooden chair, pushed by the overwhelming multitude of stars above, forcing photons upon the land. The chair tipped back and over, and Astro landed with an *oomph*. Still in the chair, his eyes filled with the spread of stars, their groupings, clusters, some twinkling in rouge loneliness, and many arcing in a wide swath across the sky. The Way and the Light, Astro had always thought of it.

Astro was a child again. He was Little Joe from Connecticut, Joey with his stocking hat covered head in the dust of the desert, but his mind, his *self*, was in the symphony of the stars.

His mouth was wide open, and it was fortunate that no digital insects had been added to this environment.

"You remember, of course," Neuro said, "our night under the stars."

285

"Oh, absolutely! But I remember another night, also."

"As I knew you would."

"This is glorious!"

"It is important sometimes to see things not just as a scientist, as a professional, but as a human."

"To realize, not analyze."

"Yes. A good way of putting it."

"But did you have to make these chairs wooden? I am very uncomfortable in this position." Astro got himself up and righted the chair. "I mean, I know you are really sitting in some comfortable recliner. Couldn't you have altered history a little and—"

"Aloysius Ignatius?"

Yes, Dr. Kinyanjui?

"Give the man a recliner chair."

The wooden chair melted into the wooden deck of the platform. Then it rose up, altered into a fat, leather recliner.

"Wonderful!" Astro said. "I'll come here to relax my little spongy self."

"Actually, you'll find it much more useful than just that," Neuro said.

"In what way?"

"This is actually going to be your observation deck. That sky above will change as you travel to reflect what's outside of *Shoeless Joe*. When you come up to Saturn, for example, you will be able to sit here and see it all above you as if you were just floating in space. You will be able to travel along and through the rings and note each particle of matter. No view through a telescope. No stream of data. Just a view of what is as perceived by the naked human eye. It will be as if you're flying in space. You will be able to fly right up to and stick your head in Uranus."

Astro took his eyes off the stars, looked at his friend, smiled, and said, "Is that a joke? From Dr. Kinyanjui?"

"Yes. Feye made it up. He thought you might enjoy it."

"Normally I would, but…." Astro returned his eyes to the sky. Or, rather, to beyond the sky. "Right now…" Astro could think of nothing more to say. For the moment, he was a creature of pure feeling.

~

This is mission control. We are now at fifty-nine minutes and counting.

The voice seemed to come from the stars above and the savanna below.

"Well," Neuro said. "Less than an hour. Let us have a drink."

A table appeared between them. Upon it were two glasses and a bottle of twenty-five-year-old single malt Scotch. Or at least a reasonably intoxicating facsimile thereof.

Astro took his eyes off the stars again and looked over to his friend, and watched him pour the Scotch. As he accepted his glass, he said, "You know, some meteor might just smash into the *Shoeless Joe*, and then I'll be as dead as you're going to be. Cheers!"

"You know better than me how unlikely that is. Cheers! But thank you for the morbid thought."

"It's not morbid. On the contrary, it gives me some solace that... Well, that someday we will somehow *not exist* together on the same plane."

"Surely you do not mean heaven?"

"Of course not, just… Oh, I don't know. Just a thought that I find not unpleasant."

They both fell silent as they drank in the Scotch and the universe. After they had two glasses each and were convinced that they could now hear the music of the spheres, Neuro asked. "Do you remember my definition of luck?"

"What?"

"That night—the night of your unfortunate accident—we were pretty drunk in that bar."

"The one where I hacked into their computer and stopped a stream of some stupid sport?"

"Yes, that night. I never did find out who won that game."

"I'm sure you can look it up."

"Yes, I could, assuming I wish to waste time on the now truly irrelevant. But what is not irrelevant to the moment is, do you remember the definition I came up with?"

"Definition of what?"

"Of luck!" Neuro said with some pique.

"Ah. Wait a minute… Yes! That luck was being born a transsexual, specifically a female inside a male body—then turning out to be a lesbian. Now, why the hell would I remember that?"

"Yes, it was probably not worthy of devoting neurons to."

"So why did you bring it up?"

"Because I have changed it."

"Your definition?"

"Yes."

"Okay. So what is it now?"

"Us."

"Us?"

"I mean life. Complex life. Especially us. We who are conscious, creative with it, and grow intelligent because of it."

"Oh. Is that luck? Or a curse?"

"Do not be cynical. Only those who have it can even ask that question."

"True."

"Do you know how many different things had to happen for life to arise here to evolve to us?"

"Of course, I do, Neuro. I'm a highly educated individual, you know."

"And I do not just mean Earth being lucky to orbit in the Goldilocks Zone."

"Of course not. That goes without saying. But you might as well say it."

"A nice rocky planet. Life needs a rocky planet. Our kind of life, at least."

"And what other kind would you want?"

"Exactly!"

"And don't forget the magnetic field. From our very active spinning molten core. It keeps the cooties away."

"The what?"

"The high-energy particles from the solar wind."

"Why did you not say that, then?"

"Cooties is a fun word."

"But not accurate."

"But fun."

"Okay. I will give you that." Neuro took a long drink and then said. "And what about plate tectonics?"

"So important, plate tectonics," Astro agreed.

"No plate tectonics on Mars."

"Poor Makena."

"How rare might plate tectonics be?"

Astro offered his empty glass to Neuro for filling. "How rare is this Scotch?"

As Neuro filled Astor's glass, he said, "And what if we did not have an atmosphere?"

"No atmosphere, no me, no you." Astro drank lustily from his glass. "And not just any old atmosphere," Astro said through wet lips.

"True."

"And our early atmosphere—so good with its oxygen and ozone shielding all those early prebiotic thingies from radiation. Nucleic acids and proteins and such. No prebiotic, no biotic, I've always said that!"

"And water!"

"Water! Water for life! But not for Scotch."

"No, not for Scotch."

"Any more Scotch?" Astro asked.

"Aloysius Ignatius, please fill the bottle," Neuro called out. The bottle was filled, and Neuro poured, and Astro was appreciative.

The two sat back, sipped their whiskeys, and looked beyond the platform. Astro to the stars. Neuro to the savanna. It was a quiet few moments until Neuro said, "Dinosaurs."

"Dinosaurs?" Astro queried because he thought it was such a queer thing for Neuro to have said.

"Dead Dinosaurs."

"Okay."

"Dead dinosaurs becoming fossil fuels."

"Neuro!" Astro was aghast.

"What?"

"You must have skipped that day in school."

"What is the implication of your damning statement?"

"Dinosaurs did not become fossil fuels. Everyone knows that."

"They do?"

"Well, everyone who didn't skip that day in class. Old myth. It's dead plants that became fossil fuels."

"It is?"

"Aloysius Ignatius, what became fossil fuels?"

Aquatic phytoplankton and zooplankton that died and sedimented in large quantities under anoxic conditions millions of years ago began forming petroleum and natural gas due to anaerobic decomposition.

"You mean dinosaurs died for nothing?" Neuro asked.

"Everybody dies for nothing," Astro said, depressing the moment.

"Well, be that as it may actually and not mythically be, my point is the same."

"Your point?"

"It is the same."

"It may be the same, but it is also unstated."

"Oh. My point is that energy-dense fuels are a possible requirement for technological life. Our civilization was absolutely dependent on access to energy-dense fuels. You know, oil, coal, petroleum. Dirty stuff, of course, but the kickstart to becoming technological. Only then can other energy sources be developed. But there is no guarantee that fossil fuels are likely to be a common feature of planets, is there? No dense fuels, no technology, no others out there like us in this lonely universe."

"Okay. A fair point. I wish I had thought of it."

"Yoshi has lectured me on it."

"Ah! I was wondering—"

"And let us not forget the moon," Neuro declared.

"So often forgotten. The moon."

"A good size, our moon."

"A fine size. In fact, perfect, I would say."

"And yet, underappreciated," Neuro sadly noted.

"Such a stabilizing influence. Spins us at just the right speed, so we're not throwing up all the time."

"And all those millennia moderating climate change."

"Not such an easy task these days."

"In Africa, we have many moon deities. What must they think of us?"

"Maybe we should have remained just prokaryotic cells," Astro said after another long drink.

"Too late now for regrets, my friend. We made our complex life bed, and now we must—"

"Die in it?"

"Let us not become morbid," Neuro said. Then addressed Aloysius Ignatius. "Aloysius Ignatius, away with the Scotch; away with intoxication.

The bottle and glasses and the table disappeared, and Neuro and Astro were now stone sober. Finally, after some quiet contemplation, Astro spoke.

"So, we are the definition of luck. We are the outcome of a crapshoot. Of several crapshoots, in fact. Do we really want that on our gravestone?"

"That is not the point, my friend. The point is it makes us rare. Even if life, our kind of life, intelligent, creative, questioning, technological life. Even if such life has happened before—and, as you know, we still have no evidence of that. Even if it has happened before somewhere in the galaxy, even somewhere beyond our galaxy, the big question is, Where? How far away in this vast universe? Will the twain ever meet? Even if we are not alone, we are as good as

THE DEFINITION OF LUCK

alone. Living, breathing, replicating mass, all alone in this cold universe. Does that not make us precious?"

"Not to us, apparently."

"Yes. That has been our mistake."

"And you are trying to make up for that mistake?"

"No. *We* are trying to make up for that mistake. My friend—we. We are trying to preserve what little of the precious we can so that later, maybe much, much later, minds far greater than our own, can —"

We are now at T-minus sixty seconds.

Time had slipped away.

Only enough time left to say goodbye.

Astro and Neuro stood and hugged. Always a silly display, one being so tall and one being so short. But there was no one in the universe to see it at the moment; no one to laugh at it. Or possibly be charmed by it.

They broke, then stood slightly apart and said in unison, "Goodbye, my friend."

Then the sky above and the savanna below announced *T-minus ten, nine, eight, seven, six…* as Neuro faded from the scene.

…five, four, three, two…

End

"What is more impressive than the entire universe is life, as matter and process, life as inspirer of thinking and creation."
— Antonio Damasio

Acknowledgment

I would like to acknowledge fellow authors Jean Rabe and Donald J. Bingle, who held this author's hand during a frightening period of technological panic and who, through swift action, solved the problem and made the panic go away. Readers of this book should google both writers without hesitation to discover them and their fine novels.

ABOUT THE AUTHOR

Before publishing ten critically acclaimed novels, award-winning and Amazon Bestselling author Steven Paul Leiva spent over twenty years in the entertainment industry as a writer and producer. He worked with such talent as Academy Award-winning producer Richard Zanuck; director Ivan Reitman; literary legend and screenwriter Ray Bradbury, and *Star Wars* producer Gary Kurtz; He even lent his voice to the Academy Award shortlisted (placing in the top ten) animated short, *The Indescribable Nth. https://vimeo.com/14857442*

Leiva produced the animation for *Space Jam*, putting together an ad hoc animation studio for Warner Bros in three days over the phone.

During this time, he wrote novels and a play, *Made on the Moon*, which premiered at the 1996 Edinburgh Festival Fringe, receiving a four-star review from *The Scotsman*.

After *Space Jam*, Leiva decided to concentrate on writing novels. Since 2003, he has published ten novels, a novella, and a book of essays.

His work has been praised by literary great Ray Bradbury, Oscar-winning film producer Richard Zanuck, NY Times bestselling author and Pulitzer Prize finalist Diane Ackerman, and *Star Trek: Enterprise* actor John Billingsley, the greatest bookworm in Hollywood.

Leiva received the Scribe Award from the International Association of Media Tie-in Writers.

You can find more about Leiva and read his blogs at https://tinyurl.com/ydgpkps8

BOOKS BY STEVEN PAUL LEIVA

Blood is Pretty: The First Fixxer Adventure

Meet the Fixxer—with wit and aplomb he works the fruitful fields of Hollywood fixing the sins and correcting the stupidities of the denizens therein. In *Blood is Pretty* he comes to the rescue of "the most beautiful woman I have ever seen" to extricate her from the grip of the soul-sucking sexual desires of a producer born in slime, and takes on the task of buying off with money and muscle a film geek who won't cooperate with a director of minuscule talent who simply wants to claim "V"—the geek's "Holy Grail" of a film treatment—as his own.

Hollywood is an All-Volunteer Army: The Second Fixxer Adventure

What those in the know in Hollywood really know is that if they need a dark deed done, if they need a sticky personal or professional problem "fixed," they can call upon the mysterious and dangerous Fixxer. Whether you are a successful comedy film director whose "art" has never truly been appreciated because the country's most important film critic has held a grudge against you since college, or you are a neophyte and naïve screenwriter who resents the professional blackmail she has just suffered, you call upon the Fixxer.

Traveling in Space

A unique first contact novel from the aliens' point-of-view.

The last thing the factfinders—who call themselves Life—expected to find while traveling in space in "The Curious" on a mission from their planet, The Living World, was other life. But one day they stumble upon the third planet out from a backwater sun and find it teeming with a vast diversity of life in- cluding one sentient and cognizant, if primitive, species that they dub: Otherlife.

Being not only from "The Curious" but inherently curious themselves, they begin to study the Otherlife and their alien culture, discovering such strange things as: marriage, intoxicating drinks, weapons of minor and mass destruction, the gleeful inhaling of toxic substances, two-parent families, layered language, genocide, non-nude bathing, and—the strangest thing of all—religion.

This first contact between Life and Otherlife, disconcerting for both, has moments of humor and moments of horror—and neither escape the encounter unchanged.

12 Dogs of Christmas - A Novelization

Winner of the Scribe Award from the International Association of Media Tie-in Authors
Based on the beloved independent family film.

12-year-old Emma O'Connor is sent to live with her "aunt" in the small town of Doverville. Emma soon finds herself in the middle of a "dog-fight" with the mayor and town dogcatcher. In order to strike down their "no-dogs" law, Emma must bring together a group of schoolmates, grown-ups, and adorable dogs of all shapes and sizes in a spectacular holiday pageant. The *12 Dogs of Christmas* is a fun, heartwarming story, featuring a diverse canine cast and is perfect for all those who love dogs, kids, and Christmas.

By the Sea: A Comic Novel

A modern comic adult fairy tale with an ensemble cast of Cinderellas. Instead of a kingdom by the sea, our story takes place in and around a residential hotel by the sea. The architecturally eclectic Briers Hotel is situated on Leech Beach, a not particularly inviting beach, being often fog-bound and always scruffy. But it's the perfect setting for our Cinderellas, male and female, who put up with the scruffy-ness of life while striving to make it through their various personal seaside fogs. Theater; art; antiques; old movies; sex; more sex; death; fast and slow cars, chicken shit and cow poop; military bearing and erotic emissions—not to mention the wicked witch, the sea serpent by the sea shore, the village ogre, the village idiot, and several Prince Charmings—all figure into this merry tale with a multitude of happy endings.

IMP: A Political Fantasia

Thomas P. Powell's ascension in politics was both unusual and yet very American. From traffic cop to Vice President of the United States, his climb up the ladder of public service was often due to the push of random acts and not-so-happy accidents—although Thomas held the opinion that it was due solely to his singular innate moral authority. What matters is what's within, that's the Powell political philosophy. Then, on the cusp of his grasping the last rung of the American political ladder, something truly within suddenly appears. A horrible homunculus, an impetuous imp, climbs out of Thomas's right ear to bedevil his nights and confuse his days and take him on a crazy, wild, nauseating, and nuclear journey. It's as if The West Wing was done as a Twilight Zone episode.

And you thought our last political nightmare was surreal.

Journey to Where: A Contemporary Scienic Romance

When a radical experiment into the nature of time is sabotaged, the scientific team finds themselves in an alternate universe, where humans never became the dominant life force. Instead, dinosaurs evolved into intelligent bipeds, developing language and societal structures.

The scientists have to learn to communicate with this alien species, who view them as unusual pets, and figure out how to recreate the original experiment in a non-industrialized world, so they can go back home—assuming there's a home, or even a universe, to return to.

But the scientist who sabotaged them is trapped in this new world with them. And he's looking to rise to power, even if his quest means the death of his traveling companions. A contemporary scientific romance in the tradition of H. G. Wells and Jules Verne

Creature Feature: A Horrid Comedy

THERE IS SOMETHING STRANGE HAPPENING IN PLACIDVILLE!

It is 1962. Kathy Anderson, a serious actress who took her training at the Actors Studio in New York, is stuck playing Vivacia, the Vampire Woman on Vivacia's House of Horrors for a local Chicago TV station. Finally fed up showing old monster movies to creature feature fans, she quits and heads to New York and the fame and footlights of Broadway.

She stops off to visit her parents and old friends in Placidville, the all-Ameican, middle-class, blissfully normal Midwest small town she grew up in. But she finds things are strange in Placidville. Kathy's parents, her best friend from high school, the local druggist, even the Oberhausen twins are all acting curiously creepy, odiously odd, and wholly weird. Especially the town's super geeky nerd, Gerald, who warns of dark days ahead.

Has Kathy entered a zone in the twilight? Did she reach the limits that are outer? Has she fallen through a mirror that is black? Or is it just—just—politics as usual!

Bully 4 Love: A Rather Odd Love Story

Adolphus Seruya is a happy, middle-aged, unambitious, bachelor, and History professor at a prominent community college. Then suddenly SHE walks into his classroom. Lavinia Carson is beautiful in a unique yet compelling way. And radiant almost beyond description. Thus begins a rather odd story of love rejected, love ignored, love found— and cuttlefish pizza.

Extraordinary Voyages

What if a man wanted to go to the moon from the time he was an infant? Not a toddler, not a child, not a young man, but a babe in his mother's arms? What if Baron Munchausen traveled from 1790 to 1641 to take Cyrano de Bergerac to Mars? What if the man who wanted to go to the moon from the time he was an infant wrote some rude poems? What if the author of this book wrote his own

Wikipedia page that he was sure Wikipedia would never publish? What if you bought this book and found out?

Includes the critically acclaimed novella *Made on the Moon*.

The Reluctant Heterosexual

With *The Reluctant Heterosexual,* Steven Paul Leiva concludes his thematic trilogy: **The Love, Sex and Pursuit of Happiness Novels**. All three novels look at these essential aspects of the human condition, with each novel focusing on one of the three. *By the Sea: A Comic Novel* looks at our unease when unhappy. *Bully 4 Love: A Rather Odd Love Story* takes a skewed view of this most revered emotion. And now, *The Reluctant Heterosexual,* as the title predicts, concerns sex, which is not always the same as love, nor is it always a happy situation. Subtitled *A Tragicomedy in Four Movements A Prelude And An Interlude,* each section of the novel, as in a musical composition, has its own tempo, mood, and form as it tells the story—and stories—of Robert Leslie Cromwell and Sandy Smith. Two *Homo sapiens sapiens* surviving and striving in the late 20th-Century.

Robert and Sandy are intelligent, creative, not unattractive, wealthy, married to each other, and in love. And yet their procreating bodies might as well be standing naked on a savanna in Africa in the late Pliocene Era. It's the sometimes comic conflict between ancient bodies and modern culture. Can there possibly be a happy ending?

Searching for Ray Bradbury: Writings about the Writer and the Man

Includes the title piece written for the *Los Angeles Times*, and "The Man Who Was Himself," Leiva's memorial appreciation of Bradbury commissioned by the Science Fiction & Fantasy Writers of America for the Winter 2012/13 edition of their quarterly magazine, *The Bulletin*. Other pieces were originally written for *Neworld Review*, KCET.org, and his personal blog.

With a special foreword by Hugo and Nebula Award-winning author David Brin.

Printed in Great Britain
by Amazon

86533320R00182